# GRIEVOUS ANGEL

By *Quintin Jardine and available from Headline*

*Bob Skinner series:*
Skinner's Rules
Skinner's Festival
Skinner's Trail
Skinner's Round
Skinner's Ordeal
Skinner's Mission
Skinner's Ghosts
Murmuring the Judges
Gallery Whispers
Thursday Legends
Autographs in the Rain
Head Shot
Fallen Gods
Stay of Execution
Lethal Intent
Dead and Buried
Death's Door
Aftershock
Fatal Last Words
A Rush of Blood
Grievous Angel

*Oz Blackstone series:*
Blackstone's Pursuits
A Coffin for Two
Wearing Purple
Screen Savers
On Honeymoon with Death
Poisoned Cherries
Unnatural Justice
Alarm Call
For the Death of Me

*Primavera Blackstone series:*
Inhuman Remains
Blood Red

The Loner

Quintin
# Jardine

# GRIEVOUS
# ANGEL

headline

First published in 2011 by
HEADLINE PUBLISHING GROUP

1

Cataloguing in Publication Data is available from the British Library

ISBN 978 0 7553 5692 8 (Hardback)
ISBN 978 0 7553 5693 5 (Trade paperback)

Typeset in Electra by Avon DataSet Ltd,
Bidford-on-Avon, Warwickshire

Printed in the UK by CPI Mackays, Chatham, ME5 8TD

Headline's policy is to use papers that are natural, renewable and
recyclable products and made from wood grown in sustainable forests.
The logging and manufacturing processes are expected to conform
to the environmental regulations of the country of origin.

HEADLINE PUBLISHING GROUP
An Hachette UK Company
338 Euston Road
London NW1 3BH

www.headline.co.uk
www.hachette.co.uk

This book is dedicated to the memory of Eddie Sanderson, my dear friend, who was never all that keen on Christmas, and made his point in his own special way, by leaving us on December 25, 2010.

This is my story, or part of it. A memoir, and a confession, by Robert Morgan Skinner, chief constable. And this is how it came to be written.

I love my wife, unequivocally.

I knew that from the off. On the morning that I met Aileen de Marco, in a conference room, around a crowded table, I understood that things were going to happen between us that would reshape my life.

Few would take me for a romantic, that's not my image, but I can be. I believe in the existence of the soul. I believe that when two people who are meant for each other come face to face, their eyes lock and in that time, something passes between them, a bond is formed that transcends . . . everything. I believe in soulmates.

That's how it was with Aileen and me. It took a little while for her to realise it, but I knew instantly. For I'm one of the lucky ones; it had happened to me before.

Not that I understood at the time. I was only a kid, and so was Myra Graham, but when we met at that party something shifted inside me.

You might not believe this if you know me, but until that point in my life I was an introverted lad. From the age of four or five, I'd been bullied and abused, in secret, by my furtive beast of a brother. I was too scared to complain to my mother, not that it would have done me any good, for as far as she was concerned, in what I didn't know at the time was her alcoholic haze, her Michael was followed by his own wee patch of sunshine, everywhere he went. As for our dad, he was a busy man, with ghosts in his own past that made him remote in my early years . . . and I'd been warned by my oppressor that if I opened my mouth to him, I could kiss goodbye to my two front teeth. Even at that, why did I stay silent? Let's just say that shame came into it.

If I hadn't met Myra when I did, in a dark corner at a Saturday-night sixteenth birthday bash for the older brother of a schoolmate, whose name is lost to me now, who knows how it would have ended. Today, my guess is that the sly beatings, the Chinese burns, the arm-twisting, the finger breaking, and yes, okay . . . it took forty years before I could admit this to a living soul, and even now, only Aileen knows the whole truth . . . the sexual attacks, would have carried on until I'd done something terminal either to myself, or to Michael. (The latter more likely? Possibly. I can't say for certain.)

He was ten years older than me, and by the time I found Myra, he had gone into the army, his absence affording me physical, if not emotional, relief. She changed me, just by looking into my eyes, that brave, reckless, lustful, dark-haired girl.

My class marks had always been good, and I had made the school football team easily, but in spite of that, I was a kid with few friends and no self-esteem, living in a fog of fear of my brother's frequent home leaves, and in dark, undefined guilt over things that I knew were wrong but couldn't rationalise. I was a damaged, troubled, introverted boy. Who? Bob Skinner? Come on! Yes, honest to God, that's how it was.

But in the moment that our souls bonded, Myra's and mine, a hot wave surged through me. It took me years to define it properly, but now I know that it was my first realisation that I was, after all, a person of value, and that someone could appraise me without pity or disgust.

Then she took my hand. 'You're not odd at all, Bob Skinner,' she said. 'Louisa in your class told me you were weird. I reckon she's the daftie. Actually I think you're quite dishy.'

I didn't know what to say. I didn't know how to reply. So I kissed her, hard. I didn't know how to do that either. On the day I die, I'll still recall the way her tongue licked my teeth and opened my mouth. She will always be the boldest person I've ever known. It was her strength, and her weakness, all in one.

'Silly Louisa,' she whispered, as we came up for air.

She made me walk her home, and she made me take her to the cinema, which was still clinging to life in Motherwell, on the following Friday. During those six days, I did a lot of thinking; it was confused at first but gradually I reached conclusions. I couldn't express it, but I was in love. I wanted Myra, but to have her, I knew that I had to be more than 'dishy'. I had to become someone she could admire truly. That meant that I had to become someone worthy of my own respect. I had to fight back against Michael. I had to stop being afraid. I had to turn my shame into anger.

I was nowhere near full grown, but I was fourteen years old, big for my age, my voice had broken and the hair was sprouting on my crotch. I was beginning to be aware of my body, and of its potential. Even before my first proper date with Myra, I did two things. I joined the YMCA, so that I could use its gym, and I joined an amateur boxing club. The coach there threw me in at the deep end with an experienced lad around my own age and size, to see what I could do naturally, before he started teaching me anything.

I should have been nervous, but I wasn't. All my knowledge of boxing had come from television so I decided to imagine I was George Foreman and that the other kid was . . . Michael. Someone rang the bell, and thirty seconds later they were hauling me off him.

I trained four times a week after that, twice at the gym, twice at the boxing club, where the coach took me in hand and taught me proper technique. When my sadist brother came home three months later, I bided my time, for a couple of days. I stayed up late one night after my parents had gone to bed, waiting for him to arrive home from the Electric Bar. I knew he'd have a bellyful in him but I wasn't about to give him an even chance. I was there when he stumbled into the kitchen, in my jeans and my boxing vest. He blinked when he saw me; by then he wasn't that much taller than I was, and I'd put on muscle in the gym. I stepped in close and hit him in the gut. The breath left him first, and then the beer. I left him lying in it.

I lay awake all night waiting for him to sober up and come looking for me, but he didn't. I expected vengeance next day and I was ready for it, but nothing happened. Michael rarely spoke to me after that, or came near me. Bottom line, he'd been a coward all along.

Our relationship did end in violence, a couple of years later, after he'd been found out by, and kicked out of, the army, and alcohol had taken over his life completely. He hit our mother, and I walked in on the scene. By that time I was sixteen and serious; I beat him senseless with her screaming in the background. In the wake of that, he was institutionalised, and I never saw him again, until a few years ago, when I identified his body.

All of that stayed secret, locked up within me. I never told my parents, or Myra. The first person to hear any of the story was Andy Martin, my closest friend. I had to tell him because Michael was found drowned in his territory, but even then I withheld the most personal truths.

My first soulmate changed me from a scared, scarred little boy, and put me on the road to becoming what, for better or worse, I am today.

She set me free; without her influence . . . Who knows? But of this I'm certain. I wouldn't be telling this story, in this form, today.

I didn't change her, though; I never curbed that recklessness, or that self-indulgence of hers. If Myra wanted something and it was within her reach, she would have it. The same applied to men. Make no mistake, she loved me as much as I loved her, but for her, love and sex were separate things. I wasn't perfect either, mind; at university, I had a relationship with a charismatic, talented girl, who went on to great things later. It might have flowered, but the guilt was too much for me, and so I ended it. Myra never felt such qualms though. I don't know how many lovers she had in our time together. I told myself, and my daughter, that I knew nothing of them until after she was dead, but if that were true, I wouldn't be the detective I am. Of course I had suspicions over the years, but I kept them secret, within myself. I'm good at that: it may be a legacy from the horror years with my brother.

If Myra hadn't died? If, if, if, if . . . hell, 'if' I could eliminate a single word from our language that would be it. Truth, she did bloody die, she did, and so did part of me, the place where my compassion dwelt. It was lost for years, and so in a way was I, all the way through a later loving relationship, and then a doomed second marriage that I could have saved, maybe, with a little more kindness and generosity and a little less self-obsession.

Do I feel guilty about that failure? Yes. Do I regret it? No. For Sarah is where she wants to be, and so am I. She and I were never soulmates. We were lovers who settled for what we had, and in our case that wasn't enough for a lifetime.

And now I'm with Aileen, my second chance, my second redeemer. For, yes, she saved me too. She took a hard, bitter, obdurate man, and she softened me. It didn't happen all at once, but gradually she restored

5

my inner warmth and she stopped me from applying my expectations of myself to everyone around me.

There are moments in my life now that, honestly, I've never known before. I'll walk in on her when she's busy, doing something that requires her full concentration . . . clothes-filing, for example, or shoe-arranging, or saving the planet . . . and I'll gaze at her without her being aware of it, and I'll smile. Then she'll look back, her eyebrows slightly raised in puzzlement, and she'll say, 'What?' and I'll laugh out loud and take her in my arms and lift her up and say, 'Nothing, baby, nothing. You make me happy, that's all.'

But oh, if only it could be like that all the time. There are still the black moods, and they will never leave me. I've seen terrible things in my life, work and private, and I've done some too, the sort that would not look good to the world outside. But that brings me back to my unwitting gift from Michael, that capacity for secrecy so deep that it's been known to lead me to hide things even from myself.

A few months ago, even though I've risen to the rank of chief police officer, and theoretically I'm above the messy end of the job, circumstances took me to a couple of crime scenes, two of the nastiest I've ever encountered. Experiences such as those have led me to develop a ritual. It's very simple. Once all the smoke has cleared or the blood has been swept away . . . or substitute the metaphor of your choice . . . I will sit down in the garden room in our house in Gullane, preferably in the dark unless it's high summer, when the daylight in the north never quite fades, and I will kill a bottle of very good red wine, maybe a Pesquera or a Mas La Plana. If that doesn't do the trick I will open another, and a third, if that's what it takes. Next morning I will rise early, feeling too bad to be allowed into hell, and I will run along the shore to Dirleton and back, or beyond, to North Berwick . . . if that's what it takes. It's my way of purging myself, and it's always worked . . . until those two horror scenes a few months ago.

We all have our limits . . . even me, for all that I've tried to deny it. I tried my hardest to chase the memories of the couple, incinerated in their kitchen, and of the men in the isolated barn, tortured relentlessly before they were killed. I followed my ritual: we were low on wine, so I drank countless Corona beers, until I fell asleep in my armchair. I woke just after six, and ran fifteen miles, sticking to the roads because it was dark when I set out. I assumed that I would be fine after that, but . . . wrong.

That evening, I sat silently through dinner, drinking water rather than alcohol, then watched television, a replay of *Lewis* on a nostalgia channel, not caring that I'd seen it before. As I looked at the screen, gradually the images began to fade, and were replaced by others, from that house, from that barn, from other places, a first-hand documentary of the evil that I had witnessed and known, all the way back to my childhood and Michael, my own true scream movie, all of it put together from my own life, suffering seen, suffering inflicted, suffering endured. I squeezed my eyes closed, as tightly as I could manage, but I couldn't kill the images. I shoved my knuckles into the sockets until they hurt, but it made no difference.

And then Aileen slid on to my lap, tugging at my wrists. I resisted, but she kept on pulling, until my forearms were resting on the arms of the chair, and she was kissing my closed, moist eyelids, until gradually I relaxed and I could open them and the daymare was over and I could look into her face, and take in her distress.

'What is it, love?' she whispered.

'Everything,' I said, hoarsely. 'All the . . . all . . . everything. My life. It's caught up with me.'

'Tell me.'

'Tell you what, love?'

'Everything. Everything that you've got bottled up inside you. Talk to me, Bob. You don't, you know.'

'I do,' I protested. 'I talk to you all the time.'

'Sure you do, but you set your limits. There's a part of you that's locked up, that's closed to me.'

I tried to fob her off. 'You wouldn't want to know what's in there.'

It didn't work. 'I need to know,' she insisted. 'I'm sitting here watching you have a breakdown, before my eyes. I've seen it coming for the last couple of days, and it's just about the scariest thing I've ever known. You think the kids haven't sensed that there's something wrong? Mark's noticed too, and so has James Andrew. "Is Dad okay?" he asked me last night. I want to help, Bob, but I can't as long as I'm on the outside. Tell me, love. Tell me everything about you that I don't know already. You have to. I'm not moving from here until you do.'

And so I did. I began from my earliest days, with Michael's reign of terror. I tried to downplay that as much as I could, but Aileen didn't buy it. She made me set out every detail of his torture, and of his violations. When I told her the worst of it, we were both in tears. 'You're a very special person,' she said.

'Me?' I gasped. 'How do you work that out? How does being buggered by your brother when you were seven make you special?'

'You survived it, and you didn't kill him.'

'Ah, but I thought about it. I knew where he was, afterwards, and there were times when I thought about finding him and finishing him. I could have done it, being what I am, without ever being found out. I could simply have made him disappear. The very fact that I didn't became part of my guilt. I have no idea whether he ever preyed on other kids. I should have thought of that, and removed the possibility, even if it was only by discussing my own experiences with another officer, in another force. But I didn't, I kept it to myself.'

'There's no evidence that he ever did that, is there?'

'None that I know of. I like to think that he redeemed himself, that his banishment made him a better person.'

'Then stop beating yourself up. It happened, it's long in the past, and now you've shared it with me, it makes me love and admire you all the more.' She wiped her eyes with the back of her hand. 'So move on; go on. Tell me the rest of it. Open yourself to me.'

And I did. I set out for her all my secrets, shared with her all of the evil memories I had gathered and stored through my career, those things that I've seen because of the job, those deeds that I've done because someone had to, told her where all the bodies were buried . . . in a couple of cases, literally so. I talked, and she listened, for two hours. When I was done, I was spent . . . and so was Aileen, exhausted and shaken.

'Do you feel the better for that?' I asked her.

'No. But that wasn't the idea.' She paused. 'That man you shot,' she whispered. 'In your cottage. Did you have any other option?'

I thought about her question carefully. 'Probably,' I told her, when I was ready, 'but the guy had gone rogue, he'd already killed a couple of people . . . not to mention the fact that he'd already shot me.' I added, 'If he'd walked out of there, it would have been embarrassing for those who sent him. I made the call, and to be frank, it's been a long time since I even thought about him. In the same situation, I'd do the same thing. To be even more frank, I don't regret anything I've ever done to someone else . . . apart from that unfortunate kid in the boxing ring in Motherwell all those years ago. It's the cruelty that I've seen human beings inflict on each other; that's what tears me up. Now you've made me share it with you, but I'm not sure that it will help. A burden shared might be a burden halved, but now you're stuck with one you never had before.'

'Then write it down. And don't worry about me; I'm tougher than I look.'

'You're not serious,' I exclaimed. 'There's things I can't ever write down, can't ever mention outside this room.'

'Then stick to the stories you can tell. They don't need to be for publication, but maybe as you examine each one at length, you'll be able to put them in a better perspective.'

And so, that is what I'm going to do. They won't be chronological, these . . . memoirs, I called them earlier, and that's as good a word as any. They'll be stories that my wife reckons need telling, for therapeutic reasons, before I become a psychological basket case.

But where to begin? Basket cases? Why not? Let's start with the man in the wheelchair, the Stephen Hawking of crime, as a chum of mine once called him.

# One

'*W*hy *were we created to suffer and die?*'

'Why the hell not?'

I stared at her, fork halfway to my half-open mouth. I'm closer to my older daughter, my first child, than anyone else in the world, even Aileen . . . that's how it is, in truth . . . yet she's always had the capacity to surprise me. I gasped, not just at the bluntness of her reply, but because she'd nailed down the answer to my metaphysical question, one hundred per cent.

'You . . .' I began, and then the phone rang. 'Bugger,' I grunted. She frowned. 'Not you,' I added, quickly.

When? It must have been fifteen years ago that I read a spoof sci-fi story about a space wanderer who travelled the universe, looking for its Maker, so that he could put to Him/Her the Primal Question.

Yes, that's right, it was fifteen years ago, for Alexis Skinner was at that unmercifully awkward stage, not quite a woman, I thought, but on the other hand definitely not Pops' wee girl any more. The attitude that's characterised her ever since was in its formative stage, with all of the sharp edges that time would smooth away, still, then, at their most abrasive.

We were having our evening meal, she and I, the two-person family unit that we'd been for almost a decade, since Myra had died in a tangle of metal. Daisy Mears had gone home for the night. She'd been a part of our lives for the previous eight of those years. More than a part: in truth, she'd been the saviour of mine, professionally.

Daisy lived in Gullane, in a cottage, as we did; hers was on the other side of the main street from Goose Green, in Templar Lane. She was five years older than me, just past forty, divorced, childless, and with no intention of ever getting involved with another man in any way, other than business. She was an artist, and a pretty good one at that; her landscapes, and stormy, brooding sea-scapes, sold for upwards of a grand a time through an Edinburgh gallery, and for not quite as much to collectors who approached her directly. She hadn't always done that well, though. When she'd become Alex's day-carer . . . my daughter did not care for the term 'childminder' and corrected anyone who was foolish enough to use it . . . the money had come in handy, in the wake of her acrimonious split from the heavy-handed skinflint she'd made the mistake of marrying.

She'd joined us after a succession of short-term failures. At first Myra's mother insisted on helping me out, but after only a year she was diagnosed with non-Hodgkin's lymphoma and went back to Lanarkshire to die. After her came a series of women who'd promised that my unpredictable working hours would be no problem, only to discover that they were. At that time, I was still in my twenties, widowed, with a five-year-old kid who was the centre of my world. It might not always have been apparent . . . indeed, today I have an ex-wife who'd take issue with the assertion . . . but through my life my career has come second to my family.

With the resignation of the most recent 'carer', I had a problem, but I had an option open to me, one which I almost took up. When Daisy answered the ad that I'd placed, in desperation rather than hope, in the *East Lothian Courier*, I was probably within three months of leaving the police force and moving back to Motherwell, to add a law qualification to my arts degree and join my father's firm.

She was made for us. Her creative hours were completely flexible, and could be shaped to meet our needs. She'd come in every morning, to get Alex ready and take her to school, then pick her up at the end of the day and bring her home, or if I was working late, take her to her place until I called for her. On the odd occasion when an investigation turned into a crisis, she'd look after her overnight, always at Templar Lane, for Daisy and I agreed early on that she would never sleep over at Goose Green. Villages are villages, even the nicest of them; we knew there would be talk as it was, without our feeding it.

I thought about letting the answer-machine handle the incoming call, but only for a fraction of a second. I've never been able to do that. If the phone rings more than three times, in my home or in my office, it means that I'm not there, unless I'm sound asleep or locked away taking care of private matters. Even then, I once ruined a perfectly good mobile by answering it while taking a piss and letting it slip from my grasp. I stood up from the table, and snatched the handset from its cradle on the sideboard.

'Three two nine one,' I answered. My phone number. That's my way. I never give my name when taking a call at home. My life is about having an edge; I've always liked to know who's calling before giving anything of myself away.

'DCI Skinner?' Male voice, deep, young, just on the confident side of arrogant.

'Who's this?'

'PC McGuire, St Leonards.'

I frowned. The name meant nothing to me. 'This is Skinner,' I conceded. 'It's quarter past seven, and I finished a ten-hour working day just over an hour ago. So why are you interrupting my dinner, Constable?'

'Because my boss told me to, sir.'

'And who would that be?'

'Detective Superintendent Jay.'

Greg Jay; arrogant prick. I didn't like him, and I wasn't alone. 'I thought you said you were a PC,' I snapped. 'Why are you gophering for a CID officer?'

'I was nearest the door; got seconded.'

'And Jay gave you my ex-directory number, just like that?'

'I didn't know it was X-D, sir. He just told me to call it.'

'And?'

'And to ask you to meet him at Infirmary Street Baths, as soon as possible.'

'That's how he put it?'

The PC hesitated, but only for a moment. 'Actually, sir, he said, "Tell him to get his arse along to Infirmary Street Baths, now." Those were his exact words.'

I cut off my retort, just before it left my mouth. Alex was watching me, with a frown on her face. 'In that case, Constable McGuire,' I replied instead, '. . . what's your first name?'

'Mario, sir.'

'Now there's an odd mixture.'

'Father Irish, mother Italian.'

'Indeed? Well, Mario, please give Detective Superintendent Jay my compliments and tell him that my arse is going nowhere until he calls me himself and gives me a good reason why it should.'

'Will do, sir.' Something in the lad's tone hinted that he would enjoy it too.

'And one other thing,' I added.

'I know, sir. Forget the number I just called.'

My daughter looked at me, a little anxiously, as I came back to my seat. 'Can you do that?' she asked. 'He's a superintendent and you're only a chief inspector.'

'Nobody's "only" a chief inspector, love,' I told her. 'Nobody's "only" anything. "Only" isn't a word I like to tag on to people.' That said, I could have added that if you made chief inspector at thirty-three . . . I'd held the rank for three years by that time . . . then somebody who'd taken twelve years longer to make super would know that at some point down the road he'd be calling you 'sir', and thus wouldn't be taking too many liberties.

I didn't say it, though; instead I concentrated on finishing my lasagne before the phone rang again. I felt myself grin as I wondered whether that young constable had the stones to deliver my message verbatim, suspecting that he did.

It didn't take Jay too long. I was in the kitchen when he called; Alex picked up in the dining room, before I could stop her. She answered in the same way I did, number only, as I'd taught her.

'Yes, my father is at home,' I heard her say. 'Who's calling, please?' She paused. 'I'm sorry,' she continued, switching into young woman mode and sounding frighteningly like her mother. 'Either you tell me who you are or I hang up. That's what my father says I should do with anonymous callers.' She waited, taking the phone away from her ear slightly, as if she was getting ready to put it down. 'Thank you,' she said, eventually, then turned to look at me. 'Dad, it's Detective Superintendent Jay.'

'How soon can we start her on our switchboard?' he drawled, as soon as I took the phone.

'We'll be minding hers before she's done,' I told him.

'You finished your tea then, Bob?' The sarcasm in Jay's tone was only one of the reasons for my dislike of him.

'And done the dishes.'

'You ready to obey orders now?'

I didn't want to upset Alex, so all I did was grin, when I really wanted to bite his ear off. 'Since when were you my line manager?' I asked him, quietly. 'You're at St Leonards, CID; I'm drugs squad commander. So please stop puffing out your chest and tell me exactly what the hell it is you want.'

'Listen . . .' he growled.

'I'm listening.'

I heard a deep breath being drawn. 'I've got a crime scene,' he continued, eventually.

'Infirmary Street Baths,' I said. In the Victorian era Edinburgh's civic leaders built several public swimming pools to combat the scourge of cholera. When I was young, my father took me to see his grandfather's grave in a cemetery in Wishaw, Motherwell's neighbouring town; as we approached it he pointed out a green area, without memorial stones, and told me that it was the site of a mass grave for victims of a cholera epidemic.

'That's right,' Jay confirmed, brusquely.

'I thought they were closed.' A hundred years on, we weren't so bothered about Biblical plagues.

'They are. They were shut down about a year ago; they've been mothballed while the council tries to find a new use for the building, or for the site, if it comes to that. There are jannies going in every so often, to check the place out, make sure that everything's all right.'

'But today something wasn't?'

'That's right. They found a guy in the pool.'

'What stroke was he doing?'

16

'Very funny. There's no water supply to the building, but even if there had been, this one wasn't swimming. He was at the deep end; right under the high diving board. His neck was broken.'

'He took the plunge, eh?'

The superintendent allowed himself a grim chuckle. 'That's how it looks. But we don't know for certain whether he dived off it or whether he was chucked off.'

'What makes you think I can tell you?' I asked.

'If what Alf Stein says about you is right,' I could see the sneer on his weasel face, 'you probably could tell us just by looking at him.' Detective Chief Superintendent Stein was our head of CID, Jay's boss and mine. I'd heard myself described, with undisguised jealousy, by someone who didn't know I was within earshot, as his protégé, but Alf had never told me that I was. 'But the reason I'd like you to look at him . . .' he hesitated, '. . . this has got drugs overtones to it, Bob. There's no ID on the body, but Alison Higgins reckons she's seen this bloke before. She thinks that he's one of Tony Manson's crew.'

I could have said that I'd look at him next morning in the mortuary, but in truth, if Jay had done that to me I'd have been seriously upset. And there was something else: Alison wasn't wrong too often. I told him to hold, and put my hand over the phone's mouthpiece. 'Do you know if Daisy has anything on tonight?' I asked my daughter.

She nodded. 'She's taking some pictures to show to a private buyer in Haddington.'

'Do you have much homework?'

'I've done it.'

'Fancy a quick trip into town?'

'Aw, Dad! *Top of the Pops* is on in a minute or two.'

'We can record it. I need to do this.'

'New jeans?'

'Are you trying extortion on a police officer?'

'It's always worked before.'

'Okay.' I put the phone back to my ear. 'I'll be about forty-five minutes, give or take a couple,' I told Jay.

'Our guest will wait for you,' he replied.

I let Alex set the VCR; we had no empty tapes so she and I had a brief argument about which to use. She won in the end, because I wasn't really interested in catching up on Juventus winning the Champions League on penalties. She didn't get to choose the music in the car, though. I never could stand R Kelly, and Wyclef's language on one of the Fugee tracks was . . . well . . . 'Mista Mista' had become the anthem of the Edinburgh drugs squad, but it wasn't for my daughter's ears. Instead I forced her to listen to 'Aria', a strange, contemplative blend of opera and chill-out music by the Cafe del Mar maestro, that a friend had given me in Spain a few weeks before, at Easter.

Although it was a Thursday, most of the late evening shoppers were heading for home by the time we came into the outskirts of the city. I was thinking about Infirmary Street Baths, and what was waiting for us there. Alexis was thinking about something else; we were on Milton Link when she turned the volume down.

'Dad,' she said, abruptly, reclaiming my attention. 'Why don't we have a dinner party?'

'What?' I spluttered. 'Why the hell would we do that?'

'Why shouldn't we? You never invite friends to the house. It's as if we're hermits. You're a good cook, and I'm not bad at some things. We could manage.'

'Who would we invite?' As I thought about it, I conceded the point; we did live a secluded existence. Alex wasn't my life in its entirety, but I didn't have a legion of friends, not outside the job. Yes, I was invited to parties thrown by people who'd been part of our circle when I was half of a couple, but nobody expected me to take a turn as host myself, not with a kid . . . but she wasn't any more, was she?

'You could invite the Lloyds,' she suggested. Jack Lloyd was my usual foursomes partner in the golf club. He and his wife were more than ten years older than me. 'And Aunt Jean could come.'

I smiled. I must have looked condescending, for she frowned. 'When you're a lawyer,' I told her, 'and you have an opposition witness on the stand, you'll need to take your examination more slowly than that, or you'll have no flexibility left, no wiggle room. It's the biggest mistake defence counsel make when I'm in the box.'

'I don't know what you mean,' she snapped.

'Yes you do. You're matchmaking, and you're not very good at it.'

Alex and her aunt, her mother's younger sister, had always got on. So had Jean and I, for that matter. But neither my daughter nor I could stand her husband Cameron, one of the very few men that Myra had ever detested absolutely. Jean had joined our camp a couple of years earlier. She had celebrated her thirtieth birthday by chucking him out, and had called a week before to tell us that her divorce had been finalised.

'Okay, so what if I am? Dad, it's been a long time. You've got to . . .'

'Move on?'

'Yes.'

'Alex, I have moved on.'

She looked across at me. 'Do you have a girlfriend?'

'You know that I don't.'

'I know that you never bring any women home, but that's all.'

'Well I don't.'

'None at all?'

19

'No.'

'You mean you've been celibate since Mum died?' She pronounced the bombshell word carefully, as if she'd just learned it.

'Hey!' I protested, laughing. 'Jesus, kid, what sort of a question's that for a thirteen-year-old to be asking her father?'

'That means you haven't. If the answer was "yes" you'd have said so. People prevaricate when they have something to hide; that's what you told me.'

'I've got nothing to hide,' I insisted.

I had, of course. Nine months before, I had left Alex in Daisy's care and gone to Spain for a long weekend, to do some maintenance on the house that I'd bought with part of my father's estate, and to commission an extension. I'd flown from Glasgow to Barcelona and Jean had come with me. Her suggestion, not mine; nothing had been said in advance about the sleeping arrangements, but I suppose we'd both known what was going to happen. It wasn't a disaster, but it did feel a little weird. We had some laughs, the sex was good, and I didn't imagine for a second that Myra would be turning in her grave, but when Jean made it clear at the end of the trip that it would be a one-off, I felt relieved rather than slighted. She hadn't been my only fling; there had been other women, a few over the years, but always away games, work as far as Alex was concerned, the truth and nothing but the truth with the understanding Daisy.

'Tell you what,' I offered her. 'No dinner party, but we'll have a barbie in the garden, one Sunday afternoon. We'll invite friends from the village, you can ask some of yours from school, if their parents are okay with it, and I might ask some from work. You can invite our Jean if you like, but don't you be surprised if she wants to bring a man.'

The notion that her aunt was capable of independent thought and action sent her into silent contemplation. 'You up for that?' I asked, as I negotiated a troublesome roundabout.

'We'll see.' The idea of a joint adult-kids party left her underwhelmed, as I had guessed it would. Negotiations were suspended, and I drove on, letting the music fill the void.

Infirmary Street had been closed at either end as I turned into it off the Cowgate. The uniform on duty waved a 'get on your way' gesture at first, but he was looking at Alex rather than at me. He knew me well enough; his name was Charlie Johnston and he wasn't going anywhere other than towards retirement and a PC's pension, his objective from the start. He and I were contemporaries. The first thing he'd done on joining up was to learn, off by heart, the book and how to play everything by it without ever risking his head above the parapet. After a closer look, he stepped aside and moved a traffic cone.

Jay was waiting for me on the pavement outside the old building, sucking on a cigarette. Even now, it's difficult for me to paint a word picture of the man. He came closer than anyone I've ever known to being a walking definition of 'nondescript'. The only feature that stopped him from going all the way was the colour of his eyes, as grey as the stone of the bathhouse behind him.

They flickered as Alex stepped out of the car, and I didn't like what I saw in them. She was tall for her age, and dressed as she saw fit. That evening her choice had been jeans, ripped at the knee, and a baggy, custom-made, white T-shirt that one of her friends had given her the Christmas before. It had 'WARNING! CID brat!' emblazoned on the front.

'Bob,' he said, his face twisting into what passed for a smile. 'Glad you could come. It might help us get a head start.'

'I know that.' There was a cop standing in the doorway behind him, a PC in his mid-twenties, around my height, six two. Modern police tunics make some officers look fat, but not this guy; he just looked massive. He had to be McGuire, even if he did look a lot more Italian than Irish. His hair was darker than dark, the purest jet black, and his eyes, a complete contrast to Jay's limpid puddles, were deep blue pools which twinkled with laughter and excitement. I'd seen him around but hadn't put a name to him before. He was usually to be found in the company of another young plod, his equal in size if not in temperament.

'Mario?' He nodded. 'You've got an important and dangerous job.'

'What's that, sir?'

'Look after my daughter while I'm inside.'

He beamed. 'She couldn't be in safer hands, boss.'

'It's your safety I'm worrying about.' I winked at Alex. 'I won't be long.' She shrugged; at that moment she was more interested in her new minder than she was in me.

'Come on then,' Jay grunted. He led the way inside, past what had been the ticket booth, and up a few steps into the pool area. There was plenty of natural light, from a window that ran along the full length of the roof, but not enough for the scene of crime people apparently; four big lamps, on stands, had been set up in the drained pool. I took a look around, reacquainting myself with my surroundings. I had been in the baths a couple of years before, as a user. When I had taken over command of the drugs and vice squad it had been based in Gayfield Square, and I had gone there to swim on a few lunch breaks. The pool was flanked by individual changing cubicles, women on one side, men on the other. The designer had left gaps at the top and bottom of the doors, a sign that the building dated back to a time before electric lighting. There was an upper tier, with more cubicles, for individual baths, relics of the days when all there was in many homes was a tin tub in front of the fire.

A ladder had been placed at the deep end, where the tiled floor was flat. A red-haired guy stood at the top, a DS called Arthur Dorward; he was a graduate, as was I, but his degree was in chemistry. He was wearing a scene of crime suit, and handed one to me. 'What about you?' I asked Jay, as I put it on.

'I've seen all I want to see down there,' he retorted.

I climbed down the ladder, jumping off with a couple of rungs to go. The body was lying as the superintendent had described it; it was that of a young man, a big bloke, white, dressed in black trousers and shirt, with shiny lace-up brogues and patterned socks. It was face down, the limbs were splayed out and the head was at the sort of angle you'd expect from a well-executed hanging. There was a little blood, but no more than a smear.

I looked up, towards the diving platform which jutted out above my head, a solid structure and wide enough to accommodate at least two people and possibly three. It was fifteen or sixteen feet higher than the edge of the pool, add on another couple for the water level then twelve for safe diving depth; yes, the guy could have fallen thirty feet, more than enough to do the job.

Two officers stood beside him. They were both dressed as I was, in one-piece sterile suits with hoods, but I knew them both. Alison Higgins had just made DI; she had been a sergeant on my team until a year before. I had engineered her move, without her ever knowing about it. She had chummed me to Infirmary Street once or twice . . . on lunchtimes when we weren't back at her flat in Albert Street, banging each other's brains out. Our thing had cooled off since then . . . not that it had ever been red hot . . . but we were still good friends.

The other suit was a detective constable, new to CID; his name was Martin, Andy Martin. He was from Glasgow, and he was reckoned to be a high-flier, not necessarily by Jay, but by me. He had helped me out on an investigation a few months before, when he was still in uniform, and I had recommended to Alf Stein that he be fast-tracked into CID. Jay thought that he had been favoured because he had a degree of fame as a rugby player, but if that had been so he'd have deserved it. The young Martin had played for Scotland B and had been a certainty to make full international status, until he had made it clear to the head coach that his job came before any squad training session, even in the newly dawned professional era.

'So you think I might have an interest in this, Alison?' I asked.

'I'm sure I've seen him before, sir.' She was always impeccably formal with me, on duty, when there were others around. 'And I'm sure, too, that it was in my time on the drugs squad.'

'Has the body been moved?'

'No, not at all.'

'So you've only seen him in profile, as he is now?'

'That's how sure I am,' she replied, confidently.

'Has the doctor been yet?'

'And the pathologist,' Martin volunteered, 'and the photographers.'

'Then turn him over.'

The young DC nodded, squatted down beside the corpse and rolled it on to its back, then straightened the arms and legs. The left side of the face had been smashed by the impact, but it was still recognisably human. And recognisable as . . .

'Marlon Watson,' I said, loud enough for Jay to hear, above us at the poolside. 'Fucking hell, but that's one unlucky family.'

'Marlon?' Martin echoed.

'Age twenty-three or twenty-four, born in nineteen seventy-two, when *The Godfather* was the big film of the year. Mr and Mrs Watson didn't have a lot of imagination when it came to naming their kids. This one had a brother called Ryan; he was born in nineteen seventy, the year *Love Story* came out. There was a sister, too, so I've been told, older than either of them. Her name's Mia; spot the movie.'

'*Rosemary's Baby*.' Alison was a movie buff.

'That's right: a movie about the spawn of Satan, and Bella Watson called her kid after its star.'

'Why did you say they're unlucky?' Jay asked.

I looked up at him. 'Don't you remember? Maybe not; it's a few years back now. I wasn't long on the force when it happened. This one's brother was at Maxwell Academy, that hellish school they pulled down a few years ago, and his uncle, a bad bastard called Gavin Spreckley, had him selling heavily cut smack to the other kids, under the protection of the janitor. The *Saltire* newspaper got on to it and ran the story. We didn't have enough on Gavin to lift him, but Ryan was arrested and remanded to a secure unit. He disappeared from there; he didn't break out, though, he was snatched. The staff were careless, or maybe somebody was bribed. Anyway, a day or so later a parcel was delivered to the *Saltire* newspaper office. It was a box, with two right hands in it, the boy's and the uncle's, cut off after they'd been killed. We never found the bodies, but Tommy Partridge . . . he led the investigation . . . reckons that he knows what happened to them.'

Jay scowled. 'That's not bad luck as far as I'm concerned; it's good luck for the rest of us.'

'The boy was fourteen,' I barked at him. 'A year older than my daughter is now; he never stood a fucking chance, being brought up in that environment.'

'Tough shit. I remember the wee swine now; he carried a razor, and cut somebody with it, one of our guys.'

'Sure, and you carry a spring-loaded baton in your jacket pocket, Superintendent.' His face flushed with anger, and I stopped short. I'd been drawn into an argument with the guy in front of his own troops, not a smart thing to do. 'But the family trouble didn't end there,' I went on, cutting across any potential retort. 'We all remember that,' I glanced at the DC, 'apart from you, Martin.'

'What happened, sir?' he asked me.

'Mayhem. Partridge and his team knew who did for the pair of them; there wasn't much doubt about that. Spreckley was a known dealer; his supplier was a guy called Alasdair Holmes, the younger brother of a man called Perry Holmes. I won't give you Perry's life story, but you can take it that he was a man of many business interests, some straight, others criminal on a national scale. Every cop in Scotland wanted him, but none of us could get near him. Anyway, the Holmes brothers knew nothing of what had been going on in the school, and when they found out . . .' I felt my eyebrows rise.

'The belief was that uncle and nephew were killed by Al Holmes and a big German monster who worked for them, called Johann Kraus, and Partridge's bet was that they were cremated in an incinerator on a smallholding that Perry owned and where Kraus lived. He also believes that they made Gavin's brother Billy watch the executions. If Gavin was small-time then Billy was tiny, a gopher, no more than that.'

I smiled, but I wasn't laughing inside. 'However,' I continued, 'there was a wee bit more to him than they thought. It took him a few years to work up the courage, but one day he walked into the Holmes business office just off Lothian Road and shot both the brothers. Alasdair was killed instantly and Perry took four bullets. He should have died, but he didn't; instead he wound up in a wheelchair, paralysed. As for Billy, Johann Kraus saw him off, then he went berserk himself and killed an innocent bystander. There was a short siege, before one of our snipers blew his brains out.'

'So what do you think this is?' Higgins asked. 'The next round?'

'Perry Holmes exterminating the Watsons? No, I don't see that. Perry's a quadriplegic; from what I've heard he's looked after by a couple of male nurses. He still runs his kosher businesses, but that's all. The other side of his life ended when that bullet lodged at the base of his brain, where it is to this day. It all seems to have passed over to Tony Manson now.'

'So is DI Higgins right?' Jay interrupted. 'Did this Marlon guy connect to Manson?'

I knew where he was heading, from the tone of his voice. 'Closely,' I told him. 'He was his driver.'

'So it is one for your drugs squad,' he exclaimed, beaming at the prospect of spin-passing a tricky investigation to someone else.

'Maybe yes, maybe no. Tony does other things, as you know very well.'

'Sure, among them prostitution, which still makes it your baby.'

I sighed, because I knew that one way or another, he was right: but I wasn't for letting him know it. 'We'll let the boss decide that,' I declared. 'How did he get in here?' I asked Alison, to avoid any debate.

'There's a door at the side. It's been jemmied. The building isn't alarmed, so there was no risk.'

'Time?'

'The janitors call in twice a week. The entrances were all checked and secure on Monday. The pathologist is sure he's been dead for at least thirty-six hours, because rigor mortis is starting to dissipate.'

'So we're looking at something that could have happened overnight on Tuesday. There's a pub across the road, and steady traffic through this street, so we ought to start with the premise that the break-in happened after closing time.' I gazed up at Jay. 'Do you know when that boozer closes? Does it have a late licence?'

'Only at weekends,' Martin volunteered. 'It shuts at eleven through the week.'

'Okay, that indicates a window from around midnight Tuesday onwards.'

'Maybe he was in the pub before he broke in here,' the DC suggested. I glanced upwards again; Jay had gone. He was doing his level best to dump the investigation on me, and the way things were going, he was succeeding.

'That's a possibility that should be checked,' I said. 'Was he? If so, was he alone or did he have company?' I turned back to DI Higgins. 'But first things first; you should get Marlon off to the morgue . . . that won't take long, since it's just round the corner . . . and you need to find out whether anyone knew what he was doing on Tuesday.'

'Yes,' she agreed, 'but . . .' She knew the game that was being played between her boss and me, and she wasn't having any of it. She needed clear direction, unambiguous; she didn't need to be caught in the spray of a pissing contest between two guys who might be letting their dislike of each other get in the way of their judgement.

'Fuck it!' I hissed. Thing was, I knew something that none of them did: I knew about the announcement that was going to be made the next morning, at 9 a.m., on a force circular and an hour later to the press. 'Detective Superintendent Jay,' I shouted.

A few seconds passed before he reappeared, shoulders hunched in his baggy jacket, a cigarette cupped in his hand. He looked sour, ready for a fight. 'Yes?' he murmured, a challenge.

'I'm taking over this investigation,' I announced.

'Just like that?'

Perverse bastard! It was what he wanted, but not how he'd wanted it. His hope was that if he couldn't order me himself, Alf Stein would, that I'd be put in my place. His mistake was that I knew what that place was, he didn't.

'Just like that,' I echoed. 'Either I do it tonight with your agreement, or tomorrow morning, with or without it. For the sake of the investigation it's best that it's now.'

'What's tomorrow got to do with it?' he snapped.

'Tomorrow, Greg, I assume command of the Serious Crimes Unit, on promotion to detective superintendent. I'll be working alongside the Scottish Crime Squad, and my remit will include organised crime. We'll continue to have a dedicated drugs and vice unit, with Roy Old in charge, but it'll work hand in hand with my team.'

'Who defines serious crime?' Jay was deflated; I'd let some of the air out of his balloon.

'Within our force area, we do. The Scottish Crime Squad targets on a national basis, but its resources are limited. Our focus is within our own territory; we pass on intelligence when we have it, but we set our own local agenda. Tony Manson is very much part of that, and when we find his driver dead in these circumstances, that's of interest to us.'

He shrugged. 'Good luck to you, then. I'll be off home. Higgins, Martin, you can knock off too.'

Christ, the man's lifetime mission seemed to be to rile Bob Skinner. 'Normally, I'd have no objection to any of that,' I said, 'but in this case I need a team on the ground, now. So I'm commandeering yours, or some of them, at least. Higgins, Martin, you're with me, and I'll have the lad on the door as well.' I looked him in the eye. 'Before you ask, yes, I have the power to do it. Call Alf, if you doubt me.'

He could have called the chief constable too. I'd been called to a meeting in his office, that morning, without being given a clue to the subject in advance. It had been James Proud, Alf Stein and me, that was all. The chief had told me of my promotion, and of the reason for the strengthening of my unit. It had existed for a while, and I'd spent some time there as a detective sergeant, but it was being beefed up. 'I don't want my force to be marginalised,' the chief had said, 'or to see any of its investigative role being handed over to a central crime-fighting unit. One or two of my fellow chiefs would like to see that happen, but it won't, not while I'm behind this desk.' There was a school of thought within the force that Proud was more politician than policeman; I was pleased to learn that he was both. 'For the moment, you'll have the squad that Tom Partridge built up, but you can add to it, straight away or whenever it suits you.'

I kept on staring up at Jay. 'I'll let you know how the investigation goes, Greg,' I told him. 'If I need anything else from your division, I'll let you know.' I didn't feel any guilt about putting him down in front of his own officers; that's what he'd have done to me, if he'd been able.

He sloped off, without another word. Policing is no different from any other profession, or from humanity for that matter. It has those people with that little bit extra, or who exceed their natural ability by their effort and enthusiasm, and it has its great majority, those who do what's expected of them competently, the people who, in the end, make it all work, life's Poor Bloody Infantry. Then there are the others, those who want the ride for free, and whose weight is carried by the rest. Occasionally, one of those will climb the ladder through lack of proper scrutiny. Greg Jay wasn't a typical example, he'd gone higher than most, but he'd been on my radar for a while, and with me having risen to the same rung as him, he knew that his card was marked.

I climbed the ladder out of the pit, beckoning to Higgins and

Martin to follow. They'd both stood silent while Jay and I had our gunfight. At the top, I called out to the lead crime scene officer. 'DS Dorward,' I said, 'I know this place must be a fucking mess, with council staff walking all over it twice a week, but I need you to get as much as you can out of it. First off, I need to know how many people were in here with the dead man.' The SOCO opened his mouth but I cut him off. 'Yes, I know it's possible that nobody else was here with him, that he was off his face on something and thought he was Greg Louganis, but I do not believe that. I want everything there is. Start with the door that was jemmied.'

Red hair poking out angrily from under his tunic hood, the man stared at me as if I'd asked him whether he regularly had sex with pigs. 'That's the first place we went, sir,' he retorted. 'It's covered in prints. If the victim's are there, we'll find them.'

'Of course you will. Sorry. Give me everything you can, as soon as you can, but without compromising thoroughness.'

'What does "compromising" mean, sir?' he drawled. 'Is that a CID term?'

I laughed. Dorward's path and mine hadn't crossed too often, but every detective in the force knew of his prickliness.

'Nah,' I replied, 'it's a general term, as in "compromising your promotion chances". Sarcasm can be good for that.'

He smiled, calmly. 'I'll bear that in mind, sir. Now will the three of you please fuck off and let me get on with it.' Dorward was untouchable and he knew it. He was a genius at what he did, and rank meant nothing to him.

We peeled off our sterile gear and stepped back outside, where Alex was waiting with McGuire. 'Where's Mr Jay gone?' she asked, frowning as if she knew.

'Home. I've taken over the investigation.'

'What is it?'

'It's a suspicious death.' I was always matter-of-fact about my job when I discussed it with my daughter. I didn't believe in euphemism . . . not that she'd let me get away with any since she was five, and she'd forced me to use the 'D' word when I tried to explain why her mother wouldn't be coming back from the hospital. For almost a year after the accident, that's where I'd said she was, but with kids such deceits don't survive a week at a village primary school.

'You mean a murder?' she persisted.

'We don't know yet. Nothing's ruled out till we can prove it couldn't have happened.'

'So what happens now?' She seemed excited by the situation.

Good question, kid. If I'd been any good at delegation, I could have given my three subordinates orders and taken Alex home; but I'm not, and never have been. I wanted to be the one who did what had to happen next; I wanted to see the expression on Bella Watson's face when I told her that her second son had died a violent death.

I took a few steps away, nodding to Alison to follow. 'Would you do me a big favour,' I whispered, 'one that's completely unfair of me to ask a colleague of your rank? And don't fucking call me "sir" when you answer.'

A faint grin touched the corners of her mouth. 'Sure, Bob. I'll do it.'

'You know what it is?'

'Of course. You want me to take your daughter home and wait till you get back there.'

'You don't mind?' I said.

'No, but so what if I did?' The grin became a wide smile, reminding me of how attractive she could be. 'You can hardly send her home with a uniformed cop, and I wouldn't trust my mother's cat with Andy Martin.'

I didn't expect Alex to make a fuss when I told her what was happening, but neither did I expect her to be quite as enthusiastic as she was. She'd met Alison once before, by accident, when we were on a clothes shopping expedition in the junior designer section of John Lewis, and for a while after that she'd looked at me curiously.

The two of them headed off towards Alison's car, which was parked at the top of the street, leaving me with Martin and McGuire. 'You were in this at the start,' I told the PC, 'so you can stay for the ride. You and DC Martin are both seconded to Serious Crimes . . . temporarily, I stress . . . so you can lose that uniform for a while.'

The Irish Italian beamed. 'Yes, boss. What do you want me to do?'

'What you're told, and no more. You are not CID yet, so don't let it go to your head.' I checked my watch: twenty minutes to nine. 'There's a mugshot of Marlon Watson in the drugs squad office at headquarters. Have it faxed to St Leonards, then take it into all the pubs in the area, not just that one across the road. There's the cellar bar in Chambers Street, the Irish pub along South Bridge, and a couple more; you'll have time to check them all before last orders. Show it to the staff and any regulars they point you at. Ask whether anyone saw him on Tuesday, or even Monday. We shouldn't rule that out, he may have died earlier than we think.'

'What if someone saw him on Wednesday?' McGuire asked. (He was flippant from the start; it's one of his strengths, funnily enough, for it encourages people to underestimate him.)

'Then arrest him, because he fucking killed him! Report to me at headquarters tomorrow morning, in the SCU office. Andy, while Mario's doing that, you and I are going to find the mother, to break the bad news.'

Martin looked back at me. 'What about the father?'

'He hasn't been around for donkeys. He was a seaman; worked the trawlers, they said. As far as I know he sailed away twenty years ago and never came back. I doubt if he even knows that Ryan's dead. That's if he isn't himself.'

'Wife?'

'Marlon? Not that I've heard of; last time he was lifted he gave Bella's address.'

'Do you know her?'

'Oh yes,' I said, heavily. 'When Billy shot the Holmeses, there was a whisper from an informant that it was Bella who bought the gun and told him to do it. DCS Stein, the head of CID, put it to her himself. I was there at the time. She told him to either prove it or fuck off. Perry made one of his rare mistakes there. He should have told his brother to kill all three Spreckleys, not just Gavin. If he'd ever met Bella, maybe he would have.'

# Two

The Watson family home was in a crumbling council estate on the south side of the city. It was one of the urban sores that Scottish Homes had been set up to eradicate, and it should have been high on its agenda, but wasn't. The police station that had been built there a few years earlier might have been the work of an architect who'd seen *Assault on Precinct 13*. Indeed that had probably been in the design brief.

There were a few kids hanging out in the street as I parked in the gathering gloom, and I cursed myself for lack of foresight. I had two cars, a BMW 3 Series saloon that I used socially, and a battered, scratched six-year-old Land Rover Discovery that was my work car. Since Myra's death I'd always gone for solid vehicles with good all-round protection. When I'd left home, because Alex was with me, I'd taken the Beamer, without thinking ahead. It was a nice car, gunmetal blue metallic, and it drew admiring glances, even in Gullane, where upmarket was the norm. Where we were, it was more likely to draw gunfire.

We got out, and as I locked up I looked around; a few yards away a group of half a dozen boys and youths stood, some eyeing me up, a couple looking at the car and almost salivating as they did. 'Just a minute,' I said to Martin. I walked up to them. The oldest of them might have been sixteen, maybe a year or so younger, but he was a big

35

lad. He was cocky with it, didn't flinch as I approached, but looked at me as if he was thinking of having a go there and then.

I held his gaze. 'If you haven't guessed,' I began, 'we are the polis. We're going into that building, and we'll probably be a while in there. You lads are appointed to watch my motor.'

'What's in it for us?' the gang leader grunted. I felt a wee bit sorry for him. In his environment face was important and he was about to lose some, in front of his crew.

'We'll discuss that when the job's done. But if, when we come out of there, I see one mark on my car, as much as one fingerprint on the windscreen, I will pick you out, yes you, son, personally, and I will knock seventeen different colours of shite out of you. There will be no point in doing it over then getting off your mark, because I will come back, and back, and back until I've found you. My name is Skinner, and I'm a man of my word.'

I left them to consider my offer and rejoined Martin; he'd been watching from the other side of the road. 'What was that about, sir?' he asked.

'Personnel management. Come on.'

The houses in the street were all in tenement blocks, but Bella Watson's house was ground floor, with a main door that opened out on to a narrow, untended garden, with beer cans, cigarette packets and other garbage littering what might have been a lawn with a little interest, imagination and effort. I'd been there twice; after her brother had re-enacted the OK Corral gunfight, and a year or so later to take Marlon in for questioning that I'd known would be pointless but had to be done.

The door was painted grey, with a quarter panel of dappled obscure glass. The DC stepped in front of me and pressed the buzzer. 'What the hell are you doing?' I chuckled. 'She'll think you're the rent man.

Fat chance of her answering then.' I leaned forward and pounded the woodwork, hard, with the side of my closed right fist, once, twice, a third time. 'Now she knows. Count to thirty, slowly.'

'Why?'

'To give her time to hide anything she doesn't want us to see.'

He had reached twenty-eight when we saw the handle turn.

Bella Watson was better dressed than she had been on my previous visit. She'd never been scruffy, but the casual house-wear that I'd been expecting had been replaced by a short-sleeved blouse with vertical cream and brown stripes, a close-fitting brown skirt, and shiny high-heeled shoes; none of it looked as if it had come from Littlewoods catalogue. It was the first sign she'd ever given me that she had a body, and it took me by surprise. Her hair was different too; the grey streaks that I'd seen before had gone, it was a lustrous auburn and it had a Charlie Miller look about it. She was around fifty, I knew, but with the new style and a tan that was way out of place in her neighbourhood, she could have passed for at least five years younger.

The mouth was still the same, though. 'Aw fuck, it's you,' she moaned, as she looked up at me. 'What do you want now? Ma boy's no' here.'

'We know that,' I told her. 'He's with us. Invite us in, Bella.'

She knew it wasn't a request; and she stood aside to let us past and into the hallway. The house had had a makeover too. There was a new fitted carpet in the living room, and a white three-seater settee and armchair that had a leather look to it. The telly in the corner was bigger than mine. I glanced at the sideboard, at the two framed photographs that stood upon it; Marlon and a boy who hadn't grown much older than he'd been when it was taken. There wasn't one of the daughter, I noticed. 'Marlon's earning good money, surely,' I remarked.

'This has got fuck all tae do wi' him,' she snapped.

I stared at her. 'You're not telling me you've got a job, are you? There would have been a story in the *Evening News* about that.'

'Smart bastard.'

'So what is the story? Or is this all knock-off? Would you like to show us receipts for this lot?'

Her eyes blazed at me. 'Piss off, Skinner!' she snarled. 'If ye must know, it's our Mia. She's been lookin' after me. She's doing all right for herself.'

I didn't know Mia; I'd never met her. But as far as I knew she hadn't broken the mould and gone straight to Oxford from Maxwell Academy. She wasn't the business of the evening, though. 'Does Marlon still live with you?' I asked her.

'Aye. Why? Did he tell you lot different?'

I shook my head. 'No, he hasn't said a word to us. When did you see him last, Bella?'

Her eyes narrowed. 'Why?'

'Listen,' I said, 'we're not trying to do him for anything. I need to know, that's all.'

'Tuesday,' she muttered, grudgingly. 'Tuesday afternoon, before he went out.'

'Had he been in all day?'

'No, he'd been at his work.'

'With Tony Manson?'

She seemed to draw herself up to her full height, about five eight in the heels, and a look of pride shone in her eyes. 'Yes, wi' Mr Manson. He's his prodigy.'

'I think that might be protégé, Bella; who told you that?'

'Mr Manson did.'

'Manson came here?'

'No. I'd to go to his place one day. Marlon had left his mobile at home, and he needed it.'

A question suggested itself. 'Are you working for Manson too, Bella?'

'No.'

I didn't believe her. 'Bella!'

She folded. 'Okay, occasionally.'

'What sort of work?'

'In one of his launderettes.'

Tony Manson had a range of commercial interests; they included low-rent offices around the West End of Edinburgh and in Leith, two discos, one in Fountainbridge and another in Bellevue, a pub chain that was incorporated and traded as Bidey Inns, several saunas, a private hire taxi company, and a string of launderettes. It was believed that much of what was laundered there was money from Manson's other business activities, drugs, prostitution, protection and loan-sharking. I knew all those places and I'd never seen anyone in a launderette dressed as the new-look Bella was.

I shook my head. 'Try again?'

She snorted. 'All right, Skinner. God, you're a fuckin' bastard. Ah do a few shifts in the saunas, when Ah'm needed.'

'I didn't know you were a qualified masseuse.'

'Ah can massage a cock as well as most, although probably no' as well as one of you polis shites.'

Beside me, young Martin seemed to recoil with distaste. I saw his hand go, subconsciously, to the crucifix on his neck chain, as if he was warding off an evil spirit, and maybe he was. 'Back to Marlon,' I said. 'You're saying you haven't seen him since Tuesday?'

'That's right.'

'Does he often stay away for a couple of days?'

'Naw, but he said that Mr Manson had gone tae Newcastle, so I suppose he's gone too.'

'He'd no other plans for Tuesday?'

'None that he told me.' Finally she seemed to realise that I was stringing her along; she folded her arms tight across her chest and glared at me. 'Look, Skinner,' she hissed. 'What the fuck is this about?'

She was a nasty, vicious cow from a family without a detectable moral code, but there is one part of the job that no cop ever enjoys; doesn't matter who's being given the news. 'Sit down, Bella,' I murmured.

And she did, hard, on the leather settee. I didn't have to say another word; she knew well enough, for she'd had the same news before. Under the tan her face went ashen, then her back straightened and her mouth set in a thin white line; but her eyes stayed dry. 'What happened?' she asked. The edge on her voice could have shattered diamonds.

'He was found dead late this afternoon,' I replied, 'in the old swimming baths in Infirmary Street. We're not certain how long he'd been there, but we think since Tuesday night.'

'How did he die?'

'It seems that he fell off the high board. Our guess is that he had help.'

'Was it just him?'

'What do you mean?'

'What about Mr Manson? Marlon wasnae just his driver, he was his minder as well.'

'No, Manson wasn't there; we still have to speak to him. But he'll keep. Bella, do you know if Marlon might have upset him in some way?'

'Naw. No chance of that. Marlon worships the ground that man walks on. And Tony,' she corrected herself, 'Mr Manson, likes him too. This is someone else.' Her expression changed, turned into one of pure savagery. 'That bastard Holmes! I should have done that fuckin' job myself, no' trusted our Billy!'

'Stop right there, Bella,' I warned her. 'Whatever Holmes was in the past, he's out of it now. The man can't even wipe his own arse. Now, if you've got any idea who might have done this, tell us now, and we'll nail them. But you do nothing yourself; you've lost enough of your family to the life you chose to live.'

Her eyes blazed up at me. 'Chose? You fuckin' ignorant toffee-nosed bastard. You come and live here. You bring your family here and see what sort of a fuckin' choice you've got.'

I didn't have a glib response to that one. All I could offer was, 'People do move out, Bella.'

'Aye, most of them in the back of a Panda car, the rest in boxes, like ma boys and ma brothers. Thank God our Mia's made it.'

'Where is she?' I asked. 'Married?'

'She's had better luck than that. She's got a good job; she's on the radio.'

Back then, I was a cynic, so my life wasn't full of surprises, but every now and then . . . I couldn't hold back a gasp. 'Eh? As what?'

'She's a presenter. A disc jockey, like. She calls herself Mia Sparkles. Watson or Spreckley didnae sound showbiz enough.'

'Where? What station's she on?'

'Airburst,' Martin volunteered.

I looked at him. 'Never heard of it.'

'Maybe not, boss, but I'll bet your daughter has. There were some new licences issued the year before last; it started broadcasting last August. They're targeting a young audience. The advertising profile's ten to twenty-five. It's doing well, from what I've read. Mrs Watson's daughter does what they call the "School's Out" slot, three hours, four to seven.'

'You sound like a regular listener.'

He shrugged his shoulders, encased in a shiny new leather jacket. 'Why not? I still fit their listener profile . . . just.'

'Where can we contact Mia, Bella?' I asked.

'You don't,' she growled. 'She'll hear this from me.'

'Were she and her brother close?'

'Aye, of course they were.' She didn't convince me. If the family unit was so tight-knit, why was Mia missing from the sideboard?

'Then we'll need to interview her,' I told her.

'Well, you can find her at the station, I suppose. I'm no' helpin' yis.'

On another day I might have pushed her harder, but I let it go. 'We'll do that. There's something else; we'll need a formal identification of Marlon's body. Either you or Mia could do that.'

'Ah'll do it!' she said, firmly. 'Where is he?'

'In the mortuary. We'll take you there just now if you like.'

She snorted. 'Ah'm no' leaving here wi' you two bastards. Ah ken where it is. Ah was there before, for oor Billy, remember.'

I nodded. 'If that's what you want. I'll delay the post-mortem until ten tomorrow morning. Be there for nine thirty, please.'

She stood, and we turned to leave. Unexpectedly, I felt a sudden rush of admiration for her stoicism. 'Bella,' I murmured, 'I'm sorry.'

She sighed. 'No, you're fuckin' not. A year from now you'll have forgotten about Marlon, just like everybody's forgotten about poor wee Ryan, and ma brothers.'

I didn't tell her, but she was wrong. I've never forgotten, not a single one of them, nor any of the others.

The young team was still outside, standing across the street from my car. I walked around it slowly, examining it. It was spotless; I wouldn't have been surprised if they had polished it. I nodded approval.

The leader walked across. 'Okay then, boss?'

'Fine.'

'What's in it for us?'

'My appreciation.' His eyes narrowed, angrily. 'Listen, son,' I went on, 'and think about this. There are people in this street that are capable of killing you if they see you taking money from a cop. That's one reason for my hand staying in my pocket. The other is that if I did pay your lot, you'd take it as a licence to extort money from any dumb stranger who parked here. I will give you this, though.' Quickly, so that none of the others could see, I slipped one of my business cards into the pocket of his shirt. 'What's your name?' I asked him.

'Clyde Houseman.'

'Well, Clyde, if it ever occurs to you that it might be a good idea to get out of this hellhole and get a life that gives you a chance to be different, you call me, on one of those numbers, and I'll show you how.'

I unlocked the pristine Beamer, started the engine, and drove off. In the mirror, I saw that Clyde was still looking after me as I turned at the junction and passed out of his sight.

# Three

I dropped Martin at the St Leonards police office, where Jay's team were based. I looked into the CID suite, but its detective superintendent was long gone, and the place would have been empty, save for a young woman PC who was covering the phones, Martin's job, I guessed, if I hadn't snaffled him.

'When do you finish?' I asked her. She looked at me, severely, as if I was going to ask her on a date. 'Just curious,' I added.

'Officially I haven't started yet,' she replied. 'I'm night shift, ten to six, but I got here twenty minutes early and DS Bryce borrowed me from the front desk.' She was an attractive girl, in the same age bracket as Martin. Her hair was as distinctively red as his was blond.

'Coke and Mars bars,' I said.

'Excuse me?'

'Stock up with Coca-Cola and Mars bars. There's instant energy in both. They're murder on your teeth, but when you need them they help you make it through the night.'

She threw me a sideways look; I guessed that she gave away her smiles reluctantly. 'I'll bear that in mind, Mr . . . Sorry, I don't know who you are.'

'Bob Skinner, DCI, until tomorrow morning, then it's detective super. I work out of Fettes.'

'Drugs squad, I assume,' she added, solemnly. 'That explains why you know a lot about stimulants.'

'Most are legal, PC . . . ?'

'Rose. Margaret Rose.'

'Have a good night, PC Rose. When you feel your eyelids begin to droop, remember what I told you.'

I told Martin to be at headquarters for half past eight next morning, and to be prepared to witness a post-mortem. 'Have you been to one before?' I asked, cautiously. I'd learned the hard way to stand well clear of inexperienced colleagues while watching Joe Hutchinson at work.

He nodded. 'A couple, with DI Higgins.'

'See you tomorrow, then.' I'd noticed before, the guy had vivid green eyes, unusual in itself, but these were really different.

I must have been staring at him. 'I wear contacts,' he said. 'They're slightly tinted, for the sun.'

It was pushing ten thirty by the time I got home, but barely dark, for high summer was approaching. Alison's car was parked on Goose Green alongside my Land Rover, opposite the cottage. The curtains were drawn in the living room, but a silver sliver showed through a gap. There was no light, though, in the attic dormer, Alex's room.

I tapped my watch as I walked in. 'What's this?'

As a teenager, my daughter set her own hours, within limits, but she tended to begin the process of bedding down for the night around ten o'clock. 'I couldn't let Alison sit on her own, could I?' she declared.

'Maybe not, but she's not on her own now.'

'Okay.' She jumped out of my armchair. 'Goodnight, Alison, goodnight, Pops.' She gave me a quick kiss on the cheek, then headed for the stairs.

'Thanks,' I said, as soon as the living-room door closed, 'a million thanks.'

'Don't mention it,' Alison replied. 'I should be thanking you.'

'Why?'

'You could have sent me to see the bereaved mother, instead of doing it yourself.'

'If I'd done that, I'd have had to second you to Serious Crimes.'

She was holding a mug in both hands; she raised it and took a sip. 'But you're not going to?'

'No, I've got a DI there already; besides, I've already made up my mind to take young Martin from your squad. If I said I wanted you as well, Jay would scream bloody murder.'

'You were hard on my boss tonight,' she murmured.

'Your boss is a double-dyed, chromium-plated shite, and you know it. If he ever gets to be head of CID, we're all fucked.'

'Do you think he might?'

I grinned, and winked at her. 'Not a chance.' I walked into the kitchen; Alison rose from her seat and followed me. I took two bottles of Becks from the fridge, popped the caps and handed one to her.

She smiled as she laid down the mug and took it from me 'You know, Bob, you can be really devious, when you set your mind to it.'

'Now what does that mean?'

'Cunning, crafty, wily, Machiavellian; I could go on.'

'I know what the bloody word means, woman; I'm asking why you're hanging it round my neck.'

'Because you're an operator. You make things happen without people knowing that your hand's behind them . . . at least you don't think they know. You're driven by ambition, and you won't let anyone stand in your way. I'll bet you've got your whole career planned out.'

I took her hand and led her back through to the living room, sat on the sofa and drew her down beside me. 'No,' I said, 'I haven't. But Alf Stein and the chief have; they spelled it out for me yesterday. I do two years in this new job, then I make chief super. I go back into uniform for a year, or do a secondment somewhere . . . James Proud has contacts that you would not believe . . . then Alf retires and I succeed him. After that . . . they did not elaborate.' I put an arm around her shoulders, and she settled in against me. 'But honest to Christ, Alison, it's their plan, not mine. I don't suffer fools, and I cut corners when I have to, but I'd never stand on anyone to get to the top.'

She squeezed my hand. 'I didn't mean that you would. I was talking about me. You got me off the drugs squad, didn't you? My move back into mainstream CID, you told me it was routine, career development, but it wasn't, was it? You guys in specialist units, you can do what you bloody like; I've seen you. You had me moved.'

She had me there. 'Yes, I did,' I admitted. 'Confession time; I fixed it up. But you know why. I don't have to spell that out for you, do I?'

'Maybe not, but Bob, I've hardly seen you since. I know it's difficult for you domestically, but . . .'

'You were the one who told me it wasn't going anywhere,' I reminded her. 'I distinctly remember you saying that, one lunchtime at your place.'

'Maybe so, but . . . Bloody men! I didn't mean you to take me so literally. Whoever said that I wanted it to go anywhere beyond where it was. I don't want to marry you, Bob, don't worry about that, but the way it was between us, it suited me. Now I feel as if you've dropped me.'

I ran my fingers through her hair; it was dark, but with blond highlights. 'Don't think that, Ali, not for a minute. Look, you see the way I am here; you see the way Alex and I are. I've always tried to keep my life with her separate from everything else, and I've succeeded. I wouldn't have brought her with me tonight if I'd had any other option. Well, maybe I did, maybe I could have told Jay to fuck off, that I'd look at his body in the morning.'

'No, you couldn't,' she contradicted me. 'It's against your nature.'

'Be that as it may, one side effect of us being in different offices . . . our thing started out of proximity, and that way it was easy to maintain, but . . .'

Her gaze dropped to her lap. 'I get it. You only want low-maintenance women.'

'No! Fuck, I'm tripping over myself here. What I'm trying to say is that I'm sorry I've neglected you, and now you think I've dumped you, but I haven't. You want proof, yes, I could have told you and Martin to go and see Bella yourselves, but I didn't. I wanted you to be here when I got back.' I nudged her. 'See, you're right; I am a devious bastard.'

'Well, you got what you wanted. Now I must be going.' She made as if to rise, but I held on to her.

'You're not going.' I tapped the empty bottle in her hand. 'We both knew that, when you took that beer.'

'But Alex . . .'

'Sleep in the spare room if you like, but as you drop off think on this: my daughter tried to pair me off with her auntie earlier on tonight because she couldn't think of anyone else suitable. If you're still here in the morning, you'll see those blue eyes of hers light up.'

# Four

And did they ever, when she came into the kitchen in her dressing gown and saw Alison cramming a slice of toast into her face, as she slipped on her jacket. No, she hadn't slept in the spare room, but she had gone in there, crumpled the sheets and punched a head-sized hole in one of the pillows. She was gone by seven thirty; I spent the next fifteen minutes before Daisy arrived waiting for the cross-examination, but it didn't happen. It was only when I was leaving myself that Alex whispered, 'She's nice.'

I had reached the Land Rover when something that had slipped my mind slipped back in. I went back to the cottage. 'Hey, kid,' I called out from the door. 'Does the name Mia Sparkles mean anything to you?'

She stepped into the hall from the living room. 'Yes! Airburst FM. She's good!'

'How does she sound?'

'Smooth . . . but not too smooth, not phoney. Plays really good music. Why, Dad?'

'I'm probably going to be meeting her today, that's all.'

'Get me an autographed photo.'

My new team was ready and waiting when I walked into the Serious Crimes office for the first time as their leader. I'd been presented to them the day before by Alf Stein, but none of them were strangers to me. The DI was a sound, forty-ish guy called Graham Leggat . . . everybody called him Fred; he told me why once, but I can't remember now . . . I had a DS named Jeff Adam, who had 'competent' stamped all over him, and a couple of time-serving DCs, Macken and Reid. They were all wondering who Martin and McGuire were, and what they were doing there. I explained what had happened the evening before, and that the pair had become caught up in it.

'In theory, they're both on secondment, but you can regard Andy as permanent. Mario's still on the uniform strength, but if he earns his spurs, he might get to wear them here. What did you get last night, PC McGuire?'

'No sightings in any of the pubs, sir; I'm sorry.'

'Don't be too bothered. Half the IDs we get from mugshots are wrong anyway; some are people trying to be helpful, others just taking the piss.'

'There was one thing, though.'

'Oh yes? Enlighten, please.'

McGuire looked untypically diffident. 'Well, it might be nothing, boss, but the manager of the Irish pub on the South Bridge, he told me that he'd locked up on Tuesday and was walking home past Infirmary Street, a bit after midnight, when he saw something happening down there. He described it as a scuffle, two men grappling with a third.'

'You showed him the image?'

'Sure, but he didn't recognise it.'

'What did he do?'

'He kept on walking. He's no have-a-go hero, boss.'

'Maybe as well for him. Did he give you any sort of a description?'

The PC nodded. 'He said that two of them were wearing suits. He thought at first that they were pub bouncers, but there was nothing still open then. The third guy he thought was dressed in black, shirt and trousers.'

'Good. Well done.'

'He gave me a wee bit more, though,' he continued. 'He said they were up against a Transit van, and that one of the back doors was open.'

I was impressed. 'We should get the guy in and show him some photos, just in case. Take care of that, please.'

'Can I wait till he's really busy, sir?' McGuire asked.

I smiled, puzzled. 'Sure, but why?'

'He deserves it. If he'd been a bit braver, even if he'd only made a noise, yelled at the guys, they might have legged it and Watson, if that was him, might still be alive.'

I nodded. 'Do it in your own time, Mario. But don't ever let Marlon's mother hear that story. I don't want her paying a call on the guy. Meantime, I want you to get on to the council. Check out all the street cameras in the area and get their tapes for Tuesday evening. Maybe we'll get a sighting of the van and, better still, the two guys.'

I was about to send everyone off to work, and take Martin with me to meet Bella Watson at the morgue, when I paused for second thoughts. If I did that, I'd be marching into my new unit with my own small team and sidelining everyone else. 'Listen, guys,' I said to Leggat and Adam, 'there'll be time later on today for you to brief me on the team's current workload, but we have an immediate situation. The man who was found dead last night was Tony Manson's driver, and I don't need to set out the questions that throws up. Fred, I'd like you and Martin to find out where Manson is. Bella Watson told us that he's out of town. Is that true? If it is, what's the reason for the trip? Is it genuine, or could he simply be putting distance between himself and what happened in Infirmary Street Baths? I'd suggest that you talk to his lawyer.'

'That shifty wee bastard Cocozza?'

'That's the one, Fred.' I looked at the two DCs. Most probably they were going to be moved on, but they were what I had to work with at that moment. 'While that's happening, I want you gentlemen doing the rounds of Manson's known associates. Talk to them and see if they let anything slip about Tony's territory being under attack from outside. Fred, have a word with the Scottish Crime Squad and the NCIS. I wouldn't put it past them to be sitting on something they should have passed on to us.'

'Do you want to involve them?' Leggat asked

'Not until the investigation moves out of our territory, and even then only as far as I have to. DS Adam, I want you with me.' I caught Martin's glance out of the corner of my eye. 'Nothing personal,' I whispered, as I walked past him towards the door. 'Work it out and tell me later.'

I let Adam drive to the mortuary. We'd crossed over on a few investigations when I'd been working with Alf Stein. He was never going to drop the ball, but he'd used up all the original thoughts he'd ever had in his head. I liked him, though, and his absolute trust-worthiness meant that he was going to stay on my team. 'Do you know the Watson and Spreckley families?' I asked him, as we crossed Heriot Row.

'I wasn't around when Gavin and the kid got it,' he replied, 'but I saw the colour of Billy's brains after big Kraus spread them all over Perry Holmes's office. I never met him, though; he dropped out of sight for a while. I did interview Bella, though, with Tommy Partridge. We were both sure that she put him up to it.'

'She told me as much last night. Ancient history, but still, that's why I don't want her hearing the story McGuire was told.'

'That lad,' Adam murmured. 'Do you know who he is?'

'Sure. He's a police constable on my team.'

'Yes but . . .'

I held up a hand to stop him. 'Jeff, of course I know McGuire's back story. He's the nephew of Beppe Viareggio, and the grandson of old Papa Viareggio, who snuffed it about ten years ago, after he'd built up a very successful deli, importing, and property business. His mother married an Irish building contractor and founded one of the most successful secretarial employment agencies in the city. I know also that over the years there have been stories about the Viareggio clan having links to the Mafia. There isn't a prominent Italian family in Scotland that hasn't had that whispered about them at one time or another. It's a load of bollocks in most cases, and most certainly in theirs. Yes, the old man and his wife, who's still full of beans, incidentally, were first-generation immigrants from an Italy where secret societies were rife, but they came here to get away from that, not to import it. You would never, ever, have fucked with Papa, but he was absolutely straight. Same with Beppe, only he's a wimp who would crap himself if he was ever in the same room with the faintest scent of organised crime. This was all established years ago, when I was here last, and if I should find that the Serious Crimes Unit has been wasting resources monitoring McGuire's family . . .' I took a deep breath. 'If it has been, the files will be useless, so if they exist, shred them before I come across them, or before McGuire does. Understood?'

'Yes, boss.' He smiled. 'Not that there are any such files, you understand.'

They were ready for us when we arrived at the mortuary. Marlon Watson's body was in the viewing room, laid out on a trolley under a sheet, face uncovered, with the right, less damaged, side of his face in profile. The pathologist was there too, with a young assistant, one of his PhD students, I suspected.

Joe Hutchinson was every cop's carver of choice, occupant of the Chair of Forensic Pathology at Edinburgh University, and top man in his field. The force booked him whenever it could, even for jobs that didn't appear at first sight to need his special skills, just in case there was more to it than we thought and we wound up facing him as an expert defence witness.

'Didn't you get the message, Joe?' I asked. 'I said ten o'clock start.'

'Busy day, Bob,' the diminutive professor replied. 'We'll get under way as soon as you've got the formal identification over with. While you're doing that I'll take a look at the photographs, and at the report of my colleague who attended the scene.'

He'd barely gone when Bella Watson arrived. We met her in the anteroom. She was wearing a different outfit, a dark trouser suit over a white blouse; not her working clothes, of that I was sure. 'Have you got them yet?' she snapped, even before the door had closed behind her.

'Them?' I repeated.

'Ma boy could take care of himself. It would have taken more than one.'

'Not if he was shot,' Adam pointed out.

She glowered at him. 'Another blast frae the fuckin' past,' she growled. 'Where's the other yin, the fair-haired lad?' she asked me.

'Doing other things.'

'Pity. He had a bit o' sympathy about him.'

I let that pass me by. 'If you're ready,' I said. She nodded and I led her into the viewing room, Jeff Adam behind her. 'Is this the body of your son, Marlon Watson?' I asked her, for the record.

She didn't flinch when she looked at the trolley; there wasn't a sign of a tremor, but in truth, I hadn't expected her to collapse at my feet. After all, this was a woman who'd once identified her brother by the tattoos on the knuckles of the severed right hand that was all they had to show her. 'Yes,' she replied, then turned on her heel and walked out.

'Thanks, Bella,' I said, outside. 'I know, from personal experience, that couldn't have been easy for you.'

I was trying to be sympathetic, but she looked at me with disdain. 'You know fuck all,' she sneered.

I gave up trying. 'But you know a fucking sight more than you've told us,' I barked. 'You can't expect me to believe that Marlon didn't tell you anything about his job with Manson. What was going on there? For that matter, you're hocking your mutton to punters in the saunas. No prizes for guessing which ones or who owns them, so, how did a woman your age get taken on there? You're not doing it to pay off drug debts. I can tell a serious user just by looking at her, and you're not one. But you're not a kid either; you're about fifteen years older than the norm, even if you don't look it. Come on, did you get the gig through Marlon, or did Manson take you on himself?' I thought I saw the faintest twitch in the corner of one eye. 'Hey!' I exclaimed. 'You've been shagging Tony, haven't you?'

'Fuck off!' she shouted and stormed out of the building.

'Well, well, well, Jeff,' I murmured. 'How about that for a connection!'

'For sure,' he chuckled. 'How did you stumble on that?'

'It wasn't that difficult. Manson's a famous sexual athlete. He owns those saunas, all fronts for brothels, and the girls that work in them are on call. He wants laid, he phones. My guess? Marlon asked him if his mother could work there, Tony had a look, and gave her the okay; almost certainly test-drove her himself. It fits, all of it. She catches Manson's eye, and before you know it she has nice new furniture, she's clothes shopping in Jenner's, and her son goes from being one of the boss's several message boys to being his personal driver. Tell me a part that doesn't fit.'

'I can't,' he admitted. 'But what does it tell us, boss?'

'Nothing for sure, but it makes me wonder. If Marlon's death is down to a potential rival of Tony's, does that make Bella a target too?' I mused. 'It might.'

'What can we do about it if she is?'

'We could pity the guys that go for her. If she's not carrying a shooter in her handbag I'd be surprised. Of course we could find it and lift her for that, but it wouldn't get us anywhere. No, I'm going to put her under surveillance.'

'Who will you use?'

I looked at him. 'I'll need to think about that. She knows us, she's seen Martin, and McGuire would stand out like a lighthouse. Macken and Reid? What do you think?'

Adam hesitated. 'To be honest . . .' he began.

I let him get no further. 'Don't ever be anything else. We'll use new talent, then. I'll take care of it. Come on, we'd better get suited up for Joe's performance.'

By the time we took our places at the back of the autopsy suite, Marlon had been moved to the dissection table. 'All present?' the professor asked. 'Then let's begin.' He beckoned towards him. 'Before we begin, gentlemen,' he said, 'I want you to take a look at these X-rays.' Several images, covering the full length of the body, were set out on a long viewing screen. He didn't have to tell me what he wanted us to see. There were obvious fractures of every limb, of several ribs, of the right collarbone, and of the skull.

'Christ, Joe,' I murmured, 'he looks as if he's been hit by a bus.'

'Travelling at quite a speed. I've had the length of the drop from the diving platform measured: thirty feet and seven inches. That means that he would have hit the deck at just over twenty miles per hour. An anomaly, certainly.'

'What does it say?'

'Let me do a full examination,' he said, 'and then I'll give you a wholly informed opinion. You go back over there and give me some breathing space.'

By that stage of my career I was a post-mortem veteran. They'd been a regular part of my time on the drugs squad. That doesn't mean to say I was permanently inured to the gore, the exposed bone and organs, and the smell. I had a sell-by date, as I found out more than a decade later; I believe that every police officer has . . . or should have. Today, I cannot continue reading a novel in which the author goes into a detailed autopsy description that has no real bearing on the narrative, but seems to be there only to shock or to show off. Back then, though, in my mid-thirties, I was able to stay detached. That's not to say what I saw had no effect. Years later, Alex told me that she always knew by my mood in the evening when I'd been to a post-mortem during the day. It was the only part of my job that I ever brought home even though I didn't know it at the time.

Joe Hutchinson was famously meticulous. He had never been caught out in the witness box and he never would be. But even by his standards his examination of Marlon Watson took a long time. I'd hoped to meet Alison for a quick lunch, but by mid-morning I could see where it was headed, so I called her to cancel. As it happened she was busy too, unexpectedly. I wondered if Jay was giving her a hard time.

The professor broke for coffee after two hours, but wouldn't give us a progress report. By the time it ended, the subject looked like a turkey on Boxing Day.

I was so relieved when we were able to peel off our suits and get out of there that I didn't mind waiting another twenty minutes for Joe to get himself scrubbed and dressed. He rejoined us in the reception area, looking tired, but satisfied, having left his assistant to reassemble the jigsaw.

'I would say, gentlemen, under oath of course, that whoever killed this man, they were very sadistic and very determined. I am not able to tell you how many times he was tossed from that platform, but it was, beyond doubt, more than once. You saw the X-rays for yourselves, but what they didn't indicate was that there are fractures to both the front and the back of the skull; conclusive proof. They simply kept chucking him off until he was dead. Hell of a way to kill someone,' he murmured, in a tone that almost sounded respectful. 'After the first couple of falls, he would have had to be carried or dragged back up to the platform, and that of itself would have been excruciating. The body is massively damaged, but there is bruising to the wrists and ankles that's consistent with him being gripped hard, lifted and tossed over the edge. In my view he was already dead, or dying, the last time this was done. He hit the floor of the pool skull and face first and there is no sign of any resistance to the impact on that occasion, but several of the fractures, to the wrists and arms for example, indicate that there was earlier. If it's important for you to know how often he was dropped, you might have your crime scene team examine the pool for damage to the tiles. It'll be there, it'll be considerable, and it might give you an answer.'

'It won't tell us why, though, Joe,' I pointed out. 'Could they have been trying to get information from him?'

'That's not a hypothesis I could advance in evidence. You'll have to catch the perpetrators and ask them.'

'And we will,' I said, 'but can you say as a pathologist whether you'd expect someone to survive a thirty-foot drop on to a hard surface?'

He pondered my question for a few seconds; eventually he nodded. 'A young, fit man, hands and feet unrestrained: yes, I would, but I'd expect fractures, even if he managed to land feet first.'

'So what we're dealing with here is a form of torture, not just an attempted murder that took a while to succeed?'

'That's one way of putting it, yes. To be frank, the only thing I can rule out is suicide.'

# Five

Leggat, Martin and McGuire were all in the office when we got back. The two DCs were still on a late lunch break; not a great way to impress a new boss, and even less so on the first day of an investigation.

I let Jeff Adam give them the blow-by-blow of the autopsy. 'They bounced the poor bastard off the swimming pool floor until he was dead,' he summarised, as neat a description as I could have offered.

'Somebody must have been seriously upset with him to do that,' the DI said.

'Or very keen for him to tell them something,' I pointed out.

'Could he have been double-crossing Tony over something? Or could he . . .' he stopped, in mid-sentence. 'Here, he isn't on anyone's informant list, is he?'

'Bella Watson's son? No way. No, Fred, when he was just running for Manson we . . . the drugs squad, I mean . . . had him in often enough. If he'd been a grass, I'd have been warned. Mind you . . . have a word with the Scottish Crime Squad crew, in case they were cultivating him.'

'Without telling us?'

'Roles reversed I wouldn't tell them,' I pointed out, 'unless they needed to know. Yes, do that, but we won't hold our breath for a response. No, first priority is finding Tony Manson. Did you check his house?'

'Yes, I sent a car out there. It's locked up, and the phone's on auto answer.'

'How did you get on with that wee shit of a lawyer?'

'He stonewalled us.' Leggat sighed. 'Said he doesn't know where his client is, or how to get in touch with him.'

'Did you believe him?'

'The first might be true, the second won't be.'

I turned to McGuire. I couldn't help but admire his suit; pale blue mohair. 'Mario, cameras?'

'They have tapes for us, boss. They've promised them by this afternoon.'

'Fine. Chase them up if they're not here in half an hour. When they arrive, review them; you know what you're looking for.'

'Yes, sir.'

'And one other thing. The suit; when I said you could lose the uniform I didn't mean you to replace it with Savile Row. This is CID. We do unobtrusive here.'

The big guy looked crestfallen. 'Sorry, boss.'

I smiled. 'That's okay. It might come in handy if you ever go undercover in the New Club. Who's your tailor, by the way?'

'A friend of my cousin Paula's,' he said, morale restored. 'She gets me a deal.'

'Mmm,' I murmured. 'Maybe she could get me one too.'

'I'll ask her.' Then he frowned. 'One other thing, sir. DCS Stein asked if you'd go and see him.'

'Urgent?'

'He didn't say so.'

Whatever, a summons from the head of CID wasn't something to be pushed to one side. I had a small private office at the far end of the suite. I headed for it, and asked Leggat to come with me. I'd been

61

shown it the day before. My predecessor, Jock Davey, had taken early retirement on health grounds, and a couple of his possessions were still on the desk, a calculator, and a heavy glass paperweight. I put them on the window sill and eased myself into the well-worn chair; Leggat took one of the visitor seats.

'Fred,' I began, 'before I go and see the boss, there are a couple of things we need to discuss. First, the media haven't happened upon this yet, not for what it is. Someone from the UNS news agency called St Leonards last night asking about activity in Infirmary Street and the desk sergeant told him it was a break-in, for at the time that's all he thought it was. But we have to come clean now. I'd like you to have the press office put out a statement telling the media that we're investigating the death of Marlon Watson . . . you can name him . . . and treating it as murder. No more detail than that, though. You should add on the usual appeal for witnesses. Anyone who saw Watson on Tuesday, or who saw anything unusual in the Infirmary Street area around midnight that night.'

The DI nodded. 'I've got it drafted already, sir.'

'I thought you might have. By the way, in this wee room, it's Bob. That's item one. Next, what's your view on our two DCs?'

'Macken and Reid? Not my choice, either of them; they don't know what initiative is. They were old cronies of DCI Davey; he brought them with him when he took over here.'

'Right. They'll be replaced. I don't plan to piss off Roy Old by emptying the drugs squad, but there's a DC there I want to bring in. His name's Brian Mackie. He's only a couple of years older than McGuire and Martin, but he's cool under pressure, plus he's firearms trained. I want to set up surveillance on Bella Watson. I'm going to put him on that, him and one other new boy.'

Leggat was surprised. 'Surveillance on the mother?'

'Yeah, for two reasons. I'm pretty certain that she's servicing Tony Manson, but I don't know how close they are. I'm also sure that the guys who killed Marlon didn't just do it for fun or revenge. They were trying to get information out of him. If his mother knows what he knew . . .'

'It makes her a potential target.'

'Precisely. But there's more than that; if she's in the loop, it's possible she has an idea who did for her boy. If so, they're in trouble themselves. Bella's tougher than any of her family were, and probably more dangerous.'

'I see,' he murmured, thoughtfully. 'Who have you got in mind for the second bod on surveillance?'

'Nobody. You got any ideas? Bear in mind that when the operation's over, Macken and Reid will be out and they'll stay.'

He leaned back in his chair. 'Male or female? There's that lass in DCS Stein's office. I rate her, if he'd let us have her.'

'Mmm. We're not supposed to be sexist, Fred, but where Bella lives a woman would be very obvious. We can fit her in, possibly, in the future, but for this job, a guy.'

'Age?'

'Don't care.'

'In that case,' he began, 'there's a young lad called Steele, DC Steven Steele. We were looking closely at Jackie Charles a couple of months ago, after an armed robbery, and I borrowed him from Leith. I saw a lot in him. Charismatic's not a word I chuck around, but it applied to him.'

I had to laugh. 'In that case he'll blend in well with Mackie. Big Brian's had a charisma bypass.' I rose. 'I'd better go see the boss, since he's asked. I'll fix those transfers with him.'

I left the suite and went down one floor, to the lair of the head of

CID. His exec . . . her name was Shannon, DC Dorothy Shannon . . . was behind his desk in the outer office. DCS Stein and I both liked to work with junior officers who were young enough not to have found a comfort zone. She looked up as I entered. 'Afternoon, sir,' she said, briskly.

'And you, Dottie, and you. Is he in?'

'Yes, sir. He's expecting you.'

He was standing by his coffee machine when I opened the door. He'd heard me, for there were two mugs beside it and he was filling them from the pot that stood there, ever ready. When he retired, he gave the contraption to me. To this day, I drink too much coffee and it's down to Alf.

'I hear you've had a baptism,' he murmured as he handed me a brimming mug, emblazoned with the image of his namesake, the late great football manager.

'Yes indeed,' I agreed. 'I had to take up the reins early,' I felt myself scowl, 'or rather I had them thrust into my hands.'

'I heard that too. You shouldn't be so rough on Greg.'

'Greg's a bam-pot,' I growled. Stein shared my west of Scotland origins; he knew what the word meant.

In fact he knew better than I did. 'No, son,' he chuckled, 'he's a bam-stick. A bam-stick is used for stirring a bam-pot, and that's what makes him useful.'

'Either way, he's shit.'

He looked at me sharply. 'Bob, you listen to me. The one thing that will hold you back in the job is letting personal feelings screw up your judgement. I don't like the man any more than you do. Indeed I know things about him that you don't, things I could use to bounce him off the force tomorrow. I'm not saying that he takes backhanders. Hell no, he dislikes criminals even more than he dislikes you, but he's got other faults. I keep him, though, because he's actually a better detective than he's given credit for. Of all the divisional CID commanders, he's got the best clear-up rate.'

'I gather you've had a call from him.'

'No, I've had a visit. He complained about you walking into his crime scene and kicking him off his own investigation. He complained about you bringing your daughter with you. He complained about you commandeering three of his officers. He complained about you having personal relations with one of them.'

'He did what!' I roared.

'Calm down, now, while I tell you. I yelled at him too when he said that, and asked him what the hell he meant by it. He told me that Higgins never went back to St Leonards. He said he called her at midnight, and then again at six in the morning, and got no reply, so he drove out to Gullane and saw her car parked outside your house.'

'I'm going to kill him,' I declared, quietly and sincerely.

'No, you're not.' Alf smiled. 'I forbid it.'

'Boss, I took Alex with me last night because I had no option. Jay effectively dumped the investigation in my lap, and Alison took her home as a favour to me. Yes, she stayed the night, but she was never part of the investigation team, so what's that to Jay? You know about the two of us, anyway. As for Martin and McGuire, I seconded them because I needed them and because you and the chief made it clear I've got the power to do that.'

'You don't have to explain yourself,' he told me. 'I'm not asking you to. Bob, I sent Jay out of here with his tail between his legs and the threat of organising traffic patrols in Hawick ringing in his ears. The only reason I'm telling you about it is to emphasise what can happen when you make enemies. You're a bull, son, and you've got to develop colour blindness when somebody waves a red flag at you.'

I nodded, chastened. 'Point taken, boss.' I frowned. 'But now you've got me worried about Alison. She works for Jay.'

'Not any more. I've told him that he's forfeited all rights to her confidence as a manager. I'm transferring her to Torphichen Place. She's going places and he's not getting in the way.'

'Good. Thanks.'

'I did it for her, son, not you.' He paused and looked at me, not as a colleague, but as the concerned friend of two people. 'Be easy with her, though, will you?'

'Of course.' I didn't want to prolong that discussion, so I moved on. 'I want to keep Martin and McGuire.'

'Fine, I'll sort it.'

'And I need two more guys, urgently.' I gave him a rundown on the murder investigation and explained the Bella Watson situation, then gave him the names of the DCs I wanted.

'Agreed,' he said. 'I'll order the transfers as of now.' He frowned. 'Somebody's rattling Tony Manson's cage?'

'Looks like it.'

'I don't like that. Tony's a ruthless, evil, drug-running, murderous bastard, and all the rest, but he's the status quo. He's the devil we know, and you know the saying. If we've got a new one on our patch, I want to know who he is. Any rumours?'

'Macken and Reid have been asking around.'

The DCS snorted. 'Those two wouldn't have a clue where to ask, Bob. But you do, and you've got the presence to make people talk to you. So has that boy Martin. I saw him play rugby a couple of weeks back, for Edinburgh against Borders. He's a fuckin' animal; brute strong.'

I hadn't picked that up, the night before, or when we'd worked together earlier. He didn't take it off-field. In truth, when he'd grasped for his cross in the presence of Bella I'd marked him down as a wimp. *I'll bear that in mind*, I thought.

'Where's your next call?' Alf asked.

'I need to interview Bella's daughter, Mia the deejay. She talks to people for a living; I'll have to find out if that extends to the police.'

# Six

I had no idea where Airburst FM was based, but Martin did, so I took him with me to meet Mia Watson. The studios were located in an anonymous, flat-roofed building on a commercial estate in Sighthill. I've noticed that local radio stations tend not to advertise their presence, as if it's okay for their listeners to phone them but bad news if they turn up on the doorstep. There was no neon sign above the Airburst premises, only a small brass plate on the door, although the cars parked outside, bedecked in the station logo, did give the game away.

The entrance was secure, with a videophone beside the door. Andy Martin announced our arrival and a girl came to let us in, a tiny wee thing with purple hair, a silver stud through her right nostril and another through her eyebrow. Facial ironmongery was starting to become fashionable then. I've never been a fan, or even understood it; Alex has had pierced ears since childhood, but has no ambition to go further.

The kid led us to a tiny reception area and asked us to wait there; we did, until she returned and led us through what looked like the newsroom, to an office beyond. It had glass walls, with black slatted blinds that were wide enough open to let us see, as we approached, a young woman, seated at a long table.

Our escort opened the door for us, but didn't follow us in. Mia Sparkles, née Watson, stood as we entered. She had brown hair, short, with an Audrey Hepburn look, and brown eyes; she wore very little make-up, a little blusher and lipstick, that was all, and she was dressed in white cotton trousers and a T-shirt bearing the station logo; she displayed it well.

I have this belief, that I can look at people and know what they're made of, under the skin. As I gazed at Mia, and imagined her mother, it came to me that they couldn't have been less alike. While Bella radiated hostility and hatred, her daughter was the complete opposite; I couldn't pin it down completely, but to me, she showed as provocative, enticing, exciting, a person who could connect with anyone she chose. She sparkled, simple as that; I found myself wondering if she'd chosen her radio name or whether it had been given to her.

Not that she was smiling at that moment. Her expression was solemn, for she knew why we had come. 'I'm Bob Skinner,' I told her. 'And this is DC Martin.'

She looked at Andy. 'It was you called me earlier?' she asked. He nodded. 'Sorry, I didn't catch the name.' Her attention, and those magnetic eyes, turned back to me. 'Is this about my brother?'

'You know, then.'

She nodded and blinked. 'Yes. My mum called me, this morning.' Her accent wasn't a bit like Bella's either: Scottish, but with no rough edges. Smoother than my Lanarkshire tones, that was for sure.

'We're sorry for your loss,' I offered.

'Thanks; I have a feeling that you mean that, and I appreciate it. It's terrible that a thing like that could happen to somebody.'

'Are you going on air this afternoon,' I asked her, 'or will someone stand in for you?'

She shook her head. 'No, that wouldn't be fair to the station, or to my listeners. I won't have a problem; I won't break down on air or anything like that. I don't mean that to sound heartless, Mr Skinner, but I haven't seen my brother since he was twelve years old. I never knew him as an adult. Nobody in here even knows I have a brother.'

'Our press office is issuing a statement about now,' I told her. 'It doesn't mention Marlon's connection with you. If that's something you want to keep private, we'll respect that.'

'Thanks. I'd be very grateful if you would.'

'So you haven't seen him at all lately?'

'No, as I said, never.'

'How about your mother?'

'Occasionally.'

'Did she ever talk about him?'

Mia smiled, but I sensed that it was false. 'She has two topics of conversation: money and herself.' She glanced at her watch. 'Listen, I hate to rush you, but I have to get my act together; I'm on in fifteen minutes.'

'Understood,' I said. I took out one of my calling cards; they'd have to be reprinted following my promotion but my Fettes extension number wouldn't change, it would move with me. As an afterthought I found a pen and scrawled my mobile number on the back, before I handed it to her. 'If anything occurs to you, something Bella might have said, for example, call me.'

She smiled. 'You know my mum?'

'Oh yes, I know your mum.' I had a quick memory flash. 'By the way, I've got a request from my daughter; she's a fan. Can she have an autographed photo?'

'My pleasure,' Mia replied. 'I'll attend to it after my show. I'll post it to the address on your card, yes?'

'That'll do fine. Her name's Alex.'

'Will I include her mother and you in the dedication?'

'She doesn't have a mother, not any more.'

She frowned. 'Oh. I'm sorry.'

I shrugged, awkwardly; a strange gesture, I know, but I couldn't help it. 'It was a while ago.' In a way that was a lie; to me it was the day before yesterday. 'Just "To Alex" will be fine.'

We left her to get ready to brighten the airwaves. Andy Martin mirrored my thoughts as we climbed into my Land Rover. 'Quite a contrast,' he said, casually. 'I wish I had a card to give her.'

'You just keep your mind on the job, mate.' I was about to start the engine when my mobile sang its song. I checked the oncoming number; it was Alison. 'Yes,' I answered, discreetly.

'Have you been at it again?' she asked.

'What do you mean?'

'I've been transferred to Torphichen Place.'

'None of my doing,' I told her, honestly. 'Are you annoyed about it?'

'It's a crap building compared to St Leonards, but no, I'm not. I like Detective Superintendent Grant. But it's a bit of a coincidence, you have to admit. You stomp all over Greg Jay last night in my presence, this morning he treats me like dog shit, and this afternoon I'm out of there. Was it him had me shifted, do you think?'

'No, it wasn't him.' Too certain, Skinner! I knew it as soon as I'd spoken.

'Ah, so you did know about it!'

I'd walked into that. 'Alf Stein told me,' I confessed.

'Is it connected to you and me?' She pressed. 'Does Mr Stein know about us?'

'DCS Stein knows everything about everybody,' I chuckled. 'I reckon he could blackmail the Pope. Look, come out tonight and have dinner with Alex and me. I'll tell you the story then.'

'Bob, I don't know . . .'

'Have you had a better offer?'

'No, but . . .'

I brushed her hesitancy aside. 'Come, and bring a bag. Relax, just a small one. About seven, okay?'

'Okay.'

I put the phone away, without saying a word to Martin, although I knew that his mind was working and that he'd probably figured out who was on the other end of the conversation. To head off further conjecture, I asked him a straight question. 'What's with the cross? You seemed to be very attached to it when we were in Bella's den yesterday.'

'I'm a Roman Catholic, sir,' he replied, quietly.

'Devout?'

He took time to consider his response. 'Practising,' he said when he was ready. And then he added, 'But I'm a sinner too, just like most people. I draw the line at killing, stealing and coveting my neighbour's wife, or his ass . . . especially his ass . . . but I'm not above fancying his . . . sister.'

I threw him a sidelong look. 'You almost said his daughter there, didn't you?'

He nodded. 'I confess that I did, but I'm neither wicked nor suicidal.'

'They're all someone's daughter, Andy, the most precious thing a man can have.' I didn't want the mood to get heavy, so I moved on. 'They tell me you don't turn the other cheek on the rugby field.'

'That doesn't pay.' He grinned. 'Our Blessed Lord would have made a lousy flank forward. Mind you, He'd have got a game as long as He stood His round in the bar afterwards.' He paused. 'My being a Tim isn't a problem for you, is it?'

'Shit no. I might have been born a Proddy in Motherwell, but my dad outlawed bigotry in our house. I've left all that behind anyway. I'm nothing now. I haven't been on speaking terms with God since he let my wife die.'

'I don't imagine it was His fault,' Martin murmured.

'Fucking was. He could have made her drive slower.' I turned the key in the ignition. 'Come on, let's get back to the office.'

# Seven

There were two newcomers in the outer office when we walked in. One of them I knew well.

'Afternoon, sir,' said Brian Mackie, tall, dark-suited, sombre, his dome-shaped skull giving the impression that it was trying to push its way out through his hair; eventually it would succeed. 'Short time, no see.'

Less than twenty-four hours earlier, I'd said my farewells to him, along with the rest of the drugs team. 'You can run away back there if you want,' I told him. 'I've got a really lousy job for you.'

He shrugged. 'I wouldn't expect any more of you, sir.' That was as close as Mackie ever got to humour.

I looked at the man who stood beside him. He was a little younger, and shorter, but trim, with a capable look about him, and the face of a born lady-killer. 'DC Steele?'

He nodded. 'Sir.' His handshake was firm and confident. I liked that.

'Welcome to your new home, gentlemen,' I said, 'but you won't be seeing much of it for a while. I need you to keep watch on someone for a few days.' I paused. 'Actually, it's part surveillance, part bodyguard, but it's discreet, and the subject mustn't get a whisper that it's happening.' I gave them a rundown on the Bella situation. When I told them where she lived, Mackie grimaced, and I guessed why.

'I know, Brian, it's not the sort of place where you can just sit in a car all day. We'll get you a cover story; there's a manhole in the street.' I glanced towards Adam. 'Jeff, set it up, please; get on to the council and get it opened, and screened off. You two can be working there.'

'It's the weekend tomorrow, sir,' Stevie Steele pointed out.

'Is your social diary full?' I asked him.

'Nothing I can't get out of, boss, but won't it look odd to have guys working then?'

'Anyone asks, say it's an emergency. Tell them that if you don't get it fixed their toilets will back up. Go on, get it under way, now, you two and DS Adam. DC McGuire,' I said, moving on. The big guy blinked at the rank I'd given him, but I'd already decided that he was staying, it was a CID unit, and I didn't want anyone to think of him as less than a full member. 'You got those tapes?'

He had and he was keen to show me something. He had a video-cassette player and a monitor set up in a corner of the room. 'I found this, boss,' he said as he led me towards it. 'I've already shown the DI.'

The tape had been paused. I looked at the time and date that were frozen on the screen: eight minutes before midnight on the previous Tuesday. The image was monochrome, and slightly blurred, but the camera seemed to be located in the Cowgate, looking east in the direction of Holyrood. McGuire pressed the 'play' button and the action started. A couple of cars came into view moving towards the camera, jerkily, since it was shooting at no more than one frame per second, then passed out of shot; the road was clear, until a box-shaped van appeared, at the bottom of the screen, then took a sharp right turn into Infirmary Street, and disappeared.

'We've got that,' the newly minted DC murmured, then pressed the 'fast forward' button, running the tape on. I watched the time readout, as he must have been, for when it reached three minutes past twelve, after one day had moved into the next, he slowed it to normal speed. Another car appeared heading west and as it passed, another van, no, the same van, surely, slowing this time to make the same turn as before.

McGuire stopped the tape and looked at me. 'That's a Transit,' he said, 'for sure. It doesn't show again on that tape, but there's another camera looking along the South Bridge.' He reached for another cassette box, but I stopped him.

'That's okay; just tell me.'

He did. 'The image doesn't cover the other end of Infirmary Street, but an identical van appears in shot at six minutes to midnight, heading north, towards the city centre. And there's another sighting, at seven minutes before one. Again it's heading away from the camera.'

'Go on. Your conclusion?'

'It backs up the pub manager's story, boss, doesn't it?' he declared, confidently. 'I'd guess that Marlon was in the van. The first time the driver turned into Infirmary Street, it was busy, so he drove on. Then he did a loop up the High Street, left at the Mound, down Victoria Street and into the Grassmarket . . . even with only a wee bit of traffic that would have taken him ten minutes . . . and had another look. Second time it was all clear, so they hauled the lad out, forced him into the baths, and played with him.'

'What about the pub manager guy? Did you get any more out of him?'

'He's with a photofit operator now, but I'm not sure how good he'll be. I fear he'll give us something just to get us off his back. He was right about the Transit, though.'

'You and I know that, but to a prosecutor, it's as you said, a guess.

We need to find the van and prove Marlon was inside it. I didn't notice any livery on the side. Have we got a number?'

McGuire winced. 'I don't think so. The turn it makes in the Cowgate is very tight to the camera; it doesn't show the number plate. The South Bridge shots do, but the focus is pretty crap. I've frozen it, frame by frame, but I can't get close to reading it.'

I looked at the still image on the screen. 'I can see that. Tell you what, there's a technical department upstairs, run by a whiz called Davidson. Take the tape to him, and ask him to do what he can to enhance it. Tell him I sent you.'

'Yes, sir.'

I left him to get on with it and looked into the far corner of the suite, where DCs Macken and Reid sat at facing desks. I hate to admit it, since they were on my team, if only briefly, but I never did get to know their first names. As I walked across to them, they were deep in conversation. When I heard Macken say, 'Frankie Dettori,' I knew that the subject wasn't work-related.

I've always had a temper, I confess. For the first fourteen years of my life it was probably suppressed for fear of the consequences, but it's always been there. The only plea I'll offer in my defence is that normally, the fuse is quite long. No, I have one more piece of mitigation: it's non-existent with my kids. With them, and Aileen, I'm a big pink bunny rabbit. With anyone else, though, when it's lit, there's no stamping it out.

Reid glanced at me as I approached; he was a couple of years older than me, had been buried in Special Branch for a few years, photographing harmless students at protest rallies, and probably thought he was fire-proof. My presence didn't seem to register with the other fellow at all.

'Gentlemen,' I said.

Macken leaned back in his chair and looked at me as if he was appraising me. He was a couple of years older than Reid, and it was rumoured that his wife was the cousin of the wife of his retired patron, Jock Davey. 'Yes?' he replied, stifling a half yawn.

He was a goner then, but he didn't know it. Fred Leggat did though; he'd been speaking with Mackie and Steele, and I heard him stop in mid-sentence.

'You two with me, my office, now!' I ground the words out but shouted the last, then turned on my heel and walked away. Behind me I heard the noise of chairs scraping back. I was relieved; I'd have hauled Macken to his feet if I'd had to, but that wouldn't have been good boss form. I was sitting behind my desk when they joined me. Reid reached for a chair. 'Don't bother,' I barked. 'Standing.' The door was still ajar, but that was their problem.

In the outer office, everyone else seemed to have found something to do, apart from McGuire, who seemed to speed up as he headed for the door. I suspected that he didn't want anything to splash on his nice suit. I launched into them. 'As far as I know,' I bellowed, 'in this job, DC stands for detective constable, and that's four rungs down the ladder from detective superintendent. That means that when I give you a task, you report to me when it's finished, not the other way round!'

As they gazed back at me, Reid was apprehensive, but his sidekick still had a truculent look about him, that of a man who'd had a couple of pints for lunch and maybe one for the road as well. 'So? Tell me. What do you hear about Tony Manson? Is his business under threat? Does he have a new rival? Where the hell is he? Or have you just been in the pub all bloody day?'

'No, sir,' Reid protested. 'We did what you told us, we asked around. We got nothing. Nobody's heard anything about new feet on the ground, no new drug dealers, no new hookers on the streets.'

'Who did you ask?'

'Informants,' Macken drawled.

'What the hell does that mean?'

'Guys we know. Dealers we've lifted; users we've spotted. Hoors.'

'Street level? Druggies and prostitutes?'

'Aye.'

'Aye?' I shouted. 'Would that be as in "Yes, sir"?'

'Aw, fuck.'

I jumped out of my chair, walked round my desk and got right in his face. He was reeking of beer, and scraps of food clung to his teeth. 'You are an idiot,' I told him. 'I told you to talk to known associates. Folk like that have never even seen Tony Manson,' I shouted. 'He hasn't been on the fucking street for years. Your so-called informants . . . if they exist . . . don't have a clue about his world or what happens in it. They only find out about it afterwards, once it has happened. You're experienced officers, on a specialist unit; you're required to know that.' I kept my eyes on him, quelling his belligerence, leaning in ever closer until he took a couple of steps backwards.

'Keep on going,' I snapped, 'out to your desk. Clear it, go home, and don't come back here. I could suspend you for drinking on duty, Macken, but I can't be arsed with the paperwork that would entail. It would distract me, and quite frankly you're not worth it. You are finished in CID. On Monday morning, you'll be told where you'll be working. Wherever it is, you'll be in uniform for the rest of your police career. Now go!'

As I spoke, I hoped that he'd take a swing at me, but he wasn't quite that stupid. He turned, stumbling slightly, and left. I'd have to square his transfer with Alf, and he'd probably have to route it through the ACC. Placing him wouldn't be easy; being booted off Serious Crimes and out of CID as well hung a sign round your neck as visible as a rotting albatross. Wherever he went, my bet was that he wouldn't last a month before handing in his warrant card.

'You're out as well,' I told Reid, 'but I'll get you a move within CID.' I knew where he'd go too. Greg Jay was running short-handed at St Leonards. 'You can go home now too.'

I hadn't wanted to end my first day with an axe in my hand and blood on the floor, but some things have to be done. I could have handled it more gently, but I'd been provoked by that waste of a chair Macken. I waited until they'd both left before rejoining the rest of the team. 'I'm sorry you had to witness that,' I told them, 'but I believe in the job, and I can't stand people who just don't give a fuck.'

I glanced at the clock. It was ten to five. 'It's Friday night, but this is a murder investigation. Brian, Stevie, you've got your weekend mapped out for you. Fred, Jeff . . .' as I spoke, the door opened and McGuire came back into the room, '. . . and you, Mario, I want you to be ready to follow up any responses from the press appeal for information. Go back to Marlon's street. Don't blow the guys' cover but talk to Bella again and see if you can get anything out of her about her son, where he drank, who his pals were. Ask the neighbours as well. Jeff, see if you can find that boy Clyde; he and his team are the eyes and ears of the place. If you have to slip them a tenner for information, do it, but not where anyone can see you. Andy, I want you here tomorrow morning, ten o'clock, Saturday or not. You and I are going to talk to a couple of the people that Macken and Reid didn't know.'

# Eight

There was one of those, one of Manson's 'known associates', that I had to see on my own. I knew that if I turned up as one half of the traditional CID twosome, he would give me the time of day, politely, as much as he ever gave anyone, unless he poured them a drink or his boss told him to be less than courteous.

When I left for home, I took a different route from usual, down Leith Walk. Near the foot, I parked in an empty space, and crossed the road. My destination was a pub; it was called the Milton Vaults and it was owned by a company whose sole shareholder was Tony Manson. Once upon a time, its clientele had been so wild that the place was known locally as the War Office, but those days were over. They had ended when Manson had installed a new manager with instructions to clean things up.

He was behind the bar, with two of his staff, when I walked in. He registered my arrival before the door had swung behind me, and nodded a greeting. It was five fifteen, the weekend had started, and it was busy; the customers were all regulars, for they stood in groups, drinking and talking. Every one of them was male. Tradition died hard in that part of the city. I made my way to the far corner of the bar, drawing the occasional look, but ignoring them all. 'How're you doing?' I said.

His name was Lennie Plenderleith, and his height was a matter of debate. He was either six feet seven, six feet eight, or six feet nine, by varying accounts, but one thing was not in dispute: he was built like a whole row of brick shithouses. He had been a gang leader in Newhaven in his youth, not that he had needed the gang. He'd picked up the usual string of convictions, until finally he had come to the attention of Manson. He'd gone to work for him and had been clear of arrests for almost ten years.

That was not to say he had become a pacifist, no way. His boss was a very powerful figure within the city, but every so often someone made the mistake of crossing him. Soon afterwards, the transgressor would be admitted to the Royal Infirmary. We knew pretty much for certain that Lennie had driven the ambulance, figuratively, but none of the patients ever said a word about their misfortune.

'Fine, thanks. What can I get you, Mr Skinner?' he asked. His voice was quiet. People like him don't need to be loud; their very presence commands attention.

'I'll just have a Coke, thanks, Lennie.' I shoved a couple of pound coins across the bar as he filled a glass from a nozzle, but he pushed them back as he laid the glass in front of me.

'Have you had the radio on this afternoon?' I asked.

He nodded. 'I know what you're talking about. Marlon Watson, yes?'

'Got it in one.'

'I need to talk to his boss, to eliminate him from our inquiries, so to speak. He doesn't seem to be around.'

'That's self-evident. If he'd been around, nothing would have happened to Marlon.'

'So they hadn't fallen out?'

Lennie managed to frown and smile at the same time. 'No chance. Marlon wasn't the sort of lad to fall out with people. Besides . . .'

'Tony shags his mother?'

The smile widened. 'Among others,' he said.

'Do you know where he is, Lennie?'

'Yes.'

'Are you going to tell me?'

He shrugged. 'Why not? He's in the Gran Hotel, in Ibiza Town.'

'Not on his own, I assume.'

'No. He's got a woman with him. They're away for a week. I can't give you a name, though, Mr Skinner.'

'Not even if I insisted?' I ventured; not that I planned to.

'No, because I don't know it.'

'Marlon told his mother he was going to Newcastle.'

'He flew from there. But Marlon didn't even know that. He drove him to Newcastle Station on Sunday morning, and dropped him off. As I understand it, the bird went down on the train and met him there.'

'I imagine Tony didn't want Bella to know,' I said.

'Not just her,' Lennie chuckled. 'He didn't want anybody to know. Look, he likes Bella . . .'

I was sceptical. 'She told me she works in his saunas. That's hardly a sign of his affection.'

'She might have let you think so, but she doesn't in the way you mean. He uses her as a sort of inspector. She'll drop in unannounced, to make sure that the places are being run okay. She takes no shit, and he likes her for it.'

'How's he going to take Marlon's death?' I asked the giant.

'How do you think? Badly, very badly.'

'In that case, Lennie,' I told him, 'no offence, but we'll be watching you for a bit.'

He shrugged again, massively, shoulder-rippling. 'No offence taken, but you'll be wasting your time.'

I raised an eyebrow. 'Yes?'

'Yes. Work it out for yourself.'

I let the comment lie. 'We do need to talk to Tony,' I repeated.

He sighed. 'I know; but you'll need to wait till Sunday. He's due back then. Marlon was supposed to pick him up; from the station again. You could fly out to Ibiza, of course, but I'd have to warn him, so that would be a waste of time too. He'd be gone.'

Plenderleith was nothing if not honest. 'Okay,' I conceded. 'I know you're going to call him anyway to let him know about Marlon. So, when you do, tell him I'll be at his place first thing on Monday morning, and I won't be pleased if he's not there.'

'I'm sure he will be, Mr Skinner.'

I finished my ersatz Coke and left. More punters had come in while I'd been talking to Lennie, and more of them studied me as I made my way to the door than had done when I'd arrived. They were the ones who'd made me as a cop; I stared them down so they'd remember me, and recognised a couple as I did so.

As I pulled out into traffic, I was wondering about the big guy. He was closer to Tony Manson than I'd realised, trusted with the secret of his Ibiza tryst, and to know what Bella Watson really did for him. I'd worked out straight away why it would be a waste of time keeping tabs on him as a way to the guys who'd killed Marlon. When Lennie passed on a message from the boss, the recipient always walked away . . . eventually. He was telling me that those two were dead men, and that he wasn't given that sort of task.

Even as I cruised along Salamander Street, I knew that he would have called Manson by then, and that if he had the faintest idea of who the torturers were, or of who had hired them, then things were liable to happen fast, and I had to keep pace. Of course I did have another option. Shut up and do nothing: stand back, let rough justice be meted out and pick up the leavings afterwards. Sure, and then we might wind up with an all-out gang war on our hands, the sort of mess in which innocent bystanders can get hurt.

I pulled off Seafield Road into the forecourt of a car showroom and called Alf Stein, mobile to mobile. I brought him up to date with the investigation, as it stood, and told him what my team was doing. 'I should have known,' he sighed. 'I move you to Serious Crimes and they get really fuckin' serious. Press, Bob, press, until something cracks; that's all you can do. Do you need any more manpower?'

'For the moment, no. I like what I have. By the way, I've addressed the Macken and Reid problem. I'll send you a memo for the record, but I've booted them.'

'Good grounds?' he murmured.

'They'll hold up.'

'Okay, I'll deal with it.'

'Macken's got to go from CID, completely,' I added.

'I get the picture. Shitty job in uniform.'

I headed back to Gullane. I picked up some stuff in ASDA and made it home by six forty, later than usual, but not enough to start Daisy fretting. 'Alex is excited,' she told me, as she put a sketch pad into her bag.

'Why?'

'Let her tell you. She's in her kingdom.' I'd guessed that; I could hear the radio.

I went upstairs to the attic as soon as Daisy had left, and knocked on her door. 'Clear!' she called, her way of saying 'Come in'. She had a school pal with her, a lass called Susie something, whose dad was in PR, and whose mother taught in another village school along the coast.

'What's the story?' I asked.

'Didn't Daisy tell you?' She had her impressionable child face on, the one I didn't see too much of any more, and her eyes were gleaming. 'I had a dedication on Airburst. Mia Sparkles played a song for me. "Wonderwall". Did you ask her to?'

'No, it never occurred to me. That was off her own bat.'

'What's she like, Mr Skinner?' Susie bubbled.

It was on the tip of my tongue to say that she was one of the most attractive women I'd met in a long time with a body that not even a radio station T-shirt could disguise, but I cut that down to, 'She's very nice. Alex,' I told my daughter. 'We're having company for dinner.'

'Same as last night?' She'd become a bold adolescent in an instant.

'Same. She'll be here soon.'

Susie took her cue. She looked at the clock and exclaimed, 'Gosh, is it that time?' and jumped to her feet. I led the way downstairs and went into the kitchen while Alex walked her to the door.

'What's for dinner?' she asked.

'Smoked salmon, fillet steak and salad, then ice cream.' Typical menu for a single man when entertaining.

'Can I cook the steak on the George Foreman grill?'

'No way. You might burn yourself, then the cruelty people would be after me.'

'There's more chance of you doing that.'

She had a point. 'Okay,' I said, 'but remember to ask Alison how she wants hers done.'

I'd laid the smoked salmon on plates and was slicing Chinese leaves for the salad when the bell sounded. Alex beat me there. 'Hi, Alison,' she said, as she opened the door, like someone greeting a peer, not someone who was eighteen years older than her. 'Nice to see you again.'

'And you. Sorry I'm a bit late,' she added, looking towards me, at the back of the hall. 'There was more traffic than I expected.' She had a small bag in one hand and a bottle of wine in the other. She held it up. 'I brought this. Is it okay?' It was Spanish; Sangre de Toro, by Torres. I'd bought a couple of the same in ASDA. *She knows me*, I thought.

'Perfect. Ideal for what we're having.' I kissed her, chastely, took both from her, dropped her bag in my bedroom and went back to the kitchen. Alison came with me, leaving Alex to switch on the television.

I offered her a beer, while I finished assembling the salad. 'Help yourself if you want one,' I said. 'They're in the fridge.'

'Can we go for a walk?' she asked. 'It's a lovely night.'

She was right. Through the window I could see my back garden flooded with evening sunshine. 'Why not?' I said. 'We'll need to take Her Ladyship, though.'

'Will she mind?'

She didn't. She was so intrigued by Alison and by the possibilities of a relationship that if I'd said, 'Get your jacket, we're all going to the dentist,' she'd have followed without a murmur. We walked the short distance to Gullane Bents, then, instead of going down on to the beach, took the path that runs along the fringe of the golf course, then climbs up to the summit of Gullane Hill. I'd brought a pair of binoculars, so that Alison could enjoy the view properly, a panorama stretching from Berwick Law, along the Fife coast, to Edinburgh, the Forth bridges and the distant Trossachs beyond.

Once she'd had her fill, we headed back, down the southern side of the hill and along the Main Street. We were all hungry by the time we reached home, so Alex switched on the Foreman and set it to warm up while we attacked the starter, and the Sangre de Toro . . . at least Alison and I did; I allowed my daughter an occasional small taste of wine with dinner, but only white, so she was restricted to Shloer apple juice. She did a damn good job with the steaks . . . three medium, but not bloody . . . but she left the cleaning of the grill to me, as I'd told her to. She and Alison did most of the talking around the table, their chat ranging from school, to pop culture, to fashion, and to village life. I let them get on with it, for I felt a weight upon me that I hadn't anticipated. As I looked at the two of them, and listened to them talk, I realised that it was the first time I'd ever heard my daughter in conversation with a woman who was old enough to be her mother, other than Daisy, and when I was around they never said much more to each other than 'Hello' and 'Goodbye'. I was overcome by a wave of the sort of sadness that I'd thought was behind me, and, hard as I fought against it, I could not prevent myself from seeing Myra in Alison's place.

When I couldn't stand it any longer, I stood up, abruptly. 'Alex,' I said, 'isn't there something on TV that you wanted to watch?' It was twenty-five to ten, and we both knew that there wasn't, but she took the hint.

'Oh yes,' she exclaimed, maybe a wee bit theatrically. 'I've missed the start. Good night, Alison. Good night, Pops.'

'Night, kid. Remember you're going to Daisy's at nine tomorrow.' I'd fixed it before she'd left.

'Yes. I'll be ready.'

'You working tomorrow?' Alison asked, as she left, and I set about wiping down the grill.

'A couple of doors to kick open. Doesn't mean you have to rush off though.'

She frowned. 'Yes, it does. You've got a lovely kid, Bob, but I don't want her to start making assumptions. That's how you drift into places you might not really want to be.'

'That's a fair point. Honest truth, Ali, after eight years I still haven't a fucking clue where I want to be.'

She put her hands on my chest, palms flat. 'Right now,' she said, firmly, 'you want to be with your daughter; any woman would have a tough time wedging in alongside you. In four or five years' time, once she's off to university, it'll be different, but until then, you have to finish what you had to start when her mother died.'

'You reckon?'

'I know so. Now, what about the story you were going to tell me? What about my transfer?'

I smiled. I'd forgotten about that. 'You pour us some more wine,' I told her, 'take it into the sitting room, and I'll join you when I'm squared up here.'

'That sounds like a plan.' She waited while I uncorked a second bottle of Sangre de Toro, picked it up and went off to find our glasses.

I was putting the last of the cutlery in the dishwasher when my mobile sounded. I took it out, flipped it open and looked at its small screen. No name, which meant that the caller wasn't logged in, and the number meant nothing to me. I thought about rejecting it, until I realised that it might be Mackie or Steele, or any one of my new boys.

But it wasn't a boy. 'Is that Mr Skinner?' the voice asked.

'Yes. Enlighten me.'

'This is Mia, Mia Watson.'

Out of the blue. 'What can I do for you?'

'I was doing that autograph for your daughter, and I thought it might be safer to send it to your home address rather than to the office.'

I didn't hand that out to strangers, not even when they were drop-dead gorgeous, with a chest that got the most out of the word 'Airburst!!!'

On the other hand, she was doing me a favour. I compromised. 'Send it "Care of the Mallard Hotel, Gullane". That'll get to me.'

'Okay, no problem.' I was about to thank her and end the call, when she continued, a little less confidently. 'Mr Skinner, when I saw you earlier on, I'm sorry, I wasn't very helpful. To be honest I was still in shock; it still hadn't sunk in. Maybe there are things I know that might help you without me even realising it. So, if you'd like to meet me again . . .'

'If you think it would help,' I replied; not too enthusiastically. If only I'd stayed that way.

'Who knows? It might, it might not.' She sounded vulnerable, alone.

'Do you have a time in mind?'

'Tomorrow?'

'Okay. At the studios?'

'No, I don't go in there at weekends. Could we meet in town, somewhere discreet? How about the foyer of the Sheraton? I go there for coffee quite often. The sort of people who'll be there on a Saturday aren't going to recognise the likes of me.'

I thought about my plans for the morning. A couple of calls. How long would they take? 'Twelve thirty?'

'That'll be fine. I'll see you there.'

I closed the phone and went to join Alison. 'Trouble?' she asked. 'You're frowning.'

'No. Someone I have to interview for the Marlon investigation, that's all.' I don't know why I didn't tell her that it was his sister, unless it was because I didn't want any questions that I couldn't answer.

She didn't follow it up. 'So,' she said, instead, 'my surprise transfer. If you weren't behind it, who was?'

'Indirectly, Greg Jay.'

She sat up straight, her mouth falling open. 'You mean he had me bumped!'

I shook my head. 'You're not listening. "Indirectly", I said.' I told her the story of Greg Jay's visit to the head of CID, of his litany of complaints about me and of his accusation of an improper relationship between the two of us. I left out the part about his early morning drive-by. If either of us chose to make that a disciplinary matter, Jay might have found himself wearing sergeant's stripes again. Alf didn't want it to go that far, but I couldn't be sure that Alison wouldn't insist on it if she knew.

As it was she was angry enough. 'The swine,' she hissed. 'Next time I see him . . .'

I turned her face towards me. 'You'll say nothing, and you'll think how lucky you are not to be working for the son-of-a-bitch any more.'

'Are you going to let it lie?'

'What did a friend say once? "All rights reserved, all wrongs revenged." A nice turn of phrase, but it's not necessary in this case. The boss has dealt with it, Alison. He threw Jay out of his office and he got you out of his reach. What more should I do?'

She sighed, pouting a little. 'I suppose . . .'

'Listen,' I said, 'I've been told that I have a few virtues to counterbalance my faults, but patience is the one I've had to work hardest at. I'm getting there, though. There may come a time when Mr Jay's career is in my hands. And then . . .'

She pulled me towards her, and kissed me, for quite a long time. 'You'll do nothing,' she whispered, as we surfaced. 'I see you with your daughter and I know that as hard as you are on the outside, you're a softie at heart. You won't do anything in cold blood.'

'No?'

We kissed again. 'No,' she repeated, after we'd paused for breath once more. 'On the other hand, my dear, I am as ambitious as you, and if the day should ever come when his career is in my hands . . . I'll rip his balls off and enjoy listening to him squeal.'

I grinned. 'You're quite a scary lady, aren't you?'

'Mmm. Just as well you're not in love with me.'

'That isn't everything. Close and comfortable's good too. I know plenty of couples who've built a life around that.'

'You'll never be among them, though. You have to be in love, Bob. You still are, even after eight years; I could see that in your eyes tonight. That's why we're safe with each other. I want sex, not love, and sex is all you have to give.'

I drained my glass. 'In that case,' I murmured, 'let me be generous.'

# Nine

It was good, no denying that. Sex with Alison was energetic, enthusiastic, strenuous, and a whole lot of other adjectives, with the exception of acrobatic. We tired each other out after a while and fell asleep, with a window left open slightly to let us breathe.

I don't know how long I'd have slept if my bed-mate hadn't been wakened by the sound of the milk truck skidding round Goose Green, just after half past seven: in those days we had the fastest milkman in the east. I came to with my hand on her breast, my thumb massaging her nipple, very gently. 'Bob,' she murmured, 'it's morning.'

'And?' I mumbled. 'Since when did you only do it in the dark?'

We were out of bed by eight, though, at least I was, having insisted on first go in the shower so that I could get breakfast under way. By the time Alison emerged at eight fifteen, her short, blonde-tinted hair still in damp disarray, Alex was up too, scrambling eggs and grilling bacon and tomatoes, while I made tea and toast. 'Not for me, please,' Ali said. 'I'm a cereal only girl.'

She relented, though. My kid has always done very good scrambled eggs. It's an undocumented fact: one-parent families do not have room for a bad cook.

Breakfast over, we got on with our weekends. Alex left first, to walk to Daisy's place. She told me they were going food shopping in Haddington so I gave her forty quid and a list and told her to pick up some stuff for us. At thirteen I'd have trusted her with a debit card on my account, but legally she was too young to sign the slips. After she'd gone, I tidied in the kitchen, while Alison dried her hair, and packed her bag.

'You don't have to go,' I pointed out, once more. 'You could just chill out here, and wait for me.'

'No, I can't. Apart from anything else, I was air-dropped into a new office yesterday, and unlike you, I had no warning. I'm going in this morning as well. I need to read up on our current investigations. We've got a couple of pub break-ins on our hands, and one serious assault that might turn into murder. That's a break from the norm. Two young male victims, stabbed, last Saturday: one's unconscious, on life support, but the other's wounds were superficial. At first he said they were attacked, but the story kept changing. Eventually he admitted that he and his mate tried to mug a gay bloke, but got it badly wrong.'

'In Grove Street?'

'Yes. The witness thought he was a dead man, but someone turned into the street and the guy ran off.'

'I read about that in the *Saltire*,' I recalled. 'There was no mention of the poofter aspect, though.'

'Poofter?' she repeated, raising an eyebrow. 'Are you homophobic, Bob?'

'Do I have a fear of homosexuals?'

'You know what the word means.'

'Alison,' I told her, deadpan. 'I treat everyone the same, regardless of creed, colour, gender or sexual orientation.'

'Good,' she said. 'Just for a second, I thought you sounded really bitter. No,' she continued. 'Mr Grant held that back from the media. He's got officers out tonight going round the gay pubs and discos. The two would-be muggers said they saw their prey coming out of one in Morrison Street and followed him.'

'Have you got a description?' I asked.

'Orange hair and heavy eye make-up, that's all.'

I laughed. 'You may take it that by now the hair will be a different colour and the kohl will be gone.'

'That's what I thought,' she agreed, 'but I'm the new girl, so I kept it to myself.'

I considered the situation. 'Between you and me, I'd have given the press everything.'

'Why?'

'Because all kidding aside, this man sounds dangerous. Your two victims probably intended no more than to rough him up a wee bit and nick his wallet, but what they got in return . . . Gay man out on a Saturday night tooled up? That's hardly typical of our pink community.' I paused. 'You're not part of the pub trawl, are you?'

'No, it's boys only, Superintendent Grant said.'

'So you could come back here tonight?'

She shook her head. 'No. I've got something on. I'm going to my friend Leona's for dinner. She's married to an MP, he's away to South America on some parliamentary jaunt or other, she's pregnant, and we're having a girlie night.'

'What's his name?'

'Roland McGrath. He's a real prick; I can't stand him.'

I sensed bitterness. 'Let me guess: he tried it on with you.'

Her eyes turned grim. 'A week before their wedding. The stag and the hen nights merged into one later on. Everybody was a bit pissed and Roland caught me in a quiet corridor of the hotel and offered me what Leona was going to be getting for the rest of her life; that was how he put it. He wouldn't take no for an answer, so . . .'

'So? So what?'

She laughed, suddenly, beautifully. 'So I threatened to arrest him. He didn't believe me until I cautioned and cuffed him.'

'You took your handcuffs to a hen night?' I gasped.

'I surely did. We'd been going to have a rag with Leona, but we thought better of it. Yes, I cuffed him and it was only then that he said he'd been joking all along.'

'How did it turn out?'

'Eventually it was me that made the joke of it. I left the cuffs on him for the rest of the night and told everyone I was showing him what marriage was all about. I've never told anyone the real story until now.'

'Not even Leona?'

'Especially not Leona. She thinks that the sun shines out of his fundamental orifice.'

'Will you tell her about you and me?' I asked her.

'I have done, a while back, when we first started . . . seeing each other.'

'What did she say?'

'Well,' she began, 'she wanted to know if you were a good shag, and I said you are, then she wanted to know if I was in love with you, and I said that I wasn't. She said that was a shame, because you were probably looking for someone just like me. And I told her that was absolute bollocks, because you were looking to make chief constable, just like me, and that we both know that any relationship that competes with that ambition in either of us will be doomed to failure.'

I wasn't sure I'd wanted to hear myself summed up so bluntly, or so accurately. Oh yes, she was right, but still, there was one difference between us that she'd overlooked. Elvis had never sung about her. She'd never woken crying in the night, from a dream of grievous loss, to the realisation that it had all been true. She'd carried her ambition from the start, untarnished. Mine was a substitute, even if it did burn bright in those days.

I smiled, though, and ruffled her carefully composed hair. 'You keep on telling her that, but be sure you add that I'm going to get there first.'

'Oh I do, but the glass ceiling's there to be shattered.'

'And you're the woman to do it. You have a good night and don't spare the gossip.'

'No danger of that. Call me.'

We left together, each in our own car, but her Nissan was out of my sight in the Discovery by the time I reached Aberlady.

I arrived in the office at quarter to ten. McGuire, wearing black jeans and a muscle-hugging polo shirt, was at his desk, and Martin was waiting for me, his green eyes full of life. 'It's Saturday,' I said, 'and the rugby season's over. But if it wasn't . . .'

'The job comes first, boss. I still play rugby at top club and district level, but I've told the national selectors that I'm no longer available.' Recalling the awe in Alf Stein's voice when he'd described the young man's playing style, I realised that if he had taken that step, then I was looking at someone whose career ambitions matched Alison's and mine.

'Okay. I promise I'll do my best not to let work interfere. What other games do you play?'

'Squash and golf; that's all.'

'Me too. There's a squash court in this building; we'll need to work each other over some time.' I turned to business. 'Any calls since you got here?'

'One from Stevie Steele. He and Brian have been down that manhole since eight. Bella's been down to the shops for rolls and milk and the *Daily Record*, and there was someone with her. A very large bloke; a Chieftain tank on legs, Stevie said.'

I grinned at the answer to a question I'd been asking myself. How would Tony Manson have reacted to the news of Marlon's murder? I'd come up with one proposition. He'd have had the same thought as me: like son, like mother? But he wouldn't be relying on the police to protect his woman.

'In that case, we don't need to bother about her safety.'

McGuire looked at me. 'You know who he is, sir?'

'I do. He's the best insurance policy I can think of.'

'Did Manson send him?' Martin asked.

'Yes. I know where Tony is, Andy, and when he'll be back. I'd like this business sorted out before he gets here, otherwise it will get messy.' I headed for the door. 'Come on, let's knock a couple of doors. I'll drive.'

I'd parked the Land Rover in front of the building rather than round the back. As we stepped outside I saw that the chief constable had arrived after me, and thanked my stars that I hadn't nicked his space.

Martin tried to stay impassive when he saw my wheels, but couldn't quite cut it. His eyebrows rose, very slightly, but they did. 'Pile of old shit,' I told him, 'but it doesn't stand out in a crowd. I put a couple of the dents in it myself, for added authenticity, so to speak. It's reliable under the bonnet, though; our garage makes sure of that.'

The DC smiled. 'It'll never catch a getaway vehicle, though.'

'It doesn't have to, son,' I pointed out. 'It's got a police radio in it.'

As I drove out of headquarters, into Fettes Avenue, my mind went back to Alison's division's open investigation. 'Andy,' I began, 'do you live in Edinburgh?'

'Yes. Haymarket.'

'And you're a young single guy, so you'll get out and about?'

'Yes.'

'Got any gay friends? Or doesn't your faith allow that?'

The question took him aback. 'I'm not that Old Testament, boss. There's a gay couple that are regulars in Ryrie's Bar, part of the crowd. We're not bosom buddies . . . bad choice of phrase . . . but we talk. Why?'

'Do they ever say anything about anti-gay prejudice in Edinburgh? We've got this image as a tolerant society, but there are bigots everywhere. Is there a problem that we don't know about?'

I glanced at him and saw him frowning. 'Well,' he replied, thoughtfully, 'those blokes are body-builders, both of them, but one of them did say something about there being parts of the town where they always go together, just in case. Look, is this important? I've got a date tonight, but I could go into Ryrie's early on, check if they're there.'

'Nah,' I said. 'Don't do that. It's not our business, just something I heard.'

'Okay, but if it would help anyone, I'll do it.' He paused. 'Where are we going, sir?'

'We're paying a house call,' I told him, 'on a man called Douglas Terry.'

'Are you sure he'll be in?' he wondered.

'A practical man, eh, Andy. I'm not certain, but I don't think that Dougie sees much of the day before noon, not at the weekends, at any rate.'

'What does he do?'

I had to think about that. 'Do you read much?' I asked him.

'A bit.'

'My dad brought me up on short stories,' I said, 'almost all of them

American. He liked Thurber, Dorothy Parker and Damon Runyon, but his number one favourite was William Sydney Porter, who wrote under the pen name O Henry. Of all his stories, the one that's stuck in my mind is called "Man about town". That's what I would call Dougie Terry . . . a man about town. You might call him a freelance. He does a bit of everything for everybody, but mostly he's involved with a man called Jackie Charles.'

'I know that name,' Martin murmured.

'You should. For a start, it's over a big car showroom down in Seafield Road, specialising in high-value vehicles. But that's his public face; he also owns a chain of bookie's shops under the name John Jackson, and a couple of taxi firms, Carole's Cabs, and Sherlock Private Hire. The first one's called after his wife, the second he bought from Perry Holmes, the guy that Bella Watson's brother Billy tried to kill.'

'You seem to know a lot about him.'

'Oh, I do.' I felt my mouth tighten as I thought of Jackie Charles. He had been a neighbour of mine at one time, out in Gullane, before he went upmarket and bought a big pile in Ravelston Dykes. Myra and Carole were part of the same crowd of young women in a group called the Housewives' Register . . . God knows who came up with that name . . . so we often went to the same parties. I'd found them a bit awkward, though, and eventually I stopped going; I'd stay home and babysit while Myra went without me. My hesitancy came from what, by that time, I'd learned about Jackie's other activities. He was what might be called a business angel, in that he put up the capital, and lent organisational skills to entrepreneurial ventures. The problem was that these ventures were armed robberies, not just in the Edinburgh area but all over Britain, but Jackie was too smart ever to be linked to any of them.

I didn't tell any of this to my young colleague though, not then, because it would have taken him into areas of my life that I wasn't ready to share with him. 'Dougie Terry works for Jackie,' I said. 'He looks after the below-the-parapet businesses, but he does other stuff as well, disciplinary matters, let's say.'

'Charles is bent?'

'Charles is one of the two big players these days in organised crime in Edinburgh, the other being Tony Manson.'.

Martin frowned. 'Are you saying that he might have had Marlon killed?'

'That's what's perplexing me,' I confessed. 'There's a loose business relationship between Jackie and Tony. Charles stays out of the pubs, drugs and prostitution and Manson doesn't step on his toes.' As I spoke I pulled up outside a house in Clermiston Road. Once it had been council property, but now in the aftermath of the Right to Buy, it had been augmented with every build-on imaginable, save for a machine-gun turret. I parked behind a Ford Mondeo and across the driveway, blocking the exit of a Mercedes S class saloon, with a personalised registration plate.

I walked up to the door and gave it the policeman's knock. Martin started to count, but I told him not to bother. 'There'll be nothing to hide in here.' And then I smiled. 'By the way, there's something I forgot . . .'

Before I could finish, the door was opened by a slim woman in her late thirties with a soft perm and hard eyes. 'Morning, Jane,' I said. 'We'd like a word with Douglas.'

'I'm sure you would. Come in then.' She didn't argue about it; she'd got past that stage years before. 'Douglas,' she shouted, at the foot of the stairs. 'Police.'

She opened the door to a well-furnished sitting room. 'I'll be off out,' she declared. That was par for the course. On the three or four occasions that I'd rousted Dougie at home he'd always made her leave, so that under no circumstances could she be called to witness anything that might be said: super-cautious.

We waited for five minutes, before Terry appeared. He was around forty, stocky with heavy chiselled features and a chin that was in want of a shave. 'Mr Skinner,' he greeted me.

I nodded an acknowledgement. 'This is DC Martin.'

Terry turned to him and offered his hand. As they shook, he said, 'Good morning, son. Do you know what kippers are? Fish that need a lot of sleep. Did you like my wife? I first met her in the tunnel of love. She was digging it at the time.'

'Dougie!' I shouted. 'Enough! What I was telling you on the door-step, Andy; we call this guy the Comedian. Whenever our colleagues have him in for a chat, they ask him a question and he tells them a joke. That's how it goes until they get pissed off and chuck him out. Chic Murray's his favourite.'

'Not always,' said Terry, looking at me. 'Did you hear the one about the couple in the old folks' home?'

'Dougie,' I told him, seriously. 'I am not your local CID; I've got no sense of humour. You try that routine with me, and I will knock your fucking head off. Then you'll wish you'd had breakfast before we arrived.'

'No fun you, big man,' he grunted. 'Sit down then.' He sat, we followed suit. 'What can I do for you?'

'You can convince me that Jackie Charles didn't have Tony Manson's driver killed.'

I studied his face. His eyes widened, and his mouth opened for a second in a gasp. He didn't put that on. 'Now it's you that's fucking joking,' he muttered.

'You know me better than that.'

'When?'

'Very early Wednesday morning, in Infirmary Street Baths.'

'That dead bloke was Tony's guy?' he exclaimed. 'Are you fucking serious?'

He was scared, and that interested me.

'That's who it was. Whoever did it was very determined.' Slowly and deliberately, I described how Marlon had died.

'Jesus Christ,' he said, when I was finished. 'Are you sure it wasn't Tony himself?'

'I can't be a hundred per cent certain that it wasn't, but Tony's rogering the boy's mother. Plus, he's sent big Lennie Plenderleith to bodyguard her until he gets back. So, Dougie, go on, tell me. Is Jackie upset with Manson over something?'

'No,' he insisted. 'No way. Jackie's fine wi' Tony.'

He was rattled all right. If I had turned up on his doorstep asking that question, then it could only be a matter of time before Manson came to ask it as well, and his interrogation techniques weren't subject to the same limitations as mine.

'Then prove it to me,' I challenged. 'Get out there and ask questions. Two guys in a Transit van; we don't know the colour and we don't have the number, but that's what they drove. Who are they and who were they working for? You'll find me at Fettes; Serious Crimes office. Make it soon.'

We left him in his armchair, pondering the gloom that was darkening a sunny day outside.

'Will we get anything from him?' Martin asked.

'We've got something already. From Terry's reaction in there I know for sure that Jackie Charles isn't involved. That's a start. He might come up with something on the van. To be realistic, he's got more chance than we have. There isn't a door in Edinburgh that's closed to him. He's tight with Charles and he's on fairly good terms with Manson. That gives him a lot of clout.'

I unlocked the Land Rover. The Mondeo had gone, probably in the direction of Jenners: Jane Terry was a designer dresser. 'On to the next,' I said.

'Where's that?'

'Slateford.'

'What's in Slateford?'

'The new generation.'

I drove across town, with the volume on the CD player turned up so that I didn't have to talk. I was too busy thinking about Marlon, and what he'd known, or done, for him to die that way, thinking about Alison, and thinking about our next port of call. Eventually I pulled up outside a pub in Slateford Road. It was called Caballero's, a fanciful name if ever I'd heard one, and it occupied much of the ground floor of a tenement building with three storeys of flats above.

'Ever been here?' I asked Martin.

He nodded. 'About a month ago, with the rugby team, after a game at Myreside.'

'You didn't cause any trouble, I hope.'

'None, boss. Most of the tales are exaggerated.' He laughed. 'Most of them.'

I led the way inside, and looked around. The place had been refitted since my last visit. The old island bar had gone, and had been replaced by one that ran most of the length of the back wall. There were booths on either side, but the floor was clear apart from two raised platforms, about four feet high, each with a pole in the centre running all the way up to the ceiling. There were no dancers in place though, too early for that, only a couple of barmen, one per customer.

'What can I get you gents?' one of them asked, in an accent that had not come from any part of the city or its environs. His black hair was slicked back and he wore a uniform that might have looked vaguely Spanish, to someone who'd never been to Spain.

'You can get us Tomas,' I replied.

'He's no' in.'

'My car's parked next to his. Please don't piss us about, mate, or I'll be checking your immigration status.'

The barman's face flushed, but before I had to lean any harder, a door opened beyond the serving area and a man stepped through it. He was young, still in his twenties and not much older than Martin, but he had the air of a leader about him, and a hint of danger too. 'Mr Skinner,' he exclaimed, in an accent similar to that of the barman, but with more edges knocked off. He extended a hand that carried, on the back, a tattoo of a man on a horse. We shook. 'I saw you on the TV in my office. Welcome to Caballero's. It's good to see you.'

'And you, Tomas. This is DC Martin; remember the name and the face.'

'I do remember it; the face at least. You were in here a few weeks back; you chinned one of your rugby pals when he got out of order with one of my dancers. You were very impressive.'

I looked at Martin; he shrugged, as if to say, 'Rather I did it than his bouncers.'

'Andy, this is Tomas Zaliukas. If you ever heard anyone mention the name Tommy Zale, he's who they're talking about.'

'Please, Mr Skinner; I used to think that name was macho, but now I'm trying to shake it off. I'm proud Lithuanian, proud of my name.'

'You'll never manage that, Tomas. It'll always be hanging around. Now, take us somewhere private, please.'

'Sure,' he said, 'come through the back.' He led us into an office that was furnished more like a sitting room. On a long sideboard were three television sets, but two were monitors fed by cameras in the bar. One of them was trained on the till. I smiled when I saw it, and he read my mind. 'You can never be too careful, Mr Skinner,' he chuckled.

'I hope you mean that, Tomas,' I replied. 'I put my judgement on the line when I backed you for the licence of this place and for your pub in Leith, and I don't want to be proved wrong.'

He looked offended. 'What do you mean?'

'Once upon a time, when you were younger and wilder, you were Tony Manson's driver, yes?'

'You know I was. But like you say, I was younger then, not long ashore from jumping ship in Edinburgh. I moved on since then.'

'And you're doing well for yourself, I'll give you that.' He nodded his thanks. 'But,' I went on, 'as part of moving on, after the Iron Curtain was pulled aside, you brought in a crowd of your fellow countrymen. We both know that some of the stuff they did, for Manson and others, would have landed them in jail for a hell of a long time if it could have been proved, and that you'd have been alongside them, if we could have nailed you for setting it up.'

He frowned, and went tight-lipped. 'I say nothing about that.'

'No, and I'm not asking you to. We're past the bullshit stage, you and me. I don't pursue lost causes; I prefer to concentrate on keeping you straight.'

'Okay.' He was showing more signs of irritability. 'But now I straight, so?' he grumbled.

'Do you know who's been doing your old job lately, chauffeuring?'

'No. Why should I? I keep my distance from Tony, and he's okay with that.'

'Marlon Watson,' I said.

'That's who?'

'Yes.' I sat and waited, watching Zaliukas's mind work.

It clicked. 'The gadgie that was found swimming in an empty pool?'

'That's the one.'

His eyebrows rose. 'Poor lad. Who did he upset?'

'That's what we're trying to find out. Whoever it was, he used two guys to make his point, unless he didn't subcontract the job, and that's not usually how it goes. What I want to ask you, Tomas, without throwing any accusations your way, is this. How sure are you that all your Lithuanian associates are under your control? Would any of them take on freelance work?'

'If any of them did . . .' he murmured.

'. . . you'd give us their names.'

'Sure I would,' he said, instantly, but I wasn't convinced. 'But I trust them all, Mr Skinner, I trust them all. Two of them, you said?'

'That's right.'

'Anything else?'

'They used a Ford Transit for the job, unmarked.'

Zaliukas shrugged, and grinned; the edginess between us was gone. 'That's my boys off hook then. None of them would drive shit like that.'

'Is he really legit, boss?' Martin asked, as we left. 'He seemed to have . . .' He stopped. 'I don't know quite how to put this, but I've come across a couple of people in the short time I've been on CID. One was a paedophile and the other was crazy; he had strangled his sister. They both gave me the same feeling, that they were different from the rest of us; it seemed to come off them in waves. I've just had it again.'

I was pleased to hear him say that, although I didn't tell him; it was a big step along the way to being a good detective. 'I remember the two you're talking about,' I said, 'although I was nowhere near the investigation. Psychopaths, both of them, and very obviously; they should have been stopped before they got as far as they did. It's not always that simple though. About eight years ago, there was a robbery homicide. It was three or four years before it was solved. Three people were involved. One disappeared without trace; the other two, a man and a woman, were both psychopaths, and classically so, yet they were successful people with conventional lives, and had given no hint of their real selves, even after their crime. Yes, Tomas gives off a vibe, and he might be diagnosed as psychopathic too, that's possible, but he's highly intelligent and he's worked out that the best way forward for him is by putting his brains to legitimate use.' I frowned. 'There's another saving grace too; he's on my radar, and he knows it.'

I drove Martin back to Fettes. There were no reports of progress from anyone, so I stood him, and McGuire, down for the rest of the day, told the rest of the team to reach me on my mobile if anything did come up, then headed for the Sheraton.

It took me a while to find a parking space, but eventually I nailed one, opposite the Lyceum Theatre. I was ten minutes late when I passed through the Festival Square entrance doors and into the hotel. I kept walking, through the foyer and into the lobby area. It was busy; I couldn't see an unoccupied table, but I could work out why Mia had been so confident that she wouldn't be recognised. The Saturday customers were almost exclusively female, not her fans, though, but their affluent mothers. I looked around for her, and spotted her at a table in the furthest corner. She was wearing a sleeveless brown dress, and her arms and legs showed off a golden tan.

I apologised for my lateness. 'Bloody Edinburgh,' I muttered, as I sat. 'The Castle Terrace car park was full so I had to cruise for a bit.'

She smiled, and I couldn't help noticing, once again, how attractive she was. 'I thought,' she chuckled, 'that policemen had special signs they could leave on their cars.'

'Like "Doctor on call", you mean? We can do it in an exceptional policing situation, but we'd draw complaints from Traffic if we tried it on. Plus there's a further consideration. There are wee neds out there, wherever you turn, and most cars work best with all four tyres inflated.'

'Neds? Is that not a Glasgow word?'

'I'm betraying my roots,' I admitted, 'but the type is universal.'

A quick frown knitted her brow. 'Don't I know it. My late brothers were two classics.'

'Maybe so, but it's not a capital offence. Most of them can be cured by having their arses kicked hard enough by the right bloke.'

'That wasn't an option in their case, not for offshoots of the Spreckley family. Christ,' she exclaimed, bitterly, 'were those boys ever touched by Fate.'

'You've broken free. How did you escape?'

Before she could answer, a waitress appeared by my side, pad in hand. I hadn't looked at the menu, but when Mia ordered a club sandwich and coffee, I told her to bring that twice.

'Initially,' she said, when we were alone again, 'by keeping my head down, staying apart from the nonsense and working hard at school. I didn't have a problem childhood, I won't say that. I was older than my brothers, so I had a bit of authority over them, and rough as the neighbourhood is I was never bothered by anyone because I was Gavin Spreckley's niece. Uncle Gavin was a real animal. Uncle Billy was weak, always a follower, never a leader, but Gavin, oh, he thought he was Al Capone. He made my flesh creep, but he was useful in that way . . . until he got Ryan into even bigger trouble than usual and they both disappeared.'

'Or most of them did.' The comment escaped; it slipped past the censor sensor in my brain, and was out there before I could stop it. 'God, Mia, I'm sorry. I shouldn't have said that.'

'Don't worry, Mr Skinner,' she assured me. 'I'm not the sensitive kind. It was true, anyway. When that happened, it was the end of it for me. I was sixteen by that time, and I could make my own choices, so I went to live with my dad.'

'I thought he was long gone,' I said.

'He was,' she replied, 'but not forgotten. He kept in touch with me, sent me money, and presents and such. Only me, though, not the boys, and he never spoke to my mother.'

'Why did he leave?' I asked as our sandwiches and coffee arrived. They must have been lined up in the servery, ready made.

'He and Uncle Gavin had a big bust-up when I was about six. I learned all the details about ten years later. Dad found out that Gavin and Billy were involved with people who were dealing drugs. Not long after that, Dad was beaten up himself, by a gang of men he didn't recognise. He wound up in hospital and when he was there, Mum went to see him with a message from Gavin, that if he didn't clear off, next time they'd kill him.'

I poured the coffee, and then looked up, catching her eye. 'Are you sure the message was from Gavin?'

'Are you trying to suggest that it might have been from Mum herself?'

'I'm not saying that.'

'It's possible. She wasn't upset when he left, that's for sure. We had quite a succession of "uncles" after he'd gone.'

'Where did he go?'

'Peterhead. He moved up there, and sailed out of there. He worked on the trawlers.'

'Yes, I knew that.'

She smiled again, but there was a wry sadness in it. 'So the police have always taken an interest in our family, have they?'

'I'm afraid so,' I admitted. 'But it has drawn itself to our attention over the years. What about you, though? How did you get where you are?'

'More by luck than judgement,' she replied. 'I stayed on at school in Peterhead and got my Highers, then went to Sunderland University and did a degree in broadcast journalism. I brought it back to Peterhead and got a job in the newsroom in a radio station in Aberdeen. I might have stayed there, but my dad died.' She stopped, and was silent for a while.

'How?' I asked her, quietly.

'His job. He was washed overboard, and lost, about three years ago. So was I for a bit; lost, that is. I had nobody else up north, so I looked around and found myself a news job with the station in Stirling. I was doing okay, liking it, then one day they had a crisis. One of the presenters was injured in a car accident on the way to work, I was on duty, and I was told to fill in for him. Because I was known as a reporter, they asked me to choose another name. I said "Mia Sparkles", because believe it or not, "Sparkles" was what my dad used to call my mum. I turned out to be good at it; the girl who was injured was going to be off long-term, they wanted a female replacement, so they gave me a longer run. The audience figures went up. That's what counts, start to finish, so I wound up with a career change. When Airburst won the new licence, they asked me if I would join to present a show called "School's Out", and . . . here I am.'

'Well done,' I congratulated her. 'You're a role model for a lot of kids.'

'Oh please, Mr Skinner,' she protested. 'Don't burden me with that.'

'Then don't you burden me with "Mister". The name's Bob. This isn't a formal police interview. Come to that, it isn't any sort of an interview. You asked to meet me, remember?'

'True,' she conceded.

'So you don't see yourself as an example to others?'

'Hell no!' She laughed, spontaneously. 'I've got a very healthy following among nice middle-class kids, like your daughter, with real spending power through their parents. That makes me Airburst's golden girl, but these kids like me because they think I'm one of them, a big sister. If they knew I was a schemie from a low-life family, that would change, and fast.' Her face darkened. 'That's why I'm so grateful to you for not associating me with my brother's death, and it's one reason why I steered clear of him while he was alive, the other being the fact that I never could stand the little shit, him or Ryan.'

As she broke off to attack her sandwich, one thing puzzled me. 'Why did you contact your mother?' I asked.

'I didn't,' she replied, when she was ready. 'She contacted me. As soon as she heard "Mia Sparkles" on radio, she knew that it was me. That didn't happen until I moved back to Edinburgh. The signal from the Stirling station doesn't reach this far. But I should have anticipated it.'

'What did she want?'

'Money, what else? I pay her to keep from selling the story of my family background to the tabloids.'

'How much is she into you for?'

Mia winced. 'A hundred and fifty a week.'

'Don't say if you don't want to, but is that quite a lot for you?'

She nodded. 'We're a new station. I'm not on huge money.'

'Seven and a half grand a year, after tax.' I felt outrage welling up in me. 'How do you pay it?'

'Standing order, my bank to hers, every week.'

'She's not that bright, then. What's her phone number?' I asked.

'She doesn't have a phone. She uses a mobile.'

'There's no phone in the house?'

'No.'

'What's her number?'

'Why?'

I was steaming mad. 'Just give me it.' She did, I took out my own mobile, keyed it in, and called it. A man answered, a quiet voice, but I knew who it was. 'Lennie,' I said, 'it's Bob Skinner. Put Bella on, please.'

'Okay. Did you recognise my voice,' he asked, 'or are you . . .'

'That's a "yes" to both questions. What did you expect? Now, let me speak to her.' Obstructing the police wasn't part of his brief; I heard him call her.

'What do you want, Skinner?' Bella snapped. 'Have you caught the fuckers?'

'No, but I've caught you.'

'Whit d'ye mean?'

'Do you want to upset me?' I snapped.

'I'm no' fuckin' bothered, pal, one way or the other.'

'Well, you should be, lady, because you have done. I'm with your daughter.'

'Lucky you.' Opposite me, Mia was looking alarmed, but I motioned her to stay silent.

'Yes, but not so lucky you. Don't you have the brains to collect the money in cash when you're blackmailing somebody? This stops, Bella, it stops now, and you repay the money you've had so far or, I promise you, I will arrest you and charge you with extortion.'

'Oor Mia would just love that,' she sneered.

'It wouldn't bother her one bit, or affect her, because in cases like yours, the court won't let the media say who the victim is, or why they were blackmailed. So you believe in my promise, you slag, because if I have to I'll keep it. But I'll do more than that. While I'm at it, I'll make very sure that the papers know who you work for, and who you're shagging when he isn't in Ibiza boning another bird. We both know how much he dislikes publicity, so unless you want big Lennie there tapping your shins with a baseball bat instead of looking out for you, you will fucking well behave yourself! Understood?'

I heard a long intake of breath. 'Understood?' I repeated, loudly enough to draw a glower from a blue rinse at the next table.

'Aye,' Bella hissed. 'Okay.'

'Wise woman. Remember what I've said, and don't you think, not for one second, that I won't do everything I've threatened.' I slapped my phone shut, ending the call. 'Sorry about the language,' I told Mia, 'but it was your mother I was speaking to. You can cancel that standing order.'

'Have you always been that angry?' she asked me quietly. 'I don't know what you did to my mum, but you scared me.'

I looked at her. 'Angry? Me? That was just me in cop mode, don't worry about it.'

'No, it was more than that. There's real rage in you, Bob.'

'No, really, I'm a big soft nelly at heart. You should see me at home with my kid.'

'I'm sure, but you're not at home just now. You couldn't see the look in your eyes when you were lacing into my mother; I could. They were full of . . . fury, almost.'

'Nah,' I scoffed, lightly. 'You were imagining some other bloke.'

She wouldn't be deterred. 'You told me your daughter doesn't have a mother any more,' she said. 'What happened? Did she run off?' I shook my head and sought refuge in a large bite of club sandwich. She took it as a snub. 'I'm sorry,' she murmured. 'I have no business asking.'

'It's okay,' I told her. 'It's no secret. Car crash, eight years ago.'

'Were you involved?'

'No, she was alone. It was a silly wee car with too much power. She lost control.'

'Poor woman. Poor man. It must have hurt you so badly.'

I looked away. 'That's a fair assumption. You know the damnedest thing, though? The mind must have some sort of a safety valve, for I've got very little memory of the accident itself, even though they told me that I arrived on the scene not long after it happened. There's before, and there's after, but the detail of the . . . the thing itself, it's not there.'

'I wonder if that's what makes you angry,' she mused. 'Or could it be that when you have to deal with people like my mother, and you must have, all the time, you feel it's unfair, for them to be alive while your wife isn't.'

I held my hands up in mock surrender. 'Hey,' I exclaimed, 'I thought you did a broadcast journalism degree.'

'I did, but there was a psychology element: to help us with interviewing, let us work out what our subjects' reactions meant.'

'I'll bear that in mind next time I'm interviewed on the radio.' I turned the spotlight back on to her. 'But what about you? Don't you feel any anger about your brothers or your uncles?'

'About Gavin and Billy, no. Not a bit. They had no regard for life. Ryan? You could say he never had a chance, but I could see that Uncle Gavin was a beast, so why couldn't he? But suppose he had, it wouldn't have made any difference. He worshipped him, and copied everything he did. Marlon, maybe I feel a bit of pity for him, but not enough to let his death screw up my life. He could have done what I did, if he wanted, got out.'

I found myself thinking of the kid in her mother's street, Clyde Houseman. He was playing the role of tough guy because he had to, because he knew no other way of making the place survivable. Maybe one day he'd call me; but probably not.

Mia broke through my contemplation. 'That man you mentioned when you were talking to Mum; who is he?'

'Lennie Plenderleith? He's minding her.'

'No, the other one, the one you said she's . . .'

'His name's Manson. He's . . .' How to put it? '. . . a person of interest to us, and your brother was his driver. How does that relate to his death? As of this moment we have no idea.'

Her eyes widened, and she put her hand to her mouth, to stifle a grin. 'I'm sorry,' she said. 'It's terrible of me to laugh, but are you saying that my mum's a gangster's moll?'

I smiled at her amusement. 'An old-fashioned term but appropriate. She doesn't have exclusive rights to the territory, though, Manson spreads his favours far and wide.'

'Why does she need a minder?'

'She probably doesn't, having met her; but her boyfriend might know more about your brother's death than we do.'

'He might think that somebody could be after her too?'

'Not really, but we're covering the possibility. I'm not just relying on Lennie to look after her. I've got people there too. If they see anyone nosing around . . . She's safe. But most important of all, she's off your payroll.'

She gazed at me, and her eyes seemed to soften even more. I felt as if they were embracing me. 'I can't thank you enough for that,' she said. 'It started off at a hundred a week, then she wanted more. She'd have bled me dry.'

'It's my job,' I assured her. 'I let her off lightly. You let me know if you don't get that money back.'

'I don't care about that. I'm glad she doesn't have her claws in me any longer; that's the main thing. She's a bad bitch.'

That was an understatement: I wasn't going to tell her daughter but I had Bella marked as the most evil of the three Spreckley siblings. I'd met Gavin only once, in my very early days on the force. He'd been dangerous, yes, but thick with it, so thick that he'd crossed the Holmes organisation and got himself and his nephew killed. His sister, on the other hand, was as amoral as him, but as I was discovering, she had a brain. The truth was that I'd have been struggling to convict her of extortion; a half-decent lawyer would have got her off. No, my real threat to her was in using her to embarrass Tony Manson. 'You made a smart move when you left home,' I told Mia. 'Your mistake when she put the bite on you was in not calling her bluff.'

'You reckon?' She was sceptical.

'Absolutely. You need some good PR advice. You're underestimating your audience. If your story was told properly and sympathetically, you'd be a role model for thousands of kids who are just as you were, trapped in awful domestic circumstances, and afraid to do anything about it. I'm not saying that you should do it now, with your brother's murder still a hot media topic, but once that's all blown over, the right piece in the right newspaper will give your career another shove forwards, rather than hurting it. You'll be a media darling. You'll be on telly before you know it.'

'You're very sure of yourself, Detective Superintendent.'

I grinned at her. 'Is that your way of asking who the hell I am, a cop of all people, to be advising a broadcaster on public relations?'

She laughed in return. 'You said it.'

'You think you're the only one who's studied psychology?'

'Are you a uni graduate?' She sounded surprised.

'As it happens, yes I am. It's the coming thing with the polis. The lad who was with me yesterday, he's one; my girlfriend's another.'

'You've got a partner?'

'No,' I said, quickly. 'We're not that serious. We see each other, that's all. It suits us both.'

'I'm sorry, Bob,' she exclaimed. 'I was being nosy.'

'It's okay. But . . . to be accurate, psychology wasn't part of my university degree. I studied that on a senior command course at the police training college, for much the same reason you did at university. Not only that, we were given some training in how to deal with the media.'

'Who trained you?'

'Consultants; a couple of television journalists. To be honest I wasn't all that impressed by them.'

'Some of it must have rubbed off, for you to be passing it on to me. I will think about it, honestly,' she conceded, 'but I've still to be convinced that it's worth taking the chance.'

'It could be taken out of your hands, Mia. The bigger a name you make for yourself, the more the press are going to be interested in you. Life is about control. Lose it, and you're vulnerable.'

'Wow!' She chuckled. 'Angry and a control freak. I'm glad I'm not . . .' She stopped short, and her eyes left mine.

'Married to me? Is that what you were going to say?'

'Mmm.' She nodded. 'Sorry.'

'Then don't be. I wouldn't wish me as a husband on any woman. Still, I'll make one plea in my defence. The only place where I've never had control is my own house. In reality Alex runs that, just like her mother did before her. It used to be that her needs as a child dictated everything. That's still true to an extent, but she's pushing fourteen now, so her adult personality's developing. She can play me like a guitar.'

'I'll bet,' Mia said. 'That reminds me.' She reached into a capacious handbag that lay at her feet, and produced a stiff, cardboard-backed envelope. 'I brought this.'

I was about to take it from her when my phone sounded; headquarters, the screen told me. I excused myself and took the call.

'Skinner?'

'Yes.' I wasn't sure of the voice.

'It's Davidson here, technical services. I've got something for you.'

'Oh yes? Go on.'

'One of your underlings left a tape with us to see if the quality could be enhanced. Well, we've excelled ourselves. I've got a partial number for you.'

'How partial?'

'All but one digit. It's N two seven, D something N. We can't quite get the middle letter of the suffix. It may be that the plate is damaged. We've done bloody well as it is.'

'I'm not complaining,' I told him. 'I'll take that, thanks.'

I cut him off and called Leggat's number. 'Fred,' I began as he came online, 'we've got something on the vehicle.' I read out the number that the techies had retrieved. 'I need you to dig out the licensing authority in Wales, and try to fill in the missing letter. It shouldn't be too difficult; the odds are against there being more than one Transit van in the range of possibilities.'

'Will do, Bob. Where'll you be?'

'Possibly at home by the time you get back to me, but use the mobile anyway.'

'Sorry,' I said to Mia. 'I'm never completely off the radar.'

'That's almost comforting to know.' She handed me the envelope. 'Autographed picture, for your daughter.'

'Why don't you give it to her yourself?' The invitation was completely spontaneous. It came out of the blue. There was something about Mia, and I didn't want to say 'So long' and go on my way.

'What do you mean?'

'Come with me and meet her. Or do you have other plans for the day? Boyfriend waiting somewhere, for example?'

'I don't have one of those,' she replied. 'I don't have any other plans for the day either, and I'd love to meet your daughter, but are you sure?'

'Absolutely. Think of it as audience research.'

She laughed. 'Nice way of putting it. On that basis, yes, thanks. Let's go. But I'm paying the bill for these.'

She wouldn't have it any other way. By the time our waitress had brought the check and picked up the money, it was almost two. While Mia went to the ladies' room, I called Alex's mobile to let her know I was heading back home . . . I'd bought it for her thirteenth birthday, on security grounds. She also carried a personal howler alarm, a police-issue pepper spray that she wasn't allowed to talk about, and she'd been going to martial arts training since she was eight.

'This is exciting,' Mia bubbled, as we passed out of the lobby area. 'You wouldn't think so, given my background, but I've never been picked up by the police before.' My hands were in the pockets of the denim jacket that had been my Saturday choice; she took my arm. I'd been ignored by the Ladies Who Lunch on the way in but, with my new companion, heads turned as we passed.

There is this thing in my life . . . only my private life, I should stress. Whenever I try to plan a surprise for a near and dear one, be it a party or a present, it never quite works out. I say something by mistake, or somebody else does. But, if ever there is a rabbit that I want to stay in the hat, the furry little bastard is almost guaranteed to jump out and crap all over my day. I'm sure that Parkinson had a law that applies, or if not him, Murphy.

We were approaching the exit when the doors swung open and who walked through them but Alison, with Detective Superintendent Alastair Grant, her new boss.

She saw me, and her face froze.

'Alison,' I began. That was all she let me get out.

'Good afternoon, sir,' she replied, evenly, then strode on. Grant offered a brief 'Hello' but was more or less pulled along in her wake.

Mia didn't seem to notice the exchange. 'You haven't told me where you live,' she said as we stepped outside into the square.

I pulled myself together. 'East Lothian,' I replied. 'Gullane.'

'Lucky you,' she exclaimed, then winced. 'God, I shouldn't say that to you, of all people. What I meant was, it's lovely out there.'

I slid an arm around her shoulders and squeezed, lightly. She was quite tall, even in heels that were no more than a couple of inches high. 'Mia, you don't have to treat me like I'm an emotional cripple. It is lovely out there, and choosing to live there is one of the smartest things I ever did.' I let her go as we reached the pedestrian crossing in Lothian Road, and waited for the green man.

'Sorry about the transport,' I said, as I unlocked the Land Rover. I pointed to a sticker that Alex had put on the rear window; it read, 'My other car is a BMW.' 'That's true,' I told her.

She peered at the radio as I drove off, heading up Johnston Terrace rather than for the Grassmarket, even though that would have been quicker. I didn't want to take her past the mortuary, where her brother was still in a cooler. She wouldn't have known, but I would. She played with the controls until she found Airburst FM. It wasn't one of my presets. 'They want me to do a Sunday morning show through the summer,' she murmured. 'Ten o'clock to one. We get thumped by

Radio One on Sundays, and they want to change that.'

'I know of at least one listener you'd have,' I said. 'How do you feel about that?'

'For the money I'm on, I feel that five days is plenty, thank you very much.'

'Can they make you?' I asked.

'Under the terms of my contract, they can, but I don't think they'll push it. It can be terminated by a month's notice on either side, and I've already been approached by Radio Forth. If they really want it, we'll negotiate. I've got a pay review coming up in a month. If they double my salary, I'll do the Sunday slot.'

'Do you have an agent?'

'I don't need one, not at this stage of my career. Why pay someone twenty per cent when I know what I'm worth already?'

*Beauty, body, brains*, I thought. And I felt myself getting hard.

That made me wonder about Alison. I'd have to apologise to her, I knew, but for what? No commitment, she'd said, even more firmly than I had, so why the frost? To hell with it, let DI Higgins stew for a while. *Good afternoon, sir*, indeed!

We were on the A1, almost at the Tranent junction, when my phone sounded again. I pulled on to the verge to answer, activating my warning flashers. Fred Leggat was excited. 'We've matched that plate,' he announced. 'The missing letter is a C; that makes it a Newcastle-on-Tyne number. The van's red in colour and it's registered to a man called James Pearson, of South Shields.'

'Excellent! Fred, standard practice, get a stop-on-sight request out to all traffic cars. We want to be talking to this man as soon as we can, but first, let's find out about him. Run an NCIS check, and have a word with our colleagues on Tyneside. Who is he and why would he be interested in our territory?'

'I'll get that under way,' Leggat promised. 'How do you want to play it afterwards?'

'Ask our friends, very politely, to lift him, and impound his van. If they're well disposed towards us, they'll bring them both up to Edinburgh. If they're not, or they're tight for manpower, we'll meet them at the border and take them off their hands.'

'Very good. Do you want to be involved?'

'Every step of the way, once we've got him in our hands.'

'Even if it's tomorrow?'

'Even if.' I pocketed the mobile and rejoined the traffic.

'How do you manage?' Mia asked.

'Manage what?'

'Life. Don't you ever have any time to yourself?'

'Not really,' I admitted, 'not in the job I do.'

'Drugs Squad, it said on the card you gave me.'

'Not any more. I'm Serious Crimes Unit, now.'

'But you don't work alone.'

'No,' I conceded. 'I have a team, but I'm two days into the job and I'm still sizing people up.'

'So our Marlon's murder is a serious crime.'

'All murders are, Mia. But his becomes of interest to my unit because of the job he did.'

'Driving for my mother's fancy man?'

'That's right.'

'Is he a killer, this man?'

'Not personally, no more than the Governor of Texas.'

She twisted round in her seat and gazed at me. 'What do you mean by that?' she asked.

I considered my reply. 'Well, when George Bush Junior,' I began, 'signs off on the execution of some unlucky bastard on his death row list, he doesn't go along to Huntsville and give the injection himself, but it happens as surely as if he did. It's the same with Tony Manson, and people like him. They give the word and somebody dies. The man your Uncle Billy shot, Perry Holmes, he was the same as Manson.'

'Why did Billy shoot him? I was a journo in Aberdeen then. I wasn't party to the details, and my dad didn't discuss it.'

*Shit!* I thought. *Why did I mention Holmes? She doesn't know anything about it.*

'You don't want to go there, honey.'

'I think we're beyond that option, Bob, aren't we?'

We were. If I clammed up, she'd find out. 'We believe that it was Holmes who had Gavin and Ryan killed. He had them executed; they'd been freelancing drugs, and to him that was a capital offence. Billy hadn't been involved, but we understand he made him watch what happened to them.'

'And Billy executed him in his turn?'

'It didn't work out that way, not quite. He killed his brother, but Perry survived. He's a basket case, though, and out of that life. Now please, let's not talk about it any more. These are the people I have to work amongst. I'm nearly home now, and I don't allow that part of my life in there.'

She reached out and squeezed my hand. 'Poor love. I'm sorry.' At that moment, we were passing the bend where Myra died.

The mood had changed by the time we passed the quarry corner and the Gullane skyline, beyond the golf courses, came into sight. 'Oh!' Mia exclaimed. 'That's beautiful.'

'That's what most people say the first time they see it. I remember I did. We had to put ourselves in hock to live here, but not doing so wasn't an option.'

**124**

'I've been here before,' she confessed. 'When I was about eight. Gavin brought Mum and us out here one day. I remember, he left us all on the beach and came back for us after a couple of hours. It was about this time of year, 'cos it was quiet. I wanted to go in the sea, but we didn't have swimsuits or anything, not even towels. I made such a fuss, though, that eventually Mum told me to go in the nuddy if I was that keen. So I did, then ran up and down the hard sand till I was dry. Gavin did his nut when he came back and saw me. I remember him screaming at Mum that she was letting me make an exhibition of myself, even though there was hardly anybody else there but old couples walking dogs.'

'I could hazard a guess about why he got humpty. He was probably out this way on business, and didn't want attention drawn to himself in any way.'

'You don't have drugs in Gullane, do you?' she exclaimed.

I frowned. 'My ego isn't so big that I'd assume there are none just because I live here. But I do keep my eyes and ears open. If anyone was pushing hard drugs I'd know about it, and I'd come down on them so hard that folk would talk about it for years afterwards. There was one clown a few years ago, along in North Berwick, selling pills to kids out of the back of his car. A concerned parent told me about it, and he's still inside.'

Instead of going straight home I cruised past Daisy's place and blasted the horn. A few seconds later, Alex appeared in the doorway, Tesco bags in both hands. I waved to Daisy, then reached behind me to open a back door. I wish I'd taken a photograph, for the expression on her face, as she saw that the front passenger seat was occupied, should have been preserved for posterity. It was a mix of curiosity and concern. I could read her mind; no women for eight years and now two in two days. Was her old man having a mid-life crisis?

'Hi, kid,' I said, as if it was just the two of us. 'Had a good day?'

'Yes,' she replied. 'Tesco was heaving, though.' Her eyes were fixed on mine in the rear-view. Her reaction puzzled me until I worked out the obvious, that Mia was a radio star and relatively new on the scene, so there was no reason why she should recognise her.

'This is Miss Watson,' I told her, deadpan. 'She's come to visit us. Miss Watson, this is my daughter Alex.'

Mia reached back and they shook hands. 'Pleased to meet you,' Alex said, but I wasn't convinced. She liked Alison. I began to wonder if I'd made a big error of judgement.

I was still unsure when we arrived home. I pulled the tank alongside the BMW. 'The window sticker does not lie,' I pointed out. Our guest smiled, but said nothing. I guessed that she might have been spooked too by my daughter's reaction, so I put an end to the game.

'Alex,' I said, 'Miss Watson has a first name, and I don't think she'd mind you using it. She's called Mia.'

She stared at me and dropped the bags, then looked at Mia and back to me. 'Mia Sparkles?' she exclaimed.

'You got it in one. I told her all about you and she wanted to meet you. She doesn't get too many chances to meet her listeners.'

'Why didn't you say so from the start?' she scolded me. 'Instead of playing childish bloody games!'

Maybe I should have told her to mind her language, but mine wasn't always perfect around her, so all I did was wink and say a very meek, 'Sorry.'

I unlocked the front door and ushered Mia inside. I didn't think that the cottage was anything special, but it seemed to appeal to her. I've never thought of myself as a romantic, but it struck me that the feeling was mutual. With her in it, my comfortable but well-worn living room seemed to be enhanced. Or had it become again what it once was, was that it? Or was it all my imagination?

'I'm going to put the kettle on,' I announced. 'Alex, show Mia around the house. I'll be in the garden when you're done, with tea on a tray . . . if that's all right with you ladies.'

'Fine by me,' Mia responded. She fished the envelope out of her bag and presented it. Her fan's eyes lit up again.

They were talking, animatedly, when they rejoined me, ten minutes later. By that time I'd dug the garden chairs out of the shed, their first airing of the year, and made a pot of Darjeeling and Earl Grey blend . . . to me, tea is tea, but Alex liked that mix.

'What do you like most about the station?' I heard her new friend ask, as I passed round the mugs.

'I only listen to you,' she replied with the candour that she's never learned to tone down. 'You play the music I like, you talk about interesting things and you don't treat me like a kid.'

'Interesting things?' I butted in. 'Such as?'

She frowned at me. 'Things I can't talk to you about. Clothes, because you're all stuffy and conservative when we go shopping. Movie stars, because you think they're all a bunch of useless tossers. Women's things, because you're my dad and it makes you uncomfortable.'

She was right, on every count. 'You talk about all those things?' I asked Mia.

'Of course.'

'Including . . .'

She smiled, and her eyes seemed to engulf me again. 'Including that. Bob, my audience are predominantly young women; that's what our research shows. Young women have periods. They're an inevitable part of life, so why shouldn't I talk about them on radio? Puberty's easy for you guys; your voices squeak for a bit and that's it. One day you're Macaulay Culkin and the next you're Tom Cruise.'

'I'm much too tall to be Tom Cruise,' I complained.

'Okay, Russell Crowe, if you prefer.'

'Who the hell is Russell Crowe?'

She laughed. 'Wait and see. But take my point; no problem for boys, once it's done it's done. But for girls it's still a taboo subject with most people . . . even some girls themselves, because that's the attitude they inherit from their mothers, or in this case from Dad.'

I didn't have a counter-argument. Daisy had seen Alex through the onset of puberty and I had left them to get on with it. I'd never even bought her Tampax while doing the supermarket shopping. Thinking back, it hadn't been a topic of conversation between Myra and me either.

'I'm not blaming you,' Mia added, 'or saying you're failing as a dad. It's the way a girl's life is. As a result, it's a valid topic, so I air it.'

'What about your boy listeners?'

'It's got to be good for them too,' she argued. 'If you talk about issues in a matter-of-fact way, it takes any silliness out of them.'

It had been dawning on me all afternoon, and finally I was convinced. Mia Watson was like very few women I'd ever met. There was a depth to her, a seriousness, that was contagious, even across the airwaves, given the empathy between her and my daughter. 'Your father must have been a hell of a man,' I remarked, quietly. She looked at me, suddenly self-conscious.

My mobile sounded. 'Bugger!' I swore, and dug it out as I pushed myself from my chair, and walked to the far end of the garden.

It was Fred Leggat. 'Progress?' I asked him.

'Ever have one of those days when you can't believe your luck?' he replied, question for question.

I looked back towards the table. 'I think I'm having one.'

'So did I,' the DI sighed, 'until about fifteen minutes ago. NCIS came up with nothing at all on Mr James Pearson of South Shields, but the Newcastle police did. He's dead. He was a plumber, he developed mesothelioma, from exposure to asbestos, and it killed him, last year, aged fifty-four. His widow sent his van to auction. It was sold, but the change of ownership hasn't been registered yet. I've asked them to find the manager of the auction yard to get the details of the buyer, but they're not hopeful of tracing him before Monday.'

'How hard are they trying?'

'As hard as they can, Bob. They know this is a murder inquiry. We'll probably have to sit on it until Monday.'

I was frustrated but I knew that he was right. 'Okay,' I said. 'You'd better stand down. See you on Monday.'

Mia read my mood as I returned. 'Problems?'

'Delay,' I replied. 'We're trying to trace the owner of a Transit van; I thought we had him, but now we don't.'

'Has he gone into hiding?'

'In the arms of the Almighty. So he's not part of it; the van still is, though.'

I didn't elaborate, not with Alex there; she'd been in at the start of the investigation, but I didn't plan to take her with me all the way through it. Instead I sat down again and listened to them talk about radio, about Mia's daily routine, and about which music stars had visited the station and which ones were expected. 'I'm having a new band as guests on Wednesday,' she said. 'They call themselves the Spice Girls. There are five of them and their first single's due out next month. Their management sent me a couple of demo copies, on condition that I don't play it on air any sooner than a week before the release date. It's amazing; you'll love them. Would you like the spare copy? I've got them both at home; if I left them lying around the studio they'd be nicked.'

'Yes please!' Alex squealed, childlike again.

I wasn't aware that it had clouded over until I saw goosebumps forming on Mia's arms. I looked at my watch and saw that it was just after five thirty. She saw me. 'I must go,' she said. 'What time are the buses?'

'You're not taking the bus,' I declared. I didn't want her to go at all.

'I am,' she insisted. 'I didn't come out here meaning to let you run me back home. I'm a big girl; I know how to get on and off a bus.'

'Train would be better,' my pragmatic daughter pointed out. 'There's one from Drem at ten past six.'

'That'll do then.'

I was tempted to ask her to stay and eat with us. We always went out on Saturdays, usually somewhere within walking distance, so that I could have a glass of wine, or two, or three. That evening we were booked into the Roseberry and I knew that they'd have fitted in a third, but I didn't want to push it with her. I drove her to the station, with Alex in the back seat.

'It's been a lovely afternoon,' Mia said, as we saw the approaching train in the distance.

'Would you like to do it again?' I asked. 'Maybe just the two of us,' I suggested, 'to give you a break from the interrogation?'

'What about your girlfriend?'

I thought about the doorway of the Sheraton. 'I'm not sure she is any more. In any event, the accent's always been on the friend part of it.'

'So you tell yourself, I'm sure,' she murmured. 'Tell you what, call me at the studio on Monday, when we've both had time to think about it. Unless you're too busy, that is.'

'I'll do that,' I promised.

Alex was silent, all the way home, and for a while after that. I switched on the TV and caught up with the news. The weekend offered a break from stories of parliamentary sleaze, but the news bulletins were dominated by a disaster on Mount Everest, where storms had killed up to eleven climbers, while the main sports headline was Manchester United's victory over Liverpool in the FA Cup final, thanks to a late goal by Eric the Red. I'd forgotten that the game had been on telly, live.

My preoccupation wasn't lost on my daughter. 'You like Mia, Dad, don't you?' she ventured, finally.

'Sure,' I replied. 'Don't you?'

'Of course I do, she's brilliant.' She hesitated. 'I like Alison too.'

'And so do I.'

I was watching the third rerun of Cantona's volley when she pulled over the footstool I never used and placed it between me and the screen. 'Pops, can we have a grown-up talk?' she asked.

'I thought we always did.'

'Don't try to get out of it,' she scolded, impatiently.

'Sorry. You first then. Go ahead.'

'Something's worrying me.' That gained my full attention· I reached round her with the remote and switched off the TV. 'It's been a long time since Mum died, hasn't it?'

'You know it has. Eight years; you were five when it happened.'

'And now I'm thirteen. Does that make me different in some way?'

I was puzzled. 'No, why should it?'

'Are you worried about me,' she pressed on, 'about my emotional development?'

'No. Come on, kid, stop throwing big words at me. What's your problem?'

'This is. We've come all this way together, Dad, and you've been brilliant. But I know you're lonely too. Have you finally had enough of bringing me up on your own?'

My reaction was instant. 'No way!' I protested.

'Or do you think I need a mum?' she asked. 'Because if you do, you're wrong. I don't need anybody else; just you. If you think you've met somebody you really want, that's good. But if you're thinking it's what I want, you're wrong. Honestly, I don't think I'd like to share this house with another woman, not even Alison.'

Another woman! This was my baby talking to me, but that's how I'd better get used to thinking of her. I reached out and took her hand. 'That's me told, good and proper. For the record, I haven't been running auditions, honest. I promise you, if I ever think about getting married again, and you're still living at home, I'll let you pop the question to whoever it is. In the meantime, though, does it make you feel awkward when Alison stays the night?'

She looked at me as if she was the adult and I was the child. 'Pops,' she sighed. 'I watch *EastEnders*. I know what sex is. If you must know, you bringing someone home made me feel more grown-up. It makes me feel that you're starting to treat me more like an adult. But,' she said, firmly, 'if you bring different people home, don't expect me to keep one of them secret from the other.'

I leaned back in my chair and looked at her, a little awestruck. 'God,' I whispered, 'what did I do to get you?' She opened her mouth to answer, but I held up a hand. 'Enough! Let that stay unsaid at least. Go on,' I told her. 'Get your glad rags on. We're due at the Roseberry at seven thirty.'

As she left, I ran my hand over my chin and decided that I'd been a bit too far from my Philishave that morning. On my way to my bedroom, I noticed for the first time that the light on the phone was flashing, indicating that I had a message. In fact, there were two: the first was from Alex's sole surviving grandparent, Thornton Graham, my father-in-law, asking whether he could visit next day. The second was from Alison. 'Bob,' she'd begun, but gone no further before hanging up. I called her back from my bedroom extension. She sounded impatient when she answered.

'Sorry,' I said.

'What for?' she snapped, then took a deep breath. 'No,' she said, 'I should be apologising. You caught me on my way out the door, that's all.'

'You rang me.'

'Yes, then I lost the bottle to say what I meant to.'

'You want to try again?'

'Mmm.' She'd begun to sound like herself again. 'It's another sorry, for my ridiculous performance at the Sheraton, flouncing off like that just because I catch you with a poppet on your arm. I wanted to warn you before she finds my knickers drying in your bathroom, that's all.'

I laughed. 'Don't worry, I checked. Alison,' I said, quickly, before she took me seriously, 'do you want to know who she is?'

'If you want to tell me.'

I did. 'She caught the six o'clock train home,' I finished, 'after she'd promised Alex a copy of the hit single of the year, on top of the autographed piccie.'

'And now I feel like an idiot,' she moaned. 'Thanks a bunch.'

'Just as well we're not serious about each other, eh?'

'I wasn't kidding about that, Bob.'

'Me neither. Now that's off our chests, do you want to come out here tomorrow night?'

'Let's see how hung-over I am in the morning after a session with Leona.'

'Okay,' I told her. 'Call me when your head clears.'

Before changing to go out, I phoned Thornie to confirm his visit. Alex was pleased when I told her; we had virtually no extended family (she didn't know that she had an uncle on my side) and that made her cherish her grandfather and aunt even more.

He was an early riser, was Grandpa Graham. Alex and I had barely cleared away the breakfast things when he arrived, at ten thirty, having driven all the way from Carluke, by a slightly longer route than necessary. He never drove past the accident site; instead he took the A198 to Dirleton Toll, and stopped off at the cemetery to lay flowers on Myra's grave, before heading for Gullane.

Alex was looking out for him, and went to greet him as his car pulled up outside. I strolled out after her. 'Hey, Thornie, how you doing?' I asked, as we shook hands. He was sixty-eight, but his grip was still strong, a relic of his younger days as a steel worker, before moving up to management, and a reminder that he had spent most of his retirement on Lanark golf course. 'Have you brought your clubs?' I asked, rhetorically, I assumed, for he always did whether I'd told him to or not.

'No,' he replied, taking me completely by surprise.

'What's wrong?' Something had to be.

He nodded towards his granddaughter, who was leading the way down the path. 'I'll tell you later.'

The day was warming up, and the early summer that often comes to Scotland in May was holding firm, so I decided that the garden was in play again. 'Alex,' I said, 'you're on coffee duty . . . proper coffee too, not instant.'

'Aw, Dad.'

'No arguments. It's your turn. And don't use the stuff in the packet either. I bought some beans in the deli; grind them and use them.'

Thornton came to help me as I fetched the chairs from the shed, and set them around the patio table. As he unfolded the third, I took a closer look at him; I couldn't miss the dark circles under his eyes, a new addition to his weather-beaten features, and noticed for the first time that his breathing was laboured. 'Tell me,' I murmured, as we sat.

He looked at me, and smiled. 'Did it ever occur to you that statistics are always about other people?'

It hadn't, since I lived with crime stats, and targets, but I nodded nonetheless.

'I thought that, until I heard someone on telly discussing road accident figures after my daughter had died, and I realised that she was one of them. In time, her mother fell ill, and became one too. Even after that, though . . . we're bombarded with statistics, so many that we disregard them. For example, there are the figures about smoking, and what it does to people. Not to you yourself, though, always other people. I often used to wonder whether it was one particular cigarette that did the damage, and eventually I decided that it was, and that the odds against you pulling that one from the packet were still pretty long. When I go to the bookie's, Bob, I always back favourites, yet I'm not a rich man, so I should know that they don't always pay off.'

By that time, I knew what he was going to tell me, but I waited, I let him take his time. 'Mine's finally come up, son,' he said. 'I've drawn the fatal fag. I've been diagnosed with lung cancer.'

I looked up at the blue sky, expecting to see dark clouds moving across it, but it was clear and unblemished. 'What are they going to do about it?' I asked him. 'Surgery?'

'They say no. They say it's a big tumour and that it's already spread to my lymphatic system; when that happens, the knife isn't an option, they say.'

'Who's saying this, exactly?'

'It seems to be the unanimous view. I asked to see a surgeon as well as the physician who examined me first, but she told me the same thing; so did my GP. Instead, they want to give me chemotherapy, and maybe radiotherapy as well.'

'Good,' I exclaimed. 'That means they're being positive about your chances.'

'That's the buzz word, Bob,' he murmured. 'Positivity. They said that about Mina, even as they told me she was going to die within a week. But, now that I'm a statistic myself, I'm more interested in them, ye see. I really interrogated my GP, like you do with a baddie, but he stuck to the party line, then he started to go on about prolonging life. So I went to the library. You can get on this internet thing there. It's got a lot of information, and the library people show you how to look for it. What it told me is that statistically . . . back to that word again . . . I'm a rank outsider, twenty to one against lasting even a couple of years. I've never backed a twenty-to-one shot in my life, son. And that's with the treatment,' he added, 'which is no picnic, as I saw when Mina was ill. The chemotherapy makes you sick without other drugs to control it, and they don't always work.' He touched his silver head. 'The radiation makes you sick too, and it makes your hair fall out. So what will I be if I have it? A baldy old man that can't stop throwing up, and can't get any further than the practice putting green on the golf course.'

'You've got to try, though,' I insisted.

'Why? Jean, and Alexis, and you are all I've got to live for. But I don't want any of you, least of all that wee one in there, to see me like that. I wouldn't wish it on you, and I've got too much pride to want to look in the mirror and see a bloke I don't recognise staring back at me. So I'm going to take the other option. They call it palliative care; that means giving me painkillers and such as and when I need them, and keeping me as comfortable as possible, while the disease runs its course.'

'And how long will that be?'

'That's the beauty of it,' he chuckled, an action that triggered a long, racking cough; it hurt me just to hear it, so God knows what it did to him. 'It might be longer than if I had the treatment. They can't say for sure that it won't. However, when I pressed my own doctor, he guessed three months, maximum.'

I was struggling to take it in. Three days earlier, I'd looked, close to, at Marlon Watson's broken body and accepted it as part of my daily routine, yet this, out of the blue, was overwhelming. 'Jesus, Thornie,' I murmured, feeling close to tears. 'What are we going to tell Alex?'

'Well, what are you going to tell me?' she asked as she emerged from the kitchen carrying a tray, with a coffee pot, three mugs, a milk jug and a packet of the chocolate ginger biscuits that I thought I'd stashed out of her sight.

'That Grandpa's going away for a while,' Thornton replied.

'Away?' she repeated, looking at him, full of curiosity as she held the tray for me to unload it. 'Where?'

'Places I've never been. I've decided to go on one last great journey.'

'To where?' she persisted.

'That's the beauty of magical mystery tours,' Thornie had been a Beatles fan from their earliest days, 'you never know where you're going until you get there.'

'How do you know you'll like it?' She was intrigued.

'That's called faith, love. But I will. That's why they're always magical. Think about it. If anyone organised crap mystery tours, how long would they stay in business?'

She laughed, and hugged him. 'Were you a hippie when you were young, Grandpa?'

'Lassie,' he chuckled, and only just caught another paroxysm, 'when I was young we didn't have hippies. We had ration books and national service. It's only now I'm old that I'm getting a chance to catch up on that stuff.'

'Will you send me a postcard?'

'Sure. Now give me some of that coffee, Alexis, before it gets cold. It's the only reason I come here, you know, your coffee.'

The truth sank in, and hit me hard: he'd come to say goodbye. I had to get up from the table and go back indoors, quickly, before my daughter saw my face. I went to my bedroom, knowing that she wouldn't follow me in there, even if she did wonder why I'd left the two of them. It took me a few minutes to pull myself together. Before I went back outside, I changed my shirt, giving myself a cover story if she was wondering why I'd gone so suddenly.

I didn't need it. When I rejoined them, Thornton and his granddaughter were in full flow. 'What's this she's telling me?' he said. 'About you turning into a Lothario?'

'Certainly not,' I protested. 'He was a very shifty type, the original.' *And what was I yesterday?* I thought.

'I must listen to this new friend of yours, Alexis.'

'I don't know if you can, Grandpa. She's on a local station.'

'But you never know, the signal might reach Carluke, even if it's not supposed to. They can't put up walls to keep radio waves out.' My mobile sounded. 'Any more,' he continued with barely a pause, 'than you can keep them from reaching those things. They can be switched off though, Bob.'

'Not this one, Thornie. It has to stay on.'

'You should nag your father into smelling a few of those roses,' I heard him say, as I flipped it open and headed for the foot of the garden.

'Yes,' I grunted, irritably.

'Is it a bad time, boss?' Jeff Adam asked.

'It's as good as it's going to get for a while,' I replied, 'but not your problem. You're the guy in the office on a Sunday while I'm in my garden. What's up?'

'That Transit van's been found,' he announced.

'Progress, thank Christ. Where?'

'Newcastle, but don't get excited. It's not going to be any use to us; any personal traces that might have been in it are destroyed. It was found in the early hours on a piece of open ground near St James's Park, set alight. The fire brigade turned out, but it was practically melted by then. They're taking no chances.'

'Do we know who "they" are yet? Any joy with the auctioneers?'

'Afraid not; we'll get nothing from there before Monday. So no progress, I'm afraid, other than we can stop looking for the van.'

'I wouldn't say that, Jeff. The very fact that the thing was still in Newcastle, that tells us something. Unless they went all the way down there to borrow it for the job . . . and that's unlikely: it would have been easier to steal something local . . . then Tyneside is where they're from.'

'Does Tony Manson have a Tyneside connection?'

'Not that I've ever heard of. Maybe that's the problem; maybe somebody there wants to connect with him. But that's something I'll ask him when I see him tomorrow. While you're on, is all quiet with Bella Watson?'

'Yes. Steele and Mackie are still down the drains, but they've had nothing to report. Big Lennie's still there, so that's hardly surprising.'

He was right. 'Fuck it,' I said. 'Pull them, Jeff. Tell them to stand down. It's a waste of overtime. I'll see you tomorrow.'

I ended the call and went back to the table. My coffee was stone cold, so I made a nonsense of the expensive beans by sticking the mug in the microwave to warm for a few seconds. Thornton and Alex were still chatting and laughing, and I was pulled back to the realisation that this peaceful family scene was never going to be repeated. I'd been expecting to play golf with my father-in-law, so I'd made no plans to entertain him. I phoned the clubhouse, and managed to get the last table for Sunday lunch. The dress rules required a jacket and tie, but Thornton was clad appropriately. Just after twelve, I sent Alex off to dress like a lady, and he and I were left alone again.

He spelled it out for me. 'This is how I want it to be, Bob, her last memory of me. Unless there's a remission, and they've barely mentioned that notion, I won't see her again. She thinks she's grown up, but she's not ready to handle Grandpa dying in a morphine haze, and I don't want to see her cry. You can come, son, when it gets near the end. Jean'll need your support. But not Alexis; not my wee girl. Okay?'

'Okay, Thornie. It's your death; it'll be as you wish.'

'Good lad. One thing though; make sure they play "Magical Mystery Tour" at my funeral. I wasn't kidding; that's how I think of it.'

Indoors, the phone rang, then stopped. I assumed that Alex had picked it up.

'How are you, son?' he asked.

'Me? I'm fine.'

'And the girlfriend?'

'Her too.'

'And the other one?'

'Someone I met in the course of an ongoing investigation, then spoke to again, yesterday.'

'Then brought her out here to meet and confuse your daughter.'

I nodded. 'Yes, I probably shouldn't have done that. We had a talk, though, and I think she's all right.'

'Of course Alexis is all right! It's you I'm bothered about. You're vulnerable, Bob. You haven't a clue how to handle women, and I don't want to see you get hurt. You've had enough o' that for any man's lifetime. Be careful, lad. That's all I'm saying.'

I nodded, and he said no more, until Alex rejoined us, in a navy blue dress with a matching short-sleeved jacket, an outfit that I hadn't seen before. She might not have been old enough for me to give her a credit card, but I had an account in John Lewis and she was able to charge things to it.

'That was Alison on the phone, Pops.' She smiled. 'She said that her head's clear and she'll see you later.'

I didn't offer to drive to the golf club. It's less than a quarter of a mile from the cottage and that would have seemed distinctly odd to Alex. So we walked, round the corner, along the path beside the Anglican church and through the car park. Thornton was steady on his feet, but I let him set the pace, and it was slow. He covered it up, though, by pausing every so often, to admire the church, to point out a tree in blossom, and to question Alex about some of the big houses on the skyline. Even then, she knew a lot more about the village than I do.

He was still eating well, though. He always had done, and when I saw him tuck into Mrs Mann's famous steak and kidney pie, I could understand why he had rejected the offer of chemotherapy. It would have been torture to him.

We had a table in the bay window; as we ate he was able to look out across the first and eighteenth holes of Number One golf course, at the steady stream of players starting and finishing their rounds.

'Anybody who's a member here is a lucky man,' he declared. 'Will you put my name forward?'

'Of course I will,' I replied, taken by surprise.

'Then please do. I know that the waiting list here's as long as God's arm, but it does no harm to have ambitions in life. The day you run out of things to look forward to, you might as well be dead.'

My spirits were lifted. Thornie might be making preparations, but he hadn't given up. Whatever he might have said earlier, he had a few quid on at twenty to one.

'Isn't that right, Alexis?' he continued. 'What are you looking forward to?'

'Getting that CD from Mia,' she replied, instantly.

He laughed. 'I was thinking more long-term.'

She shrugged. 'Being older. Being sixteen so that Pops doesn't have to get someone to be with me all the time he's not there. Leaving school and going to university. Being a lawyer and having my own money.'

'What about boyfriends?'

She frowned. 'I haven't seen anyone I like yet, Grandpa.'

'Good answer. There's no harm in being hard to please. But what about exciting things? When I was your age I wanted to play for Rangers. I made it too, but it was only Cambuslang Rangers, not the big team.'

She shifted in her seat; Alex didn't show diffidence very often. 'I'd like to be a singer,' she admitted. 'Next year I'm going to try to get into the High School musical.' That was news to me. 'Mrs Medine, the music teacher, thinks I'm good enough.'

'Then go for it, my love, but remember this: never let your dreams cloud your judgement.'

As we walked home, steadily, along the main street, the weather was breaking, and storm clouds were gathering in the west. Thornton decided that he would head for home, before the worst of it hit. We stood on the green to see him off; just before he turned the corner he waved, and that was the last his granddaughter ever saw of him.

I was still shocked, profoundly, by everything that had happened, when Alison arrived a few hours later, although by that time I'd made some phone calls and found a seconder and additional nominees for Thornie's membership application.

She cheered me up, as soon as she stepped through the front door, by walking straight into the kitchen and looking round, including behind the door, then doing the same thing in the bathroom and, finally, the bedroom.

'What are you doing?' I asked her, puzzled.

She grinned. 'Checking for another woman.'

'No women have been here today,' I promised, 'other than Her Upstairs with her headphones on. Just one elderly gentleman, her granddad, but he's gone now.'

'I didn't know she still had one.'

I almost said, 'Not for much longer,' but stopped when I realised that it wouldn't be fair to load her with a secret to be kept from Alex. It was going to be tough enough for me to do that. 'Yes,' I replied, instead. 'She's the apple of his eye, and vice versa.'

I led her back into the kitchen and opened a bottle of New Zealand pinot gris that I'd been persuaded to try by the nice lady in the upmarket grocer opposite the golf club, to go with the chicken salad that I'd knocked up. 'How did the girlie night go?' I asked as I handed her a glass.

'It was the quietest we've ever had,' she confessed. 'Leona wasn't drinking, since she's great with child, and I was still a bit morose after making such a tit of myself in the Sheraton.'

'Get over that,' I told her. 'I've never had a woman throw a wobbly at me before. I'm beginning to see it as flattering.'

'Well, don't. If you want to screw little Miss Radio Star, you carry on. I'll get over that too. In fact, why don't you put your name on that "Two's Company" dating thing they have in the *Scotsman*. I'll write the ad for you. "Thirty-something vulnerable widower, GSOH, own teeth, two cars, one nice, one crap, seeks twenty-something lady with ample tits with a view to companionship, hill walking, fine dining and lots of shagging." You'll be amazed by the responses you get.'

'Vulnerable,' I murmured. 'You said "vulnerable". It's the second time that word's been used about me today.'

'But you are, my dear. It's part of your attraction. You are so patently lonely and bereft that every woman who sees you wants to give you a great big hug, then carry on from there. If you like, I could take the word out of your matchmaking ad copy and substitute "big dick", but it wouldn't get nearly as many replies.'

'I really don't have a clue, do I?'

She took my arm and led me to the living room. 'No, Bob, you don't. It's just as well you've got your daughter to look after you. She's the best minder you could possibly have. Nobody will take advantage of you while she's around.'

'That's good to know. So back to last night; sounds as if you had a real fun time.'

She shook her head. 'No,' she murmured. 'I hate to see my pal being taken to the emotional cleaners, but she is, by that shit of a husband. She's vulnerable too, Bob. You'd make a great couple, if it wasn't for Roland.'

'I doubt that. She married a politician. That shows a lack of judgement in my book.'

She giggled. 'Don't be cruel to my friend.'

It was time to eat so I called for Alex, but had to go upstairs and pull the headphone jack from her CD player to get her attention. She had been singing along to something by Reba McEntire . . . yes, I hear you ask, what the hell was a Scots thirteen-year-old doing listening to Reba? . . . and her face flushed when she realised I'd heard. 'You're a cert for the school show,' I told her, 'but country music might be a bit risky for the audition. Something more mainstream, maybe. How about Kim Wilde?'

'She's your generation, Pops.'

Whether she wanted to get back to band practice I knew not, but she went upstairs again almost as soon as supper was over, leaving us to watch a crime drama on television that soon had us laughing at its ineptitude. The storm had passed over, so we gave up on it, and took a couple of beers outside.

'What does GSOH mean?' I asked her, in the twilight.

'Good state of health, man. You do have your own teeth, don't you?'

I bared them in a wolfman grin. 'Vulnerable, eh?'

She put her head on my shoulder. 'Afraid so. Sometimes, I wish I loved you, Bob, but if I did, I'd only wind up getting hurt.'

'I'd keep you safe.' As it turned out I couldn't, but that was a few years down the road.

'Nobody's safe,' she whispered. 'Not one of us. You should know that.'

I did. Thornie's visit had reminded me of that. I held her to me, as if I was shielding her . . . but equally, I might have been hiding behind her.

We turned in early, and fell asleep quickly; deeply too, for when the mobile sounded on the bedside table, Alison didn't stir, and for me it seemed to be part of a dream. It wasn't though, and as I came to, I realised why I'd been so slow to react. Of course, it wasn't my ringtone; it wasn't my phone, it was hers. I shook her, but all she did was mumble and roll over and into me. So I took the call myself.

'Alison's phone,' I growled. 'This better be serious.'

'It is,' a male voice replied: a voice I knew, Detective Superintendent Alastair Grant.

And he knew mine too. 'Bob? Is that you?'

'Yes. Now hold your fucking horses and give her time to wake up.'

I switched on the light and watched her climb slowly out of sleep. I waited until she could focus on me. 'It's your gaffer,' I told her. 'He says it's serious.'

'What time is it?'

I had no idea. I looked at my radio alarm. 'One twenty-two.'

'Shit.' She took the phone from me. 'Yes, sir.' I watched her as she listened. I was thinking that she'd been excessively rank conscious for someone sitting up naked in bed in the middle of the night; the situation would have made me laugh, but for the look on her face.

'I understand,' she said, eventually. 'Yes, I'll get there as soon as I can.'

By the time she'd pushed the 'end call' button, I was out of bed and reaching for my dressing gown on its hook behind the bathroom door. 'What's happened?'

'There's been another stabbing, fatal this time, in Jamaica Street. He thinks it may be linked to last weekend's.'

'Jamaica Street?' I repeated. 'That's not your area.'

'No, but it's just round the corner from that pub, the Giggling Goose.'

I knew why she'd been called. 'That's a gay bar, isn't it?'

'That's right. Mr Stein's told the boss to get involved; he wants me to meet up with the Gayfield Square CID team.'

'Why the fuck's Grant not going?' I complained, as she headed for the bathroom. 'You haven't been involved in the Grove Street investigation.'

'Because he's been at a family party in Perth, and he's staying there overnight.'

'Who's in charge from Gayfield?'

'DCI Pringle. I've never worked with him before. Do you know him?'

'Yeah. Dan's a sound guy,' I added. 'He's old school, and he looks a bit like PC Plod, but underestimate him at your peril. You get ready, and I'll make some coffee.'

She was showered and dressed inside ten minutes. Her hair was still damp, but it would dry in the car. She was flustered. 'Be cool,' I told her as she took a wolf-sized bite from a slice of toast, 'and don't go charging in there. As far as Dan's concerned, it's his crime scene; you'll be there more or less as an observer.'

'Fine by me. All I've done is read the paperwork on our inquiry. A fat lot of use I'll be.'

I handed her a mug of Nescafe, strong, and heavy with sugar; I didn't want her nodding off at the wheel. 'You don't need to be any use. Keep your head down, take notes and compare the scene with the photos you've seen of the other one. Were there any exceptional factors about that?'

'One that struck me: the witness statement from Grove Street. I told you that the guy, Robert Wyllie, kept changing his story, yes? He started off by saying that he and his mate, Archie Weir, were attacked, no more than that, but finally admitted that they were out to rough up a gay bloke. However, he maintained that they never actually got that far. What he claims is that their target rumbled them.'

'That he didn't act in self-defence?'

'Not according to Wyllie; his final account reads as if they were lured into Grove Street. He says that the man was heading up Morrison Street, then took a quick turn. They followed him but he was nowhere to be seen. They went a few yards and then he was on them. Wyllie was stabbed first, in the leg. He went down, Weir started to run away, but the man with the knife pursued him and went to work on him. Seven stab wounds in all, two in the back, one in each arm and three in the abdomen. He turned back towards Wyllie, who was still on the ground holding his leg, but just then the fourth person came round the corner and the attacker ran off.'

'Okay,' I said, as she gulped her coffee, pulling a face at its sweetness. 'You have that background knowledge, they don't. So go there and find out what they do have. Another live witness would be a good start. How's the guy Weir, by the way?'

'On a ventilator. They don't expect him to make it.'

'Mmm. Not good.' I took the empty mug from her, and kissed her; on the forehead, to avoid smearing her lipstick. 'On you go now. You're a star, and you're going to leave us all behind.'

'Thanks,' she murmured. 'I'll see you.' I thought she'd go then, but she stayed in my arms. 'Not for a while, though. I've got to be careful; waking up with you could be habit-forming.'

I'd been thinking the same thing. I locked the door after her, then went back to bed, but I was done with sleep for the night. I lay there, aware of Alison's scent on the duvet and on the pillow, my mind working, contemplating the crime scene that she was driving towards. My curiosity wasn't idle. I found myself hoping that by the time they got there it would have been wrapped up, plenty of eye witnesses and an arrest made, either a gang killing or a dispute between a couple of macho guys that had gone too far, and nothing to do with the Grove Street attack that sounded as if it was going to become a full-scale murder inquiry before long.

But if it wasn't, if the evidence pointed to a link between the two, then it would be a single homicide investigation, crossing divisional boundaries. I had no intention of volunteering, but I knew there was every chance that Alf Stein would decide that it fell within the loose remit of my unit and thus would dump it in my lap.

I could see the headlines as I lay in the darkness . . . 'Gay Blade Strikes!' . . . and I didn't fancy it at all.

# Ten

I gave up trying to sleep just after six; apart from my pressing work problems, Thornton's visit was weighing heavily upon me. He was the last of our parents' generation, mine and Myra's, and such a hearty fit guy, that it had never occurred to me that he wouldn't be around for my fiftieth birthday, and for a few after that. I tried to imagine what I would say to Alex when 'It' happened, but I couldn't. Instead, I had a vision of Jean, Alex and myself in the front row of the church where Myra and I had been married, and my eyes filled with tears.

I rose and took my time about getting ready for the day. The face that I saw in the mirror as I shaved was creased and lined, with dark bags under the blue eyes. My hair was all over the place, and looked greyer than ever. I could still find a few dark strands, but they were as outnumbered as the Spartans at Thermopylae. They had begun to retreat on the day that I cut off a lock and put it in Myra's coffin, and had been quickly overcome by the silver hordes.

'Vulnerable?' I grunted. 'No, you're just a sad old bastard.'

I chose a suit, a pale cream linen thing that was meant to look crumpled . . . or so I'd been told by a dickhead in Austin Reed, who hadn't bothered to tell me that it would need dry cleaning after almost every wearing. I complemented it with a black shirt, but didn't bother with a tie. I remembered my admonition to McGuire about flashy dressing but disregarded it; I wanted to leave my image with the man I'd be seeing that day long after I'd left him.

I was on my second coffee, and had run almost half a loaf through the toaster, when Alex joined me, also dressed for action. 'Why did Alison go?' she asked, a little anxiously, as she filled a bowl with cereal. 'Did you have a row?'

'No, of course not,' I reassured her. 'She had a work call.'

'Oh,' she said, relieved. 'That's all right, then.'

I laughed. 'There will come a day in your life, kid, when you get a business call at half past one in the morning. When it happens, I promise you that it will not be all right.'

'Lawyers don't get calls in the middle of the night.'

'No? I reckon that if this career choice of yours is definitive, it's time I introduced you to a couple I know. There's a man called Mitchell Laidlaw, one of my five-a-side football chums. I'll ask him if he'll have a talk with you. And there are a couple of advocates that you ought to meet.'

She shrugged. 'If you want.' Then she turned to what was really on her mind. 'This trip of Grandpa's, Pops. Do you know where he's going?'

'No,' I said . . . honestly, I believe. 'I haven't a clue.'

'I think it's weird, going on holiday and not knowing where you're going.'

'Not at all. People used to do it all the time, before the days of packages to bloody Benidorm, back when you went on holiday in your own country, not in other people's. When I was a kid, we went to Fife.' That was the only place my mother would go, but I didn't tell Alex that. She looked at me with a kind of pity.

I was in the office by quarter to nine, but I wasn't first. McGuire was there before me. He raised an eyebrow when he saw the suit. 'You really do need to meet my tailor, boss,' he said.

I waved a middle finger in his direction and retreated to my sanctum. I hung my jacket on a hook . . . no sense in creasing it more than necessary . . . sat behind my desk and called Alison's mobile. 'How's it going?' I asked. 'Has Dan got a result yet?'

'Can't talk now,' she replied, quietly. 'Office?'

'Yes.'

'Give me five.'

I replaced the phone in its socket and waited, looking out into the outer office, and waving, first to Andy Martin, then Jeff Adam, as each arrived. The DS stuck his head round the door. 'Want me to get back on to Newcastle, boss, and ask them to dig up that car auction manager?'

'No. Get them to give you his name and number and call him yourself. Cut out the middle man.'

'Will do.'

Alison called back a couple of minutes later, on my mobile. 'Sorry about earlier,' she said. 'I was with Mr Pringle.'

'Nuff said. I understand. Where are you now?'

'I'm back at Gayfield now, in the ladies. Did you get a decent night's sleep after I left?'

'Log-like,' I lied. 'How goes it?'

'No result, but we do have a witness, though. Mr Pringle's team did a door-to-door; they knocked up everyone living in the area. The owner of a mews house in Jamaica Street Lane told them that he came home just after midnight and was just closing his garage after putting his car away, when a man came running past him, heading in the direction of India Street. He gave a decent description: twenties, tall, slim, clean-shaven, black hair, khaki-coloured cotton jacket.'

'That's a start.'

'More than a start. Bob, this is the same man; I'm sure of it.' Just what I did not want to hear. 'He's changed the hair, as you said he would, but the rest of the description matches Wyllie's. And that's not where it ends. When you called earlier we'd just left the home of the manager of the Giggling Goose, a man called Ferrier. We ran the description past him. He told us that it fitted someone who'd been involved in a dust-up in his pub, earlier on. What you have to understand is, his customers aren't exclusively gay; there's no sign over the door, and his clientele's usually mixed.'

'Bet on it,' I said. 'I've had a pint in there myself before now.'

'Okay, so you know what it's like. Well, according to Ferrier, a wee bit before twelve, our man bought a pint.'

'Was he alone?'

'Yes, as far as Ferrier could tell. Anyway, as he was backing away from the bar, he bumped into two guys and spilled his Guinness all over them. It was his fault, but he started to swear at the other two, and it got a bit heated. There were a couple of homophobic remarks, and Ferrier told them to shut up. Khaki jacket wouldn't, though. He called them a couple of wankers, said they were hiding behind the barman's apron, threw what was left of the Guinness in their faces and headed for the door.'

'Did they go after him?'

'Only one of them. The other one, his pal, tried to stop him, but he shook him off. He went charging out and he never came back.'

'Did nobody go and look for him?' I asked.

'Ferrier said that about ten minutes later, his mate asked him to mind his drink and went looking for him. He came back though, and said he couldn't see him. That's not surprising. Just at the end of the lane, where it splits, there are a few steps leading down into the courtyard of the Jamaica Mews flats. The body was hidden down there in the shadows, out of sight of the lane. It was only found when a couple of girls tripped over it on the way home. It was a hell of a mess; multiple stab wounds, big ones, including one in each eye.'

'So the khaki jacket would be pretty bloody,' I suggested.

'Not necessarily. He must have died very quickly, for there wasn't as much spread of blood as the number of wounds would suggest.'

'Have you got an ID for him?'

'No, he had nothing on him. Ferrier didn't know him by name and there was no wallet found. He had one when he was in the pub, so khaki jacket must have taken it.'

'Fuck!'

'I agree, but what's it to you?'

I told her of my fear. There was a multiple murderer out there, or there would be when Weir's life support was switched off. It was always possible that Alf Stein would take over the hunt himself, but that wasn't his style, not when he had the Serious Crimes Unit up his sleeve to put a bit of PR gloss on it.

'What should I do now?' she asked.

'You should tell Dan Pringle what you know, and then bring Alastair up to speed when he gets back from Perth. They'll report to Alf, and next thing you know,' I sighed, 'I can see now, it'll be pass the fucking parcel to yours truly.'

I left her to follow my suggestions, or not, as she chose, and went back to my own day. Once everyone had arrived I pulled my team together, and brought everyone up to speed on developments in the Marlon murder investigation, the van, the Newcastle connection, my Friday visit to Lennie Plenderleith, what he'd told me about the reason for Tony Manson's absence, and the speed with which he'd been moved in to 'babysit' . . . some baby! . . . Bella.

'What do we read into that?' Fred Leggat wondered.

'It says to me that Marlon's death was as big a surprise to Tony as it probably was to the boy himself. We can expect that the man will be taking it very seriously, now he's back. I'm going to see him this morning to make sure that he knows he's in our thoughts.'

'But are we any closer to understanding why Marlon was killed?'

I shrugged. 'I don't know about any of you guys, but I'm not. Newcastle: that's all we've got.' I looked across at Jeff Adam; he was at his desk, seated, leaning forward, shoulders hunched, phone pressed to his ear, in his left hand, scribbling in his notebook with the other. I waited till he was finished.

He turned in his chair as he replaced the phone, with a small involuntary jump as he realised that every eye in the room was focused on him. 'What?' he exclaimed, provoking a round of laughter. It made me feel good. I was brought up to believe that a happy team was usually a successful team. (Too bad that my dad didn't realise what was happening within his own small squad.)

'A name,' Adam announced. 'I have a name. The Transit was bought by one Glenn Milburn, number seventeen Woodvale Avenue, Wallsend, Newcastle.'

'Real name, or could it be a fake?' I asked.

'Not very likely, boss. The auction house insists on proof of identity from all buyers. Milburn produced his passport, so unless that was a phoney, it's him. The manager even gave me a description. Big bloke, face like a front-row forward, he said. Whatever that means.'

'Usually it means that only a short-sighted mother could love it,' Martin chuckled.

'Excellent, Jeff,' I told the DS. 'A good start to the day.'

'How do we play it, boss?'

'You talk to your Newcastle CID contacts; check with NCIS to see if this Milburn has a record, known associates, and so on. You'd better get down there.' I looked around the team and settled on McGuire. 'Take Mario with you. I want this guy lifted, I want a name for the second man, and ideally I want the pair of them in our custody by this evening. As a minimum, I want Milburn. Before you set off, though, you must see the fiscal's office about getting a warrant from a sheriff to arrest Milburn, and his pal if you can put a name to him, and bring them here. The rights to legal access are different in England and I don't want this investigation hindered by some fucking lawyer arguing about jurisdiction.'

He nodded. 'Understood, sir. I'll speak to Davie Pettigrew. He's my tame fiscal.' He looked at McGuire. 'Mario, you make the call to Newcastle. I'll give you a name.'

'Good enough,' I said, just as the phone rang in my room. I went back to my desk and picked it up.

'Jesus, Bob, that was a bit embarrassing last night,' Detective Superintendent Alastair Grant began. 'I didn't know about you and Alison Higgins.'

'You still don't, buddy,' I warned him.

'Sure, that's a given. But still, it was a surprise, especially after she cut you like a knife on Saturday in the Sheraton. Mind you,' he chuckled, 'it does explain why she cut you like a knife. Who was that gorgeous brunette you had on your arm?'

'A witness,' I replied, abruptly.

'She's not a hostile witness, that's for fucking certain.'

'Listen, Alastair,' I warned him, 'if all you've got to do with your day is get yourself on my shit list, you want to find something else, sharpish.'

He laughed. 'When the man of mystery gets caught out twice in two days, you can't expect it to go unremarked.'

'Fine,' I retorted, 'but if it doesn't go unreported I'll come looking for you.'

'Don't worry, my mouth will stay shut . . .'

'And nothing will be said to Alison.'

'Absolutely not, no.'

'Good. Now,' I asked, 'is there another reason for this so far annoying phone call?'

'I take it she told you what it was all about,' he said.

'You shouldn't assume that.' I paused. 'But let's say that I forced it out of her.'

'It's the same bloke in each case, we're sure,' he volunteered. 'I've suggested to Dan Pringle that we should take the lead in both inquiries, but he's on his high horse. He says that his is a murder, while ours is only attempted, or maybe even just serious assault.'

'That's a crap argument and we both know it. You outrank him; don't suggest, man, bloody tell him.'

'I would, but he's been to Alf.'

I laughed, softly, seeing a bandwagon heading in my direction. 'Go on,' I murmured.

'And Alf says—'

'That he's not holding your jackets while you sort it out,' I offered, 'and that the lead in the investigation passes to me?'

'That's right,' Grant admitted, after a moment's hesitation.

'Does he want me to go and see him?'

'No, he's at what he calls an inter-force CID exchange today, although I'm sure I heard the swish of swinging golf clubs in the background when I spoke to him. He asked me to pass it on to you, and also to give you any assistance that you need. By that, he meant manpower.'

Since I had known what was coming, I had thought it through. 'Make that woman-power,' I told him. 'I want Alison to lead both stabbing investigations, working out of your office, but reporting to me.'

'Shouldn't she move to Fettes for the duration?' he asked.

'No fucking way, man,' I retorted, 'and I shouldn't have to spell out why.'

'No, maybe not,' he conceded. 'Do you want anyone else?'

'Assistance as necessary, but for the moment I'll assign a couple of people to work with her. Tell her what's happened . . . it won't come as a surprise . . . then ask her to come up here right away, so I can brief them all together.'

As I hung up, I turned my thoughts to planning my day. While I'd been speaking to Grant, the force press officer had left a message with Fred Leggat, wanting me to update the media on the Watson investigation, but my new inquiry would have to be dealt with too, and that would grab most of the headlines. I could have done without it, but I didn't trust the press guy to handle it on his own. He was a police officer, a veteran uniformed inspector, who'd been put there to see out his time. He was known among the senior ranks as 'Inspector Hesitant'. He was fine for reading out prepared statements, but I couldn't trust him to handle questions without pissing in the soup.

I'd been lobbying Alf Stein for a while about the need for a specialist professional in that office, and he'd taken it to the Command Corridor, but he'd run up against the age-old blocker, 'budget considerations'.

I called Inspector Hesitant back and told him to call the media in for ten thirty, then went outside to see Brian Mackie and Stevie Steele. Brian knew Alison from our drugs squad days, so it made sense for him to work with her, and I wanted to see how the younger DC functioned under a bit of pressure.

I was impatient to get it all over with; I had a visit to pay that day, as soon as possible, and the enforced delay was annoying me. On top of that, there was something else I had to do, a call I'd forgotten about until Alastair Grant had reminded me, inadvertently.

I might have decided to forget about it altogether, if it hadn't been for my daughter, and a promise made to her, and . . . a tingling curiosity inside me that I couldn't quite manage to suppress.

I rang the Airburst studio, although I wasn't sure when Mia's working day began. At nine thirty, it turned out, on that day at least; she was in, and took my call. 'Hi, Bob,' she said, in the warm voice that worked so well on radio, and that tingling grew stronger. 'How've you been?'

'Good, and busy,' I replied.

'Before you say anything more,' she continued, 'I haven't forgotten about that demo CD for Alex . . . but what I did forget was to bring it with me this morning. I'm putting my programme together for this afternoon, then I'm going back home, so if you were free around lunchtime, you could call in and pick it up. And,' she paused for a second, 'we could finish that discussion we left hanging in the air on Saturday.'

I ran through my mental diary. Brief Alison; media conference; my priority visit. 'How much time do you have?' I asked. 'I couldn't make it till one, at the earliest; even then it would depend on where you live.'

'One would be fine,' she said. 'I'm renting a cottage in Davidson's Mains.' She gave me the address; it was on the right side of town for where I'd be going.

'Okay,' I told her. 'If anything gets in the way, I'll call you. By the way, I'll be talking to the press soon, about Marlon. I'll be careful what I tell them, but we do have a lead.'

I heard her sigh. 'Bob, to be honest, I don't care. Now that you've got me extricated from my mother's clutches, I don't want any more to do with my family, alive or dead.'

Ten minutes later, the door opened and Alison, all crisp efficiency in spite of her one-thirty start, came into the outer office; she looked around and spotted me almost at once, behind my desk, beckoning her to join me.

She closed the door behind her, and took the seat facing me. 'You never said you were going to ask for me,' she said, frowning. 'First you move me out of drugs, then you second me here.'

'You're not seconded,' I corrected her. 'You're working on one specific investigation . . . the Gay Blade, I've decided to call him within this office . . . and that's all. You won't even have a desk here. I'm not messing you around here, Alison. If anything, I'm giving you a real opportunity. Officially, I'm the lead officer, but in practice, you are.'

She frowned. 'It could be an opportunity to strengthen that glass ceiling if I make a bollocks of it.'

'No,' I insisted. 'I'm not going to expose you to any flak. Officially, I'm out front. If the investigation gets bogged down in quicksand, I'll take any blame that's attributed. But when you make an arrest, I'll be nowhere to be seen, and you'll be the one on telly. That's a promise.'

She looked at her hands. 'I appreciate that, Bob,' she murmured. 'But even if it does go well . . . I'm a bit afraid that I might wind up being accused of fucking my way to the top. Even if nobody says it outright, you know how sexist this place can still be.'

'Who's going to think that? There are only two people in the force who know about you and me. As of a few hours ago, Alastair Grant and, before him, Alf Stein. Neither of them will say a word. If anyone else is silly enough to even drop a hint, I will find out about it, and that sad person will find out just how ruthless I can be. Now, let me bring in your new team.'

I went to the door, and called to Mackie and Steele. They joined us, and I filled them in on their new assignment. 'You'll be working where DI Higgins determines, and operating under her orders. She's in complete charge of this unified investigation. Alison, would you like to give us an update.'

'Yes, boss,' she replied. She related the stories that I had heard already: first the attack on Weir and Wyllie, next, the provocation and ambush of that morning's victim, and then she told us something I hadn't known. 'We've got a possible ID on the latest victim. Half an hour ago, the mother of a man named Albert McCann, aged twenty-seven, called Torphichen Place to report her son missing. She said that he went out for a drink with a pal last night. He didn't come home, but she assumed that he was staying at the mate's place. That was until she had a call from his foreman in the Lothian bus garage, where he works as a mechanic, asking where the hell he was. The description she gave matches him exactly, right down to the clothes.'

'What's been done about it?' I asked her.

'Nothing yet. Superintendent Grant called me to tell me about it just before I got here. He'd asked to be told about all missing person reports as soon as they came in.'

'Then you know what to do.'

'Yes.' She looked at Mackie. 'Brian, you call Torphichen and get Mrs McCann's address. If there's a husband, find out, locate him and get the poor sod to make a formal identification. I saw the body; I wouldn't want the mother to have to do it if we can avoid it. DC Steele, Brian will get the name of the victim's pal from his mother. You take a statement from him, and ask him to do a photofit, if he's any use. Given the time of night that all this happened, his memory might not be too reliable. Once you're both done, report to me at Torphichen Place. That's where we'll be based.'

'Why not here?' Mackie asked.

'I don't want to be distracted by the rest of this unit's work,' she replied, smoothly. 'We'll focus better if we're somewhere else.' She looked at me. 'If that's all, boss . . .' I smiled as I nodded; I was relieved that she was beyond calling me 'Sir'.

When the three of them were gone I closed my office door again and thought about my approach to the media. I was left with only fifteen minutes to prepare, but I knew, pretty much, what I was going to say. I knew also that it wouldn't involve Newcastle, not until I had the man Milburn in my custody. That didn't matter, though, for as soon as I announced that the Grove Street and Jamaica Street stabbings were linked, I would be giving them their headlines for the day.

That's the way it worked out. I didn't mention McCann by name, not without a formal ID, nor did I touch on the gay overtone, but John Hunter, the city's top freelance, was shrewd enough to make the connection as soon as I said that the second victim had been in the Giggling Goose just before his death. He went down the wrong track, though, and I had to point out that there was no suggestion that either Weir, or the dead man, was a homosexual.

'But we can call this guy a serial attacker?' he persisted.

His income depended on his ability to sell news stories to his media customers, so he was always after a hook to reel them in, but I wasn't playing. 'I'll stick to suspect, John, if you don't mind, and leave it to your subeditors to add the creative touches.'

Afterwards BBC, STV and Sky wanted interviews for the telly news. It was part of the job, for all that I didn't like it. Our professional trainers had told me that I look intimidating on camera, and that I should try to be more 'viewer-friendly'. I told him in return that fearsome was all right with me, and that I wasn't after Jon Snow's lot. Still, I gave the people what they wanted, although I did try particularly hard to intimidate the bloke from Sky.

Their faffing about used up twenty minutes of my precious morning, and so it was gone eleven fifteen when I made it back to the office. Fred Leggat looked up as I entered, and I could tell that he was not about to make my day. 'It's official, boss,' he told me. 'DI Higgins has just called. We now have a double murder inquiry: Archie Weir died this morning, just before eleven.'

'Poor sod,' I grunted. 'No surprise, though. Family informed?'

'The parents were there when he died, Alison said. They approved switch-off of the life support.'

'Okay, give it to the press office and tell them to put it out.' I looked at Martin. 'Andy, you're with me. It's time to broaden your education. Have you got wheels?' I asked him.

'Yes, boss. My car's in the park round the back.'

'So's mine. Follow me; I've got a private call to make after our visit, so it's best if you travel under you own steam.'

'Fine, but where are we going?' he asked. It was a reasonable question, put with no undue deference. From the beginning, his quiet self-confidence was one of the things I liked about Andy Martin. I've never met anyone less likely to be accused of being a teacher's pet.

Nonetheless, that didn't stop me from stringing him along. 'You'll see when we get there.'

He shrugged his shoulders and slipped them into his leather jacket. 'Okay, a mystery tour,' he said, cheerfully. I thought of Thornton and turned away, heading for the door.

His car was two bays away from mine; a red Mazda MX5 convertible with 'boy's toy' written all over it. I had to smile. 'Is that for go or show?' I asked.

'A bit of both,' he admitted. 'Nice lines, and it's got the larger engine option, but it's still not a Ferrari.' He looked at my Land Rover with something that might have been either pity or contempt. 'It'll out-pull that, though.'

'That would depend on the sense in which you're using the word "pull". The Discovery was built with comfort in mind, and in my albeit limited experience, some ladies don't like to flash their minge climbing in and out of one of those things.' I tapped the Mazda's rag-top. 'Plus, I prefer a car that you can't unlock with a Stanley knife.'

I led the way out of the car park, and headed west, towards Queensferry Road, driving slowly to wind Martin up. I continued our stately progress all the way out to the Maybury junction, where I took a right turn, past the doomed Barnton Hotel. Eventually I turned into a cul-de-sac off Essex Road, and pulled up.

I stayed in my car as the young DC left his, and reached across to open the passenger door. 'Game over,' I said. 'Do you see that big house up there?' He couldn't have missed it, a big stone pile with a grey slate roof, set in an acre of ground. 'It's called "Trinity" and it's the home of Tony Manson, of whom you've heard much said over the last few days. Tony would call himself a businessman. We would, and do, call him a criminal. The thing we like least about him is his dealing in Class A drugs. I can't think of anything that would put a bigger smile on my face, professionally, than locking him up for twenty years or so, but I've never been able to do that.'

'Why not?' Martin asked, a little too directly, but I let him off with it.

'Mainly because of the requirements of our criminal justice system,' I told him, 'and that long and meaningful word, corroboration. A lone witness isn't enough to convict. If you and I took a sledgehammer to his door and found half a ton of smack in his cellar, we'd be most of the way there. But if I did it on my own, it would be my word against his that I didn't plant it; any case that was taken to court on that basis would be chucked out by the judge at the first time of asking.'

'Have you ever done that?' He gulped and added hastily, 'Searched his place, that is.'

I laughed. 'It's "no" to the other, by the way. Searched Tony's place? Of course we have; twice in my time, but purely for show, with no expectation of success. He's much too clever and too careful ever to go near any of his merchandise, or to let it be brought anywhere near him. He also follows the basic rule of large-scale criminality, and that is . . .' I made it a question.

'Never give an order to one person,' he answered, 'that a second person can hear. Corroboration again.'

'Exactly, Andy; or even overhear. That's what keeps him out of our hands. Remember the man I told you about, Perry Holmes?'

'The guy who was shot?'

'That's him. Perry was the master of discretion. In much of his life he was legit. He was a big property developer, and he still has a large portfolio. He conducted that business in the normal way, but for one thing, something he brought from the other side. He would rarely be in the same room with more than one person, unless they were architects showing him plans, or lawyers and the like, who were safe because they were covered by client privilege. Latterly he never even went to restaurants, other than with his brother, Al.'

'It didn't do him much good, though.'

'No,' I conceded. 'It didn't make him bullet-proof. And neither's Tony; so he'll be taking Marlon's murder very seriously. Let's go and talk to him.'

I started the Discovery, and drove up to the double wrought-iron gate that secured the entrance to Manson's property. There was a closed-circuit camera set on a stone pillar to the right. I opened my window, leaned out, and waved up at it. A few seconds later, the gates swung open, seemingly of their own accord. I cruised through, up the approach road, and pulled up alongside a black Bentley.

The front door opened as we approached. Two men stood just

inside; they were dressed in black, and there was a crisp look to them that suggested a military background. One of them stepped forward, raising his hands as if to frisk me. I raised a hand and glared at him. 'Don't make the mistake,' I warned.

He paused, but didn't back off. 'Easy way or hard way?' he asked.

I don't react well to threats. I feinted with my left shoulder; and the minder reacted by moving to his own left, a wrong move, as it added to the force of the fist that I whipped up from my side and into his gut. 'Told you,' I murmured, as he dropped to his knees, and as Martin stepped forward to intercept his mate.

'Hey!' The shout came from a doorway to the left of a wide central staircase. 'Leave it off, you guys. These are the polis. I wouldn't have let them in otherwise.'

Tony Manson stepped into the hallway and came towards us; he was wearing a shell suit, and his broad, lived-in, pushing fifty face sported a Mediterranean tan. He wasn't tall, but squat and powerful; nobody had ever got the better of him in his younger days. There are hard men, and then there are those who really know how to fight. He was one of the latter. 'Sorry, Skinner,' he said. 'My new help. They're not trained to be subtle.'

'You hired them in?' I asked, as one helped the other to his feet.

He nodded. 'From a security consultancy,' he said as he led us towards the room from which he had appeared. 'They came highly recommended.'

'I'd send them back for retraining, if I were you. They'd better not be armed, incidentally.' Barely two months had passed since the Dunblane massacre, and every cop in Scotland was paranoid about firearms.

'They weren't supposed to need shooters,' Manson growled. He had that air about him, that rare aura of power and potential for the extraordinary that marks some men out from the rest. He and I had met a few times before, and had sized each other up. I didn't respect him, not in any way, any more than he did me; but I couldn't say, not honestly, that I disliked him either. It's hard to define, even now, but I probably regarded him in the same way that someone else might see a business rival. Make it personal, and your objectivity's at risk. That's a maxim I've always preached to my people, but sometimes it's been difficult to hold to it myself. One thing I will say for him. When he controlled the drugs trade in Edinburgh, there was no lethal shit on the street; Tony was hot on quality control, if only because he recognised that killing his customers wasn't profitable.

He led us into his study. I'd been there before, with warrants; he'd let my team search with no attempt at hindrance, in the certain knowledge that we'd find bugger all. It was a nice, spacious room, oak-panelled, although Manson's taste in art was too modern to hang there comfortably. The Vettriano . . . original . . . was okay, but the Howson looked out of place.

I told him as much. 'I like it,' he replied, simply. 'What do you want me to do? Loan it to the National Gallery? Go on, take a seat. I've been expecting you, after Lennie told me you'd paid him a visit.' He looked at my companion, studying him. 'New boy?' he asked.

'This is DC Martin, Tony. Remember the face, for you'll be seeing a lot of it from now on.'

'Oh aye? I thought you were in a different outfit now.'

I nodded. 'Yes, but I've still got an interest in you, don't you worry about that.'

'I won't. I've never worried about you, Skinner, and I'm not going to start now.'

'You're watching your back, though. The military two-step out there's evidence of that. Marlon's murder's got you rattled.'

'What makes you think that?'

'For a start,' I told him, 'your gates are closed. That's unusual. Also, those two out there are minders. You've never needed their sort before. Marlon, poor lad, couldn't mind his fucking manners, but you were happy with him. They're signs of a lack of confidence, I'd say. What are you worried about? What could Marlon have told our friends from Tyneside to make them stop bouncing him off the swimming pool floor? Not that it did him any good, even if he did spill the beans.'

Manson growled, deep down in his chest. 'Marlon didnae have any beans to spill, the poor little bastard. I don't know what gave anybody the idea that he had.'

'Somebody seems to have thought so,' Martin said.

He glared at the DC. 'It speaks!' He turned back to me. 'Why did you mention Tyneside, Skinner?'

'Because that's where Newcastle is, and that's where we're in the process of lifting a suspect, and possibly two if we're lucky. Does the name Glenn Milburn register with you?'

'No,' he said, looking me dead in the eye. I believed him. 'Should it?'

'You might want to remember it.'

'Newcastle?' he repeated.

'Yes. We traced the van that was used to snatch and transport Marlon. It's now a pile of burned-out and tangled metal. Milburn bought it at auction about ten days ago; for that job, it looks like.'

He frowned. 'Skinner, I don't even know anyone in Newcastle, apart from a bolshie Customs bastard at the airport that gave me a hard time last night.'

'If you did, would you tell me?'

He grinned. 'No, but I don't, so I'll tell you that, no worries.' The smile was gone as suddenly as it had appeared. 'How did they get hold of the boy, Skinner? It wouldnae have been that easy. He wasn't exactly Frank Bruno, ken, but he was hefty enough and he usually had his wits about him.'

'We've got no idea, Tony. Neither has his mother.' I caught his eye again. 'What's with you and her anyway?'

'Bella and I are . . . friendly, like. As far as anybody can be friendly wi' Bella, that is. I took an interest in her after her brother shot the Holmeses. I know as well as you do that she told him to do it, and I wanted to make sure she wasnae angry with me as well. And,' as he paused, an angry gleam showed in his eyes, 'I was sorry for her as well. Gavin Spreckley was a nasty shite and deserved all he got, but it was out of order what they did tae her boy; only a kid, for fuck's sake. Bella has her uses; she's got a good brain and when she drops into any of the saunas she's fierce enough to keep everybody on their toes.'

'You let her live in that shithole, though.'

'I'm no' going to move her in here, man,' he protested. 'She's no' exclusive, ken.'

I chuckled. 'That's pretty well known. Who were you with in Ibiza, by the way?'

'You mind your own fuckin' business, Skinner. She's got nothing to do wi' this so keep her out of it.'

I could live with that; I couldn't see that it was relevant either. I changed tack. 'What was Marlon's working day, Tony? You don't have an office other than this. Where was he based?'

'Here. He came here every morning, drove me anywhere I wanted to go, in the Bentley, minded the door for me, just like those two out there, checked the mail for me . . . put it through the scanner, ken . . .'

'Scanner?' Martin repeated.

'Metal detector. You never heard of letter bombs, son?'

'While you were in Ibiza,' I resumed, 'what was he supposed to do?'

'The usual: come here, sit by the phone, watch the telly. If something was really important and he or Lennie couldnae handle it, get in touch with me. But he never did.'

'So when he left home on Tuesday morning, this is where he'd have been coming?'

'Aye, but before you ask, he couldnae have been snatched from here. He wouldnae have let anyone through the gates, and the whole place is alarmed, and monitored remotely. State o' the art. Ah've had foxes set it off before now.'

I'd known that; it was on his drugs squad file. 'Did Bella ask you to take Marlon under your wing?' I asked him.

He winced. 'No,' he replied. 'That was my idea. I gave the boy a job to keep him close to me. He had bad habits. He was always lookin' for a fight, as if he'd tae prove something . . . like we all do when we're kids, I suppose . . . and I heard he was carrying a blade. I didn't want him going the same way as his brother and his uncles, so I brought him in close, where he'd be safe.' He snorted. 'Safe! Fuckin' safe. Glenn Milburn, you said.'

'I did, and he's mine, Tony, understand that.'

'You'd better keep a close eye on him then,' he rumbled.

'Why do you think I told you his name?' I asked. 'To put you in the loop, and to protect him; because you know that if he should choke on his cornflakes in the remand wing, you will now be the very first person I'll be looking for.'

He nodded. 'Revenge is bad for business, you're sayin'?'

'Exactly. Not as bad as me, but bad enough. Listen, could Marlon have been mixed up in something that you didn't know about?'

He stared at me derisively. 'Nah, no chance of that.'

'Are you sure? Remember, he's from a lawless family. I had to rattle his mother's cage the other day. I found out that she's been extorting money from her own daughter.'

'She's got a daughter?' I stared at him; for the first time in my life I'd surprised Tony Manson. 'Christ, she's a close one. Where's she been hiding her?'

'She escaped a long time ago,' I told him. 'Tony,' I continued, 'I'm going to give you one more chance. We've got this Newcastle link, but we don't know what's behind it, not yet. Before this day's out, I hope to be interviewing this man Milburn, and I will not be holding back on him. This is a murder investigation; if you do have any information that might help us, or even any suspicions, then it's in your interests that you tell me now. If you don't, and I find out later that you've been holding out on me, then I will throw the biggest book I can find at you, as hard as I can.'

I stood; Martin followed. Manson looked up at us. 'We've been here before, Skinner, a few times, and you must ken by now that there's no way I'll ever set foot in the High Court, no' even as a witness. I'll tell you again, I know nothing about Newcastle, and I've got no idea why anyone would want to do that to Marlon. But, I've got no reason not to help you find out why the boy was killed, so anything I hear, you will, one way or another. As for this guy Milburn, give him a good one for me, and tell him no' to be stupid enough to ask for bail.'

The hired bodyguards were in the hall as we walked to the door. The one I'd banjoed gave me what I think was meant to be a meaningful look, but he couldn't hold on to it when I eyeballed him back. I made a mental note that if I ever retired and went into the security business, I'd never employ people who thought they were tough, only those who knew they were and didn't need to show it.

I drove Martin the short distance to his car. 'Well?' I said, as he opened the passenger door, 'what did you think of Terrible Tony?'

'Dangerous and resourceful,' he replied, firmly. 'How did he get where he is?'

'By moving in on a guy who was less resourceful than him.'

'What happened to him?

'They said at the time that he went into the construction industry.'

He frowned. 'Wouldn't that have been a matter of record?'

'Does euphemism mean nothing to you?' I asked. 'There was a new office block being built down in McDonald Road at the time. The story was that he became part of the foundations.'

'So where did these Holmeses fit in?'

'I told you: while Tony was king of the midden in Edinburgh, Perry Holmes was the undisputed Scottish number one. He was an importer on a massive scale; he distributed to people like Manson across the country.'

'Why did nobody cut him out?' The lad asked good questions.

'One or two tried. Perry was a property developer too; still is, from his wheelchair. On you go now, get your arse back to Fettes.'

I let him exit the cul-de-sac ahead of me, and watched him as he zipped along Essex Road. By the time I reached the Maybury roundabout, he was out of sight, so he didn't see me make the left turn into Quality Street. I'd forgotten that I was going to call Mia, but she must have been looking out for me, since she opened the door of her little single-storey house just I was pulling up outside.

She was dressed much as she had been the first time we'd met, jeans this time, and another Airburst T-shirt. 'Hi,' she said, smiling as I took the two steps that was all the tiny path from the gate required. 'Welcome.'

'This is nice,' I told her as I stepped straight into a bright living area that must have taken up half of the total floor space. It had been freshly refurbished, and twin doors led to a small conservatory that still had a look of newness.

'Isn't it,' she agreed. 'It's a bit like your place but on a much smaller scale.' She glanced at a clock on the wall, above a white painted fireplace with a high mantelpiece; it showed one o'clock, on the dot. 'You're on time.'

'My last visit didn't drag on,' I replied, 'and it was close to here, out in Barnton.'

'Handy. How much time do you have?'

I shrugged my shoulders, noncommittally. 'Some.'

'That's good, for I've made us some lunch. Ham salad okay?'

'Spot on. Thanks, Mia, you . . .'

'. . . shouldn't have!' she laughed. 'Now we've got the automatic responses over, let's get down to it.'

She led me into the conservatory, where two full plates waited, on a small round table, with a bottle of sparkling water and two glasses. It was warm in the sunshine, so I hung my jacket over the back of a chair. We sat and she poured. There was a package on the table, white cardboard about six inches square. She handed it to me. 'The Spice Girls,' she announced. 'Alex will love them; they're going to be big. They are really, really different.' She laughed. 'Listen to me: "really, really". They've got to me. You'll understand what I mean when you've heard it a couple of times. There's a phrase in there that'll live forever.'

I watched her as we ate. She seemed different from our earlier meetings, more relaxed, bubblier, more like the woman whose voice and attitude were pulling kids into her audience at a rate to rival the Pied Piper . . . 'The Pie-eyed Piper of Hamilton,' was Thornton's version of the name, and it came to me then. The thought of it made me frown and realise that I'd broken the promise to call him that I'd made to myself.

173

Mia spotted the change in me. 'What's wrong?' she asked.

'Nothing.'

'There was; I could see it. A flash of pain. What's wrong, Bob? Hard times at work?'

'It's not getting any easier,' I admitted, 'but that's not what it is. I had some bad news yesterday, family news.'

'Oh dear. Someone close?'

'The closest I have left, apart from Alex. My father-in-law. He came to see us, to tell me that he's ill.'

'Oh God,' she sighed. 'How ill?'

'Barring a miracle, terminally.' I took refuge in the salad for a while.

'How's Alex taking it?' she asked when we were both finished. She stood, and picked up her glass. 'Come on, let's sit in over here.'

I joined her, on a white cane sofa, that looked out on to the tiny enclosed garden. 'Alex doesn't know,' I said.

Mia whistled, softly. 'You can't keep a secret like that from a girl her age.'

'Thornton's insistent on it. He's told her that he's going away on a trip,' I smiled, 'to far-off and exciting places. He wants to spare her from what's going to happen.'

'That's well meaning of him but,' she took my hand, intertwining our fingers, 'he's not going to be around to pick up the pieces, Bob. He's going to be dead, and when Alex finds out that his illness was kept from her, she's not going to blame him, she's going to blame you. If you don't tell her, she'll be hurt worse than if you do, and so will you.'

'I promised her granddad though, Mia.'

'Then you have to tell him why you can't keep that promise. I don't want to sound like an agony aunt, but Bob, love, who's the most important person in your life?'

I stared at her. 'Alex, of course.'

'And what's the most important thing in your life?'

I didn't have to think about that one for long either. 'My relationship with her.'

'Then don't damage it. Her childhood is over . . . Pops. She's come through puberty, and she's starting to think like a woman. That's a process that accelerates pretty fast, I can promise you, and it's bloody difficult for any parent to keep up with it, let alone a single dad.'

I was frowning again. 'But I don't want to hurt her at all,' I protested. 'That's why I agreed to what Thornie asked.'

She touched my chin and turned my face towards her. 'She's going to be hurt anyway. It comes with the territory of adulthood.'

I sighed. 'Point taken. Thanks for that, counsellor.'

That's when I kissed her. It wasn't something that I'd anticipated, or ever imagined. It just happened, that's all, a reflex response to our proximity. She responded, very gently, her lips exploring mine, her mouth opening slightly, her tongue flicking my teeth. Until then, I'd held the private belief that kissing is overrated, no more than the opening gambit of the chess game between two people that leads to mating. With Myra and me, it had been rough and tumble, like our sex. With Alison . . . it was something we barely did, we usually cut straight to the chase. But Mia could kiss like nobody I'd ever encountered before; it was full of subtlety, tender and modest, yet inviting, too. Have you ever noticed how strong a spider's web is, how, once it's woven, it can withstand a tempest? That's the best analogy I can conjure up for Mia's kiss, the softest thing imaginable, yet once it had drawn you in, there was no escape.

'Is this the talk we were going to have?' she murmured, as we surfaced.

'What talk was that?'

'About whether we're going to see each other again.'

'I guess it is. What do you reckon?'

She flicked the first button of my shirt with a fingernail. 'How much time do you have?' she asked. I knew what she meant, but I didn't want a quickie; I wanted to be able to dive into her ocean and swim there at my leisure.

'Not enough,' I replied. 'I have to be sharp this afternoon. If all goes well, I'll be having a very tough conversation with a couple of guys from Newcastle. I won't be able to make a proper impression on them if I'm thinking of you.'

She smiled. 'Me too, I suppose. I wouldn't want to be talking to seventy-five thousand young people and have something inappropriate slip out. So? What happens next?'

'You tell me.'

'Could we have dinner one night,' she suggested, 'and take it from there? How free are you?'

'I can make arrangements,' I said. 'I have someone who looks after Alex during the day. I can arrange with Daisy for her to stay over at her place.'

'Then call me when you can fix it.'

'I'll do that,' I promised. We kissed again: just like the first time. I had to force myself to my feet.

'Go and terrify the bad guys,' she instructed me, as she walked me to the door.

'And you go and bewitch a million listeners.'

'That's the entire listening audience. We'd have to achieve a hundred per cent penetration for that.' She giggled, and a hand went to her mouth. 'But that's something we can discuss after dinner.'

For all my talk of sharpness, my mind was all over the place as I drove back to Fettes. I was attracted to Mia with a power that I hadn't experienced since before my fifteenth birthday, and I hadn't understood it then. I wanted her very badly, but I wanted the moment to be perfect, and the timing to be absolutely right. I began toying with the idea of booking a room, or maybe even a suite, in an upmarket hotel . . . Gleneagles, say, and damn the expense . . . for the Friday following. But . . . I'd left it with Alison that we'd see each other at the weekend. Alison. What about Alison? We'd been straight with each other; it was companionship and sex, nothing more expected or wanted on either side, and surely that carried the possibility that one of us might find someone we really cared about. Fine. And the incident at the Sheraton? I still hadn't worked that one out, but the one thing I did know for certain, Alison and I had two relationships, personal and professional, and she had to be treated right, on both levels. And then there was my kid. The way I felt at that moment, I had no idea how far a relationship with Mia might go, and Alex had made her feelings pretty clear about another woman . . . Mia had been right; I had to start thinking of her as such . . . moving into our house. But looming over it all was the memory of that first, spontaneous kiss.

'Jesus, Skinner!' I exclaimed, out loud, as I turned into the police headquarters car park. 'For once, will you try and think with your brain and not with your prick.'

The first person I saw when I walked into the office was Jeff Adam. Instantly, I had what my very good friend Neil McIlhenney once described, memorably, as 'a Taggart moment'. They're rarer these days than they used to be, but when they're triggered, they're unstoppable.

'What the hell are you doing here, Sergeant?' I shouted. 'You're supposed to be in fucking Newcastle picking up fucking Milburn!'

Fortunately, the rock-steady, unflappable Fred Leggat was there to intervene. 'I told him to hold on, boss,' he explained. 'Newcastle CID went to pick him up at our request, but he wasn't at home, or at work.

I didn't think there was any point in Jeff and McGuire going down there till they had him.'

I felt the hot air escaping from my balloon, fast, but did my best to keep my dignity. 'Work? What does he do, apart from being a heavy?'

'He's a taxi driver. Self-employed. He has a small office in North Shields; he runs a few cabs out of there.'

'Does he have a wife?' I asked.

Fred nodded. 'Yes. She wasn't cooperative, at first, not until our Geordie colleagues threatened to arrest her for obstruction and hand her kids to social services. A bluff, but she fell for it. Eventually she admitted that he went out late on Saturday night and hasn't been home since.'

'Did NCIS come up with anything on him?'

'Oh yes. Two convictions for actual bodily harm, one for GBH, several arrests but charges dropped for lack of evidence. He's said to work for the Newcastle big boss, a man called Winston Church . . . no hill, just Church. His known associates locally are Barton Leonard and Warren Shackleton who works for him in the taxi firm. Leonard used to, until he was given a nice room to himself in Durham jail, for being the getaway driver in an armed robbery.'

'I take it . . .'

'Yes. The Geordies went looking for Shackleton too; he wasn't at home either, and he's been missing for about the same length of time as Milburn.'

'Okay. Good shout, Fred.' I was left feeling embarrassed by my telly 'tec episode. 'Sorry I went off at you, Jeff. There was no cause for it. Do something else for me, please. Ask NCIS to go back into their computer and ask it if there are any known links between this man Church and Tony Manson. He says that there aren't, and I doubt if he would deny something that he knew we could confirm, but let's check it anyway.

I'm not saying he'd admit it either, but he wouldn't let me catch him in a flat-out lie.'

'Andy said that Manson couldn't help you,' Leggat remarked.

'He didn't tell us where to look, but the mere fact that he was worried enough to contact a private security firm and hire a couple of ex-squaddies, that tells me he thinks he's under threat from someone.' I headed for my office, motioning the DI to follow. 'Where have we got in this investigation, Fred?' I asked as he closed the door.

'Newcastle,' he replied, 'and that's it.'

'Manson did make a good point,' I told him. 'How did these guys get hold of Marlon, so quietly that we haven't picked up a trace of it? And where did they pick him up?'

'Could he have arranged to meet them?' he wondered.

'It's a thought. What's the last sighting of him?'

Leggat frowned, and scratched his head. 'When he left his mother's house last Tuesday?'

'No, Bella said he came home after that, and then went out again. She didn't know where, though. Pub, probably. Where did he drink?'

'Search me, Bob.'

'Sorry, Fred, I was talking to myself there. But there's somebody who might be able to tell us.' I called Bella Watson's mobile from my desk phone; she answered quickly, as if she'd been expecting a call. 'Do you still have your babysitter?' I asked.

'Aye,' she grunted.

'Then put him on.' I waited for the giant. 'Lennie,' I said, 'did you see much of Marlon, in the course of business?'

'We were in touch,' he replied. 'And, of course, he drank in the Vaults.'

'That's what I was hoping you'd say. When did you see him last?'

'Monday. He was in on Monday.'

'Do you remember anything about him? Was he nervous in any way?'

'No.' He paused. 'Hey, wait a minute, he was in on Tuesday, late afternoon. He brought a licence renewal application for the pub that had come in the boss's morning mail.'

'But not in the evening?'

'No. In fact as he was leaving I heard one of the barmen say to him, "See you later." But Marlon said no, that he wouldn't be in. He said he'd somewhere else to go . . . and he was smiling when he said it, as if it was a hot date.'

'It sure was, Lennie. Thanks.' I hung up. 'Progress,' I told Leggat. 'It looks as if Watson went to meet these guys, knowingly or not. How was that meeting arranged, I wonder?'

I picked up the phone again. Manson had two lines in the big house. One was in the directory; the other wasn't, but it was in my personal collection. I looked it out and dialled it.

'How the fuck did you get this number?' he growled, when he realised that I was his mystery caller.

'Please, Tony. Did you really think I wouldn't have it?'

'You lot aren't listening in, are you? I'll sue if you are.'

'No, we're not,' I told him, truthfully. 'We'd need a warrant for that. I can't speak for MI5, of course; they're taking an interest in organised crime these days.' I added that out of pure devilment. 'I need to know something. Did Marlon Watson have a mobile phone?'

There was a silence, as if he was considering whether to give me the time of day. He must have decided that he had nothing to lose by it. 'Aye, he had one. I gave it to him so I could reach him any time I needed him.'

'Contract, or pay and go?' Silly question, Skinner, I told myself. The phone would be chucked away every time its credit expired and replaced with a new one, new number. Standard practice in the hidden world, even then.

'What do you think?' Manson chuckled. I hung up on him.

Leggat was looking at me, waiting for the outcome. I nodded. No more was needed. 'I'll check with the mortuary,' he said. 'It should be among his possessions.'

'It should,' I agreed, 'so why do I have a feeling that it won't be?'

It took him less than five minutes to confirm that my hunch had been spot on.

'Maybe Milburn will still have it on him, when they find him,' he suggested.

'He might, if he's a hoarder, but the SIM card will probably be ashes by now, and that's where all the call information would have been.'

Fred's scepticism showed in his face. 'Does that not strike you as pretty thorough for somebody whose crime file doesn't mark him out as a thinker?'

'It does, but let's wait till we have him in our custody. How did you leave that with Newcastle?'

'They're checking all likely haunts, plus the passenger manifests of all recent flights and ferries out of the city. They're going to give us a progress report at five, if they haven't found him before then.'

'Meanwhile we just sit on our hands. I'm bloody useless at that.' Through my door's glass panel, I saw Jeff Adam approach. I waved him in, keen to mend a broken fence.

'NCIS do not have any record of connection between Winston Church and Tony Manson,' he reported, 'directly or indirectly. They don't have any shared associates. Church doesn't have any known links to Scotland at all. Indeed the intelligence is that he has enough on his hands just keeping control of his own territory without looking to move in on anyone else's. He's getting on, and some of his younger associates are reckoned to be hungry. For example, the job that the man Leonard's doing time for was a robbery of a pub in Durham that's owned by his brother-in-law.'

That was interesting. 'So it's possible that Milburn and Shackleton . . . let's assume that he's the second man . . . were operating independently of Church?'

'That could be,' Adam said. 'Nature abhors a vacuum.'

I laughed. 'Hell, Jeff, that's a bit profound. I know it's still a while to five o'clock but go and rattle Newcastle's cage for me.'

'Meanwhile,' I murmured as he and Leggat left, 'what about the other?' Of course, as soon as I turned my attention to the 'gay blade' murders, I thought of Alison, and that made me think of Mia. If I'd known that Milburn and his mate hadn't even been found, far less on their way into my tender hands, I might not have left her place, and . . .

Distance had lent me a bit of objectivity, but the old saw about enchantment was working as well. I wanted Mia, no question; she filled me with an excitement that I'd forgotten. But Alison: she meant a lot to me, safety, security, friendship, comfort, plus we were there already, a couple of sorts, even if it was only part-time. 'She isn't Bella Watson's daughter either,' I whispered, then cast the thought aside, as quickly as it had appeared in my mind. I relived that kiss, and I felt myself tingling all over again. Yes, I wanted the woman, but did I have the bottle to take her, and to live with whatever consequences that brought?

I jumped when the phone rang. I snatched it up, barked, 'Skinner,' and felt my face flush as soon as I heard Alison's voice.

'Sorry,' she said, cautiously. 'Are you busy with something?'

*Nothing you'd want to hear*, I thought. 'No, sorry, I was miles away.'

Indeed, I'd been at Gleneagles, mentally. 'Whassup? Where are you?'

'I'm at the mortuary. Professor Hutchinson is just finishing the post-mortem on Albie McCann. I thought it might be a good idea if he went straight on and did Archie Weir's and he's agreed.'

'That's an excellent idea.' But it would be tough on her; sitting in on two autopsies, back to back, so to speak. 'Do you want me to come up?' I asked. I had an ulterior motive; if wee Joe Hutchinson's workplace didn't stop me thinking about peeling Mia Sparkles like a grape, nothing would.

'That would be good,' she admitted. 'We still don't have absolute confirmation that they were both killed by the same man, and I'd welcome your input.'

'Plus you'd like me to hold your hand.'

'No!' she snapped, then hesitated. 'Well . . .'

'Hey,' I told her, 'if I'd been through the first one, I'd be calling you for company. Besides, depending on what Joe finds, it might be useful for both of us to be there.'

I picked up my phone and my car keys and stepped into the outer office. I told Fred Leggat where I was bound, and confirmed with Jeff Adam that the Geordies had yet to turn up any trace of Glenn Milburn and his mate, then headed for the door.

I was fitting my seat belt when my mobile sounded. I fished it out awkwardly from my jacket pocket. 'Hi,' Mia said, quietly, as I connected.

'Hi yourself,' I replied. 'Shouldn't you be getting ready to entertain my daughter and her peer group?'

'I am. I'm in my studio now, getting my playlist and ads sorted, but before I go on air I wanted to talk to you again. That dinner we discussed . . . can we skip it?'

What? In that first instant, I managed to feel both disappointed and relieved at the same time. 'Sure,' I murmured, slowly. 'If that's what you want, no harm done, and maybe I'll see you around.'

She chuckled, huskily. 'I'd never have taken you for someone with low self-esteem where women are concerned. I didn't mean that I didn't want to see you again. The opposite, in fact. Can you make it back to my place tonight, once my show's finished?'

I felt a trembling in the pit of my stomach. Nerves? Jesus Christ! 'Maybe,' I said. 'I'm not sure. Thing is, I've got a work commitment that could go on for a while. Plus, it's a bit late to spring a sleepover on Daisy.'

'Tomorrow?'

I sighed, audibly, and wondered what she'd read into that. 'Mia, don't you want to take time to think about this?'

'I have done. I've been thinking about nothing else since you left. Tomorrow?'

Low self-esteem, no willpower. 'Tomorrow.'

'Seven thirty?'

'Seven thirty.'

'Lovely. By the way, I'm not on the pill.'

# Eleven

'Are you on the pill?'

'Fuck me, Bob,' Alison exclaimed; appropriately. 'It's a bit late to ask me. What brought that on?'

I shrugged. 'A moment of panic?'

'Of course I am. Do you think I'd have let you go bareback otherwise?'

'I suppose not.'

She laughed. 'Bloody hell! You suppose?'

Fortunately there was nobody close to us in the autopsy room, and our exchange was muffled by our surgical masks. Nevertheless Professor Hutchinson frowned at us from the other side of the examination table. 'Pay attention in class, you two,' he said. He tapped the microphone above his head; it was there to pick up his commentary as he worked. 'And remember, this thing is extremely sensitive.'

I hoped we wouldn't have to ask him to edit the tape.

'Since you've just joined us, Detective Superintendent Skinner,' he continued . . . a little archly, I thought, 'I'll recap what I told DI Higgins following the examination of the body of Albert McCann. The young man was in excellent physical health, although somewhat intoxicated at the time of his demise; he had recently consumed at least four pints of beer, India Pale Ale from its colour and odour, none of which ever made the journey to Seafield. My assistant and I found that death was due to a single upward stab wound that skewered the heart, piercing both chambers. The indication is that the attacker was either male, or an exceptionally strong woman, and right-handed.'

'We know that,' Alison volunteered, 'from a statement by a surviving witness. And he says it was a man.'

He glowered at her. Joe didn't like to be interrupted while in full flow. 'There were twelve other wounds in total,' he continued, 'but we believe that these were all inflicted post mortem, and that the massive wound I have described was the first, and almost instantly fatal. The attack on this man was of the sort that usually attracts the adjective "frenzied" in the popular press. At the very least anyone who continued to attack what would have been a fairly obviously dead body with such force can be described as "determined". Regrettably, I have seen in my career many victims with injuries similar to those of Mr McCann. Similar . . .' he repeated, and his eyes twinkled, telling me that he'd been leading up to a major moment . . . 'but not identical. There is a shape, a pattern, to these wounds that I haven't seen too often before. The weapon that inflicted them was razor-sharp in its tip and on both sides of the blade, but what makes it different is its shape. It's broader than the norm, although to be honest the range of objects that people stick into other people seems to be expanding all the time these days.'

He stopped and looked at me. 'Alison tells me that you believe that McCann and Mr Weir here are both victims of the same man. A little patience on your part, and I may be able to advance that theory, or knock it down.'

'We await your findings, Joe,' I told him, 'enthralled.'

He went to work, and I thought about something other than what I was going to have for dinner.

'How are you getting on with Marlon?' Alison asked, sotto voce, as we looked on.

'We've got a suspect, probably two,' I murmured.

'Excellent.'

'It will be when Northumbria CID manage to find them.'

'Are you sure they're your men?'

'If we're lucky we might have a witness to place them with Watson.' Before I'd left, I'd told Mario McGuire to take the photos of Milburn and Shackleton that had been faxed from Newcastle and show them to his pub manager pal. An identification under those circumstances might not stand up to heavy cross-examination by a defence brief, but it would be enough to let us charge them and hold them on remand.

'Good luck.' She looked at me. 'Bob, is something bothering you? Something you're keeping from me?'

I found it difficult to return her gaze. 'What makes you think that?'

'I don't know, exactly, but last night, when I arrived at your place, I thought you were preoccupied.'

If it hadn't been for the mask, my sigh of relief might have been audible. 'I was,' I told her. 'I didn't want to ruin your night with it, that was all. It was my father-in-law's visit.' I led her across to the furthest corner of the room and told her why Thornton had come to see us.

When I was finished, she took my arm, and hugged it. 'Oh Bob,' she sighed, 'that's awful. The poor chap.'

'There's more,' I said. 'I'm in a real dilemma.' I explained Thornie's view about keeping it from Alex until it was all over. 'I agreed,' I added, 'but now I'm not so sure.'

'Nor should you be,' she said, firmly. 'You don't have the right to do that. Neither does her grandfather.'

'But Ali, love, she's so young,' I protested.

'Jesus Christ, Bob,' she spluttered behind her mask. 'Emotionally, she's older than you are. Do you think she isn't ready to deal with death? Is that it? The girl lost her mother when she was barely school age. Yet now she's one of the best adjusted, most mature thirteen-year-olds that I've ever met. She's faced her tragedy and she's come to terms with it . . . which, perhaps, is more than you have.' Her forehead was wrinkled with concern as she spoke. She really was a good woman, better than I'd appreciated, and better than I deserved; suddenly a randy night with Mia Sparkles seemed less of an imperative. 'You're very close to him, aren't you?' she said.

'Truthfully? Closer than I was to my own dad.'

'Then this is going to affect you just as much as it does Alex, and probably more. You helped her to deal with her mother's death. Now it's her turn to help you.'

I smiled at her, but she probably didn't realise because of the damn mask. 'Thanks.'

'Any time.' She paused. 'Have you got next weekend planned?'

'Are you kidding?' I replied. 'I don't have tonight's dinner planned. Why?'

'I was wondering; would you like to go crewing?'

'Say that again?'

'Crewing, Bob, crewing.' She shook her head. 'Bloody men! Have you ever done any sailing?' she went on.

'Cross-Channel ferries; that's all. Boats are not my thing.'

'In that case . . . the thing is, my brother Eden has a yacht. He keeps it at Inverkip Marina. It's quite a big boat and sometimes I help him with it. He's asked me if I'll go out with him next weekend. Would you and Alex like to come?'

I wasn't sure. My weekends usually involved golf unless the weather was too rough, and for a real golfer there is no such thing. Then there was the potential embarrassment of being seasick. The ferry to France had never bothered me, but there had been an occasion when I'd gone on a fairground waltzer with Alex, and come very close to chucking my cookies. Then there was the prospect of Gleneagles, with Mia.

The last of those swung me. 'Okay,' I agreed. 'That would be good.' Accepting Alison's invitation was a means of chickening out of something that for some reason was making me far more nervous than an inshore yacht on the Firth of Clyde, but she wasn't to know that. Besides, I might actually enjoy it, and I knew that Alex would. 'When do we leave?'

'Ideally,' she said, 'we'll drive across on Friday evening and stay the night on board with Eden and Rory . . . my nephew . . . so that we're ready to cast off early. It'll be a two-day voyage, then back on Sunday.'

'Sounds good,' I agreed, 'subject to . . .'

'I know: the demands of the job. Try not thinking about things that might get in the way and maybe they won't.'

'What age is Rory?' I asked, casually.

She laughed. 'Back off, Dad. He's only ten.'

'Officers!' The call was imperious. 'If I might have your renewed attention,' the wee professor continued.

We moved towards the table, where a once-functional human being lay, turned more or less inside out. For anyone present during an autopsy, it's essential to remain completely detached. The worst thing you can do is allow your mind to personalise the situation, to imagine, for one second, a loved one of your own in the place of the thing under examination. As I've said before, I had mastered that by that stage of my career, but Alison had put in less mortuary time than I had. As we approached the body I felt her shudder, and put my arm around her waist to steady her.

Joe saw and understood. 'Do you want to take a break before we carry on?' he asked. 'The atmosphere in this place can be rather overpowering.'

By that time she was over her lapse. 'No,' she said, brusquely. 'Let's get on with it.'

'If you're sure.'

'I am,' she snapped. I let my supporting arm fall to my side.

'Very good.' The pathologist looked up at me. Behind him his assistant was . . . doing something else with a piece of Archie Weir, and I didn't need to know which piece or what he was up to. 'This is a similarly forceful attack to that on Mr McCann. Seven wounds this time; attacker also right-handed. None of them was instantly fatal, as you know, but the overall effect was massive organ damage, liver, lung and kidney, and blood loss, sufficient to cause brain damage. While the wounds were not as deeply penetrative as those on the earlier victim, this may have been due to Mr Weir putting up more of a struggle, initially at least. In any event they are deep enough, and wide enough, for us to have established a pattern identical to those inflicted upon Mr McCann, and to say with authority that they were caused by the same weapon or by its identical twin. Therefore, Bob, Alison, you may proceed with your investigation on the basis that you are looking for a single assailant. No doubt the tabloids will say, "Police seek frenzied knife killer," or some such; in this case they won't be exaggerating. I must tell you that I hope you catch him soon. This is an extremely dangerous person.'

'That was quite a statement for Joe to make,' Alison mused as we left the morgue. 'What's our next step?'

'I'll have Inspector Hesitant issue a press release tomorrow confirming that we're looking for the same man in each case. I don't know if we can go much further than that. We don't have a description worth a light beyond youngish, tall, slim, and it's pointless putting that out; it covers thousands of men. As for issuing a general warning . . .' I stopped and thought that over. 'Christ, all we can say is that both victims were in their twenties, as are most of the guys that are out and about at the weekend.' I looked at her. 'Have you got a name for McCann's pal yet?'

'He didn't say who he was meeting. His father gave Steele a few possibles; he's working his way through them.'

'Let's hope he finds him quickly then. If not I'll use the media to ask him to come forward. Meantime, there's our other close-up witness, Weir's mate, Wyllie. You haven't interviewed him yourself, have you?'

'Not personally. That was done before I joined the division.'

'Okay, why don't you have a talk to him?' I suggested. 'Go see him. From what I've been told, he's been a bit evasive about the circumstances leading up to the attack. Maybe press him a bit on that, get as much detail as you can.'

'Will do.' We'd reached our cars. 'Let me see your hands,' she ordered, suddenly. 'I should know them well enough by now, I suppose, but let's have a close look.'

Puzzled, I held them out. She turned them over and examined the palms, running her thumbs over the hard pads of skin left by thousands of golf shots: I've never worn a glove when I play. 'Not too bad,' she murmured. 'You shouldn't have too many blisters come next Monday.'

'Blisters?'

She grinned. 'Didn't I mention that? It's not a motor yacht, Bob. It's a schooner, Eden's pride and joy; sail-powered all the way.'

'Does that mean climbing masts and such?'

'Don't you worry,' she assured me, 'I'll do all the macho stuff; you'll just have to pull on the odd rope.'

'What about Alex?' I asked. 'What'll she have to do?'

'Sunbathe, if she's lucky. Maybe cook, if she fancies it. What's the matter? Cold feet?'

Actually, the more I thought about it, the more I fancied the idea. I'd lived by the sea for over ten years, and my place in Spain was near a large marina, full of gin palaces, but as I'd confessed to Alison, messing about in boats wasn't something I'd even thought about. 'No,' I told her. 'My feet are well warm, don't you worry. Will there be hammocks?'

'No, dear, there are cabins.'

It occurred to me as we spoke that I knew much less about Alison's background than she knew about mine. 'Your brother,' I said. 'Where did he get a name like Eden?'

'It's been in our family for two hundred years; he was stuck with it.'

'What does he do for a living? No, let me guess; he runs a garden centre.'

She pursed her lips. 'Everyone's a comedian. He is in retail, but not that sector. Ever heard of a chain called Dene Furnishing?'

Who hadn't? It was the biggest in Scotland. 'Sure, big warehouses, aren't they? All over the place.'

'Yup. That's him. That's my bro.'

I whistled. 'Jesus! No wonder he can afford a big boat on the Clyde.'

She nodded. 'And a spoiled Barbie doll wife who fancies herself as an interior designer. Rachel's as much use as a chocolate teapot as far as I'm concerned, but Eden thinks she's pure fucking Dresden.'

'Will she be there?' I asked.

'No chance. She only goes on the boat when it's firmly moored. Honest to God, Bob, Eden's a real player, a formidable guy, just like you are. Yet he was blinded by this inappropriate woman at first sight. There's no telling, is there?'

I chuckled quietly. 'No, babe, there isn't. Now, can I do something completely inappropriate?'

She frowned. 'Such as?'

'This.' And I kissed her, long and tender, right there in the car park of the house of the dead.

'Wow!' she murmured, when we were done. 'There was nothing inappropriate about that, big boy. But what was it for?'

'It was for reminding me of who I am.'

I stayed that way for at least a minute. Then I climbed into the Discovery and headed on my steady way home. I hadn't gone very far, though, before I was feeling completely, utterly confused. I really did not know what the fuck I was doing, woman-wise.

I had a hot date, probably involving breakfast, with Mia the following night, yet it had been on the tip of my tongue a few minutes before to ask Alison to come home with me. Sensible and secure, red-hot and risky, they couldn't have been more dissimilar, and here was I, a serial widower with a fast-growing daughter who didn't really want another woman in what she was coming to see as her kitchen, entangled with them both.

Looking for a distraction, as I cleared the Jock's Lodge lights, I reached out and switched on the clunky old radio; I'd no other entertainment option, since the cassette player had chewed up a tape and refused to spit it out. I'd had it on Radio One in the morning, to catch a news bulletin. Some rapper with a daft name was shouting at me, so I pressed the next of the preset buttons. The previous owner of the tank had been an orderly man and the six stations were tuned in numerical order, first four BBC, then Radio Forth, then Classic FM. I expected the Radio Two drive-time show, but it wasn't what I got.

Mia must have changed the settings when she'd been in the car on the previous Saturday, because instead of the usual Identikit late afternoon presenter, whoever it was then, whichever of the bland leading the bland, the ridiculous rapper was replaced by what I was coming to realise was one of the sexiest voices I had ever heard.

'So what are you doing this evening, Alex?' Mia Sparkles asked.

'What?' I exclaimed.

'Right now?' my daughter said, her voice slightly distorted by the phone but still recognisable. 'Finishing some Spanish homework and waiting for my dad to get home. After that, helping him make dinner, then some French homework. Usual stuff, Mia, you know how it is.'

'Yes, I know. My dad was a single parent too, when I was around your age. He was a better cook than me, though. How about yours?'

'My dad's a very good cook,' she replied, making me feel as proud as she sounded.

'What's he best at?'

'He makes amazing spaghetti sauces. There's one he does with fish.'

'Oooh,' Mia murmured. 'He can make me some of that any time he likes. Nice talking to you, Alex. And now all you Airburst kids . . . are you ready for . . . Oasis?'

I wasn't; can't stand them. I switched the radio off.

'Finished your Spanish?' I asked, as she jumped into the car outside Daisy's.

'You heard me?' she squealed.

'Obviously so. How did that happen?'

'Mia asked me on Saturday if I'd like to be on a phone-in.'

'But you didn't think to tell me?'

'I thought you might be sniffy about it,' she confessed.

'The only thing I'm sniffy about is you keeping it to yourself,' I told her. 'I'm sure that Mia's got more sense than to let slip any clues about where you live or to say that you're a cop's daughter. If I'd known you were on, I'd have heard the whole thing, instead of coming in halfway through it.'

'Sorry, Pops.'

I reached out and ruffled her hair, as we drew to a halt at home. 'G'roff,' she said, grinning and batting my hand away.

'I've got another treat for you,' I told her as we went indoors. 'Or Alison has, to be accurate. Fancy being a cabin girl? We're going sailing.'

Her mouth gaped open. 'We are? When?'

As she spoke, I saw the message indicator on the phone, flashing red. 'Tell you in a minute,' I said, as she headed for the stairs, and her sanctum, and I pressed the play button. It was a female voice, familiar; Jean, my sister-in-law.

'Bob, phone me please.' That was all she said; I had the feeling it was all she could say. A spasm of dread ran through me.

I snatched the handset from the cradle and pressed in her number. Normally she was quick on the draw, but I counted half a dozen rings before she answered. 'What's happened?' I asked.

'It's Dad,' she replied. 'He's gone.'

'Gone?' I repeated.

'He's dead, Bob.'

I had not expected that. A turn for the worse, perhaps, an admission to hospital ahead of schedule, but no, not that, not Thornie, not so quickly. I was struck dumb. I'd spent part of my afternoon looking at death, in its most graphic state, but I was unprepared for its invasion of my own home. 'Jean,' I whispered. 'It can't be. He was here only yesterday.'

'And he told you about his illness, didn't he?'

'Yes, but he was still active,' I protested, 'still on his feet.'

'But very slowly, you must have noticed that, Bob.'

'Yes,' I conceded, 'but still . . .'

'I know,' she said, gently. 'I didn't expect it so quickly either. But his consultant did warn me, privately, that things could come to crisis point unpredictably, in a number of ways.'

'How did it happen? How did he . . .'

'I had a call from him on my mobile, around three forty-five, in the office.' Jean was a hospital manager, in Wishaw. 'His number showed on my phone but he couldn't speak. I called his doctor and headed for his house. He got there just before me. He was ringing the bell and getting no answer. I used my key, and we found Dad dead on the kitchen floor.'

'Oh shit,' I sighed. 'What a way to go.'

'I know. I can't get my head round it either, someone so loved, dying alone.'

'Your sister did,' I reminded her, tactlessly, but I wasn't thinking straight. 'You never get your head round it. What did the GP say?'

'There was some blood,' she told me, and then had to pause.

I tried to soothe her. 'It's okay. I'm sorry. I shouldn't have asked.'

'No, it's all right. It won't be undone by not talking about it. The doctor says that he coughed it up, after he had a massive pulmonary haemorrhage. It would all have been over very quickly. He would almost certainly have died wherever he was, at home or in a hospital ward.' She gave a strange sound; it might have been a snort. 'You know what? I'm cursing myself for not insisting on driving him through to yours yesterday. This could have happened when he was at the wheel. He could have taken people out with him.'

'But he didn't,' I said, 'so don't dwell on it. He did what he came to do, and he left contented. Just you focus on that. Now, what do you want me to do? Can I help in any way? Do you want me to come through?'

'No, Bob. There's nothing to do. He's been taken to the mortuary, and I'll see the undertaker in the morning. I'll let you know when the funeral will be. Are there any dates you'd like me to avoid?'

'That's thoughtful of you,' I told her, 'but don't you bother about us. We'll be there, whenever. Are you really sure you're going to be okay?'

'Yes,' she replied, firmly. 'I won't be alone, Bob. I have a friend, a man friend that you don't know about; he'll be with me.' So my prophecy to Alex had been right, I mused. 'Anyway, you've got something to do at home. You concentrate on my niece. This will be very hard on Alexis.'

'Indeed,' I sighed. 'Keep me informed. So long for now, and again, I am so sorry.'

I hung up, and turned, slowly, towards the stairs. Alex was sitting on the third step from the bottom, but she stood and came down into the hall. Her face was solemn and, the strangest thing, she seemed a little taller than she'd been before.

'It's Grandpa, isn't it?' she said, and all I could do was nod. I made to hug her, but she turned away and walked into the living room. I followed her, watching her, ready for her to break down. But she didn't. She turned and looked at me, frowning and waiting for me to find the words I was after. That was the moment when I knew, beyond doubt, that I didn't have a child any longer.

'He died this afternoon, love,' I told her, feeling my chin wobble. 'Very suddenly, at home.'

'He was ill, though,' she murmured, 'wasn't he?'

'Yes, my darling, he was. It was only a matter of time, but I never imagined it would be so soon.'

'He told you yesterday, didn't he?'

'Yes.'

'But you didn't tell me.'

'He didn't want me to. In fact he insisted that I didn't. But I was going to anyway; this evening, in fact. I'm sorry, love.'

She took my hand. 'It's all right, Pops,' she whispered. 'You didn't have to tell me anything. I could see that he was ill. And I knew as soon as he said he hadn't brought his golf clubs that it must be serious. I didn't believe any of that stuff about the mystery tour.'

'Maybe not, Alex, but that's where he's gone, on the greatest mystery tour of them all.'

She smiled, and her expression said that if I wanted to believe that, it was all right with her.

'You can cry, you know, kid,' I whispered.

'I might,' she replied, 'but not just now. I've been crying since I was five, Pops. I'm only just learning not to. Besides, Grandpa wouldn't want me to, and if I did, it would only upset you more.'

I let myself slump on to the couch and she joined me there, nestling against me as she always had done. 'Are you sure you're only thirteen?' I asked.

'No,' she replied. 'Alison says I'm going on twenty-five. And speaking of Alison,' she added, 'what did you mean about us going sailing?'

I told her about our invitation for the weekend.

'Can we go?' she asked.

'Do you want to, given what's happened?'

She pushed herself upright and stared at me. 'Are you kidding? What would Grandpa tell us to do?'

I couldn't argue with that thinking. 'Okay,' I promised, 'unless his funeral is on Saturday, we will join Alison's brother's crew.'

'Where will we be going?'

'That'll be up to the captain.' I nudged her side. 'See, kid? Mystery tour.'

'Maybe we'll meet Grandpa at the end.'

'In this world, love, who knows? Hey,' I went on, 'fancy going out to eat? That's all there is on offer unless you're cooking, for frankly, after the day I've had, I cannot be arsed.'

# Twelve

Neither could she, but the options on a Monday weren't that great so we settled for fish suppers from Aberlady. A bad move on my part; the batter was heavy and I ate too many chips, a recipe for indigestion and a restless night. Not that I'd have slept much anyway; my mind was in danger of overload, a whirlpool of thoughts, each of them a crisis of sorts: the two murder investigations that I was heading up, and the two women with whom my life had become entangled. As I struggled with the intricacies and implications of them all, I kept coming back to Thornton. Myra's death had been as great a bereavement for him as for me, yet he'd been my rock in the aftermath, my wise counsellor in the dark hours when I thought I wouldn't be able to cope . . .

Jesus, I hate that word now. Cope. All those well-meaning people, who looked at me anxiously and asked, 'Are you coping?' I found myself hating them for their pity. I hoped they would choke on their own kindness. I wanted to rage at them, to shout, 'What fucking choice do I have?'

It was Thornie who got me through, for all that his own heart must have been breaking. I might not have made it without him. My own father was no help to me at all; I didn't know it then, but he was in the last couple of years of his life. He was working too hard, and the diabetes that he hadn't bothered to tell me about, and was neglecting, was about to lead to irreversible heart difficulty. My dad had always been a remote figure to me. Now I'm inclined to blame him for a lot of things, but in those days he was someone I barely saw, and as I found out after he died, and I learned just a little of the truth about his war, someone I barely knew.

How I wish now that I hadn't been so self-obsessed in my youth, and so angry over Michael, that I let him maintain that distance between us. If I had known of the war service that had earned him one of his nation's highest honours, and had taken the time to ask him about it, to ask him what it was he had done or seen that, I realise now, haunted him forever afterwards, then today I might feel a lot differently about him.

I never loved my father; yes, that's the sad truth, and I doubt that he ever loved me either. There's nothing I can do to change history, but maybe I can find out a bit more about it. I've made myself a private promise, that one day, when I'm a man of leisure, I will seek out his past, and find out what it was that he did on his country's behalf that marked him so badly. He left Alex and me comfortably off when he died, but that meant little to me, for he had left me nothing of himself, nor given me anything when he was alive.

Thornie was my real dad, and it was him I cried for in the small hours of that night, something that I never did for William Skinner, GC. But no, it wasn't just for Thornie, but for everything that he had given me as well, for she who had been taken away. My daughter was learning not to cry; I still had a way to go.

I felt grim in the morning, and in a state of turmoil so deep that I did what I had decided against the afternoon before. I told Alex that I'd be very late that night, and I fixed it for her to sleep over with Daisy. Before I left, I packed an overnight bag and slung it in the car.

I was flying on autopilot, but the damn thing was faulty and I was heading for a mountaintop.

I didn't go straight to my desk; it wouldn't have been fair to my team. Instead I told Fred that I'd had a family bereavement and wanted some space. I went to the gym and lifted some weights, then put on my running shoes and spent an hour and more taking out my anger on the streets. I must have covered about ten miles around the city centre. By the time I'd cooled out and showered, I felt more human, and more able to face my colleagues without the near certainty of turning into Mark McManus.

I did a quick catch-up. There was no news from Newcastle; Milburn and Shackleton were off the radar completely. Our Northumbrian colleagues had run out of ideas, and places to look for them. However there was a message from Alison, asking me to call her when I could.

I did, there and then. I took care to keep my tone professional. I reckoned that if I did I wouldn't be overcome with guilt about where I was headed that evening. *And anyway, Skinner, why should you feel guilty? No strings, no commitment, careers first and foremost, remember.*

'What have you got?' I asked her, briskly.

'A name for McCann's mate: Charles Redpath. Steele managed to have a chat with him over the phone, but all he could do was confirm the barman's story.'

'Description?'

'The clothes match what the man from the mews house told us, but we've got nothing more to go on. Redpath isn't a fighting man from the sound of things. Stevie reckons he didn't look too closely at the guy, just in case he took an interest in him as well as McCann.'

'Any other leads?'

'No,' she said, candidly. 'We've got names for a few of the other people who were in the bar, some from Redpath and some from the bar staff. Steele and Mackie are going round talking to them all, in the hope that somebody might have seen the killer and known him.'

'Aye, maybe,' I murmured sceptically.

She read my mind. 'I know, anybody who could might think twice about it.'

'So where do you go now?'

'Back to Wyllie, as you suggested,' she replied. 'I've read his statement again. It's one of the vaguest things I've ever seen. I do not believe that it's a straightforward account of what happened, so I am going to give him another chance to get it right.'

'That's good,' I told her, 'but don't you go to him. Have the bugger lifted; have him brought to Torphichen and tell the uniforms who pick him up to have their serious faces on. Let's get him as jumpy as we can.'

'That was what I was planning. But I thought we should give him the full treatment. So, how are you placed?'

I frowned. 'Ali, I told you this was your gig.'

'I know, but I want your help.'

She didn't sound desperate, or indeed anxious in any way. What she was asking was logical: the more weight we could put on Wyllie, the more we would squeeze out. 'Yeah, fine,' I agreed. 'Tell you what. Let's bring him here. Do you know where he works?'

'Same place as Weir did. B&Q at the Jewel.'

'Right, I'll send my boys Andy and Mario to lift him there. Those two would scare cheese. Speaking of which, come for lunch at one, and we'll see him at two, two thirty, once he's had a wee sweat in our smelliest interview room.'

'When you say lunch, do you mean senior officers' dining room?' she asked, with the smile in her voice that always managed to put one on my face, even then.

My promotion had opened its door to me, although I hadn't had time to take advantage of the privilege. 'If that's what you'd like,' I replied. 'But if you'd prefer it, I could get a takeaway from Pizza Hut.'

'You'd be wearing it as a hat, my dear.'

I'd done it again. I'd begun my conversation with Alison fighting off guilt about my date with Mia, and ended it by inviting her to lunch. But the fact was, she'd lifted my spirits in those few minutes; she'd taken the last of my anger away. Instead of replacing the receiver, I pressed the button in the cradle to get the dial tone. I tried to dial Mia's mobile number from memory so that I could call her to cancel, but I lost my way after half a dozen digits, so finally I did hang up and reached for my mobile, where it was in the memory. I was scrolling through my directory when the thing sounded; 'Jean', it told me.

'How are you doing?' I asked, before she could speak.

'How did you know . . . oh, these bloody clever mobiles. I'm doing all right, thanks, Bob. I stop for a cry every now and again, but there are things to be done after a death. You just have to get on with them. The undertaker's been to see me. The funeral's arranged for Friday afternoon, two o'clock at Daldowie Crematorium.'

*That's good*, I thought, instantly. *We'll still be able to go sailing*. My face flushed as quickly as my reaction, at its selfishness.

'You know how to get there?' she continued.

'My God, Jean, I haven't lived in the east for that long,' I reminded her. 'My parents were sent off from there, remember, and your mother.'

'Of course, I'm sorry, Bob. Will you be bringing Alexis?' My sister-in-law never shortened her niece's forename.

'Of course, to that question as well.'

'It won't be too much for her?'

'You've got some catching up to do, Auntie. She would drive cocktail sticks under your fingernails if you asked her that question. At her age, a day's a week in maturity terms.'

'Mmm,' she sighed. 'I keep forgetting. You're right, I should see more of her, Bob, I know.'

'I hope you will now that she's your closest blood relative.'

'God, you're right there too,' she exclaimed. 'I hadn't thought of that.'

'Come and visit us,' I said, 'when we're past all this. Bring the new man too.'

'I'm not sure if he's ready to meet you,' she replied, cagily.

'Why shouldn't he be?'

'Because he's a policeman too; a sergeant, uniform, stationed in Hamilton. He's heard of you.'

'What's his name?'

'Lowell Payne.'

'What's he heard?'

'That you're a hard bastard. His words, not mine. I told him you're very gentle, really.'

'I'll look out for him if I'm ever through in that direction and he can make his own mind up. But he'll meet me on Friday, remember, whether he's ready or not.'

'True,' she conceded. 'Will you be bringing anyone, other than Alexis?'

The idea hadn't occurred to me, but given the timing and the geography, we'd be heading for Inverkip Marina after the funeral so . . . 'It's possible,' I told her. 'But if I do,' I warned, 'don't read anything into it.'

'I'll reserve judgement on that. You can read anything you want into Lowell. I like him. You will too.'

'It won't make any difference if I don't; it didn't the last time, when you married that arsehole.'

'True,' she admitted. 'But Dad liked Lowell, and that's enough for me. On second thoughts, Bob, you should come to Dad's house on Friday; the cortège will be leaving from there at one twenty.'

I promised that I would. As soon as we had said our farewells, I rang a guy I knew in Strathclyde Special Branch and asked him if he'd do me one of those favours that he owed me, by checking up discreetly on Sergeant Lowell Payne, and his reputation within the force. Thornie had started off by liking Cameron, I recalled; he'd always given people the benefit of the doubt, until there was none. If there was anything on Payne's file that I didn't like, I didn't want Jean to find out about it the hard way.

I went outside into the main office . . . yes, I'd forgotten about the call I'd been about to make when Jean had phoned. McGuire and Martin were both at their desks, making their way through files of continuing investigations that Fred Leggat had given them. I tasked them with picking up Wyllie. 'Don't smile,' I warned. 'DI Higgins has a feeling about this man, so I don't want him brought in here full of confidence. If he wants to speak while he's waiting for us, don't let him. If he asks for tea or coffee, give him water. If he wants to pee, go with him.'

'What if he wants to take a dump, boss?' McGuire asked, cheerily.

'Wait outside the cubicle door.'

'Can I go back to St Leonards?'

I patted him on the back. 'And to that nice tailored uniform?'

'Mmm,' he mused. 'What's a wee bit of methane against that? Maybe not.'

They'd been gone for around twenty minutes when Alison arrived. I hung her light raincoat . . . it had been drizzling slightly while I ran . . . in my room, and we headed for the Command Corridor, where the dining room is located.

'On Friday,' I said as we walked. 'I'd been thinking that we'd all go in my car.'

'Me too,' she agreed, readily.

'In that case . . .' I told her about Thornton's death.

She was shocked. 'Bob, that's awful. So sudden. How did Alex take it?'

'Better than I did. I won't go into detail just now, in case it makes me cry. That wouldn't look good in here.'

She squeezed my arm. 'I don't know about that. It's a new man thing, and new men are all the rage.'

'I'll stick to being an old one,' I said, 'or middle-aged . . . young middle-aged . . . approaching middle-age. Anyway, the funeral's on Friday afternoon, in Lanarkshire. Will you come with Alex and me? We can head for the boat afterwards.'

She stopped walking, and whistled. 'Are you sure about that, Bob? This is a family funeral after all.'

'A very small family now.'

'Still, I'm not part of it. What would Alex think?'

'What should she think?' I asked.

'Well, that we were . . . more than we are.'

'She knows how we are, and she's happy with it. Ali, I'd like you to come.' I realised that it was true; I wasn't just saying it because her presence would have been convenient. I hadn't gone to anything with a partner since Myra died. Indeed, I'd never gone to anything with a partner other than Myra.

'If that's what you want, I'll come, depending of course on . . .'

'I know, I know, I know: the fucking job. That goes for us both. If there's a crisis, everything comes second.'

'What would you be if you weren't a cop, Bob?'

That was a question I'd put to myself, often. As I've said, a few years before I'd been close to becoming a lawyer, although I would have been miserable as the sort of general solicitor that my father was. Probably I'd have made my way to the Bar, with a criminal practice as my objective, or I'd have joined the Crown Office, to concentrate on prosecution. But that was then; my thinking had changed over the years, and journalism had become more attractive to me. I'd a journo friend called Xavi Aislado, a big, serious man, widely regarded as the best reporter in the country. I admired him and could have seen myself trying to fill his enormous shoes. But in truth each of those options would have been a bad second best. If I was snatched away from the job I loved, I'd have been . . .

'Lost,' I replied. 'You?'

'A lecturer in criminology,' she replied without a moment's hesitation. 'If I couldn't do it for any reason, I'd want to teach it.'

I opened the dining-room door and ushered her in. While I was a newcomer, in my own right, I'd been there often enough as a guest. I looked around. The chief constable was there, deep in discussion with his deputy. He waved an acknowledgement to me, and I nodded in return. I spotted Alf Stein too, sharing a table with Alastair Grant and big John McGrigor. John was head of CID in the Borders division. He was a massive bloke; he'd been a lock forward in his youth, and he was so much a part of his territory that he could never be moved out of it.

We took a table for two at the wall. Maisie the waitress, as much of a fixture on her patch as McGrigor was on his, gave us a minute or so to study the menu . . . comfort food, most of it; Alf Stein called the dining room 'the cholesterol highway' . . . then appeared at my side to take our orders: two ham salads, the chef's only concession to weight-watching, and sparkling water.

'So what did Alex say?' Alison asked quietly.

I told her, word for word, and I saw her eyes moisten. 'I see what you mean about crying,' she murmured. 'Bob,' she continued, 'you mustn't build her hopes up about you and me.'

'Don't worry about it. She knows where you and I are. Any problem would come if we moved beyond that.' I told her about Alex's *EastEnders* gag, and she laughed out loud, drawing a glance from big John.

'Who does she think we are? Den and Angie or Grant and Sharon?'

'Anybody but Pat and Frank.'

'Anybody but any of them, I think. But not to worry.' She looked across at me, raising an eyebrow. 'She's probably building her hopes up about you and her disc jockey friend.'

I kept my face straight. 'Oh yes,' I murmured. 'The murder victims' sister, the murderer's niece, Tony Manson's mistress's daughter, all rolled up in one. That would go down well in here.'

'Wouldn't it just?' she agreed. 'But love is blind, they say.'

'It would have to be fucking stupid as well.' The point was unarguable . . . so why was I still struggling to convince myself?

Lunch arrived, and we got down to business as we ate, planning our approach to Robert Wyllie. 'What's making you twitch most about his statement?' I asked her.

'It's the pub itself. It's called Pink's, and Wyllie described it as a gay bar. That was accepted by the interviewing officers, but when I described it that way to the station commander, he told a different story. He drinks there himself, and he told me that while it has a certain gay clientele, they're almost exclusively women. It's much the same as the Giggling Goose; gays go there because they know they're not going to be hassled by the rest of the clientele. That's the way these places are marketed.'

'Indeed? So you're thinking that if you were hanging around there waiting for a shirt-lifter to bash, you couldn't always be certain who was and who wasn't.'

She smiled. 'Your turn of phrase not mine, but yes.'

'So Mr Wyllie's been telling us porkies.' I sucked in a breath. 'Wasting police time during a murder investigation. Wait till we put that to him.'

We lingered over coffee, to keep our visitor waiting for a little longer, before I settled the bill and we made our way back to Serious Crimes. Andy Martin was at his desk, but McGuire was absent. 'Have you got him?' I asked.

'Yes, boss,' the blond DC replied. 'Mario's keeping him company; interview room three. When I left he was beaming at him like Shere Khan about to have Mowgli for dinner.'

'Have you read *The Jungle Book,* or just seen the movie?' I laughed. 'We'd better get down there or there'll only be bones left.'

Alison and I made our way down a couple of flights of stairs to the level where what we called our 'guest rooms' were located. Room three was signed 'occupied' but I ignored that and opened the door without knocking. I let her go in first, and stood just outside for a few seconds sizing up the scene. Robert Wyllie was sitting at a small Formica-topped table with a madly marked top, on which sat an ashtray . . . empty . . . and a twin-deck recorder. He was slightly built, with a pale face and pinched mouth, frowning and nervous as he faced Mario McGuire, massive and smiling. I knew as surely as if I'd been a fly on the wall that the DC had not said a word to him in all the time they'd been alone together, and from the look of relief on Wyllie's face as Alison walked in, I judged that he was well marinated. When I stepped in after her, not smiling, his expression became much less certain.

McGuire rose from his chair and went to stand in the corner, but still in Wyllie's eyeline. Alison and I took his place. I glared across the desk. There's this thing I've always tried to do with a suspect, or a dodgy witness. I lock my eyes on theirs, I never look away, and I never blink. It's surprising how effective that's been over the years. I've stared down some tough guys, until they were ready to tell me their life stories.

Robert Wyllie wasn't even a wee bit tough, however much he tried to appear so, in his biker jacket and with his dagger tattoo, carefully located so that the tip always peeked out from under his cuff. It took less than half a minute for him to look down at the tabletop, then to gaze up at Alison, timidly, and exclaim, 'What?'

'Don't look away from me,' I barked at him. 'This isn't a scene from a crime novel. DI Higgins isn't "good cop". We're all "bad cop", all three of us. We're all mightily pissed off at you, and do you know why?'

He opened his mouth, but I reached across the table and closed it for him, forcing his jaws together before he could make a sound.

'Don't interrupt me,' I shouted. 'When you were interviewed about the attack on you and Weir, you told us that it was a mugging gone wrong. You told us that you and your now deceased mate hung around Pink's bar waiting for a gay to beat up. You told the inter-viewing officers that it was a homosexual hangout and they bought that story. Okay, the bar staff in Pink's couldn't remember seeing anyone matching the description you gave in the pub that night. "Orange hair, officer? No, sorry. But it was very busy, and there was a party of students in, all in fancy dress for some daft student reason, so maybe . . ." But that's not why nobody could remember the guy you described, is it?'

I leaned across the table. 'No, Wyllie,' I continued, 'they couldn't because your story was a lie, your description was a fucking lie, and because of it you've sent an entire police investigation off chasing wild geese for a whole bloody week! Pink's isn't a gay bar, not for the men at any rate, so your loitering story just doesn't add up. You and your mate were up to something completely different. This is a murder investigation now, chum; it was serious before, but it's front page now, so you are in very deep shit with us.'

I nodded to my left. 'See that tape recorder? That is your shovel. You can use it to dig yourself out by telling us exactly what did happen, or we can just switch it on to record us charging you with wasting police time, perverting the course of justice, and public urination too, if we feel like it.'

Wyllie's shoulders slumped. 'Okay,' he whispered, 'but you've got to give me protection.'

'No, mate,' I told him. 'You've got to tell us the truth. After that we'll see what you're worth.'

Alison checked that there were fresh tapes in the deck and switched it on, then she spoke, identifying everyone in the room. 'Mr Wyllie,' she continued, 'please give us your account of what happened on the night you and the late Archie Weir were attacked. I repeat Detective Superintendent Skinner's earlier warning that any further statements you make that are found to be false will make you liable to be prosecuted.'

'Aye, okay,' he grunted.

'Speak clearly, for the tape,' she admonished him. 'Now go on, but take your time; you need to get everything right.'

'I will, I will,' he said, loudly. 'Okay, Archie and I didnae wait outside Pink's that night, like I said before. We were in the pub ourselves. So was the bloke that stabbed us. He didnae have orange hair either. It was black; everything about him was black. His jacket, his polo neck, his troosers.'

'Did he have a moustache?' I asked.

'No, he didnae; nor even a stubble.'

'What made you notice him?' Alison continued.

'It was him that noticed us. He came up to the bar for a drink, and he bumped into Archie. Then he gave him the look, like, and said, "Watch it, mate." Archie said, "What are you fuckin' on about? You bumped me." Then the guy said, "That's the fuckin' least of it. Hard man, eh." Archie just shrugged and said, "Aye, fine, have it your way," but the guy wouldnae let it go. He said to Archie again, "Fuckin' hard man, eh," and he kept on lookin' at him.'

'Did anyone notice this exchange?'

'No. The bloke was quiet-spoken, ken.'

'Did you become involved?'

'Me? No' me. I thought he was drunk at first, but I saw that he wisnae. He was fuckin' spooky though, I'll tell you. I could see that Archie was a wee bit scared, ken. He just said, "No, no' me, sorry, pal," and turned his back on him. The guy leaned over and whispered, "See you later," then he went away.'

'But not for good?'

'Ah could see him in the mirror behind the bar. He was standing at the back of the bar, near a' those students, but he'd his eyes on us too. After a wee bit, he put his pint on the shelf behind him and he went off tac the gents'. I told Archie . . . he was still shakin', ken . . . and I said, "Let's get out of here." And we did. We got fuckin' out of Dodge like, and headed up Morrison Street as far as Grove Street. I never thought he'd come after us, but he did. We never heard him though, or even saw him. The first Ah knew was when he stabbed me in the leg. I yelled and I went down, but he didnae bother wi' me after that; he went after Archie before he could move and he stabbed him, half a dozen times at least.'

'Can you describe the knife?' I asked him.

Wyllie winced. 'It was fuckin' sharp,' he whimpered. 'It was big, no a wee dagger like, or a flick knife, but that's all I can tell ye.'

'Okay. Go on.'

He blew out his breath. 'Archie stopped movin' after a while. Ah thought he was dead, then the guy came back to me and I thought I was too, but he never touched me. He just said, "Tell no one, or you're on the same train to heaven as your pervie pal there." He was walking away, when the other bloke came round the corner and found us. He never ran or anything, just kept on walking, and the bloke never even looked at him.'

'That's borne out by the other witness's statement,' Alison confirmed. 'He only referred to finding the two wounded men. He never mentions the attacker.' She frowned across the table. 'So, Mr Wyllie,' she continued, 'that's the truth, is it?'

He nodded.

'The tape doesn't have a camera,' I growled. 'You need to say it.'

'Yes,' he exclaimed, 'it's the truth. Honest.'

'So where did all that other shite come from? Why did you make it up?'

'I had tae say something. I didn't want you lot asking questions and findin' out about the guy pickin' on us in the pub, so I just made up that story about queer-bashin'. I don't want him coming after me.'

'Is . . . queer-bashing as you call it . . . something that you and Weir have done in the past?' Alison snapped.

Wyllie shifted in his chair, glanced at me, and thought better of replying.

'Had you ever seen this man before?' I murmured, just loud enough to be picked up by the tape.

He shook his head, vigorously.

'Say it!'

'No, sir. I'd never seen him before.'

'But the description you're giving us now is accurate?'

'Aye, I swear!'

'It better be, otherwise next time you see me, we'll be having an even more serious talk. Do you think that Archie Weir could have known him? Is that possible?'

'Ah don't think so. If he did, he never said. No, he didnae. I'm sure he didnae.'

'What did he call him, when he spoke to you after he'd stabbed him? Tell us again.'

'He called him "your pervie pal". At least that's what it sounded like; I could have got it wrong. Maybe he said "your pushy pal"; maybe that was it. Mister, I was bleedin', and I still thought he was goin' tae stab me again.'

'Do you know what he meant?' Alison asked him.

He shook his head, then looked at me and replied, 'No, miss,' loudly.

'That would be Detective Inspector,' she said, icily. 'Come on, Weir was your pal, you must have an idea.'

'He wasnae a big pal, though,' he protested. 'We were at the school thegither . . .'

'Which school?' I interrupted.

'Maxwell Academy,' he replied, then carried on, '. . . and we go out for a pint, but he wasnae best man at my weddin' or anything.'

'You've got a wife?'

'Aye. Ah got married three years ago; we've got two bairns.'

'So what were you doing out on the batter with Weir?'

For the first time, he seemed hesitant. 'The wife chucked me out a couple of weeks ago. I was bunking wi' Archie for a bit. But Ah'm back home now, ken,' he added.

'I see.' She paused. 'When you went out with Archie, did anyone else ever tag along, any other men?'

'No, no' really. It would be just the two of us usually.'

'Archie was single, wasn't he?'

'Aye, lucky bastard.'

'Yes, dead lucky,' she said. 'Does the name Albert McCann mean anything to you?'

'Naw, I don't think so. Naw, it doesnae. Why?'

I leaned forward, eyeballing him again. 'Because, Mr Wyllie, Albie McCann was murdered on Sunday night by the man who killed Weir and stabbed you, the man you effectively protected for a week by giving us that made-up bloody story.'

'And you havenae caught him yet?' he squealed. 'Ah want protection.'

I nodded. 'We'll protect you, Robert. You lied to us; that's a criminal offence. You're going to be charged with perverting the course of justice. You'll be held here overnight and will appear in court tomorrow morning. You can apply for bail if you like and the sheriff will probably allow it, since we'll have no real reason to object, or you can stay nice and safe in the remand section at Saughton. It'll be up to you.' I rose to my feet. 'Detective Inspector Higgins, I'll leave the formalities to you and DC McGuire.'

Alison followed me out into the corridor. 'Do you really want to be that hard on him?' she asked. 'The fiscal will probably reduce it to wasting police time.'

I shrugged my shoulders. 'He might, but my guess is he'll let it run to secure a plea to the reduced charge. I know, Wyllie was a victim himself, and he was scared, but he concocted a story, and now we have two murders on our hands. There's also the chance that he might still be in danger from this man, and we'll be doing him a favour by locking him up. If the fiscal does query the charge, refer him to me and I'll deal with him.'

'Yes, sir,' she replied, smiling.

I grinned back at her, awkwardly. 'What's your next move?'

She turned serious. 'To look for a connection between Weir and McCann. These may be two random attacks by a psychopath out for kicks, but then again, if there is a link between the two victims, it might provide the motive for both murders.'

'Absolutely. Where will you start?'

'With Maxwell Academy.'

'Logical, but if McCann was at that lunatic asylum as well, wouldn't Wyllie have known him?'

'They could have been in different years.'

'True. Okay, run with it and see where it takes you. But I'm interested in what the man said to Wyllie as well. Maybe he got it right first time. Have another look at Weir's background too.'

'I will, but I'll also get warrants to search both victims' homes. There might be things there that put them together.'

I left her to charge Wyllie and went back upstairs. I took Fred Leggat into my glass-walled closet and gave him a rundown on how the interview had gone, and on Alison's investigation in general. I didn't expect him to be involved, but he was my de facto deputy in the Serious Crimes Unit, so it was only right for me to keep him in the loop on all of its business, even that which had been slung our way for reasons of convenience, office politics and public relations. When I'd been offered the job by Alf and the chief, they'd given me fair warning that would happen.

'What's your thinking, Bob?' he asked.

'I don't have any yet. Same weapon, same killer, same approach, provoke and attack. Three possibilities: it could have been random, the man with the knife could have had a grudge against the victims, or someone else might have. I'm not going to make any guesses; Alison's are as good as mine at this stage, and she's running the inquiry.' I paused. 'How are we going on the other priority task?' I asked, without much optimism. There were no grounds for any: we were seven days from the murder, five days into the investigation, no sign of any motive and our two major suspects were nowhere to be found.

'Well,' he began; something in his tone took my attention. 'I don't think we're any further forward than we were, but this fax came in from Newcastle.' He'd been holding a couple of sheets of paper, clipped together. He laid them on my desk and pushed them towards me. 'It's the full intelligence file on the man Winston Church; there's something in there that jumped out at me.'

I picked it up and began to read through it. Church was an archetypal local hoodlum of his era. He was sixty-nine years old, and had emerged in the post-war period as a black marketeer, diversifying, when rationing ended, into just about anything that was criminal and, typically, some things that were not. He had been the top man in his city through the sixties, seventies and through the eighties, by force of arms; the feudal lord of Tyneside. His file suggested that he was the man who had got the real Carter, in the real-life gangland episode that had been fictionalised for the screen. In a biopic of his life he might have been played by Ricky Tomlinson or Warren Clarke, or even by Michael Caine.

But he was history, the file said; an old man with little power left to direct or restrain the new breed who had moved in on his patch. They tolerated him, in the same way that the outgoing chairman of a football club is made president for life, and they ignored him. Even his one-time loyal retainers, like Milburn and Shackleton, had gone freelance, their muscle and other services for hire.

I was wondering why Fred had wanted me to read his tired story when a name jumped off the page at me, one of a list of 'former associates'.

'Alasdair Holmes?' I exclaimed. 'What the fuck was Al Holmes doing with this guy?'

'Probably supplying him,' Leggat volunteered. 'If you look at the timeline in the file, Church's decline began after the Holmes brothers were shot.'

'That's of some interest,' I conceded. 'We both know that Al never did anything on his own initiative. His brother was his keeper, in every respect. But as you say, they were indeed shot. Al's dead, and even if Perry wasn't a cripple with round-the-clock care needs . . . he never went within miles, personally, of the likes of Winston Church.'

'So I understand,' Fred agreed. 'That's why I don't see it as relevant. Just a curiosity, really; that's why I drew it to your attention.'

I gazed at the report, and I smiled. 'Yes,' I said, 'it's no more than that, but given who's involved . . . I think I might just go and visit the sick.'

# Thirteen

I didn't take grapes with me, or even a bunch of the petrol station flowers that were popular in those days (and may still be, for all I know) with guys who had wool to pull over their wives' eyes. Perry Holmes might have been a basket case, but his past hadn't been erased, not in my eyes, or in those of any cop who'd seen the aftermath of some of the things he'd ordered.

My former colleague Tommy Partridge was among them. He devoted a large chunk of his career to putting Perry away but he never came close, and because of it he was a bitter man when he retired. Holmes was much, much too clever, for all of us. He never got near to the things that were his, and he was never near anything that was done in his name. When I was in my last year at secondary school, an old policeman came to speak to my debating group. In an off-the-record moment, he told us, 'You are all bright young people, with working lives ahead of you. I shouldn't give you this employment advice, but the fact is that should any of you choose to go into crime, then with your intelligence and backgrounds, you probably have a ninety per cent chance of being successful.' Holmes was living proof of the truth he spoke; he was a brilliant, ruthless man. Tony Manson had learned a lot from him, but he wasn't his equal.

I'd only ever met him once, in the Western Infirmary, two years before, after Billy Spreckley had killed his brother and shot him four times. One of those bullets had lodged in his brain, and was still there. His consultant neurologists, all three of them, for Perry wasn't a man to accept only a second opinion if he didn't like it, said with unanimous certainty that he was going to die. He was conscious and responsive, though; I was sent by Alf Stein to interview him about the shooting, and about anything else he cared to discuss . . . to take a dying declaration, in effect.

He didn't care to say a word, not a cheep. He didn't care to die either. After a few months it became obvious that he wasn't going to, not any time soon at any rate, and so he was transferred to a nursing home while a new house was built for him on an estate that he owned just outside the city, all on one level and fitted out to meet the needs of a quadriplegic.

He'd been kept under observation there, for a while, just in case his surviving old associates started to roll up to his door, but none of them had. No police time was spent on him any longer. Received wisdom, and the evidence of our own observation, was that his criminal enter-prises died with his brother Al, and, shortly afterwards, with Johann Kraus. They had been his main conduits, the means by which his orders were delivered, and executed. Without them, and with no means of replacing them, the word was that he devoted himself from his wheelchair exclusively to the legitimate side of his business empire, the vast property portfolio that he had built up with very thoroughly laundered money, and a development wing which the banks and other institutions were always ready to fund, because he was very good at it, and always gave an excellent return on investment.

The underworld vacuum that he had left behind him seemed to have been filled not by one person, but by several, of whom Tony Manson was one. He was dominant in Edinburgh, but in other areas of the country there had been a couple of turf wars, with fatalities, before the new order had established itself.

I'd met Al Holmes often enough; he was pulled in quite regularly by the drugs squad, and given as hard a time for as long as the law would allow, but Perry's system was foolproof. He swept his house and his office for bugs every day, and he never had discussions, only one-to-one meetings, with no third parties present. Al was a shit, and nowhere near as bright as Perry, but he was too scared of his brother ever to cross him.

Kraus and I had crossed paths too. He was almost as big as Lennie Plenderleith, but not in his league when it came to tough, or for that matter in the same league as me, as he found out one time when he took a swing at me in an interview room. I'd hoped he would; that's why there was no one else there. He had a fearsome reputation, but only with a gun or a chainsaw in his hand. When one of our marksmen took him down, the squad had a whip-round for the shooter.

I was thinking of him as I pulled up outside Perry's new house. Kraus had lived on a small farm that was part of the estate, and it was suspected that some of his victims, including most of Mia's brother and uncle, had gone into an incinerator there. And that made me think of Mia for the first time in a few hours; it was just gone four o'clock and she was on air until half an hour before I was due at her place. Too late to cancel gracefully . . . if I'd really wanted to.

I stepped out of the Discovery and walked up a long white marble pathway that led to the front door. It was opened before I reached it by a man in a blue nurse's tunic, a large black man, with short frizzy hair; he wasn't smiling. I glanced around looking for the camera that must have picked me up, but I couldn't see it.

'Can I help you?' the doorkeeper asked as I approached; his accent could have been from anywhere other than Scotland, and I'd never seen him before.

'I'd like to speak with Mr Holmes,' I replied.

'Then you'll be disappointed, sir. Mr Holmes does not receive visitors.'

'I'm a hard man to disappoint,' I countered. 'I apologise for not calling ahead to make an appointment, but the matter is important, and it's only just come up.'

'You'd have been wasting your time trying to call. The number here is ex-directory.'

'Those don't exist for me.' I pulled my warrant card and showed it: I'd no reason to hassle the guy, and he had every right to refuse me entrance. 'That says I'm a police officer, Detective Superintendent Skinner. You're doing your job, sir, but so am I, and mine overrides yours. So please go and ask Mr Holmes if he has five minutes to assist me in a murder investigation in which he is not, I repeat not, a suspect.'

He made his choice, and let me step into the hall. 'Very well. Please wait here.'

I did. He left through a door in the far left corner. While he was gone I scanned the place carefully for the next camera, the one that I was sure was trained on the door, but I couldn't spot that either. The guy was gone for five minutes, but I kept my patience. If he was going to ask me to leave he'd have been back sooner.

When he did return, he was brisk and to the point. I saw that he had a professional bearing, not that of hired muscle. 'Mr Holmes will see you, Mr Skinner,' he announced. 'I'm sorry for the delay, but we've been moving him to his receiving room. If you'll come with me . . .'

I followed him into a broad corridor, more of a second hall, in fact, with several doors off, all double width. The set that faced us were of dappled glass, and he led me towards them. They opened out into a conservatory big enough to accommodate a tennis court and a few spectators into the bargain. It looked into a walled garden, and was expensively but not heavily furnished, a circular table and a couple of armchairs, that was all. Its main feature was a pale blue tiled swimming pool, with a ramp rather than steps leading into it.

But no, the main feature was probably Perry Holmes himself. He was waiting for me, seated upright in a wheelchair with a high back, a head restraint, and padded arms. His right hand rested on a control pad. It moved very slightly, one finger, no more, but he started to roll towards me.

'I won't shake hands, Mr Skinner,' he chuckled, hoarsely. 'I probably wouldn't even if I could. You can sit down, though. Would you like a wee refreshment, as they say?'

'No, I'm fine, thanks.'

'Are you sure? I can't join you since Hastie here has to feed me, and we don't do that in public.' I glanced across at another blue-uniformed man who was standing close by, pale-skinned, slimmer and smaller than the other. 'But don't let that put you off.'

'No, really.'

'As you wish. You can leave us now, lads.' The two men withdrew, without a word. 'They're my carers,' Holmes said as the door closed. 'Hastie's a nurse, highly trained and very experienced; Vanburn's my masseur. I need a lot of that, to keep me going. They're good lads; they allow me a certain lifestyle, and they're with me pretty much full-time. As you can see, I have very little movement; facial muscles, fingers and toes, but that's it . . . apart from erections. Ironically, I still have those, but they have nothing to do with muscle movement. The doctors say it may have something to do with the bullet in my brain, but those people say I should be dead, so what the hell do they know?'

'Are those two your only staff?' I asked.

'No,' he replied. I noticed for the first time that his chair had high supporting pads on either side of his head. 'I have a housekeeper, a chef, both Chinese, and a personal assistant.'

'Assisting you with what?'

'My business activities, of course. My property holdings, and my other investments, take a lot of management, and I'm becoming more involved in development again, after my involuntary hiatus. Miss Young . . . that's my assistant, is a lawyer with an accountancy qualification. I recruited her from a merchant bank; I pay her a bloody fortune, but she earns it.'

I settled into one of the soft white armchairs and studied him. The Perry Holmes I'd interviewed had been wired up to half the devices in the Western Infirmary, but he'd been a solid, formidable man. Two years on, he'd lost some weight, but his eyes were keen and bright, and his life force was strong. He was past sixty, but take him out of the chair and you wouldn't have guessed; you'd have called him ten years younger.

'What do you see?' he asked. 'What are you thinking? Do I look like that poor wee professor chap? Or the Father of the Daleks? Come on, tell me; I don't have many visitors, it's useful to know what people really think of me.'

I told him exactly what I'd been thinking, and saw pleasure register on his face. 'That's good. You don't feel sorry for me, then?'

'Mr Holmes,' I replied, 'suppose you were sitting on hot coals with an imp of hell poking hot needles in your eyes, I wouldn't feel sorry for you. That bullet in your brain doesn't absolve you of all the crime you've committed, or rather that you had committed, through your brother. To tell you the truth, I had a wee bit of sympathy for him when I saw him lying dead in the mortuary, evil bastard that he was, since he was never really a man in his own right, just the instrument of your will, him and that big German pansy, Kraus. How do I feel about you? Like many people do: sorry that Billy Spreckley wasn't a better shot, and didn't put all four in your head.'

'Fair enough,' he conceded. 'I like a man who speaks his mind. If you're that repulsed by me, then how about giving me a good thump on the head? The slightest blow could kill me, so my consultants all agree. Christ, if you hit one of these support pads hard enough, and I know you could, that would probably do it. Nobody would ever be the wiser either, because there wouldn't be a mark on me.'

I frowned; and then I smiled. 'You've got a point there,' I said. I started to rise from the armchair. Just for a moment, a tiny moment, I saw a flash of uncertainty in his eyes. It was enough. I sat back again.

'Bastard,' he murmured, and then he grinned too. 'You didn't do it, though. And do you know what that tells me? That you are what you say I am . . . or I was: someone who delegates to others the things that he's too careful, or circumspect, to do himself. But that's just what you do: you delegate the shitty end. You catch your thieves, your murderers, and although sometimes your instincts may be Old Testament, as they clearly were with the late Johann, judging by the contempt with which you spoke of him, you don't act upon them. Instead you simply deliver the people up to justice; to the jailer, or half a century ago to the executioner.'

'That's my job,' I pointed out. 'If I let my own feelings get in the way, I wouldn't be doing it properly. There's this too: I work for society; you work against it.'

'Me?' he laughed. 'I'm a property tycoon.'

'Of course you are, Mr Holmes, of course you are. Now, can I ask you, as a property tycoon, or as anything else, does the name Winston Church mean anything to you?'

I had a big advantage over Perry, in his situation. He couldn't look away from me. Sure he could have turned his chair around, but I could have turned it right back. He could have closed his eyes, I suppose, but he didn't. He surprised me by holding my gaze and replying. 'Would that be Mr Church of Newcastle?'

'That's the one.'

'Yes, it's a name I recall. I've never met the gentleman, but I believe my late brother may have . . . on what business,' he added, 'I know not. Why do you ask?'

'He's connected to a couple of people we're interested in eliminating from a murder investigation. I appreciate that you're a respectable property developer, but I'm wondering, did your late brother ever mention any other people in Edinburgh who might have been acquaintances of Church's?'

His face was expressionless. 'I can't think,' he replied, slowly, 'that any of my brother's friends would have felt the need to move in his circles. Let me get this right,' he continued. 'Are you saying that Mr Church has business interests in Edinburgh, ambitions even?'

'No, that's not my view. He ran out of ambition a while back, from what I've been told. I'm trying to establish whether he might have provided services to someone who has.'

Holmes blinked. 'If that's the case,' he said, 'you might want to find that person before Mr Tony Manson does.'

'I'm aware of that,' I told him. I stood up, abruptly. A finger moved and the chair rolled backwards for a couple of feet, then stopped when it became clear that I wasn't moving towards it. 'I must be going,' I said. Another finger moved, but on his left hand; a few seconds later the door reopened and the two carers came in.

'Please show Mr Skinner out, Vanburn,' Holmes instructed. 'Do call again, Mr Skinner. You're an interesting man.'

*Takes one to know one*, I thought as I left. Even in a wheelchair Perry Holmes ranked as one of the most imposing men I'd ever met. I found myself regretting that I'd never confronted him in his prime, before he'd been wrecked by Billy Spreckley's bullet. I understood why Tommy Partridge had become obsessed by him. I'd probably have been the same in his shoes. But I'd have had a better chance of nailing him. Even crippled, he was supremely self-confident. When a guy has an ego that size, it's a weakness. Fuck, I should know.

I headed back into town. The Discovery really was a pile of shit, but it was kept reliable by our mechanics . . . and the radio worked fine. I switched it on; Airburst was still tuned in and Mia was past the halfway mark in her three-hour stint. I felt myself throb at the sound of her voice, and I knew then that I would keep our date. 'Shit!' I said aloud, as I remembered something very important. Luckily I spotted a late-hours Boots as I drove through Tollcross. I pulled up, and bought a supply of condoms . . . for the first time in at least fifteen years. *Why would anyone want them flavoured?* I wondered as I surveyed the range on offer. The answer didn't come to me until I was on my way out of the shop.

Is there a God?

I'm past fifty now, and no nearer to answering that one to my unshakeable satisfaction, but I do believe, against all logic, that there is a force that guides our daily lives and that it is one perverse son-of-a-bitch. I hadn't even restarted the car when my mobile sounded. It was six o'clock and Airburst would have been in its news break, so I thought it might be Mia, but a glance at the screen told me different. It was Fred Leggat.

'Boss,' he began, 'are you in the vicinity?' There was an urgency about his voice.

'Near enough. Whassup?'

'Newcastle,' he replied. 'It's blown up in our faces. Milburn and Shackleton have turned up. Dead.'

'Eh?' I gasped. 'How?'

'Well. It wasn't an accident. They were found in a hotel in South Shields, on the seafront. They'd been there for a couple of days, sharing a twin room. They were seen last night in the bar, but not today. The "Don't disturb" sign was left on their door, so housekeeping left them alone until about an hour ago. They knocked, got no reply and went in with a pass key. Both men were in there, dead.'

'Bugger!'

'I'll second that. What do you want to do?'

I didn't have to consider my answer. There was only one possible. 'Go there. What else? They're our prime suspects for Marlon. If we can't put them in the dock at the High Court, there'll have to be a public Sheriff Court hearing, and someone will have to give evidence of their death. I'm not bringing Newcastle cops across the border.'

'Who do you want to send?'

'Nobody.' I didn't realise it at the time, but Perry Holmes's crack about me 'delegating the shitty end' had irked me. 'I'm going myself. Is Martin still there?'

'Yes.'

'Then tell him he's won some overtime. I'll take him with me. What—' I was interrupted by a rap on the passenger window. I turned to see a traffic warden glaring at me, book in hand. I was on a yellow line. 'Hold on, Fred,' I snapped. The Disco didn't boast electric windows; I had to reach across to the handle. 'What!' I shouted.

'You're parked illegally,' the man replied. It was May, but he had a dewdrop at the end of his nose; for some reason that wound me up even tighter. 'And don't use that tone of voice to me.'

I pulled out my warrant card and thrust it at him. 'CID,' I yelled. 'And I'm dealing with an urgent call. Now fuck off before I book you, for loitering.'

'Don't you—'

'Go!' I roared. He did, shuffling away, grumbling to himself. God help his next victim. I should have regretted the incident, but like many of my colleagues, I had a sneaking dislike of our street-walking counterparts. 'The custard cops,' Alf Stein had labelled them, for the colour of their hatbands, and the name had stuck.

'Okay, Fred,' I said. 'I'll be ten minutes. Tell Martin to fire up his pussy wagon. He's driving; I want to get there tonight, and my car won't do that.'

I drove back to Fettes as quickly as I could. Mia was still on the radio. As I parked, she cued up a music track, and I called her mobile. I told her that I couldn't make our date. 'I've got to go and look at two stiffs in Tyneside. I'm sorry.'

'Work happens,' she said, sympathetically. 'When will you be back?'

'God knows. Probably midnight, earliest.'

'I'll wait up for you. Call me from the road.'

'We'll see,' I told her. 'If I haven't rung by eleven, turn out the light and go to sleep.'

Martin's Mazda probably wasn't designed with guys our size in mind, but we squeezed in, and the engine was certainly juicy enough. The traffic was light, so we made good time, but there was so much road noise in the passenger compartment that I had given up trying to talk to him before we reached Dunbar. We were through the Tyne Tunnel by eight o'clock. The Northumbrian CID had faxed through detailed instructions on how to reach our destination. I navigated, along a route that kept us close to the river, until eventually we reached its mouth. We couldn't have missed the hotel if we'd tried. There was a crime scene van right out front, and an ambulance. The entrance to its car park was partially blocked by a traffic car.

I badged the uniform who was on guard duty. He peered at my warrant card, and came to something approaching attention when he saw my rank. 'Who's in charge?' I asked him.

'That would be DI McFaul, sir. He's probably in the van.'

Martin parked the Mazda as far away from the action as he could. Getting out was a damn sight harder than getting in had been; it struck me that maybe I needed to change my exercise routine and work on staying supple. We walked across the car park, to the mobile office. Steps led up to a door in the side. Martin stood back, to let me lead the way, but I told him to go first. 'Don't be shy. You're a cop too. Recognise rank, but don't defer to it all the time.'

I followed him inside. The unit was little different from ours in Edinburgh: untidy, smelly and badly lit. There were two people, seated at desks, a man in plain clothes, thirties, tubby, dark, greasy hair, plain clothes, and a woman, younger, neater, uniformed. 'Excuse me,' Martin said to the detective. 'We're looking for DI McFaul.'

He looked up; his stress was evident. 'And who the fuck are you?' he drawled, annoyed by our interruption.

I saw my young DC's shoulders flex very slightly, inside the leather jacket. 'We're the pros from Dover,' he replied, calmly. 'I'm Trapper John and this is Hawkeye; in his case it's Detective Superintendent Hawkeye. Now who the fuck are you, please?'

The man peered up at him, dumbstruck; behind him the woman smiled, discreetly.

I laughed. 'Most people only know *Mash* from the TV series, Andy, not the movie. But you're right, I'm definitely more Donald Sutherland than Alan Alda. My name's Skinner,' I told the bloke, 'and this is DC Martin; he's got a weird sense of humour, but he's a nice lad really. I'm not; I've had a two hour drive in a matchbox, I'm stiff as a chocolate frog, and I'm not nice to know. We're from Edinburgh and we've got an interest in your two stiffs.'

Finally, the Geordie stood. 'Sorry,' he mumbled. 'I thought you were press.' In certain circumstances, there are standard cop excuses; that is one of them.

'I take it you're not the force PR officer, then.'

The uniformed woman snorted, and put a hand over her mouth.

'As a matter of fact I am,' he replied. 'Detective Constable Ranson.'

'Jesus Christ,' I whispered. The guy made Inspector Hesitant look like Bernard Ingham.

'DI McFaul's inside,' he continued. 'Interviewing,' he added.

'What were you saying about not deferring to rank, sir?' Martin chuckled, once we were back outside.

'Don't. I was taught to be careful with other kids' toys, in case I broke them, but sometimes it's hard when it's so clear they need fixing.'

I took my first good look at the hotel. It was a two-storey building, probably not that old, but in need of refurbishment. It was called 'The Seagull', but the second 'l' was missing from the sign above the door; also the paintwork and a couple of windows were streaked by offerings from the birds whose name it bore. It was no better inside; a mix of smells that I'd rather not have been experiencing, cigarette and cigar smoke that had probably become part of the fabric of the building, the unpleasantness of stale beer in an empty bar, kitchen odours that made me forget how hungry I was, and lurking in the background, but evident, drains.

My distaste must have been showing. 'It's not our finest, I'm afraid,' a man exclaimed as he walked towards us, mid-thirties, same as me, slim, grey-suited, hand outstretched. 'Detective Superintendent Skinner?'

'Correct,' I said as we shook. 'And this is DC Martin.'

'Ciaran McFaul. You guys made good time. I saw you coming out of the van and guessed who you must be. Did Scoop send you in my direction?'

'As in DC Ranson? Yes.'

The DI must have picked up something in my tone, for he smiled. 'He's best avoided when he has a press statement to prepare.'

'You actually let him do that?'

'After a fashion. He does the draft and I rewrite it. He has a brother-in-law on the police committee. Need I say more?'

'No, I get the picture. Milburn and Shackleton,' I went on. 'Are the bodies still here?'

He nodded. 'Yes. The SOCOs are done, but we kept them here till you arrived. Come on, I'll show you.'

He led the way to the upper floor then headed right, along a corridor, towards a constable, on guard outside the last door but one. He saluted and stood aside as we approached. McFaul opened the door, carefully, then held it ajar for us. A short narrow passage led into the room; its curtains were drawn but every available light had been switched on. A man was lying on his back, bare feet towards us, eyes open, arms by his sides. He wore jeans and a black crew-necked jersey. In life he'd been large and probably menacing; in death he was just an ugly pile of meat. I looked for blood, but there was none. I looked for wounds, but saw none, only what could have been a tear in the middle of the sweater.

'That's Warren Shackleton,' the DI told us. 'A man without a single redeeming feature, until now, his first one being he's dead.'

I felt something odd beneath my feet; I realised that I was standing in dampness. 'The chambermaid,' McFaul explained. 'Poor woman wet herself. Go on inside.'

We stepped past the body, carefully, into an irregularly shaped area, furnished with twin beds, two small armchairs, and a dressing table. At first there was nothing to be seen. 'Beyond the beds,' our tour guide said, pointing. We followed his sign. The second body lay on its right side, head turned, face pressed into the dirty russet carpet, clad in black trousers and a red check lumberjack shirt.

'And that was Glenn Milburn. You know his story. Small-time, muscle, cruel bastard, would have done anything to anyone for money. Anything he's ever been involved in, Shackleton's always been close by.'

I crouched beside him. Again, at first sight the body was unmarked, but when I looked more closely, I spotted a small pool of blood beneath it, flowing from a wound in the centre of his chest. I stood up and stepped back, allowing Martin to look.

'You get the picture?' McFaul asked.

'It's pretty plain. Shackleton opened the door and died where he stood. No blood, so he was killed instantly. Milburn might not even have known till the intruder reached him, for there are no signs of defensive wounds on him. What does your pathologist say about time of death?'

'Nothing for the record,' he told me, 'but he guesses between eleven last night and one this morning. He won't even go firm on the murder weapon until he's got him on the table. Either a knife or a silenced gun with a small-calibre soft-nosed bullet; that's all he's giving us for now. I'll go a bit further myself on time of death, though. The front door is always locked at midnight. If anyone wants to come in or go out, they have to call the night porter. So it stands to reason it had to be before twelve.'

'There must be emergency exits,' Martin pointed out. I noticed that he was paler than usual.

'All secure.'

'They must have been expecting him,' I said.

'You reckon?' the Northumbrian mused, scratching his chin.

'For sure. There's a spyhole fitted. If you're in a hotel room, and someone knocks on your door at that hour of the night, I don't care who you are, you're going to take a look to see who it is before you let them in. Shackleton did that and, bingo, he was dead. Look at his face. He didn't even have time to be surprised. Milburn, he was round the corner, and didn't see or hear anything. There's no sign of him having reacted when the man appeared, no signs of him struggling either. These are two fucking bruisers, Inspector, who killed a man on my patch, killed him brutally, and yet they've been despatched like sleeping children.'

'You're speaking in the singular,' he noted. 'Could it have been only one man?'

'The way I see it, yes. There isn't room in that entrance area for more than one. Here's my scenario, overall: these men were hired to extract information from a man in Edinburgh called Marlon Watson, probably about his boss, an organised crime figure. They may have been told to kill him, no, scratch that, they probably were. After the job was done, they were told to burn the van they'd used to destroy any forensic evidence, then get out of sight. When did they check in here?' I asked.

'Saturday evening. They paid cash for four nights. They used the names Hughes and O'Brien.'

'Right. They planned to leave on Wednesday, latest. My belief is that they thought their visitor was coming to pay them off. He did, permanently.'

'That late at night?'

'Yes. That bar downstairs, is it public?'

'Sure, it can be quite busy.'

'And the visitor didn't want to be seen. I don't even need to ask if there's closed-circuit TV in this place, because I know there isn't. I bet you've got no witness sightings either.'

McFaul sighed. 'No, Superintendent, we've interviewed all the staff, and nobody saw a damn thing. Clean as a whistle,' he murmured. 'We're stalled already.'

'Not quite. There's one place we can go. The NCIS computer puts these two close to a man called Winston Church.'

'The Prime Minister?' I raised an eyebrow; he grinned. 'This is Tyneside; we don't do subtle nicknames. Yes, they run for him, but not exclusively, not any more. But I'll grant you, they could have been hired out through him.'

'Then let's pay him a visit.'

'Now?'

'Right now,' I said, 'before he finds out about this.'

'I'm game for that,' the DI agreed. 'I don't see the old guy having had anything to do with these two being killed, but I'm going to have to talk to him anyway.'

'Where does he live?'

'Morpeth. It's the right side of the city for you; once we've heard what he's got to say, you can head home.'

'Depending on what he tells us.' McFaul's affability seemed to lessen, fractionally; I didn't really blame him. A couple of guys from the Met had turned up on our patch a few years before, with attitudes so bad that it had almost come to pistols at dawn. 'Not that I expect him to tell us a fucking thing,' I added. 'For the record, my interest in this is in finding the person who set Milburn and Shackleton on to Marlon Watson. I've got enough on my plate without getting involved in this mess.'

'Fair enough. Look, I know the way to Church's house. I've been there often enough. You come in my car, and my DS can go with DC Martin.'

His detective sergeant turned out to be a woman called Wilma Easton, a veteran of twenty years' service, with short, salt and pepper hair and a sturdy build, but small enough to fit more comfortably into the Mazda than I had.

We headed back the way we had come, to the Tyne Tunnel. We were heading into it when my ringtone sounded, then stopped as the signal was lost. As soon as we were on the other side, I checked 'missed calls'. Alison.

I rang her back, and explained where I was, and why. 'I see,' she said. 'In that case this can wait till tomorrow.'

'How are you getting along with linking Weir and McCann?' I asked her.

'I haven't,' she replied, 'not yet at any rate. But something's come up in the course of it, something curious. I'd like you to see it.'

'What is it?'

'Probably nothing, but it struck me as odd. I'd rather you saw it for yourself. If you call me tomorrow morning, or whenever you get back, I'll come up to Fettes and show you.'

'Okay,' I said. 'I will do . . . whenever that is.'

I slipped the phone back into my pocket. 'Business back home,' I explained to McFaul. 'I've been in my new job for five days and I'm running two major investigations.'

'Getting anywhere with either of them?'

I glanced at him. 'Are you familiar with the topography of Shit Creek?'

'Been there many times, Superintendent. No paddle, I take it?'

'Right now, your Prime Minister pal is my last hope. That's why I'm keen to see him.'

'Let's hope he can help you,' the DI said. 'But he's likely to be more of a clutched-at straw. He's never incriminated himself before, and I don't see him starting now. What do you hope to get out of him, supposing he is shocked into talking?'

'A name. He's got one old Edinburgh connection in his past that I know of, a man no longer with us. I'd like to know if there's another, or if I'm dealing with someone from out of town.'

'That's if he had anything to do with Milburn and Shack being set on your murder victim.'

'Indeed,' I conceded, 'but that past acquaintance of his . . . I don't know why, but it's making me twitch.'

'One thing I can tell you,' McFaul offered. 'Those two didn't go after the man on their own account. They weren't self-starters.'

We skirted Newcastle from the tunnel and joined the A1, then headed north. The Morpeth turn-off came up fairly quickly. I glanced in the wing mirror and saw Martin and DS Easton right on our tail. My driver seemed to know exactly where he was headed; I wondered how many times he'd stood on Church's doorstep, and whether they'd ever achieved anything. Very little, I guessed, for the sod was still at liberty, like Manson, Perry Holmes, Jackie Charles and a few others like them on my territory, men with the brains to know their way around and through the criminal law that they broke for a living.

Two or three tight turns later, McFaul turned into a street called the Crescent, and pulled up in front of a driveway with blue wooden gates, blocking it. The house beyond was detached, a mock-Tudor pile in the midst of a street of stone Victorian villas. If a dwelling can seem embarrassed by its surroundings, that one did. It was set back off the road. I looked for a CCTV camera, or any other obvious security; I saw none, but I hadn't at Holmes's place either, so what did that prove?

There was a door set in the blue gate to the right, with a recessed brass ring handle. The DI turned it, and it opened. Yes, he had been there before. We followed him inside, on to a red gravel road that approached the house. It crunched, loudly, under our feet as we walked, a pretty effective intruder alarm. There was a double garage on the left; its up-and-over door was open, revealing a blue, round-bodied Rover coupé that looked as clean as it had been in the showroom, thirty years before, if the number plate was a guide. My dad had owned several when I was a kid. Beside it sat a much newer red Rover Metro, a tatty little shit bucket. For me, it showed the depths to which the marque had sunk, but at least Church had brand loyalty. 'Is that the wife's car?' I asked.

'No,' DS Easton replied. 'That's Winston's; his wife died ten years ago. He's lived alone ever since.'

'Any family?'

'Yes. One son. He's a brain surgeon in Auckland, New Zealand. That's as far away as he could get from his father.'

McFaul had reached the pergola that covered a paved entrance area. There was a brass plate in the middle of the front door, with a button at its centre. He pushed it . . . and the door swung open. 'Hello,' he whispered, frowning. 'What's up here? That's always locked.' He leaned into the entrance hall. 'Mr Church!' he shouted. 'Winston! It's the police, CID. We need to talk to you.'

I have a keen sense of smell in any circumstances, but for some things I'm as good as any sniffer dog. I put a hand on the DI's shoulder. 'You're wasting your time,' I told him. 'You won't get a response.'

'But his cars are both here,' he replied, 'and the only taxi he ever uses is Milburn's.'

'That's not what I meant.' I stepped past him, into the house. I didn't have to follow my nose for long, no further than a big dining kitchen at the back of the house. Winston Church . . . I assumed that it had been him . . . was at home but he was in no condition to receive visitors. Outside, the daylight was fading, but I could still see what lay before me. He was sprawled, on his back, across a big farmhouse-style table, arms and legs hanging over the sides, bare feet clear of the floor. He'd been wearing a dressing gown and pyjamas when he died, no protection against a savage attack. He'd been gutted, ripped open, and his entrails had spilled out of a great diagonal tear that ran across his abdomen. As I stared at him I felt as if I was back in Joe Hutchinson's workplace, after the pathologist had finished his examination. I inched forward, but not too far; I didn't want to contaminate the place, nor did I want to get blood on my shoes. There was a slash across the dead man's face, from his right cheek, across his nose and his left eye to his eyebrow. His right hand was missing the third and little fingers. I looked around, quickly. There was a half-glazed door opening on to the back garden. It lay ajar and I noticed that one of its astragal panels had been smashed.

I realised that I was holding my breath, and let it out in a great exhalation. As I did so, I became aware of Ciaran McFaul beside me, and heard him moan softly. I glanced behind me; Easton and Martin were still in the hall, their view blocked by our bodies.

'Let's all back out of here,' I said quietly. I turned, drawing the DI with me, and heard a small squeal escape Easton as she saw what was in the kitchen. Not your everyday crime scene, even in Newcastle. 'Come on,' I ordered. 'Everybody, all the way outside.' I swept them before me, through the hall, back under the pergola.

By that time, McFaul had recovered himself, so I didn't presume to tell him what he should do. It wouldn't have been necessary anyway. He tossed his car keys to Easton, instructing her to call in an incident report, and ask for forensic, CID and uniform support, then he turned to me. 'What did you see?' he asked.

'The attacker broke in through the back door, and went out through the front, leaving it open behind him. Your SOCOs will probably find a blood trail to the door. He couldn't have done that without stepping in it and being splashed. Surmise: Church may have been in bed and heard the glass break or . . .'

'He was watching a video,' Martin interposed. 'I took a quick look in the living room while you were heading for the kitchen. The telly's on, and the player's on pause. Porno,' he added.

'One of his remaining business interests,' the DI said. 'I'm thinking the same man as the Seagull. Are you?'

'Absolutely,' I replied. 'Whoever hired them for the Edinburgh job isn't leaving any traces behind. This was our only lead and it's been well and truly closed off.'

'Was he killed before or after the South Shields pair, d'you reckon?'

'He wasn't worried about being covered in blood, so I reckon it had to be after. He broke in here, so he wasn't expected this time.'

'But why, sir?'

Martin's question took me by surprise. 'What do you mean?' I challenged.

'Isn't it a bit extreme?' he asked. 'They were hired hands, supplied by Church. Okay, but why kill them all?'

'Somebody's being super-cautious.'

'Or . . . you're looking at this from the wrong angle?'

'You what?' I snapped, then realised what he was getting at. 'Shit!' I exclaimed. 'I told Tony Manson we were looking in Newcastle. I even mentioned Milburn by name. But no, Andy, no fucking chance. Manson's more subtle than that. Mind you, if Bella was leaning on him . . . Shit, shit, shit!' Out of nowhere, I could see my fast-tracked career about to be derailed. I turned to McFaul. 'Ciaran, DC Martin might be pushing his youthful luck here, or he may have a point. There's an outside possibility at our end that I'll need to look into, if only to eliminate him. I'll get back to you when I've done it.'

'Okay.' He looked up at me. 'This place is going to be overrun in a minute, and very soon after that my boss is going to arrive. If he finds you two here . . . well, he's a bit of a stickler and he might want to know why two Scottish officers were active on his patch. If you're not here, there's no reason why I should tell him. Your choice.'

I thought about it. 'The book says we should give your SOCOs our prints for elimination,' I pointed out.

'Did you touch anything in there?'

'I don't believe I did. DC Martin, how about you?'

'I was careful not to, boss.'

I laughed. 'Boy, if you don't stop being perfect you're going to make a lot of enemies. Come on, Ciaran's right. We're out of here.' I shook McFaul's hand. 'Thanks, Inspector; I'll be in touch. You keep me in your loop as well, okay?'

'Will do.'

We cleared the exit from the Crescent just as the first of the Northumbria cars arrived. 'By the way, Andy,' I said as we headed for the A1, 'you can be as clever as you like and you won't ever make an enemy of me. But don't ever put me on the spot again in front of another officer, or you will.'

He nodded. 'Point taken, boss. I'm sorry.'

In truth I was far more angry with myself than him. I had told Manson far too much, in the hope that if he had any ideas, he would share them. I'd thought that I knew him; if I'd been wrong, I could have signed three death warrants. Either way, it was a big mistake, reckless. The saving grace was that Martin had been there as witness to the knowledge that I had given the gangster, and that of itself would have been a constraint on him. I might have let the business lie quiet, undisturbed, but by mentioning it in front of McFaul, my young DC pal had taken that option away from me, and that was his real transgression.

Suddenly, without warning, my mind was dragged back to that kitchen. I'd hit my 'detachment' button before I walked in there, for I knew it was going to be bad. That normally worked, but it wasn't a hundred per cent effective.

The things you see: the mind has ways of managing them. If you're properly professional, and experienced, it allows you to take the humanity out of the situation, and to accept the inanimate as what it is. In extreme cases, it will block out the memory altogether. But every so often, in my case at any rate, even back then when I was at my most battle-hardened, I'd see something that would return to me later, and sneak under my emotional guard. For example, something like Winston Church, his face cut almost in two, half-naked and eviscerated on his kitchen table, severed fingers in the pool of blood beneath him. I wondered how long it had taken him to die, and at the thought of it my stomach started to heave.

I looked ahead and saw in the headlights, for darkness had fallen completely by that time, that we were approaching a parking place. 'Pull over, Andy,' I said. He did, I jerked open the door and swung myself out of his awkward little bastard of a car, gulping in lungfuls of cool night air, retching violently, on an empty stomach with nothing to bring up but a little bile.

The spasms took a little while to subside, but they did. My face was covered in a cold sweat, and I was shaking slightly, but I was back in control. Martin had stayed in the car, discreetly. I wasn't ready to get back in myself; instead, I took my phone from my pocket and pressed the 'menu' key. I found Mia's number on the illuminated keyboard and called her. 'Hi,' she murmured, and at once I felt warmer. 'Twenty to eleven. The light's still on and I'm still awake. Are you close?'

'I'm the best part of two hours away.'

'But are you coming?'

I considered my options. Go home to an empty house. Crash out in the office. Call Alison and probably cry on her shoulder, since she would understand why. Go to Mira's starving, exhausted and shell-shocked, and let her see me at my worst. *Why the hell not?* I decided. *As good a way to start as any.*

Martin made good time, but even at that, it was almost twelve thirty by the time I arrived, after I'd picked up the Discovery from Fettes. The gate in the garden wall creaked, a curtain twitched, and before I could ring the bell, the door opened and she pulled me inside by the lapels of my jacket. She closed it again, with her foot, put her arms around my neck and kissed me. Fortunately, I'd refuelled on Lucozade and sandwiches from a filling station just short of Belford, and swallowed an entire box of Tic Tacs afterwards, otherwise God knows how I'd have tasted.

She looked up at me as we broke off. 'Poor man,' she murmured. 'Have you had a rough night?'

I hugged her again and let myself relax against her body, feeling hours of tension leave me, and realising that she was wearing a silk robe and nothing else. 'The strangest of the strange,' I murmured. 'The queerest of the queer.'

'Hey, I played that this afternoon,' she whispered. I knew that; I'd heard her. 'Remember how it ends? "You can touch me if you want." Well, do you?'

I let her lead me into her bedroom. It was lit by at least a dozen candles. The silk whispered as it fell to the floor, and her bare skin seemed to shimmer in the flickering light as she slipped my jacket from my shoulders. When I was naked too, she stood back and appraised my body, running her fingers over my pectorals, my abdominals, and then down. 'How old are you?' she asked.

'Thirty-six, for a few weeks more.'

'You're in pretty good shape,' she conceded, 'for an old guy . . . although that shape is changing by the second.'

She had found the condoms in my jacket. I let her put one on me, and then I let her do everything else too, lying on my back, looking up at her as she straddled me and moved, very, very slowly, smiling, until she stopped smiling and began to moan, a sound that grew in intensity until it became a howl of pure pleasure, tailing off and ending in a long soft sigh.

'Ooooh,' she whispered in my ear as she stretched her body out along the length of mine. 'It's been a while, Bob, since I've been with someone properly; it's been a while.'

I couldn't say the same, so I said nothing. Instead, I rolled over, easing her on to her side.

'Is that better?' she murmured, as I disposed of the evidence. 'I could see the pain in your eyes when you came in. Was it bad where you were?'

'Mmm,' I admitted. 'I went down there to a double homicide; it turned into three, and the last one . . . fuck! You know, I've spent the last five days looking at dead people. Even in the job I do, that's a hell of a lot.' And then I recalled something that had gone out of my mind entirely, a highly relevant fact. 'But if you want the good news,' I continued, 'the three tonight were the ones who killed your brother.'

As soon as I'd spoken, it was as if the good imp had jumped on to my shoulder and said, 'What the hell did you tell her that for? You don't mix personal and professional, Skinner.' But the bad imp didn't hang about; he was straight in there, shoving him off.

She sat up, her eyes wide. 'Really?' she exclaimed. 'Are you sure?'

'Oh yes, I'm certain. Two did it, the third was involved.'

She blinked, and shook her head as if she was trying to clear it. 'That's incredible,' she gasped. 'So . . . so . . . so who killed them?'

'Don't ask me that, love.'

'But you must have an idea. Please, Bob.'

I sighed. The waters were lapping around my chin and rising. 'Your mother's fancy man has to be a possibility, although I don't believe that. If not him, then unless they were involved in something else, something on Tyneside that the cops there know nothing about, then it has to be the person who hired them. But we do not have one clue who that is, and the trail is freezing cold.'

'It was probably my mum,' she whispered.

That was a possibility that had crossed my mind. I'd set it aside. Even if I was wrong and Bella Watson did have the stuff to take out two big thugs, alone and unaided, she'd been looked after by Lennie Plenderleith over the weekend, and as far as I knew she still was. Plus she wouldn't have had the faintest idea of where to find them . . . any more than would Manson, I supposed.

'Enough,' I said. 'Forget about that, Mia. It's my other life and it doesn't belong here. By the way, Alex says thanks for the CD. You're right; those girls will do well for themselves, until the next craze comes along.'

She settled back down beside me, and kissed my forehead. 'Thanks for coming,' she murmured. 'I haven't had a man in my bed for a long time. I was beginning to think that there was some sort of curse hanging over me.'

I laughed. 'You have to be kidding, don't you? You're one of the most . . . the most desirable . . . yes, that's a more dignified word than shaggable . . . women that I've ever met.'

She grinned, wickedly. 'Is that so?'

'Absolutely,' I murmured. 'As a matter of fact . . .'

Some time later, I fell asleep.

# Fourteen

Normally I will roll into wakefulness like waves on to a beach, steadily, in small advances, until my tide has risen and I've emerged from the last episode of whatever dream I've been having, from wherever I'd been during the night.

But not that morning. My sleep-bound adventure wasn't drawn from my imagination: it was a full colour replay of the previous evening, beginning with the struggle to escape from Martin's MX5 in the car park outside the cruddy hotel in South Shields, then taking me, step by step, back along the way, until I was standing once again in Winston Church's kitchen, staring at his ravaged body on the table.

When his intestines started to move like snakes, that's when I came to, in a hurry. Only I didn't, not completely. I sat up, eyes wide open but taking nothing in. I was awake, but my consciousness remained in that bloodbath in Morpeth. I recall shouting something. Whatever it was, it made Mia reach up and take hold of my left arm. But I didn't know it was Mia, did I? So I wrenched it free, violently, then slammed it across her chest and twisted round, forcing her down on to the bed and pinning her to it as my right hand gripped her throat.

'No,' she screamed. 'Bob, no! It's me, it's Mia, it's all right.'

That was enough . . . thanks, God, for that one . . . to bring me back. If it hadn't been, I might have crushed her windpipe. I saw the

247

fear in her eyes, and took my weight off her, then gathered her into me. 'I'm sorry, love,' I whispered. 'Bad dream.'

She wriggled in my grasp, trying to free herself. I let her go and she pulled away from me, staring at me as if she'd woken up with the Blagdon Amateur Rapist. 'I'm sorry,' I said, again. 'I thought I was . . .' I smiled, weakly, hoping to reassure her. 'Call it a Stephen King moment, eh?'

'Call it nothing!' she shouted. 'You scared me. I thought you were going to kill me. Is this normally what happens after you have a bad day at the office?'

'No,' I retorted, unreasonably irked, 'but I don't usually sleep with anyone, so maybe I wouldn't know. Calm down. I had a nightmare, okay?'

She put her fingers to her throat; I could see the red marks that mine had left. 'No,' she moaned, on the verge of tears, 'it's not okay! This is not how I wanted it to be. I don't need violence in my life! I've had enough of it. Men!' The ferocity of her sudden scream took me by surprise. 'You're all the fucking same! All bastards. Go, will you, just get dressed and go.'

'Mia . . .'

'Fuck off!'

It's impossible to be dignified when someone's glaring at you as you're trying to get the other foot into your briefs, so I gathered up my clothes, and my overnight bag, and took them through to the bathroom. I ran the Philishave over my chin a few times, then showered quickly, and dressed, same suit and shoes but a change of everything else. I was almost ready when my phone sounded.

It was Alex. I hadn't even looked at the time until then, but the readout told me that it was two minutes past eight. 'Morning, Pops,' she said, and a huge warm feeling of relief surged through me. She was my foundation, the real keystone of my entire existence. I'd lost sight of that truth for just a little while; focusing on it put everything back in balance.

'Where are you?' she asked.

I didn't want to tell her, but I couldn't lie. 'In the bathroom,' I replied.

'Possibly too much information, Pops. Whose bathroom?'

She was my daughter so it stood to reason that she'd be a persistent interrogator. 'I had to go to Newcastle last night,' I told her, irrelevantly.

'Ah, so you stayed over?'

'Well, no . . .'

She wasn't giving up. 'You're at Alison's, then?'

'No . . . Alex, don't ask, okay?'

'You're at Mia's!' she exclaimed. She sounded triumphant; she'd got me and she knew it.

'I give up,' I said. 'Yes, I am.'

'Pops, be careful.' Her sudden concern astonished me.

'What do you mean?' I almost stammered. 'You're not giving me . . . big-people advice, are you?'

'No, I didn't mean that. I meant be careful with Mia. Don't get serious or anything. She's not right for you.'

I felt just a little huffed. 'What do you mean? I thought you liked her.' I wasn't sure whether I was defending my taste in women or the woman herself.

'I do. She's a friendly person, and she's good on the radio, and she went out of her way to be nice to me which meant for sure that she fancies you, but she's different, so different from you. You don't belong together.'

'And what about Alison?' I challenged.

'I like Alison more than I like Mia, and she would be right for you, maybe, but that's not going to happen. If it was you wouldn't be in Mia's bathroom at this time in the morning.'

I was comforted. She didn't know everything, I thought, until I realised that, actually, what she didn't get was the truth about her old man, that he was as weak as most other blokes when it came to women, as easily led by his dick.

'Don't you worry yourself,' I declared. 'Neither of those things is going to happen. No kitchen-sharing, I promise. Now bugger off to school. What are you doing today anyway? A post-grad in adulthood?'

'Double maths, Spanish and English this morning, as it happens. See you tonight?'

'See you tonight,' I confirmed. 'And you're cooking, since you're so bloody grown up all of a sudden . . . and so territorial when it comes to the kitchen.'

I slipped on my jacket and ventured out of the bathroom. I'd hoped, maybe even assumed, that Mia would be waiting outside, contrite, with tea and toast, and maybe even a full Scottish on the hob if I was lucky. But she wasn't. The bedroom door was still closed. 'Fuck her,' I whispered, angry and more than a little humiliated, as I walked out, closing the door firmly so that she'd know I'd gone, but just short of slamming it like a petulant kid.

I was first into the office, but only just. Andy Martin arrived just as I was starting on my copy of that morning's *Saltire* newspaper. It was my barometer; I took its journalism and its editorial line seriously, which I didn't do always with the other blacktops. There was nothing in it about either of the murder inquiries. That pleased me in one way and worried me in another. It meant that there was no immediate public pressure on me for a result in either case, but worried me because I'd expected a harder time from them, on the Weir-McCann investigation at least. My reading was that the paper was sitting on the story, not wanting it to run out of steam, in case . . . in case there was more, in case there was a third murder. At that moment, that was my biggest fear. Two down. How many more to go?

I looked up and saw Martin standing outside my door, as if he was considering whether or not he should knock. I waved him in.

'Hi, Andy,' I greeted him. 'I thought I told you not to be too sharp getting in this morning.'

'I couldn't sleep, boss. I didn't see any point in hanging about the flat.'

'Lucky you. I wish I hadn't slept.' I'd never been more sincere.

'Bad dreams?'

I nodded. 'The worst. You had breakfast?'

'Coffee, that's all.'

I stood. 'Come on then, let's go to the canteen. When I'm feeling fucked I always refuel.'

The staff catering was just as good as that in the senior officers' dining room, and every bit as traditional. Cops need feeding properly. I filled a plate with fried egg, sausage, bacon and black pudding, then topped it off with a fried potato scone, just for luck, to be washed down with a huge mug of tea. Martin had the same, only more so. 'It's a training night at Raeburn Place,' he explained.

'Are you still serious about rugby?' I asked.

'The day I stop being serious about it, I'll have played my last game. I may have dropped out of the top flight, but I'm still as committed as ever. I owe that to the other fourteen guys in the team.'

'Think that way in CID and you'll be fine,' I told him.

We ripped through our breakfasts like a chainsaw through a tree, then turned our attention to the well-stewed tea. I looked at the DC over the top of my mug. I'd known him for less than a week, and we were hardly equals in rank, but I was starting to think of him as a friend. 'Have you got a bidey-in?'

He blinked at my question. 'A what?'

His surprise made me chuckle, and realise how far from my roots I'd travelled. 'Sorry, I forgot that's more of an east coast term. Have you got a live-in girlfriend?'

He shook his head. 'No, not just now. I did have, but that went tits up about nine months ago.'

'Whose fault?'

'Nobody's, really. We didn't fall out or anything. She wanted it to go further than I did, that's all, so we split. I still see her from time to time; we're still good friends.'

'Is she in the job?' I asked.

'Hell no. She works in PR. I would not fancy having a policewoman as a girlfriend.'

'No?'

'What else would you talk about over the dinner table, other than the job?'

'Your kids, eventually. By the way,' I added, 'you're not supposed to use that word any more.'

He was puzzled. 'Which word?'

'Policewoman. There are no more WPCs; we're all police officers now, everybody. It's no longer politically correct.'

He grinned. 'Did I catch an inference there, sir, that you don't have much time for politicians?'

'I'll say it out loud if you like. I can't fucking stand the breed. There is something completely fucking phoney about them. They'll be back soon promising us the world in exchange for our votes, and as soon as they have them they'll fuck off for another four or five years and forget about us, until it's time to be nice to us all again.'

'Don't you like any of them?' he asked.

'I admired the last Prime Minister . . . "admire" being different from "like". Balls like grapefruits. But the present bloke? I don't believe he really exists. I'm sure he's made of fucking latex, like his puppet. As for the new guy, he's all fucking bouffant and razzamatazz. He went to bloody Fettes, for Christ's sake, that fucking Gormenghast of a school across the road. "Boys Only" when he was there and now he's fixing the rules to get more women into Parliament, just because they're women. That should be a fucking gender-free zone, man. Every MP should be there on the basis of ability; no elector's choice should be restricted to people who sit down to pee. It's un-fucking-democratic, Andy, and it's the mark of the man.'

I realised that I had raised my voice, and was drawing glances from other tables; I stopped. 'Christ,' I continued, a little embarrassed and a lot more quietly, 'listen to me. You'd think I was a misogynist, yet I'm anything but. We need more women in the police force, we need them in the higher ranks and yes, we need them in politics too, but only as long as they get there the right way and not through some artificial process. Our service has been male-dominated from the start. Its thinking is far too narrow, and if I ever got to command rank, I would do everything I could to change that, but that would not include putting "Women applicants only" signs over promotion boards.'

'You lost your wife, didn't you?' he said.

Taken aback, I stared at him. 'Yes, I did. A while back.'

'Is that how you and she talked over the dinner table?'

A smile, so broad that I felt my cheeks bunch, spread across my face. 'Yeah,' I replied. 'Exactly like that. We used to go at it hammer and tongs, especially when Myra'd had a couple of drinks and her tongue was really loosened . . . not that she ever held back much.'

He nodded. 'That's the kind of relationship I want,' he declared.

'Full frontal, nothing left unsaid. That's why . . . your word . . . bidey-ins don't work for me. I want a relationship that challenges me every minute of the day. Clearly you've had one, and you'll never settle for anything else again.'

But I did, for a while. And so did Andy. We've got there in the end, both of us, but if we'd recorded that conversation and played the tape to ourselves every day, maybe we wouldn't have made the mistakes that we did along the way. But, if we hadn't, then four lovely kids wouldn't have been born, so . . . what the hell?

That morning, though, our discussion showed me something very clearly. It told me why, as much as we liked each other, Alison had been right to set limits to our relationship, to draw a boundary line over which neither of us would step. We didn't fire each other up in that way, and we both knew it.

As for Mia, she was history to me, even then. There was something about her reaction that I knew I wasn't going to get over. Sure, I had scared her; there was no doubt about that. But she'd known where I'd been the night before, and she'd even known that it connected to her, and yet there had been no shred of sympathy in her, or any attempt to understand why I had reacted in that extreme but completely involuntary way. I didn't want to reach out to her again, not after the way she'd behaved, and if she'd phoned me at that moment, I wouldn't have taken her call.

Martin said something to me, but I hadn't been listening. 'Sorry, Andy, what?

'I asked if we were going to see Manson again this morning, boss.'

'I am,' I replied. 'You're not. Nothing personal, but I may have to lean on him, and it would be more comfortable if it was just the two of us.' His eyes narrowed a little. I smiled. 'Hell, Andy, I'm not going to thump him. There needs to be some straight talking, that's all, and for that it has to be just him and me. Sometimes you have to play by their rules to make any progress.' I finished my lukewarm tea. 'Come on. We have to bring the troops up to speed.'

By the time we got back to the office, the rest of the squad, such as it was, had arrived. I knew it wasn't enough for the continuing job I'd been given, a mixture of ongoing intelligence work, active investigations and pure fire-fighting, of the kind we were involved in at that time, and staffing was an issue I'd have to address. Fred was due for a promotion to DCI, and a move. I'd meant what I'd said to Martin about broadening our thinking. Maybe Alison and I could work together after all. Then there was young PC Rose, the officer I'd met in St Leonards. She'd impressed me, for no reason that would have been clear to anyone else. I've always prided myself on being able to spot potential in an instant, by the way someone speaks, looks and acts at first encounter.

But that had to wait; for that time I had what I had. I sat on a corner of Fred's desk and gathered them around me, him, Jeff Adam and McGuire, with Martin standing alongside me. 'Okay guys,' I began. 'Andy and I had a very active evening down in Newcastle. We've got some bad news for you and then we've got some worse news.'

I gave them a detailed rundown of the scene that we had encountered at the Seagull Hotel, and of the bleak prospects of identifying the killer of Milburn and Shackleton from trace evidence left behind him. Then I told them of our call on Winston Church, and of what we had found there.

'The man didn't mess about,' I said. 'It may be that he signed his name in forensics in the old guy's kitchen, but he was efficient and thorough in the hotel and I don't expect anything else from him there.'

Leggat and Adam sat silent, frowning; it was young McGuire who spoke. 'Surely there was a big difference in the nature of the attacks, boss? One lethal wound each in the hotel, but the guy Church seems to have been killed in a frenzy.'

'Point taken, Mario,' I told him. 'But the difference can be explained. From what we saw, neither Shackleton . . . who died first . . . nor Milburn had any clue they were in danger until it was too late. Shackleton even opened the door for him. At Church's house, it was nothing like that. He broke in, the old man heard him, paused his porno movie and went to investigate. The intruder had neither the time for subtlety, nor the need; he just attacked. Church tried to defend himself,' I held up my right hand to demonstrate, then mimicked the attack, 'but had two fingers severed and his face bisected. Then he was . . .' I paused, back in the middle of my nightmare, '. . . he was just ripped open, and died of shock, or blood loss, or whatever the autopsy tells us.'

Leggat winced. 'So the investigation's stalled?'

'As of this moment, it is. We have to hope now that the victims have left something behind that links them to the guy who paid them to do the job. Fred, I didn't raise any of this last night, because the situation was developing, and because I didn't want anyone thinking I was telling them how to do their job, but now I'd like you to get on to DI Ciaran McFaul in Newcastle and ask him if he can get us access to the phone records of the three dead men, and also to the call logs of their mobile phones. I'm assuming that they had them; it seems to be de rigueur these days for hoodlums to use pay-as-you-go mobiles, in the belief that they're untraceable.'

I didn't say anything to them about my potential dropped clanger with Tony Manson. It wasn't for sharing at that time. 'Do that,' I continued, 'and ask him to send us copies of the post-mortem reports for our case files.'

'Do they belong there, boss?' Adam asked.

'Of course they do,' I retorted, just a wee bit sharply. Poor Jeff didn't have a lot of luck around me. 'Whatever the Tyneside boys may think, this is our inquiry. We started off looking for the people who killed Marlon Watson, and we found Milburn and Shackleton, and through them Church. As of yesterday we were looking to thumbscrew out of them the identity of the man who set them on him. He was our ultimate target. Now the three Geordies have been silenced. Who else did it? He did. The hired hands have been taken out of the game, but the employer remains, the man we've always been after. So you see, Jeff, nothing has changed. It's a continuous investigation, so Northumbria CID and ourselves are looking for the same man.'

Fortunately, DS Adam wasn't as smart as Andy Martin. It didn't occur to him to ask why it had taken almost a week for them to be taken out of the game.

I headed for the door. 'I'm off out,' I told Leggat. 'Call to make.' I smiled as I left them, feeling vaguely like a German spy. I'd just recalled a great line from a marvellous old war movie, *Ice Cold in Alex*, something along the lines of, 'When a man takes a walk in the desert with a spade, never ask him where he's going.' You should see it sometime, if you haven't.

I drove out to Barnton, enjoying the roominess of the Discovery, in contrast to Martin's space capsule. I switched on the radio, hoping to catch a news bulletin. Airburst FM's morning presenter was in full cry, his voice a frantic, kiddie contrast to Mia's mellow, much more adult tones. I gave him the bum's rush and switched to Radio Forth, which represented my Edinburgh, not that of another generation. I was still bitter over the way the morning had begun. I found myself hoping that Mia would phone, so that I could release my verbal safety catch and let her have both barrels. Hell hath few furies like a man who's just been left standing in a woman's bedroom with his clothes bunched in his hands, doing his best to leave with dignity.

I knew the routine at Manson's place second time round; I showed myself to the camera and, after a few seconds, the fancy gates swung wide. But I wasn't prepared for the changing of the guard. I hadn't reached the door when it was opened, not by either of the boys I'd seen before, but by Lennie Plenderleith.

'Morning, Mr Skinner,' he greeted me, as quiet and polite as ever. In those days, I used to wonder occasionally what the other side of Lennie was like, but I always decided that I didn't really want to know, unless it was unavoidable. I'd never sought my reputation as a hard man . . . and I knew I had one, make no mistake. It had been bestowed on me by the folly of others who'd thought they were tough themselves, and word had spread.

'Morning, Lennie,' I replied. 'Is the boss in?' The Bentley had been outside, so I'd assumed that he was.

'Yes. He saw you on the screen; he's waiting for you in his office. Go on through.'

Unescorted, I followed the invitation, and entered Tony's sanctum. My second surprise in as many minutes: he wasn't alone. He was at his desk, and seated alongside him as if she was taking dictation was Bella Watson. The sight of her sent me, mentally, straight back into her daughter's bedroom, but I got myself out of there in a hurry before irritation showed on my face.

'Hello, Detective Superintendent Skinner,' Manson exclaimed, affably. The clarity of his enunciation made me suspicious.

I jerked a thumb back in the direction of the door, and raised a questioning eyebrow.

He understood. 'I got rid of the A Team,' he told me. 'Pair of fucking wankers. Without their shooters they were useless, as you proved. The big man on his own is worth three or four of them, so I asked myself, why am I spending more money than I need? I don't like having him guard my door, though. He's miles too good for that. To tell you the truth,' he mused, 'I wish I could put him somewhere safe; being around me can be risky.' It was interesting; I'd never seen him in such a contemplative mood before. 'Anyway,' he continued, 'once I'd decided to move him in for a few days, it made sense to move Bella in here too.'

'I was goin' tae call you,' she said, sourly. 'When will I be able to arrange Marlon's funeral?'

'As far as I'm concerned,' I replied, as I occupied the chair that faced across the desk, 'you can do it now. It's not my call, but I don't think the fiscal's office will object. They might not let you cremate him, but it should be okay to have a burial.' I couldn't resist having a go. 'It won't be a very big affair, though,' I added. 'Just you and Tony and Lennie, by the looks of it. I don't see your daughter turning up, not after you putting the black on her.'

'She'll no' be missed,' Bella hissed. 'Jumped-up wee tart.'

'Mother of the Year,' I laughed, then turned back to her boss and mentor. 'With two extra mouths to feed you must be running short of groceries,' I said. 'I think Lennie should take Bella to Safeway to stock up. Don't worry, you'll still be protected. I'm here.'

He understood me; I'd come for a very private chat. 'Aye, okay,' he responded. He reached into the top drawer of his desk and produced a roll of twenties, peeled off a few and handed them to Bella. 'On you go,' he told her.

'Ah checked this mornin',' she protested. 'We don't need anything.'

'Well go tae the fuckin' casino then,' he snapped, 'but go somewhere.'

She flounced out, all legs and attitude. For the first time I could see that she was her daughter's mother.

Manson grinned as the door closed on her. 'Now you see why I don't have her move in,' he chuckled. 'What a fuckin' life that would be. What's that daughter of hers like then? I've only heard her on the radio. And what was that about her blackmailing her?'

'Mia's also a piece of work,' I replied. 'The other was a family misunderstanding that's been sorted out now.'

'Ah,' the gangster murmured. 'Miss Sparkles doesnae want anyone to know where she's from. I get it. I don't blame the lassie either. I must pay more attention to her.'

'I wouldn't, if I were you.'

There was something in my eyes and he read it. 'Oh aye,' he exclaimed. 'Is the detective superintendent warning me off? Has he been there himself?' He chuckled. 'I think he has, I think he has indeed.'

'Turn the tape off, Tony.'

He stared at me. 'What tape?'

I leaned across the desk. 'Do not fuck me about,' I growled. 'You've had a recorder running since I walked in here. Your voice is different, louder and clearer, and we both know why. Now, are you going to turn it off, or do I have to find it and do it for you?'

He knew when to fold 'em, did Tony Manson. 'Aye, okay,' he conceded. He opened the drawer at his left hand, produced a micro-tape recorder and disconnected it from a pen stand on his desk. 'Looks realistic,' he said. 'You'd never know the ballpoint was a mike.'

'That will bring you down,' I warned him. 'Vanity is a fatal weakness for a guy like you. And trying to get something on me would have been pretty bad for your health as well. Gimme the tape.' He removed it, without protest, and handed it over. 'And the one you made last time.' He smiled, went back into his desk drawer and handed me another micro-cassette in its box.

'There's no more,' he said. 'I promise. Now, Skinner, why are you here?'

'I want to find out how stupid you really are.'

'You know I'm not.'

'I thought I did, but something's happened to make me doubt myself, in that respect at any rate. When I was here last, I fed you some information that should have stayed within the investigation. I even ran a couple of names past you. I did that because I believed that if you could have helped me, you would have, quietly, just between us two. What I did not believe was that you would act on that information in a way I wouldn't like or in a way that would embarrass me. So imagine what I felt when I was called down to Newcastle last night and shown the bodies of the guys we had firmly in the frame for Marlon's murder.'

Thunderclouds formed on Manson's brow. 'Are you winding me up?' he asked, in a hiss that might have been the direst warning to someone other than me.

'Not for one second, Tony. Now tell me, did you have anything to do with this . . . and be fucking sure you look me in the eye.'

He did. He held my gaze and he didn't blink. I saw the real man, the near monster, not the front he'd been hiding behind until then. 'No I did not,' he replied, in the same voice. 'I swear, on your daughter's life.'

He was trying to send me a message, to say to me, *I know you, I know your weakness, should you ever push me too far, copper.* But he'd got it wrong: he didn't know me at all. I felt my volcano ready to erupt, but I kept the plug in.

'Let me promise you something,' I said, holding his gaze. 'If you ever mention my daughter again to me, or if I ever hear of you mentioning her, then I will take that as a threat to her. And . . . I . . . will . . . kill you. I'm a cop, Tony. I can find the means to do that and suffer no consequences. So let's have that clear between us.'

He considered me anew, and he nodded. 'Sorry,' he whispered. 'No threat implied. If I ever had cause to come after you, it would be you alone.'

'I can live with that.' I paused. 'You wouldn't. Now, repeat, you're giving me your word that you had nothing to do with the deaths of these three men.'

'Yes.'

'Well, somebody's hoping I'll believe that you do.'

He relaxed a little, hid behind the mask once again. 'That had dawned on me,' he drawled.

'Any idea who?'

He shook his head. 'Not the faintest, Skinner. I'm hiding nothing from you, honest . . .' he chuckled, '. . . and that's not a word you'll hear me use too often.' And suppose I did, I'd always take it with a spoonful of salt.

'Could it have something to do with Bella?'

'No. I know all there is to know about her,' he paused, 'apart from her taking protection from her daughter, maybe. It couldn't, believe me.'

'How did you get together?' I asked.

'I saw her at Al Holmes's funeral, believe it or not. She was two rows back in the crem, wearing a red dress. I liked her style, and her guts. I asked her what the hell she thought she was doing and she told me flat out that she was there to make sure he went up in fuckin' smoke. What she didnae know,' he continued, 'was that Perry had asked me to kill her. He sent for me, in the Western. It was just the two of us, in his private room. He could barely talk then, but he managed to say to me, "Favour time, Tony. I want the Spreckley sister dead." I told him that he'd have to settle for the brothers, for a man with a bullet in his head and fuck all else wasnae giving me orders.'

'Are you saying this could go back to Holmes, and that it could be his revenge on Bella?'

'No,' he replied. 'It's got nothing to do with her. I've seen Perry since; I told him that Bella and Marlon were under my protection, and that there were no more debts owed. He accepted that. He's out of that life now, Skinner, for sure. He's got lots of money, but no power. Plus, of course, he's a fucking cripple.'

'So who? Zaliukas and his Lithuanian chums?' I suggested.

'No chance. Young Tommy's trying very hard to be legit, and I'm encouraging that. He still has his faults, a bit flash, a bit reckless, but I hear he's got himself a new girlfriend and that she's bringing him under control.'

'How exactly are you encouraging him?'

He smiled. 'Let me put it this way. Your drugs team'll be wasting its time staking out his pubs.'

Meaning he had put them off limits to his pushers. 'Are you an investor too?' I asked.

'No, the boy doesn't need me anywhere near him.' The smile became a soft chuckle. 'I invest in myself, that's all. Perry's the man wi' the portfolio. Although what he's going to do with it when he dies . . . and as we both know that could happen any minute . . . God alone knows. He's never been married.'

'Neither have you,' I pointed out.

'Maybe not, but my will's made. It'll be a while before anyone inherits, though.'

I frowned. 'Are you sure about that? Maybe you're next, after Marlon.'

'It'll be an idiot that tries,' he grunted.

'You'll tell us if he does, though. That's not a request, Tony,' I added.

'Aye, I will,' he said. 'Eventually.'

I left him, lurking and pondering in his den. He had been more forthcoming than usual, once we'd got the tape nonsense out of the way; I didn't necessarily believe it all, but as far as I could figure, he didn't have a reason to lie to me.

I headed back to the office. There had been no big breakthrough in my absence. The guys were doing their best, but there was no good news, barely any at all, and the little there had been, discouraging.

'I've spoken to McFaul in Newcastle,' Leggat told me. 'They didn't find any mobile phones on any of the victims. They've been all through Church's house too, and found hee-haw. Their next step, he says, is to track the call logs for their home phones and for Milburn's taxi business.'

'That'll be a waste of time,' I forecast, 'but it's got to be done, I suppose. What about Milburn's office, and his house, and Shackleton's?' I asked. 'Are they searching those too?'

My impatience must have been showing, for Fred's look was questioning. 'Do you really want me to ask them that, boss?' he ventured. 'Remember what you said about not telling them how to do their jobs?'

His point was undeniable. He'd never had to deal with a frustrated and restless Bob Skinner before, that was all. Suddenly, I found myself wanting to go home. I hadn't been there in over twenty-four hours and the few off-duty hours I'd been able to snatch hadn't helped my general condition. I couldn't, of course, but I did have a manic need to keep moving. I cast around for things to do. I thought about going back to see Dougie Terry and giving him a harder time than before. I considered visiting my former near neighbour, Jackie Charles, and putting him through the wringer. But there was no point, in either case. It would have got me no further, and occasions such as those were best kept for when there was a real prospect of a result. Then I realised there was something I had promised to do, and forgotten with everything that had gone on. I went into my office and called Alison, on her mobile.

'Hi,' she said, making me feel good, and guilty, simultaneously. 'I thought you must still be down in Newcastle, or that you'd just forgotten about me.'

'Would I do that ever? We're going sailing on Friday, remember? I've got that to look forward to.' *And a funeral*, I thought, sombrely, *that as well*.

'Are you ready?' she asked.

'Give me a break,' I pleaded. 'It's two days away.'

'No,' she laughed, 'not that. Are you ready for me to come up and see you?'

'No,' I countered. 'You stay where you are. I'll come to you. No sense in you bringing files up here, just to take them back again.'

'Are you sure? It's no bother, honest.'

'I'm sure. At this moment, I'm better off on the move.'

She chuckled. 'Ah, it's one of those days, is it?'

'What do you mean?'

'Do you think I don't know what you're like, after the time we spent working together? Come on down then. I'll get the coffee on.'

She really was good for me. There was a stability about her that seemed to transfer itself to me whenever I needed it, whenever I became as frantic as I'd been. Again, I found myself thinking of the choice I'd made around midnight, and how fucking stupid it had been. 'Got any Gold Blend?'

'Take what you get, Detective Superintendent. Nescafe original only here.'

'I'll bring some, in that case.'

As it turned out they didn't have any in the Stockbridge grocer that I called into on my way, but they did have a pretty decent Douwe Egberts instant, and I settled for that.

There was a probationer on the desk when I walked into the Torphichen Place office from the car park at the back of the building. He didn't recognise me when I came in through the door behind him and wasn't sure whether to ask for my ID, but I showed it to him anyway. His name badge read PC Ray Wilding. He seemed a bit overawed, and I wondered whether he'd make it through training.

I was halfway up the stairs when I met Alastair Grant, coming down, wearing a Barbour jacket and with his car keys in his hand. He stopped and said, 'Hello.' Normally that would have been it with Alastair, for he was a quiet bloke, but he continued. 'When are you giving me my DI back, Bob?'

'As soon as I can, mate,' I retorted, stung slightly by his question. 'Do you think I'm spinning out this investigation just to keep Alison close?'

'No, no, no, no, no,' he insisted: four more than sincerity demanded.

He was a nice bloke, as well as a quiet one, and at once I regretted biting him. 'One "No" would have been enough, Alastair. Are you pushed, flying one short?'

'Just a bit,' he admitted. 'I'd an armed robbery yesterday, the third from a pharmacy this month.'

'Drug thefts?'

'Yes.'

'Wish I'd known earlier,' I grunted. 'I was with Tony Manson earlier; I could have told him it was becoming a problem. He'd put them out of business quicker than we can.'

'Sure,' he agreed, 'but permanently.' I think I made him nervous sometimes. 'Ah, I'm just having a moan, Bob; don't mind me.'

'I won't. The Weir murder started off as your inquiry, remember, before Alf slung it over to me.'

'Very true. I suppose all I can do is wish you luck with it.'

I smiled. 'I'd sooner rely on methodical detective work, myself. Anyway, I do not feel at my luckiest today. A door barely opens before it's slammed in my face again. I hope Alison's going to change that.'

I wished him luck, and carried on upstairs. The layout of Torphichen CID was pretty much like my own, which meant that the detective super had the private office, and the rest had desks in an open area. Alison looked up and smiled as I came in. I held up the Douwe Egberts. 'This is yours,' I told her. 'To be taken home; don't leave it here or it'll be nicked. Nothing's safe in a police office. But, before you put it in your bag, open it and make me a mug.'

'Fair exchange,' she agreed.

I watched her as she crossed the room, to the table with the kettle, the milk and the mugs. The place was empty save for a couple of DCs in deep discussion in a far corner, so my study was unobserved. She moved with the confidence of a person who was happy in her skin, on legs that were muscular but beautifully shaped, as if they'd been carved by a master from an unblemished piece of oak. The rest of her body was a good match, but it was the warmth of the being within that I found most attractive. She was too good for me, that was for sure. 'I'm sorry,' I whispered, very softly.

She turned just at that moment, and saw my lips move. 'I missed that,' she called out. 'What did you say?'

'I said, how would you like to come home with me tonight?' How weak and indecisive was I?

'Yes,' she replied, 'but that wasn't it.'

'No, I said sorry for not calling you earlier.'

She smiled as she placed a mug in front of me, on a Capital Copiers coaster, on her desk. 'You boss, me underling. I'm meant to wait until you're ready.'

'That'll be the day,' I chuckled.

'That's the rule,' she insisted. 'Anyway, you sounded completely frazzled when you did call, so I took it that you'd had a bad time. Actually, you still look pretty wired.'

I sighed, heavily. 'Do I? And here was me thinking I was supercop. Yes, we had a fairly testing experience, young Andy and I.' I told her about our visit to Winston Church and what we had found. I left out the worst of the detail, but I didn't fool her.

'So you won't be passing the crime scene photos round the table after dinner,' she said.

'No, I will not. I like my carpet the way it is.'

'I see. Is there an upside to this?'

I sipped my coffee; I'd made a good choice, I reckoned. 'For you, yes; you're not part of the investigation team. For me, no; I thought I could see a way forward, but now I can't. But that's not why I'm here. What couldn't you tell me over the phone?'

'Not tell you. Show you.'

She sat behind her desk and took a file from a tray. 'Before I get there, though, we have established a link between Weir and McCann, and it is Maxwell Academy. They were both there at the same time, but McCann was a year behind Weir, and that's why Wyllie didn't know the name.'

'Were they pals at school?'

'We don't know. Brian and Stevie are both working on that. They're interviewing all the classmates that we can find. What's more important though, isn't it, is whether they were pals after school, and that's what we're trying to establish.'

'Was Wyllie any help there?' I asked.

'I re-interviewed him this morning up at the Sheriff Court, with Stevie . . . a very dishy young man, by the way; you want to watch him . . .' She winked; I killed my idea of bringing her on to my team full time. Our intimacy had become too great to allow it.

'No,' I countered. 'If I have to, I'll just send him back to where he came from: obscurity.'

'Bully. Anyway, Wyllie stuck to his story. He didn't know McCann and he'd never heard Weir mention him, but he did admit that the two of them weren't as close as they had been since he became a family man. But there's still McCann's pal, Charles Redpath, the guy who was with him the night he died. We've still to talk to him again, and we will, soon as he gets back from his run. He's a lorry driver; works with a firm in Haddington. When we tried to contact him yesterday we were told he was away on a two-day trip to Harrogate. He's due back late this afternoon.'

'Tell his employer to hold him there when he gets back. You and I are going out that way anyway. We'll make a detour and see him together.'

'I will do,' she said. 'But are you sure you want to be involved?'

'Makes sense. Plus I'm not giving you another chance to size up young Steele.'

'Okay. Now, the main business.' She opened her folder. 'I went to Weir's flat yesterday afternoon . . . with Brian, who is in no way dishy . . . looking for something, anything that mentioned McCann. We'd done the same in reverse at his mother's place and come up empty-handed, just as we did at Weir's eventually, but there, I did find this. It was in a drawer, folded. It bears no relevance that I can see to this investigation, but it struck me as curious, and I thought you'd want to see it.'

She picked up a piece of paper, and handed it across to me. I unfolded it and saw that it was a photocopy of a single page. A quick glance at the header told me that it was from a back issue of a magazine called *Radioweek*, a trade journal, by the look of it. But it was its main article that really caught my eye. The heading was 'Adding a Sparkle After School', and it topped a feature about 'Edinburgh's newest media star, a girl on the up and up' . . . Mia Sparkles. There was a photo too, Mia with her best 'come into my parlour' look. I stared at it and felt . . . nothing. What I saw, superimposed by my memory, was the expression on that face the last time I'd seen it.

I read it, carefully. The copy made it appear that she was an Aberdonian; it didn't mention any earlier Edinburgh connection. Hardly a surprise, I supposed.

I folded it and handed it back. 'As you say, nothing to do with your investigation. A small coincidence, that's all.'

'Isn't it you who's famous for saying that you don't believe in love or coincidences at first sight?'

I smiled. 'Maybe, but I was lying about the first. That was something I said to give the *Saltire* crime reporter a good quote, and it's lived with me ever since. Anyway, we know that Mia went to Maxwell Academy as well. He saw the piece and kept it. So what?'

'She's very anxious that nobody should know about her background, is she not?'

'Yes, but so what? There's no evidence of anything but casual curiosity on Weir's part. That magazine article's months old. Weir could have sold his story to the papers at any time since then, but he didn't.'

'True. But maybe he contacted her.'

I couldn't help smiling. 'And threatened to reveal his dark secret, so she put a contract out on him? And on his pal, just in case? I don't think so, Ali.'

She chuckled, softly. 'No, maybe not. Maybe I'd just like her to have done.' She paused. 'Still, shouldn't it be followed up?'

Procedurally, she was right; but no way was I going to do it, and I didn't want her to either, for a non-operational reason. 'Yes,' I concurred. 'Tell Brian, or Hugh Grant's kid brother, to go and see her and ask her if Weir or McCann mean anything to her and if she's seen either one lately. Do it for the record, then move on.' I finished my coffee. 'I'm going back to Fettes. I'll pick you up from here at four, and we'll head for Haddington; tell Redpath's firm we're coming, and that we'd appreciate it if he waits for us if necessary.'

I went back out to the car park, past young PC Wilding, who started to give me a probationer salute, but stopped when I pointed out that he'd joined the police not the army.

I realised that I didn't feel like going straight back to the office. I needed clear space to think, and I wasn't going to find any there. I thought about going up to the castle and parking on its esplanade, but there would be buses, and tourists, hardly an oasis of calm in a sea of storms. Instead, I headed east, through the Grassmarket and the Cowgate, and into Holyrood Park, the Queen's Park as it's called sometimes, for that's what it is. I drove past St Margaret's Loch and its swan population, and up the rise until I reached Dunsapic Loch. It had less bird life because there were fewer people there with yesterday's bread. Its car park was empty and that was exactly what I wanted. I got out, leaving my jacket on the hook behind my door, and walked along the water's edge, then up a short, rocky slope to a point that afforded a view across the firth and all the way down to Berwick Law. As I approached the top I realised that I wasn't alone, as I'd thought. A couple of kids were lying on the grass about twenty yards away, oblivious of my approach. I didn't see any cycles, so I guessed that they'd walked up and stopped for what I will call, euphemistically, a wee rest. The law called what they were doing an offence against public decency, but I've never been the sort of cop who whips out his warrant card at every opportunity, and suppose I had, I was alone, and so the good old Scots law of corroboration was working in their favour. If I'd had a pebble in my pocket I might have tried to catch the boy on the rise, but I didn't, so I simply changed direction and left them to their happy distraction.

Eventually I spotted a boulder that was flat enough for me to sit on. I lowered myself on to it and looked homeward, enjoying the peace of the morning, and its sun on my face. Where was I going? I wondered. A week before I'd been chasing druggies all over Edinburgh, doing my best to keep the lid on the sales force and the consumers, knowing all the time that I had no chance of catching the people at senior executive level in the business, because they were as smart as I was and knew that the parts of the criminal code that were restrictions upon me were places of refuge for them. I'd done my time on the drugs squad, beaten all my arrest targets, banged up dozens of salesmen and users, but very few managers, and had looked forward to being rotated. In due course that had come to pass and where was I? Right in the spotlight, running two murder investigations, in which there was no subtlety, only a simple imperative: find the people responsible and take them out of society before they could do it any more damage. I sensed that I was at a, maybe the, pivotal moment of my police career. Alf Stein and the chief had laid out a future for me, but I knew what they hadn't needed to say: it was all contingent on success. There was an alternative: failure and a fall from the stairway to the stars, as James Proud, in a moment of unprecedented eloquence, had described it. I'd always tried to be honest with myself. I hadn't always been successful, but I had recognised the extent of my own ambitions. I hadn't joined the force with the aim of becoming a member of the Superintendents' Association, and I hadn't joined because I felt good in uniform. I'd joined to be, not just A detective, but The detective, the man on top, the boss, the man who drove the whole fucking analogy-strewn bus, and I'd been possessed of an ego which hadn't considered for one second the possibility that I might not be good enough.

But that was what I faced, sitting on that slab of volcanic debris, staring out across the water. Where was I in these two key inquiries that could make my career or wound it, maybe mortally? My fear was that I was stuffed, in both.

I looked for positives in the Marlon Watson murder hunt. On the face of it, we had an acceptable result. We had identified Milburn's van, and McGuire's pub manager witness, after a lot of thought, had picked Warren Shackleton from an array of mugshots as one of the men he had seen in Infirmary Street. I hadn't been sure how he would hold up against an aggressive defence advocate, but that wasn't a factor any more, since dead men can't be tried. I was fairly certain also that our scientists would find evidence that would place the two of them at the scene. DNA was coming into use then and in its era everybody leaves a trace behind.

The obvious thing for me to do, in PR terms, was to issue a statement announcing that two men who had been our prime suspects, and one other thought to be involved, were those who'd been found dead in Newcastle. I knew they'd have been the top story in the Tyneside press that morning, and expected them to make the national news, if only briefly.

Yes, I would do that, but not personally, just a couple of paragraphs put out through the press office. I had no intention of exposing myself at a media briefing to follow-up questions to which I had no answers.

On the face of it, I'd be able to close the book on the case. Show the prosecutors our evidence and they'd sign off on Milburn and Shackleton as Marlon's murderers, no further proceedings necessary. Fine, but I would know that we'd come up short, and so would my bosses. Not only that, there were half a dozen good crime reporters in the city who'd work it out too. Most important of all, though, I'd never be satisfied myself with a job half done. So, the investigation would not be closed. The search would go on, as discreetly as possible, but it would go on, and I'd be judged on the outcome.

As for the Weir-McCann murder hunt, I didn't feel in touch with that one at all. There had been an early lead in the Watson case, but no such luck with the other. We'd established that the two had been killed by the same man, with the same weapon, but we hadn't a clue why, and he was still out there. A third murder, and the press would have hysterics. Something had to tie the victims together, beyond the fact that they'd each survived the same sink-estate school, but we weren't close to finding it. The press clipping about Mia? A curiosity, that was all. No . . . I frowned . . . not one, but two: the fact that he had it at all, and the question that it posed. What was a guy who worked on the shop floor in B&Q doing with a page torn out of a communications trade magazine? 'Now that is interesting, Skinner,' I murmured. 'Where the hell would Weir have got that from?' *And who the hell's going to tell us?* I added silently, and my flicker of optimism faded. 'Bugger!' I sighed, as I stood up, my arse cold from its ancient seat.

I'd left my phone and my house keys in my jacket in the Discovery. A risk casually taken, I realised as I walked back; police officers have no personal immunity to theft. It was still there, though. I could see the car, intact, as I crested the rise. The two youngsters were gone; it could only have been a quickie. I checked the mobile as soon as I was back in the driver's seat. It showed three missed calls, all from the same number: Mia. As I was looking at the readout she rang again. I hesitated before answering. Indeed, I almost pressed 'reject', before I gave in to her persistence and hit the green key instead.

'Yes.'

'Bob, it's me.'

'I know who it is,' I replied. 'I have this clever phone that tells me.'

'Look, I'm sorry,' she said. 'I was way over the top this morning. You scared me, that was all.'

'Yes, I did,' I conceded, 'and I'm sorry for that. But you are right, you were way over the top.'

'Yes, I'm sorry.'

'Accepted, for fuck's sake!' I snapped.

'So you're still mad at me.'

'No,' I told her, regretting my flash of temper. 'No, I'm not. Mia, I don't know what I am, I don't know what to say. Nothing, I suppose.'

'I'm not usually like that. I don't know why I behaved that way.' She paused for a couple of seconds. 'But maybe I do,' she went on. 'Maybe I haven't come as far from home as I thought. Do you want to give it another try?' she asked. I didn't hear total conviction in the question.

I didn't have to think about the answer. 'No, I don't. It's not a snub, Mia. And it's not "Wham bam, thank you, ma'am" either. Last night was great, but this morning was not. Each of us saw a side of the other that we didn't like, and that's not going to go away. So best put a full stop after it.'

'I suppose,' she sighed, then she chuckled. 'You weren't so bad yourself, for a tired old thirty-something. No hard feelings, then.'

'None. See you around. Who knows, I might even send one of my guys along to talk to your audience about the evils of crime.'

'Mm,' she said. 'That DC Martin would do nicely.'

'He'd probably agree with you. So long.'

*So long indeed*, I thought, relieved, *and no damage done*. As I drove away, it occurred to me that I might have asked her whether she could recall the names McCann and Weir, then remembered that the task was being assigned to Mackie and Steele, and let it lie.

Only McGuire was in the office when I returned, minding the phones while the rest were at lunch. 'The press officer called, boss,' he told me. 'He's had a couple of people looking for updates on Weir and McCann.'

I called Inspector Hesitant back and dictated a short statement about the Marlon suspects having turned up dead in Newcastle. 'Don't go beyond that,' I warned him. 'Stick to my script; no initiative to be shown. As for the other one, you can tell them the truth, that we're trying to establish whether there's a link between the two victims beyond their schooldays.' I'd ordered him not to use his initiative; that was something he liked to hear.

I went back out to the front office and sat on the desk facing McGuire. The tailor-made suit had gone, replaced by jeans and a brown suede bomber jacket. It hung over the back of his chair. His shirt had the words 'Hugo Boss' embroidered on the breast pocket, and I was pretty certain that it wasn't a fake from a market stall. I might have been worried about the young man's expensive tastes, had I not known that he came from a wealthy family.

'What do you think of the job so far?' I asked him.

'As a whole, sir, or CID?'

'CID.'

For once in our short acquaintance he looked serious. 'It's where I want to be,' he said firmly. 'Nowhere else. When I joined the force, that was my aim. I'll tell you, sir, my folks were not best pleased when

I told them what I was going to do. I'd three different options open to me: construction like my old man, join my mother in her temp hire business, or go into the Viareggio firm with my Uncle Beppe. I did a bit in each of them, and decided that none was right for me. When it comes to building things, I'm crap. Placing secretaries by the week in banks and PR firms? Look at me, for Christ's sake. Who could take me seriously?' I studied his massive frame and agreed. 'As for my papa's businesses . . . I'll always think of them as his, not my uncle's; he's a knobhead . . . I'd have fitted in there, but I'd have wound up fighting with my cousin Paula.' I'd run across young Paula Viareggio once, in Madogs while on a date with a girlfriend of brief tenure. She looked sensational, but the word 'feisty' could have been coined for her. I could see that she and her cousin would be an explosive combination.

'So,' McGuire continued, 'I told everyone politely that I was going my own way, and I applied to join the force. Do you know how naive I was, boss? I thought you could apply just for CID. It came as a hell of a shock when they told me I'd have to wear a uniform for a while first. But I put it on. I've given myself till age twenty-eight to make it. If not, it's back to importing Italian produce.'

'How old are you now?' I asked.

'Twenty-six.'

'Congratulations, kid. You've made it two years ahead of schedule.'

His face lit up; he seemed to radiate. McGuire is the most charismatic man I've ever known, and I've met a few worthy of that adjective. 'You mean I'm staying? It's not temporary?'

I nodded. 'You're signed up. The head of CID's approved your transfer from uniform.'

'Aw, that's great, boss,' the big guy exclaimed. 'Wait till my mate McIlhenney hears about this. He will shite bricks of pure green envy. He and I had a bet on who'd make it into plain clothes first.'

'Where is he just now, this pal of yours that I keep hearing about?'

'Intimidating sailors in Leith.'

'Maybe I should take a look at him too,' I said. 'But first things first. Since you are on the strength, give me a view on the Watson inquiry. Where do we stand on it?'

He sucked in a breath. 'Well,' he ventured, 'from what I've been told, we know that the guys that wrote him off have been remodelled themselves, and we had no leads beyond them. Newcastle answered the mobile phone question while you were out. No joy there either; none found on any of them. If Milburn and his pal were taxi drivers like they say, that's beyond belief, so somebody's mopped them up too, as those guys did with Marlon's.' He frowned. 'Looks like we're up against it, sir. Down to last resort stuff. *Cherchez la femme*, and all that.'

'Say that again.' I must have spoken sharply, for he looked concerned.

'Sorry, boss,' he murmured. 'I was just being flip. Like the French say, when all else fails, look to the woman.'

I laughed. 'Maybe you were being flip, but do you know what? You're going to be a great detective, Mario. There are some, the great majority, like Fred and me, that mix methodical with a wee bit of instinct, but every so often there's someone who just relies on flair, luck and brass neck, yet gets the job done better than anyone else. You're going to be one of them; I can sense it.'

He looked at me, puzzled. 'Thanks, boss, but what the fuck do you mean? Why? What did I say?'

'Tony Manson's woman,' I answered. 'The one he took to Ibiza. We've ignored her all along. We don't know who she is, and he took pains to make sure that nobody else does either. It's time we found out.'

'Maybe, sir, but how? People sign in as Mr and Mrs Smith all the time.' His eyes gleamed. 'Christ, I do often enough.'

'Not on an aeroplane passenger list, they don't. Check it out, Mario, check it out. Manson flew to Ibiza from Newcastle the Sunday before last. Get on to the airport and find out who the carrier was, then contact them and find out who was with him.'

'There'll have been a couple of hundred people on board. How'll we know out of all of them?'

I shook my head. 'Thank God the magic doesn't work all the time,' I said. 'That would be too much to take. She'll be the one in the next fucking seat to him, son, that's how. Now go to it.'

As I left him leafing through the Yellow Pages . . . he had a lot to learn, but I couldn't teach him all of it . . . Fred Leggat, Jeff Adam and Andy Martin returned from lunch. I called the DI into my office and told him about McGuire's brainstorming, and of the instructions I'd given to the press officer. 'Make sure that everybody knows the party lines on both, Fred,' I warned. 'Nothing beyond; not even pub talk.'

'Will do,' he promised. 'By the way, DCS Stein called while you were out, boss. He said he'd like a word.'

'How about two?' I growled. 'Those being "fuck" and "off".'

Leggat laughed. 'You tell him that, boss. I've got a pension to safeguard.'

In truth, I had no reason to moan about Alf. He was my line manager, and he was entitled to be kept in the loop. I walked up to his office, knowing that he'd be there. My stomach was rumbling as I reached his door. I'd burned through my trucker's breakfast.

'Come in, son,' he greeted me. Most of the time, Alf was avuncular. 'You look fucking knackered. I can guess why. Inspector Hesitant sent me copies of the statements you issued.' He saw my expression change and added, 'Don't go and tear into him, now; it's a standing order he has. Before that, though, I had a call from my opposite number in Newcastle asking for any help we can give him. There's a lot of heat on down there. The guy they found after you'd left was a hell of a fucking mess apparently. Something of a local character too, so his death's attracted special attention. Not just in the media either. He was big in the Masons, so there's interest within the Northumbria force, at the very top level.'

'That's all I need,' I grumbled. 'Pressure from the goat-shaggers, as a chum of mine calls them.'

'Shh,' Alf whispered. 'Don't let Proud Jimmy hear you.'

'The chief? Is he one?'

'Aye. High up, too.'

'Then you must be as well,' I pointed out, 'or you wouldn't know that.'

He beamed. 'We'll make a detective out of you yet, young Skinner. Now you know about us, you'd better join yourself.'

'Not a chance,' I assured him.

'Why not?'

'I'm too secretive for you guys.'

He stared at me, and then exploded in laughter.

'Let me give you an example, sir,' I said, then described the scene in Winston Church's kitchen in all its terrible detail.

By the time I was finished he was pale, and serious. 'You were there.'

I nodded. 'Andy and I. After we'd found him, the local talent got a bit nervous about our presence, so we got off our mark.'

'Good for you. That was the best thing to do.'

'What does their head of CID want from us?' I asked.

'He wants you to share your files on the Watson case, and to take a couple of his officers on to your team. How do you feel about that?'

I bounced it straight back to him. 'You're the gaffer.'

'No, Bob, it's your call.'

'Then it's no, twice. These men were killed because of Marlon Watson.' As I set out the facts for him, my thinking began to coalesce. 'They were hired, I believe, through Church, to extract information from him, and they were given a location where they could do the job undisturbed. They did it thoroughly. I don't know what they were trying to find out, or if they succeeded, but they were not the most subtle interrogators, and they killed him in the process. They were also careless. Early in our investigation we identified the van they'd used in Marlon's abduction, traced its owner, and asked Northumbria for assistance in locating him. You with me?'

'Aye, go on.'

'Right. After . . . I stress that, after . . . we'd made that request, the van was found burning, and our suspect, the man Milburn, went into hiding with his associate. Not immediately after the murder, boss, but two or three days after it. What does that tell you?'

'Leak,' Stein growled, immediately, looking not in the least like a favourite uncle.

'Exactly. For a while I had one major concern.' I told him frankly about my conversation with Manson, including my own recklessness, but said that he was eliminated as a suspect to my satisfaction. 'It can only be inside, boss; it must have come from one of our number. I trust my people, every one of them, so my assumption is that whoever tipped them off that we were on to them is in Newcastle, not here.'

'Why didn't Church go into hiding too?' the DCS asked, shrewdly.

'We didn't have any evidence against him, we still don't and we probably never will. Sir, I can't have officers from down there on my team. If I did, I'd have to detach one of ours to keep them under observation.'

281

He leaned back in his chair. 'Point taken, son,' he murmured. 'I'd better tell my southern colleague to start looking in his own midden.'

'No!' I said. 'Don't do that. I don't want to alert anyone. I want the world to think that we're closing the Watson investigation with the deaths of these men. I want to put everyone at their ease, including the inside man, for I want him too. When I find him, I'll hit the bastard hardest of all, for he must have known that he was setting these two guys up to be killed.'

When I got back to the office, I checked on McGuire's progress. He had managed to track down the carrier, a small charter operation based in Glasgow, but its airport representative wouldn't release information without her boss's approval, and he was proving hard to find. 'If they give you any more trouble, tell him that we're friendly with HM Customs and Excise,' I suggested, 'and that a short-notice VAT inspection can be fixed up any time. That usually works.'

I left him to get on with it, for it was time for me to leave to collect Alison. I called ahead, and she was waiting for me at the front door. 'Redpath's been delayed on the road,' she told me as she climbed in. 'Tailback somewhere down the A1, his manager says.'

'When is there not?' I responded. 'That's fine. I'd rather be waiting for him when he gets there anyway. It removes any scope for misunderstanding.'

'Misunderstanding of what?'

'The fact that we're serious. You know what murder inquiries are like; witnesses tend to get nervous when we turn up. If he chose to avoid us, his company could hardly hold him there.'

The haulage depot wasn't actually in Haddington, but on the outskirts. We found it easily enough, but there was no welcoming committee. The office was a Portakabin and it was locked. A couple of red-liveried lorries were parked in the compound, but there was no one around.

'I wonder what the manager's done,' Alison chuckled. 'Looks as if he got nervous as well.'

She and I sat in the car and waited, for there was nothing else to do. I told her about the holding statement I'd issued on her investigation, and about the heat that had developed on Tyneside over Church's murder, but I kept the matter of the leak to myself.

We had been there for fifteen minutes when my mobile sounded. It was Mario McGuire. 'I've finally tracked down the travel company's managing director, boss,' he announced, but I could tell from his voice that it wasn't all good news. 'He's got no problem with giving us the name we need, but when he called the Newcastle Airport office to tell the woman there to release it, she'd buggered off for the night. He's not being obstructive; he says there's nothing he can do.'

In fact there was; if McGuire shouted loud enough, the director could have contacted his employee as soon as she arrived home and sent her back to give us what we were after. I was about to tell him that when a red articulated truck slowed at the entrance to the yard and turned in. 'Okay,' I conceded, 'but he has to get her in there at sparrow-fart tomorrow.'

'She will be, boss. The company's got a seven fifteen departure to Barcelona.'

'I wish I was on it.' I ended the call, and stepped out of the car. Alison and I waited until the vehicle was parked, then approached as the driver jumped down from the cab, a tall skinny guy with ginger hair and a full beard.

'Charles Redpath?' I began, holding my warrant card for him to see. 'We're police officers and we'd like a word.'

He didn't seem disturbed by us, in any way. 'That's me,' he said, his face expectant. 'What is it? Have you caught the swine that killed Albie? D'you need me for an identity parade?'

'No, I'm sorry,' I told him. 'We're not at that stage yet. Look, do you want to come and sit in my car?'

He glanced at it, with the air of someone who'd rather have sat in a hearse. 'Nah,' he decreed. 'We'll go and sit in the office. I've got the keys.'

We followed him across to the Portakabin. Inside, it was Spartan, but I supposed that it served its purpose. There was a small private area to the left of the door, a toilet to the right, and half a dozen full-length lockers against the far wall. Redpath unlocked one of them. A suit and shirt hung inside. He offered us each a seat, but they looked like health and safety rejects, so we declined. 'What can I do for you then?' he asked.

'What school did you go to?'

Alison's question took him by surprise. 'Knox Academy, in Haddington. What's that got to do with it?'

'Never Maxwell Academy?'

'No.'

'So you didn't know Albie McCann from school. How did you meet?'

'I used to be a Lothian bus driver; I met Albie in the garage. I didn't like it, though. Some of the runs can be really dodgy late at night. So I took this job when the chance came up.'

She nodded. 'Good. That explains the connection between you. The reason for the question is that Albie and Archie Weir, the other murder victim, did go to the same school, although they weren't in the same year. That's the only link between them, and we're wondering if it relates to their murders in some way. If it does . . . we need to find out how.'

'I see.' He scratched at his beard. A family of magpies could have set up home in there.

'So think carefully. I know you told the other officers who interviewed you that you didn't know Archie Weir. Are you still sure that Albie McCann never mentioned him?'

'Absolutely. Weir was my mother's name before she married my dad. I wouldn't have forgotten that.'

'I'll accept that,' she conceded. 'Did he ever talk about any other of his schoolmates?'

He knitted his heavy brows. 'There was one he mentioned a lot,' he murmured. 'I even met him, only a couple of weeks ago. I'd arranged to meet Albie in the Guildford Arms, up in town, for a quick one, about half five. When I turned up, this guy was there too. His name was Telfer, Don Telfer, and he was at Maxwell Academy.'

'Can you describe him?'

'I suppose. He's not very tall, about five eight, maybe. Slim guy, well turned out, clean-shaven. He's got a scar on his face but otherwise that's about it.'

'I don't suppose you know where we can find him?'

Redpath laughed. 'Yes, I do. In the middle of the North Sea. Let's figure this out. That was a Wednesday night, yes, and he said that he would be going offshore again on the Friday, for another six-week trip. He works on an oil production platform. He's the radio officer. He said that he looks after all their communications, and maintains all the equipment. He even runs an on-board broadcasting station.'

It hasn't happened very often, but that was one of the times in my career when a witness has said something that's made the hair at the back of my neck prickle with excitement. There were no prizes for guessing who had given Archie Weir that photocopied page.

'You haven't seen him since?' I asked.

'No. That was the only time. I wasn't with him for long. He and Albie left about half past six, and I went to meet my date.'

He had no more to tell us, so we thanked him and left. I drove past Haddington then turned left at Herdmanflat and climbed, heading for Aberlady and Gullane. Neither of us spoke, but we had plenty on our minds. I pulled into a parking place at the crest of the hill. 'Well?' Alison murmured.

'You tell me.'

'Let me make a call.' She took her mobile from her bag. 'Brian,' I heard her say when she was connected, 'have you or Stevie spoken to Mia Watson yet?' There was a pause. 'Okay. Tell him that when he does, he should ask her, as well as asking her if she remembers McCann or Weir from Maxwell Academy, whether the name Don Telfer means anything. Before that, though, he should trace all the Donald Telfers living in the Edinburgh area. The one we're looking for will be aged about twenty-eight, and works on an oil platform in the North Sea. We need to know which one. I want him to find out also if this Telfer subscribes to a magazine called *Radioweek*. While he's doing that, I want you to go back to McCann's mother's place. Go through his bedroom again, but this time you're looking for the same photocopy that was found in Weir's flat. It could easily have been overlooked when it was searched before, because we weren't looking for it. Call me as soon as you've done all that.' She finished, and turned to me. 'Did you get that?'

I nodded.

'Stevie's going to catch her at the radio station once she comes off air in a couple of hours. Brian'll let me know if he finds anything at the flat.'

'Good enough,' I said, as I restarted the car and swung on to the road. 'That's all we can do. You realise, don't you,' I added, 'that possession of that photocopy doesn't actually imply anything. It's probably entirely innocent, no more than Telfer finding it in one of his trade journals and saying to his buddies, "Hey, lads, remember that Watson lassie at the school? See what she's doing now?" We can't read anything more into it.'

'Are you kidding?' she exclaimed. 'If we find that same photocopy in McCann's flat, it shows a common interest in the Watson woman. We've linked all three men, I'm certain of it, and two of them are now dead, Bob. I can read plenty into that.'

'Yes, you're right,' I conceded, with the best grace I could muster. My thinking was off kilter where Mia was concerned. 'We don't even need that second photocopy to tie them together. One more chat with Robert Wyllie could be helpful, though; now we know about Telfer, he needs to be interviewed again. That should be easy. A talk with us will brighten his day at Saughton.'

'Didn't you know?' she said. 'His lawyer asked for bail after all, and the sheriff granted it.'

'His choice, but hopefully not his funeral.' I'd been bullshitting during the interview. I didn't really see Wyllie as a target. 'There's one blessing in this,' I went on. 'Unless he's gone missing too, Telfer's out of harm's way on his oil platform. As you say, two down so far. One still to go? I think we have to assume that. But why? That's the question.'

'Let's see what Mia says to Stevie; she might have the answer.'

# Fifteen

If Alex was taken aback, in the light of our morning phone conversation, to find Alison in the car when I picked her up from Daisy's, she made a brilliant job of hiding it. I felt ashamed of myself for putting her in that position, and deeply embarrassed that she should have seen me as a two-timing SoB. I had a flash of her later in life and knew what I'd do to someone who'd treated her as I had Alison. I made a mental note that I'd have to apologise to her, first chance I had. I made a second note to come clean with Alison too, but that moment would have to be chosen very carefully.

I tried to block my indiscretion from my mind as we settled in for the evening. Alison had gone out at lunchtime and bought herself a jumpsuit and fresh stuff for next day. I changed, so did Alex, and the three of us slopped around, looking for all the world like the nice wee domestic unit that we'd sworn not to become.

While my daughter went off to take care of her homework and, no doubt, to catch up on Airburst FM while she was at it, I started the evening meal, a starter of anchovies on tomato bread, Spanish style, followed by fried chicken, with steamed green vegetables. Alison stood in the kitchen, watching me at work, and sipping white wine. She was still talking shop. I tried to put her off, but she persisted. 'What happened,' she mused aloud, 'to make these three men victims? There must have been something, something serious. Could they have been dealing drugs?'

'It's possible,' I conceded. 'But how? Look at their jobs. A bus mechanic, a DIY shop assistant and a man who spends six weeks at a time out on the North Sea. None of those occupations are conducive to that business. Plus, if they were dealing, chances are at least one of them would have shown up on our radar on the drugs squad. Have you checked Weir and McCann for criminal convictions?'

'Automatically; McCann was clean, Weir was arrested at a Hibs Rangers game six years ago and done for breach of the peace. In other words, next to nothing. Maybe Telfer will throw up something, but he's got the sort of job that probably requires a degree of vetting, so I'm inclined to doubt that.'

'Let's put drugs to one side then,' I said. 'What else?'

She emptied her glass and went to refill it from the bottle on the work surface. 'No idea, but whatever it is,' she ventured, 'it may have happened within a fairly small window. Yes, it could be anything, a long-held grudge, but the only point of contact among them that we know about was two weeks ago . . .' she looked at the wall clock, ' . . . almost exactly two weeks ago, when Redpath met McCann and Telfer in the Guildford Arms, two days before Telfer said he was due back on the oil platform. So it's possible we're looking for something that happened within that period.'

'Then let's look,' I told her, 'wherever we can.'

'What would you do?'

'Well, if Telfer was off the pitch from Friday . . . I'd look at our own incident reports, for anything happening that Wednesday and Thursday that's still open, and see if I could find a line of inquiry.'

'Look where? Division by division?'

'You shouldn't have to: us department heads report everything important to the head of CID. Alf's exec should be able to show you everything within that time frame, and you can take it from there.'

My kitchen masterpieces were ready at seven thirty. Alex had just served the starters . . . one cooked, the other dished it up, that was our deal . . . when the inevitable happened. Alison's mobile ringtone sounded. 'I'm sorry,' she said, looking at its display. 'It's Mackie. I'll tell him I'll call him back later.'

'No, don't do that. Take it now, it's all right. You can catch up.'

I listened to her half of the discussion: 'Damn it! Never mind. You did? Excellent. Does he indeed? Thanks, see you tomorrow.' She ended the call, and turned to her anchovies and tomato bread.

'Well?' I asked.

'It'll keep. I'll tell you when we've eaten.'

'*Pas devant les enfants?*' my daughter murmured.

Alison blinked. 'Pardon?'

I frowned. 'She's showing off her French. "Not in front of the children?" is what she's saying. Yes, kid, exactly so.'

'I'll eat in my room if you like,' Alex snapped.

'If that's your choice,' I told her sternly.

She glared at me, picked up her plate and stalked out of the room.

'What the hell is up with her?' I exclaimed, as the door slammed.

'Given her age,' Alison replied, quietly, 'I could think of a couple of things, but the fact that she's just lost her grandpa, her late mother's father, might have quite a lot to do with it.'

Yet again, I felt like Shit of the Week. I excused myself and followed Alex upstairs. Her bedroom door was closed; I knocked on it. 'Go away!' she yelled.

'Don't pour water on a drowning man, baby,' I called to her. 'I'm here to say sorry. Can I come in?'

I waited for a few seconds, until I heard, 'If you must.' I stepped inside. She was sitting on her bed; the starter was on her desk, untouched. She looked up at me; her eyes were moist. 'What are you doing, Dad?'

'Making a complete buttock of myself, by falling out with the girl I love more than anyone else in the world.' I sat beside her and put an arm round her shoulders. 'I really am sorry, kid. I might be this great detective, but sometimes I don't have a clue what's going on inside my own head. I put you on the spot tonight without thinking about it. I'm an idiot.'

'No you're not. You're just like me. Grandpa's died, and now you can't stop thinking about Mum and you're hiding from it. Mia's not right for you, Pops.'

'I know that,' I told her. 'Maybe Alison isn't either, but she's good for me, and that's a start.'

'Then we shouldn't leave her down there on her own any longer, or she might go.'

I let her lead the way downstairs and followed her into the dining room. Our guest was still there, but most of her starter wasn't. 'I'm sorry, Ali,' I told her. 'Our little domestic is over. She can speak whatever bloody language she likes from now on.' I leaned over and kissed her: in front of the child, a first.

'I might as well tell you now,' she said cheerfully, 'while you two catch up.' I nodded, with a chunk of bread and anchovy in my hand.

'In order,' she continued, 'those three names meant nothing to our potential witness. However, Brian did find that same photocopy in McCann's room. Also, Stevie traced our Mr Telfer. He lives in Newhaven, he's a single man like Weir and McCann, he does subscribe to that magazine, by mail order, he works for Shell Exploration, and he is currently on one of their platforms in the Brent field, north-east of Shetland, where he's scheduled to remain until the end of June.'

'That's good,' I said. 'It means he can't do a runner when we go to interview him, unless he's some swimmer. Do you like helicopters?' I asked. 'Personally, I do not, but we can't wait for him to come onshore.'

'I've never been on one,' she admitted, 'but needs must. I wonder if they have newspapers delivered out there.'

I caught on. 'And if he knows about his two pals? If he does, he might be very pleased to see us.'

'Can't he come to you?' Alex chipped in.

'He's only a witness,' I explained, 'not a suspect. We've got no cause to haul him off his platform if he doesn't want to come.'

Because of the hiatus, the chicken was a little stringy and the vegetables were too steamed, but I was the only one who complained, and since it was my fault anyway, tough on me.

When we were finished and the dishwasher was stacked, Alex went off to her room to watch a TV serial she'd been following, or maybe she was simply being discreet.

'Want some music?' I asked.

'Mmm.'

I dug out an Elvis Costello hits CD and put it on. The first track was called 'Alison'. I've still got the CD, but I never play that song any more, even though it's still my favourite by either Elvis. Aileen did once, last year, and I had to explain why there were tears in my eyes.

I sat in my armchair and my Alison sat on me, folded in my lap. She wasn't wearing shoes. I took her foot in my hand, and began to massage it, very gently. 'Saw this movie with Myra,' I murmured, 'when we were both about eighteen. It was called *Stay Hungry*. It's best known today for being one of Arnie Schwarzenegger's first, but there's a scene in it where Jeff Bridges and Sally Field are sitting on a staircase and he takes her foot, just like this, and starts talking to her about what a wonderful piece of architecture it is, and . . .' I kissed her, '. . . it goes on from there. I wish I could remember the dialogue.'

'You're doing all right ad-libbing,' she purred, then gasped as I reached the soft area at the back of her toes. 'It obviously made a big impression on you.'

'And on Myra. She slipped her shoe off, right there in the cinema, and planked her foot in my lap.'

'We must see if we can find it on video.' She put her head on my shoulder. 'What do I give you, Bob?'

It took me a couple of minutes to find what I hoped were the right words. 'Peace, companionship and good, friendly sex.'

'Friendly? How about great?'

'That too, but friendly's just as important. You set your expectations there, so that when you get to great it's all the greater.'

She laughed, softly. 'You talk some real mince sometimes.'

'I know. I'm more of an action man. So? What do I give you?'

'You make me feel . . . not alone. You make me feel good about myself. You give me . . . as much as a girl could reasonably hope for. But . . .'

'Yeah, there's always a but.'

'But . . .' she continued, 'there's still a part of you that's locked away, a part of you that I'll never reach. The woman who does . . . she'll see me off, for she'll be the one for you. For now, though, there's one other thing you make me feel and that's happy. Take it as it comes?'

I nodded. The night before was the past, boxed up, and it could stay there, among my other dark secrets. 'Deal. We take it as it comes.'

Next morning Alex was up first; we were under no pressure, for we had a call to make on the way into Edinburgh. I waited until the commuter traffic had tailed off before we left. We had talked no shop all morning, but as we passed through Aberlady, Alison raised something that had been on my mind. 'With everything that's happening in this investigation,' she said, 'I hope we're all right for sailing this weekend.'

'Me too,' I confessed. 'I've got two of them on the go, remember; twice the risk. Thornie's funeral is sacrosanct. Whatever happens, we will be there. For the rest, we keep our fingers crossed.'

'But if I have to go offshore to interview this man Telfer . . .'

'It's not just you, it's the two of us; we're both going. But I reckon he'll keep till Monday. Have someone contact the platform operator . . . Shell, wasn't it . . . and make arrangements for us to fly out then. Telfer doesn't need to know we're coming either.'

'But don't all the platform communications go through him?' she pointed out.

'If they do, and Shell play ball, we'll spin him a line. We can tell him it's an equipment inspection.'

'That sounds okay.' She paused. 'But Bob, if something else comes up, there's no need for me to be at the funeral.'

'I'd like you to be there, come what may.'

'Are you sure about that?' she asked. 'We'll have to leave our whereabouts with the office. Won't it be a bit like putting a notice about you and me on the bulletin board?'

'I've already told Fred Leggat where I'll be going, but you could always tell your troops you're taking personal time, and leave it at that. That wouldn't be a lie.'

'Brian Mackie knows us both. He'll figure it out for sure.'

I laughed. 'Ali, I don't care. When we get into town I'm going to drop you right at the front door of your office, and kiss you farewell. I'm done with furtive. We are as we are.'

We drove on, joining the A1 dual carriageway and heading towards Edinburgh. We were caught up in a short tailback, at the end, but we left it when we took the roundabout outlet that led to the B&Q store. Given the time of the morning, the place was a customer-free zone. There was a customer service point just inside the entrance. Alison approached the woman on duty; they had a brief conversation and I saw her show her warrant card, before the loudspeakers boomed, 'Robert Wyllie to customer desk, please. Robert Wyllie to customer desk.'

Staff discipline must have been good, for only seconds passed before I saw him appear at the far end of an aisle. He saw me too, and stopped in his tracks. I shook my head, smiled and beckoned him on.

'What now?' he sighed, as he approached. 'You folk never let go. What are you going to charge me with this time?'

'Nothing,' said Alison, affably. 'Another couple of questions, Mr Wyllie, that's all.'

'About what?'

'That would be whom. Do you know, or know of, a man called Donald Telfer?'

He frowned, but only for a second. 'Aye,' he exclaimed, as if he was pleased to come up with an answer we'd like. 'He's a pal of Archie's. They were at the school thegither.'

'Ever met him?'

'Once or twice. He's no around all that much; he works on the rigs.'

'What sort of a man is he?'

'A clever bastard.' Wyllie's summation was instant. 'He's got a good job there, on the technical side, he told me. Likes a drink, though. They're no' allowed any when they're away, but he makes up for it when he comes back.'

'Is he aggressive on it?' I asked.

'No, he's different. He gets quiet and gets a nasty look about him.'

Alison took over again. 'We want to ask you about a couple of days during the week before last. The Wednesday and the Thursday. Can you remember what Archie Weir was up to on those days?'

He nodded vigorously. It seemed that impending prosecution had turned him into the world's most cooperative witness. 'Oh aye. We were here as usual on the Wednesday. I mind, 'cos that's our old folks' discount day. The place is always heavin' wi' pensioners. I asked Archie if he fancied a pint after work, but he said no, that he was meeting Telf, and another bloke from their old school, 'cos Telf was back off tae the rig at the weekend.' I thought he was finished, but he wasn't. 'They must have got well hammered,' he continued, 'for Archie called in sick the next morning, and he was off all day.'

'Are you certain?'

'Absolutely,' he assured her. 'Will that help?'

'We'll know in due course,' she replied.

'I meant, will it help me?'

'If it helps us make an arrest,' I intervened. 'We'll need you as a witness, so you'll be off the hook. Fair enough?'

'Aye,' he said. I'd just dealt him a 'stay out of jail' card, and he knew it.

Alison thanked him and we left him to get on with his day. 'Well,' she exclaimed. 'That was worth doing.'

'Too right it was. Next step being—'

'You don't need to tell me,' she admonished me. 'As soon as I get to the office, I'll check with the bus garage and find out whether McCann turned up for work that Thursday. And that photocopy; it still interests me.'

'Mia told Steele she couldn't remember the names,' I reminded her. 'And the article doesn't necessarily connect. The likeliest explanation is that it was Telfer showing his pals how well their old schoolmate was doing, no more than that.'

'Granted,' she said as I drove off. 'Okay, I'll have someone check on McCann's whereabouts. Mind you, if he did turn up for work bright as a button . . '

'I know,' I sighed. 'If Telfer was a suspect we could bring him to us, otherwise it means we're still on that fucking helicopter.'

'Come on, Braveheart,' she chuckled. 'They can't be that bad.'

'They are. Nasty smelly things and most of their pilots go deaf in later life. Please God let us find something reported on those days that fits the three of them.'

'Eh,' Alison ventured. 'How do I approach DCS Stein for this information?'

'I find that on your knees usually works. But happily, you don't have to go that far. He has a bright-eyed, wet-eared assistant, DC Dorothy Shannon, a friendly girl, from what I've heard. She gets the reports, and she's your point of contact. Mention my name, and she'll give you what there is.'

'As long as she hasn't been friendly to you,' she murmured.

'I only go for inspectors and above; offers of friendship from the lower ranks are rejected.'

I dropped her at the front door of her office and set her on her way with the promised kiss. It was witnessed by PC Charlie Johnston, who was many things but not a divulger of information unless it suited his purpose of the moment.

When I walked into the Serious Crimes Unit, the four guys were at their desks. Leggat, Adam and Martin were all heads down, but Mario McGuire jumped to his feet as soon as I entered. I flagged him to follow me into my room. 'You have the look of a boy with an apple for the teacher,' I declared as I hung my jacket on the back of my chair. 'Peel it for me,' I said as I sat.

'I think I've got a name, boss. That useless airport rep spent an hour airside before she got round to calling me, but finally she did, about half an hour ago. Tony Manson had an aisle seat, and the passenger sitting next to him was a bloke called Hamilton. But in seat D ... he was in C ... there was a woman called Alafair Drysalter, Mrs.'

'That's not the most common name in Edinburgh,' I remarked. 'In fact, I can only think of one.'

'That's right, boss. Derek Drysalter, the Hibs player. I've already checked with the council department that keeps the voters' roll. There's only one Drysalter household in Edinburgh. Derek and his wife, Alafair.'

'Fucking hell, Mario,' I chuckled. 'Footballers' wives. What does that old ram Manson think he's at?'

'Whatever it is, he's a lucky bastard.' He took a sheet from the file he was carrying and put it on my desk. 'I know a guy on the *Evening News* picture desk,' he said. 'I can trust him to keep his mouth shut, so I took a chance and asked him to check their library. He faxed that across to me a couple of minutes ago.'

It was a photograph taken, going on some artwork in the background, at a Hibs gathering. The couple shown were in their early twenties, both dolled up in designer evening clothes. He was tall and lean, with the build you'd expect on someone who'd scored twenty-seven goals in the season past, more than half of them with his head. She was a stereotype, all blonde bouffant with professional make-up and wearing a dress that looked as if it was held up only by her nipples.

'Jesus,' I murmured. 'Do we know where the boy Derek was while his wife was pole-dancing with Tony?'

'At a training camp with the Scotland squad, for the American trip. He'll be pissed off about missing it.'

Something in his tone made me glance up from the picture. 'What do you mean?' I asked.

He looked back at me, in surprise. 'Haven't you seen the papers this morning, boss? Derek Drysalter's in hospital. Both his legs are broken and both his kneecaps are shattered; hit and run. He was out walking his dogs last night, near their house on Blackford Hill, and somebody whacked him and drove away.'

I stared at him. 'You're kidding, aren't you?'

'I wish I was,' he sighed. 'He's a crackin' player, even if his wife is a slag.'

'Mario, I wasn't doubting your word. I'm just wondering about a hit and run driver who's so accurate that he managed to inflict exactly the injuries you'd want to put on a footballer, especially when the guy's famously quick on his feet. Were the dogs hit?'

'I don't know, boss.'

'Were there any witnesses to the accident? Did anyone see the car, or even hear it?'

'I haven't . . .' It was as if I'd eaten his apple and wanted a punnet of strawberries to follow.

'No, of course not; because you haven't had time, or been told to do it. No blame. We have to interview Derek Drysalter. From Blackhall they'd have taken him to the Royal for sure. Check that he's still there.' I frowned as I recalled something from the sporting almanac in my head. 'Mario,' I said, 'I'm no Hibbie, but wasn't he a big signing for them last summer?'

'Yes, a record. They broke the bank for him.'

'And they signed him from?'

'Newcastle United.'

'Wow,' I murmured. 'You confirm where Drysalter is, then find out who's investigating the hit and run, and tell them I want to know what they've achieved so far. While you're doing that, I've got a call to make, and then we're off to see the victim, whether he's receiving visitors or not.'

As he left to get on with his task, I picked up the phone and called Northumbria CID. DI McFaul was in his office when they put me through. I could tell by just one word, 'Yes!' that he was harassed.

'Ciaran, Bob Skinner, Edinburgh.'

'Oh, sorry, sir, didn't mean to be rude.'

'You're entitled. No progress, then.'

'No,' he replied, 'and my boss is giving me shit.'

'I know the feeling. Listen, I need to ask you something, just between you and me. It's a favour, and it needs to be handled very discreetly, since the guy involved is high profile. The footballer, Derek Drysalter. You may have heard that he had an accident last night.'

'Yes. From what I read he'll be lucky if he ever plays again.'

'I may have a say in that,' I told him. 'I'd like you to check something for me, and I repeat, very quietly. When he was at St James's Park, was he connected with Winston Church, in any way, or was a link even suspected?'

'Footballers attract a lot of hangers-on,' he said, 'and in turn some footballers hang on to a lot of funny people. I'll have a look.'

I left him to it and went back into the general office. McGuire was still on the phone, so I waited for him to finish. 'He's not in the Royal any more, boss,' he told me. 'He's been transferred to the Murrayfield, the private hospital. His consultant's a man called Jacobs.'

'Then I'd like to talk to him: the consultant, that is.'

'That'll be easy enough, boss.' He grinned. 'His secretary says that he wants to speak to us. He's due to operate on Drysalter at midday, so I've made an appointment for you at eleven.'

'For us, you mean. You're coming with me.'

He beamed; I'd never seen greater enthusiasm. 'The investigation into the accident's being run out of St Leonards,' he volunteered. 'They're still trying to trace the vehicle involved, but they've got no witnesses other than Drysalter himself, and his description's vague. He was found in a pretty deserted street, on the way up to the Royal Observatory, by a man from a house over a hundred yards away. He was screaming loud enough for him to hear above the telly, even from that distance.'

'Who's running the investigation?'

'DS Varley's in charge.'

'Not any more he isn't Tell Jock that it ties into one of ours, and ask them to send over all the paperwork he's generated so far.'

'Will he take that from me, boss? I'm just a front office plod to him.'

'No, you're DC McGuire, Serious Crimes. That's how you introduce yourself, then you ask him, nicely.'

The Murrayfield was a general purpose hospital; it catered for most ailments of the well-to-do in Edinburgh, and of those with occupational health insurance. At first sight it was a smaller version of the hotel that was its neighbour on Corstorphine Road. As we stepped out of the Discovery, an elephant trumpeted; the site was next to Edinburgh Zoo. I'd often wondered whether patients coming out of anaesthetic wondered whether they'd woken up in Africa.

At first sight Derek Drysalter's consultant might have been an exhibit himself. He was a bear of a man, about my height, and still as muscular in the shoulders and arms as a weightlifter, although he must have been pushing sixty. 'Paul Jacobs,' he said as we were shown into his consulting room.

He went straight to the point once the introductions were over. 'I'm intrigued that we should be calling each other about this, Superintendent. What prompted you, may I ask?'

I wanted frankness from him, so I didn't hold back. 'Your patient has become involved in a live investigation on our books. Whether it's as a suspect or just as an injured party, we don't know yet, but in the circumstances I need to be certain of the facts of the case.'

'I'm not surprised,' the surgeon replied. 'If this is a hit and run, then the driver's the most meticulous I've ever seen. Take a look.' He rose, walked across to a lit viewing box, and placed an X-ray exposure on it.

'This shows a fracture of the right femur, the thigh bone. The impact was from the side, so if this was a car, he was half-turned towards it. The man is six feet one inches tall, so again, if this injury came from a vehicle, it was either a lorry, or it had bull bars fitted.' He removed the print and replaced it with two more.

'This is where the so-called driver got really clever. There are fractures to the tibia and fibula of both legs, and both patellae are completely shattered, beyond repair. Since Mr Drysalter would have been unable to stand after the first impact, whichever it was, the driver must have hit him at least twice when he was in mid-air. Stuff and nonsense! The gentleman was attacked by people wielding metal bars or, more commonly these days, baseball bats, in a way that caused maximum damage without putting his life in danger. There are no injuries other than those I've shown you; no cuts, no scrapes, no broken skin. That on its own would make a nonsense of the hit and run notion. I don't have any ethical problem telling you this, incidentally. It's what I would say if I was called to give evidence in any criminal or civil hearing.'

'Have you said this to him?' I asked.

'That's not my job; I have to deal with what's on the table, not establish how it got there. I've been instructed by his employer to try to save his career, but if I do, it'll be the finest achievement of mine. Apart from rejoining the fractures, and at least two of them will need pinning, I'm going to have to rebuild both knees, repair the damaged ligaments and replace both kneecaps. With luck, he'll be able to walk without crutches in six months, maybe even jog in a further year, but football? No.'

I saw McGuire frown. 'That'll be a calamity for the supporters,' I said, 'like this one here. Can we talk to him before you operate? I don't imagine he'll be up to much for a while afterwards.'

'Yes, you may; he's still in his room. He's full of diamorphine, but he won't have had his pre-med yet, so he'll still be compos mentis.'

I thanked the consultant. His secretary led us from his office to a wing on the other side of the building, stopping at a door with the number five. 'This is Mr Drysalter's room,' she announced, and was about to open the door when I stopped her.

'Fine, thanks,' I said. 'But I need to speak to someone before we go in.' I dug out my mobile and called McFaul. 'Got anything for me yet?'

'As much as I'm going to,' he replied. 'There was a link between Winston and your footballer when he was down here. Church owned a small bookmaking chain, and Drysalter liked the horses, and the dogs, and occasionally two flies crawling up a wall.'

'Was he good at it?'

'Are those lads ever any good? The word is he dropped a million into the old Prime Minister's pocket. Most of his signing-on fee when he was transferred went to clear off his debts.'

'Habits like that are hard to kill. Thanks, Ciaran. That's very useful information.'

'Do you really think this could be our man?' McFaul asked.

'No, but at this moment, I'm not ruling him out completely. I'll know more in about ten minutes.'

I ended the call, knocked on the door of room number five and walked in. The footballer was alone, propped up on pillows in a hospital bed, his mangled legs protected by a cage. His hair was dishevelled and the stubble on his chin emphasised his paleness. He looked round as we entered and I could see chemically controlled agony in his eyes.

When I told him who we were, he moaned. 'Oh, not just now, please.'

'I'm sorry, Mr Drysalter, but it has to be. You're going to be post-op for a while and this can't wait. We need to find the people who worked you over.'

Fear mixed with the pain. 'It was a hit and run,' he protested. 'I told the other cops.'

'You lied to the other cops, son. Don't try it on with me. I'll make this as quick as I can, and then you can go to sleep for as long as you like. How did you come to know Tony Manson?'

I could see him shrink into himself very slightly, as if he was accepting something inevitable. 'I'm a member of his casino.'

'Given your gambling record in Newcastle, I'll bet he was glad to see you. How much do you owe him?'

'About forty grand. I've got a limit now.'

'Does your wife go there with you?'

'Quite often, yes.'

'Did you tell her to be nice to Tony?' I asked.

For the first time he looked something other than beaten. 'No! What the fuck do you mean by that?'

'How long has her affair with Manson been going on?'

'What do you mean?' he gasped. I had an uncomfortable feeling that I really had surprised him.

'Come on, you know she's been playing away.'

'Yes.' His voice cracked a little. 'I've suspected for a wee while. But I didn't think it was with Tony, honest to God. No, I don't believe that.'

'When did you know about her for sure?'

'I found out when the kennels rang to confirm a booking for the dogs, while I was away with the Scotland team. I took the call, and I knew something was funny. She'd never said anything about going away. I didn't let on afterwards that I knew about the booking, and she never mentioned it.'

'And you are still saying that you didn't know she was going away with Manson?'

'I didn't, honest.'

'Winston Church. When was the last time you saw him?'

'Last summer, when I gave him a wedge of money to square off what I owed him.'

'A million, I heard.'

'And a bit.'

'He let you run with that size of debt?'

'I am who I am, mister. I earn silly money.'

'I suppose,' I conceded. 'You haven't seen him since.'

'No.'

'And you don't know he's dead?'

'He's what? When?' I was looking into his eyes, and I believed him. *Fuck!* I thought.

'Yes. He was murdered, a couple of days ago.'

'Jesus.'

'So,' I continued, 'you went off to your training camp, without asking your wife where she was going?'

'Right. I was going to, but I bottled it. I . . . nothing.'

'What?'

'Nothing, flash of pain that's all.'

'When did you come back?'

'Late Sunday afternoon.'

'Where was the camp?'

'Dubai.'

'Did you go for the dogs? We know that your wife wasn't back then.'

He shook his head. 'No. I went straight to a supporters' dinner in the King James Hotel. I was picking up a Player of the Season award, and it was the only night that suited. I got home at half past ten; Alafair was home and so were the dogs.'

I pointed to the cage. 'So why this?'

'I don't know,' he muttered.

'With respect,' I said, 'that's bollocks.'

'Fuck you. I'm not saying anything about it, okay?'

'Who attacked you? Or aren't you saying that either?'

'Too fucking right I'm not. You can sit on my legs and I still won't tell you. I don't know him anyway.'

'Him?' I exclaimed. 'One man did all that?'

Drysalter pursed his lips and stared at the cage. 'Nothing,' he whispered.

'Listen,' I told him. 'You're right to be afraid of Manson, but with your help we can put him away.'

He looked up at me again, eyes narrow. 'Are you really saying this was Tony?' he asked.

'I'm like you, Derek,' I replied. 'I'm saying nothing. Good luck under the knife, and with your next career. Come on, Mario.' I turned and left him to his appointment with Mr Jacobs.

'Do you really think he didn't know his wife was shagging Manson, boss?' McGuire asked, once we were outside.

'Having seen him, I don't believe that he did. That kid's naive. He lives much of his life cloistered away with his teammates doing what he's told, eating what he's given, even sleeping to a timetable. When he's not doing that he spends his leisure time in the bookie's or the casino, so I can understand him being blind to what the wife was up to. But one thing interests me. Somebody gave him a doing, but his first thought wasn't Manson. Let's see how that one plays.'

'What do we do now?'

'We pay a couple of visits, but in the right order. Did Jock Varley give you the Drysalters' address?'

He produced a notebook from his pocket. 'Yes, sir. I've got it here.' He read it out.

'That's where we're going first,' I told him. I had a notion that Alafair would be at home, and of what we would find there. 'While we're on the way, I want you to dig out what you can about her.'

'I've got something already, boss,' he ventured, with the slightly tentative air of a man who was anxious not to appear to be a smartarse. 'The photo that my *News* pal sent me was used alongside an article. It was one of a series of features on players' wives, Hibs and Hearts, so I got him to send that as well.'

'Did it tell you much?'

'Not a lot. It said she's twenty-five, was brought up in Hamilton by a single-parent mum, who's now dead, went to the local high school, went to drama school in Glasgow, took modelling jobs between acting parts, her work name being her maiden name, Alafair McGrew, and met her husband three years ago when she did a photoshoot with the Scotland squad. Now, she says, her life is Derek and her dogs.'

'And her gangster on the side. Come on.' We climbed into the car and I headed for Blackford Hill. 'Did Varley interview her last night?' I asked when we were under way.

'No, sir. She was out last night when Derek had his . . .' he updated the situation '. . . was attacked. He was planning to see her today. But now . . .'

'It's down to us. It was convenient, her being out, Mario, wasn't it?'

'Convenient for who, boss?'

'Convenient for her not to be within miles of it.'

The Drysalter family home, a modern pile that couldn't make up its mind whether it was Rennie Mackintosh or Art Deco, stood back from the street behind a high wall, but its location meant that any paparazzo with half a brain could climb Blackford Hill and have a clear view of Alafair and Derek at play in their back garden. I parked outside. The gates were closed but, surprisingly, not locked, so I opened them and led the way up the path. As we approached the house we could hear barking from inside. The door opened, just a crack, no more, before we reached it, and a voice from within shouted, 'I thought I'd locked that gate. Look, bugger off, no press.'

I flashed my badge. 'I couldn't agree more, Mrs Drysalter. We're the police; it's about your husband.'

'I've got nothing to say to you either. Away you go and catch the guy that ran Derek over.'

'Open the door, please,' I said. The crack widened a little. 'No, all the way, please.' The dogs were still yowling somewhere in the background.

'I'm not letting you in.'

'You're not required to, but I would like to see you. I'm concerned about your well-being and I need to make sure that you're all right.'

'Rubbish,' she murmured, but she opened it, about halfway, enough for me to see that she was wearing wrap-around sunglasses, barely necessary on a morning that had begun overcast and looked like staying that way.

'Satisfied?' she drawled. She'd have slammed the door shut if it hadn't been for McGuire's size whatever moccasin blocking the way. As she pushed vainly against his strength, I reached out and whipped the shades away.

Both her eyes were blackened, and swollen, as was the bridge of her nose. I hadn't noticed before, but her lower lip was puffy as well. She snatched the Ray-Bans back from me and replaced them, but I'd seen enough. I'd expected that, or something similar.

'I'm still saying nothing!' she snapped. 'Now go . . . or I'll call your superior officer.'

'That would be DCS Stein,' I advised her. 'But it doesn't matter. You've told me everything I wanted to know. We're going to do you a favour now; we're not going to ask you anything at all.'

She took me by surprise; she slumped against the door and started to cry.

I let McGuire administer the sympathy. 'It's okay,' he said, gently. 'Is he often abusive?' She nodded. 'Do you want to make a complaint against him?'

She shook her head. 'No,' she whispered.

I leaned close to her. 'I think you have done already, kid,' I murmured, 'but not to us. Come on, Mario.'

We closed the gate carefully behind us. 'She had you going there, didn't she?' I said.

He nodded. 'I take a very dim view of domestic violence. I've seen too much of it in uniform.'

'We all do in our time,' I agreed, 'and I'm not condoning it. But remember three things: one, she's an actress; two, she doesn't know that we know she's been fucking Manson; three, everybody likes to have the police on their side. She's hoping we'll pat her on the head and go away. The bugger is, she's right; we'll have to.'

I checked my watch . . . the clock in the Discovery had packed up in the time of a previous owner. It showed twelve forty. 'The Police Federation would like you to be going for lunch now, son. But right now, as I speak, she's in there making a phone call. I don't want to give the recipient too long to digest it, once he's heard who turned up on her doorstep.'

The city bypass was fairly close, so I took that rather than head across town. The journey took me twenty minutes, and I'd probably saved the same. The gates swung open even more quickly than before, but then, I was expected. 'Where are we?' McGuire asked.

'In the belly of the beast. You'll see.'

For the third time in succession, the door was opened by a different person. Dougie Terry didn't say a word; he let us in and stood aside. I knew the way by that time.

Manson was behind his desk, contemplating what looked like two burgers, or possibly steaks, each in a big, floury bap. He looked at McGuire as we crossed the room. 'I see we've both got new minders. Skinner.'

I took the fake pen from its stand and broke it in two, then ripped its wire loose. His smile vanished. 'Hey, what the fuck are you doin'? It's not switched on.'

'Who gives a shit?' I barked. 'I'm in that sort of mood. Mario, now that you've met Mr Manson, you might want to go and have a longer chat with Mr Terry.'

'You serious, boss?' the DC asked.

'Yes, go on.'

I waited until he'd left then headed round the desk. Manson saw that I really was serious; he panicked, opened the top right-hand drawer and reached into it, but I slammed it shut on his hand and pressed hard. 'Bastard!' he yelled. I pulled him over backwards, right out of his chair, and took the gun he'd been after. He started to rise, and I slugged him with it, backhanded, across the face. He sprawled on the rug, in a bay window that looked out on to the completely secluded garden, free of onlookers. He wasn't done, more fool him. I pocketed the automatic as he got to his feet, then hit him, a big right-hander on the temple that knocked him back down, and right out.

When he started to come to, I was in his chair, pointing his own gun at the middle of his forehead, with half a burger in my left hand. 'That was the biggest mistake you've ever made in your life,' I told him, when he was ready to listen, and I had finished chewing. 'We were just going to have a chat until you went for the gun. Are you fucking mad?'

'What gun?' he mumbled. 'You brought it with you.'

'No, I didn't, but I'm taking it away. There's an amnesty on just now, post Dunblane, pre-legislation, and this is going in the river.' I put it back in my pocket (the safety catch had never been off ), picked up the other bap from the plate on his desk and handed it to him.

'Cheers,' he said, sourly.

'Actually, Tony, you did me a favour,' I confessed. 'I wanted to give you a slap, very badly. I'm angry, very angry. I've just been to see a lad in hospital. You've been screwing his wife and now you've ended his career for him. You know what? As well as being a fucking criminal, you are an arsehole of the first order.'

'Nothing to do with me,' he muttered, then winced as he took a bite from his roll and felt the pain. I'd caught him with the gun between the right cheekbone and upper jaw. His face was swelling and his eye was going to be closed before too long.

'Where's big Lennie?' I asked.

'He's gone on holiday for a bit.'

'Sure. He left last night I'll bet, via Blackford Hill.' He frowned and

I read his mind. 'No, forget that,' I told him. 'Derek's story is still that he was hit by a car, but we both know that's crap. We also know that there's only one guy in town who'd tackle a job like that alone, against a young, fit guy, and inflict the damage that he's got. You're a bastard on that score as well. You like Lennie, yet you used him to do that. What about Bella?' I continued, keeping the pressure on him. 'Where's she?'

'Back at her own place. She's got Marlon's funeral to sort.'

'And she's safe, of course, now you know there's no threat against her.'

'There never was,' he replied. 'She was upset about the kid. We both were. I just wanted her here for a while, that was all.'

I shook my head. 'I still don't get it, man. Okay, you've got a thing going with Alafair, but she's a fucking trophy for the likes of you, that's all. You don't want to marry her, for Christ's sake. A week's nookie in Ibiza and that would have been it, am I right?'

'Maybe.'

'So, she goes home, Derek finds out, they have a big fight, he loses it and hits her. And she phones you crying about it. The Tony Manson I know would have said, "Your business," and hung up on her, but instead you set big Lennie on the guy you've been cuckolding, the highest profile sportsman in town, and you break his fucking legs! I do not get that, Tony; I don't get it at all. Explain it to me, no witnesses; go on.'

He took another bite of burger, with the other side of his mouth, and I finished mine. When he was done, he looked up at me, and said, 'Just this once, okay?'

I nodded. 'Okay, if you want.'

'It was a matter of principle. A message had to be sent; now it has been and the story's over. I'll compensate the boy. His debts are wiped at the casino, forty grand's worth. I doubt if he'll ever go there again, but if he does he'll have another ten coming in chips.'

I whistled. 'That's the noblest thing I've ever heard,' I told him, ironically; I must emphasise that, in case you thought I was being serious, for irony is very difficult to convey on the printed page. 'But I don't get your fucking message.'

'It wasn't for you, but trust me, it'll have been received.'

'By whom? Derek? For fuck's sake, Tony. What good's that going to do now? Oh, and by the way, I'd sooner trust a politician.' I frowned. 'You've got a lot in common, mind you. They keep on getting away with it, just like you will this time.'

I reached out a hand and pulled him off the floor, then gave him back his chair. 'No more, Tony, no more,' I warned him. I patted my pocket. 'And no more toys either. Once this new ban on handguns comes in, if I raid this place and find any, you'll be gone for five years.'

McGuire and Terry were outside in the hall when I left, eyeing each other up, the latter more than a little warily. I sensed that something had happened. I patted the DC on the shoulder. 'And he's on our team too, Dougie. I'll bet that hasn't made your afternoon.'

The gates had been opened for us when we stepped outside. Neither of us said a word until we were off the property and back in Essex Road. It was McGuire who broke the silence. 'What happened in there, boss?'

'Tony and I had a wee chat. We're old acquaintances. Don't be offended that I asked you to leave. Some things are better one on one. I wanted you to see him before we got down to it. I'm sure you'll bump into him again before you're done.'

As it happened he did, a few years later; it was a one-sided meeting, though, since Manson was dead at the time.

'We heard a shout at one point,' the new DC said, quietly. 'Terry was for going in there.'

'Did you have to restrain him?'

'No, sir. He thought better of it.'

They usually do with him. I grinned. 'Thanks for your confidence,' I remarked. 'It might have been me that was shouting.'

'I never thought that for one second, sir. Neither did Terry, from the way he reacted. Did you get anything out of Manson?'

'I'd read the script before I heard the performance.' I summed up the sequence of events for him, but left out the more physical side of the discussion.

'If we know all that, don't we have a chance of a prosecution?' he asked.

'Of course. If . . . Derek Drysalter, who's getting fifty grand from Manson for pain and inconvenience, plus, I imagine, an insurance payment that might be in doubt if the truth came out, was to change his story and make a complaint, if . . . a couple of witnesses come forward out of the blue and make it to the trial unbribable or undamaged, if . . . Alafair confesses to everything including running to Tony after Derek hit her, and if . . . big Lennie doesn't happen to have been in a roomful of oath-taking friends at the exact moment the attack took place, then . . . yes, we might have a chance of taking it to court. The only problem is that none of those things is going to happen.'

I understood his concern. I'd been as idealistic as him ten years earlier. 'We just have to keep doing our best, Mario,' I told him. 'We get most of them in the end.'

'We haven't got Manson yet,' he pointed out.

'If we don't, the chances are that someone else will. Look at the Holmes brothers. They thought they were untouchable, until wee Billy Spreckley showed them they were only human after all.'

'Where does all this leave us with the Watson investigation?'

'Good question, son,' I conceded. 'Back at point one, unfortunately. What were those two hooligans hired to get out of Marlon? The fact that Tony and Alafair were having it away? I can't see that. At the end of the day who cares other than the Loyal Hibernian Supporters' Club? And I can't see them hiring hit men from Newcastle.'

McGuire whistled. 'I don't know, boss,' he chuckled. 'Hibbies can be very determined people when their club's involved.'

'You can joke about it, but that's all we've got at the moment. Whatever they were after, it was serious. They were brought in to do a job, we got on to them and they, for their carelessness, were killed themselves . . . to eliminate any chance of us reaching the person who hired them.' I sighed. 'And then there's the leak. How did our man find out that we had indentified the van, and the men in it?'

'We've got a mole then,' McGuire murmured.

'I'd like to think that Newcastle has, not us. But don't call him a mole; I hate that analogy. Moles are nice furry wee things. Our traitor's a reptile, a serpent in our garden.'

'Does Manson know who's behind it all?'

I sighed. 'If he does, then he isn't worried any more. Bella's no longer being protected . . . although he told me he never did think she was at risk . . . and his own security's back to normal: Dougie Terry's not exactly fucking Cerberus guarding the gates of Hell. My feeling is that Tony believes that it's over with him having sent his message, as he calls it. It might be for him, but not for us. We've still got a triple murderer to catch.'

'So what do we do now, sir?' he asked, as we neared the office.

'Us normal mortals, Mario, we just keep going, or we go back over what we've done so far and see if we've missed anything. You, I guess, just keep relying on flair, luck and brass neck.'

As soon as I was back behind my desk, I called Alison. 'How did you get on with Alf's assistant?'

'I'm no further forward,' she replied. 'She did a trawl of all the reports from divisions of incidents from the Wednesday night right through to the Friday, but there was nothing there involving three unidentified suspects.'

'Bugger. Nothing at all?'

'There was an armed robbery by two guys from a video store in Leith Walk on the Thursday night. Doesn't quite fit the time frame and we're one suspect short.'

'Nor does it sound like the sort of thing that people get killed over. Go back to Shannon, Ali, and ask her to trawl over two further days, just in case something happened that wasn't reported until after the event. And this too: get your boys to ask around discreetly for things that might have happened off our radar. For example, any word of a robbery where the victim might have had an interest in not reporting it?'

'I will do. Bob,' she seemed to hesitate for a second, 'do you think we should go back to Mia Watson on this?'

'And ask her what? She's already told Stevie that she doesn't remember any of them.'

'I know,' she sighed. 'I wondered whether, if it was woman to woman, she might push her memory a wee bit harder.'

I didn't really want Alison interviewing Mia, but I couldn't order her not to, or even come up with a convincing reason why she shouldn't. 'Try it, if that's what you want, but she goes on air soon for most of the rest of the day, and we're both off the pitch for four days from tonight, including Monday when we go to interview Telfer.'

'No,' she replied. 'We can't get to see him before Tuesday. By the time we got the train up to Aberdeen it would be too late to fly to the platform and back in one day, but as you said, he's not going anywhere. I've made all the arrangements with Shell. We go up Monday afternoon and leave at seven o'clock on the helicopter. All I have to do now is book us into the airport hotel.'

'You'd better make it one room,' I told her. 'Times are tight; we should save the taxpayer some money.'

She laughed. 'After a weekend on a seagoing schooner, you might want a suite.'

# Sixteen

'What should I wear, Pops?' Alex asked me, as she handed me a mug of tea. 'I don't have a black dress.' She was a wee bit anxious; the truth about where she was going and what we were about to do had been settling upon her since breakfast.

'They tend not to be fashion items for thirteen-year-olds, kid,' I pointed out. 'What did Grandpa like you to wear? It's not about what other people expect, it's about what he'd be thinking.'

She thought about it. 'There's the blue dress I bought with the money he gave me last Christmas. Would it do?'

'That will be perfect, my love.'

'Make-up?' Under Daisy's guidance and with my approval she had started to use cosmetics on the day she moved into her teens. She didn't overdo it, for as Daisy had pointed out, she didn't need to. 'Would that be disrespectful?'

'I'd tell you if it was.'

'Are you sure? I wouldn't want to upset Aunt Jean.'

'You won't.' Jean was going to be sending her dad off to the good fire. I doubted if she'd even notice that her niece was wearing a bit of eyeliner and lipstick. 'It's not as if you're going to be painted up like Jodie Foster in *Taxi Driver*.' We'd watched the video a couple of months before.

'You lookin' at me?' she drawled, and headed for the stairs.

'Don't come down with your hair in a Mohican,' I called after her.

The ribbing had lightened things but I was probably more tense than my daughter. I didn't like Daldowie; or rather I disliked it more than any other crematorium I knew. It was one of those places where you saw distant relations and acquaintances, promised to see them soon and then never did until the next time you were there.

I decided to match the dress code I'd recommended to Alex, so I put on the linen suit I'd worn a few days before, but with a black shirt and tie. Then I packed a bag for the weekend, full of what I imagined might be sailor stuff.

Alison had advised Alex about what she should take with her. She and I had arranged that we'd all set off from my place; if I'd picked her up, it would have taken at least forty-five minutes longer to reach Carluke. When she arrived, in a black suit, we were ready to go. She scored a real Brownie point by heading straight for the back seat of the Beamer, leaving Alex in her usual place, up front. It was thoughtful, and I loved her for it. Yes, you read me right; I loved her for it.

We got to Thornton's house just before one. There were quite a few people there, in addition to Jean, a couple of her aunts, one from either side of the family, Thornie's much older brother, Uncle Moffat, who wasn't quite sure where he was, and his best pal from the golf club. The great-aunts made a small fuss of Alex, and were polite to Alison, but mostly concentrated on sipping their Harvey's Bristol Cream, and munching their salmon sandwiches as best they could with their loose dentures.

Sergeant Lowell Payne was there too, clean-cut, about my own age, and formal in dark suit, white shirt, black tie. My Special Branch contact had called me back, giving him a clean bill of health. He wasn't expected to rise any higher than inspector, but that would give him a decent pension one day, and he had no bad habits for me to worry about. We were introduced, 'Bob, Lowell. Lowell, Bob,' but didn't say much to each other. At that stage everyone was focused on what was to come. Alex stuck close to me, tight-lipped; one of the great-aunts had insisted on pinching her cheek, and Uncle Moffat kept calling out, loudly, 'Who's that lassie? Is that our Myra?'

I was grateful when the undertaker announced that we should go. There were two limos for six passengers . . . Thornie had a vehicle all to himself . . . so there was plenty of space. Jean offered Alex a seat in hers, as a close blood relative, but she chose to stay with me. The pace was indeed funereal, but the drivers were experts and we arrived at exactly the right time.

The service took half the time that the drive had. Psalm twenty-three, prayer, hymn, prayer ending in Lord's Prayer (the Scottish version where we forgive debtors and our debts are forgiven too; that'll be right!), eulogy, committal, benediction. All crematoria seem to operate to the same tight timetable, but at least the place was full of Thornton's enduring friends, the minister knew all about him and wasn't reading from a script provided by the family, and oh, as I was reminded, those Lanarkshire Proddies sure can sing. I didn't join them; I only do that when I've had a couple of drinks and I know that somebody's listening. Alison did, though; I hadn't realised that she had such a nice contralto voice.

When it was all over, and Jean and I had shaken hands with the departing mourners at the door . . . I couldn't let her do that on her own, and Lowell was too new on the scene . . . we moved on to a hotel in Bothwell, a place that must make a small fortune from the proximity of the crematorium, for more salmon sandwiches, more Bristol Cream, stories about the departed and the laughter that always comes from the release of tension. It unsettled Alex; I could see that either she was going to cry or she'd let someone have both barrels, so I took her into a corner and explained that one day she'd be doing exactly the same herself, probably after seeing me off.

Jean saw us and came across to join us. I left them to their aunt-niece chat and walked across to the corner that Alison and Lowell Payne had commandeered. I shook hands with the sergeant properly. It had been perfunctory at Thornie's place. 'Good to meet you,' I said. 'How's Strathclyde taking to its new chief?'

'Mr Govan? He's way above my head, and I'm a long way from Pitt Street, thank heaven, but from what I hear he's shaking things up.'

'I'd expect no less,' I agreed. 'He lectured at a course I was on at Tulliallan; not a man to sugar the pill.'

'I've heard much the same about you.'

I smiled. 'I didn't know I was being watched.'

'We take an interest in you through here, since you're one of us. Ever think about coming back?' he asked.

'Not once. Not once in fourteen years.' In fact, John Govan had sounded me out, after his lecture, to see if I'd consider a move to Glasgow, but I'd declined, politely, as it pays to be with the most powerful police officer in the land.

'Shoe the other foot,' I continued. 'Have you ever considered a move east?'

'Yes,' he admitted, 'but Jean wouldn't like it, and what she wants she can have as far as I'm concerned.'

On the basis of my background check and our brief acquaintance, I'd have found him a slot, but I decided not to pursue it. 'How's Hamilton?' I asked him. 'When I was a boy, the River Clyde was like the Berlin Wall, dividing it and Motherwell. The twain never met.'

He smiled. 'It's okay. There's worse places to be . . . Motherwell, for example.'

'It wasn't always like that. There was a working-class morality about when the steel industry was at its height.'

'Yes, but with the Protestant jackboot on the neck of the Catholic minority, through its old police force.'

I couldn't argue; he knew the local history of my home town. He was an interesting guy, and forthright with it. I could see why he hadn't been earmarked for higher rank. 'Those were the days,' I said to Alison. 'I'm glad I missed them.' I looked back at Lowell. 'You'll be a Hamilton boy, then?'

He nodded. 'Born and bred.'

'Big place, I know,' I ventured, 'but have you ever heard of a family called McGrew?'

'Sure, as in Alafair. She was a budding actress, and good at her personal PR from an early age. Her name was always cropping up in the *Hamilton Advertiser*, for winning awards at the Athenaeum, or getting a bit part in *Take the High Road*.'

'What's the Athenaeum?' Alison asked.

'Royal College of Music and Drama in Glasgow,' I told her. 'Some very well-known people came out of there.'

'Alafair hasn't come up to Ian Richardson's level, though,' Lowell added. 'I haven't seen much about her lately.'

'Career change. She married a footballer.' I almost added, 'And started playing away games,' but decided to hold that back. 'But he plays for Hibs,' I went on, 'hence her absence from the *Advertiser*, and from the telly.'

Sergeant Payne was sharp. 'It wouldn't be the guy Drysalter, would it?'

'It would indeed.'

'The hit and run victim?'

'The same. Someone hit him, several times, with a baseball bat,

**322**

and ran away . . . but that information stays within our domestic group, Lowell, okay?'

'Sure, sir, Bob . . . whatever.'

Alison laughed. 'I have the same trouble, sometimes.'

'Which she's getting over,' I said. 'I'll be calling her "Ma'am" soon.'

'You will this weekend. On board my brother's boat I'm the first mate and you're a deckhand.'

'Shit, I thought you were the stewardess.' I looked at my watch. 'Speaking of which, we should be making a move. We'd better collect Alex and say our goodbyes. You know what happens at these things, Lowell, don't you? Bets are laid on who's going up the chimney next?'

He nodded towards Uncle Moffat, who was holding a large whisky in two small hands. 'There won't be too many takers,' he muttered.

'Thornie said the same thing about him after Myra's funeral, but the old boy's seen him off.'

We shook hands for a third time, as Alison went to rescue Alex from the great-aunts. 'Do me a small favour if you can. See if you can pick up any local knowledge about Alafair's family background.' I took a card from the ever-present stash in my breast pocket and slipped it to him. 'Just for fun. I'd like to know how she became the girl she is.'

The last leg of the journey was much less sombre than the first two. Alex promoted Alison to the front passenger seat, so that she could retreat into the back and listen to the Spice Girls and others on her CD Walkman.

'Well,' I began as I negotiated the complex interchange that led to the motorway network, 'what did you think of that crew?'

'What do they think of me,' Alison countered, 'that's the question.'

'Don't let that worry you for one second. You and Jean seemed to get on fine and that's all that matters.'

'She seemed all right. Was Myra like her?'

'Not much. Jean's much more reserved than she was. She's coming out of it now, though, having rectified her mistake.'

'What mistake?'

'Her first husband. Prick.' She laughed. 'Don't,' I said. 'That description was generous. But you're right about Jean and me, we've always got on.' I didn't see any need to tell her how well we'd got on at one time. 'The great-aunts, though, they've never been close to us. They didn't approve of Myra. They thought she was "flighty", a fine old Lanarkshire word for a girl with a bit of personality. She was that all right. As for old Moffat, he may be doolally now, but even when he had his wits about him he was an old cunt, pardon my French.' I glanced in the mirror, but Alex was isolated by her headphones and couldn't have overheard. 'You can tell at funerals, those who've come along out of respect and those who're there with an eye on the will. Those who were can forget it. Thornton changed his will after Myra died; he discussed it with me because he felt I should know. Before then everything was to be split equally between his two daughters; afterwards, Alex replaced her mother as a fifty per cent beneficiary. It'll be a tidy amount too; she and I will need to discuss how it should be invested. If the aunts had known that they wouldn't have looked in her direction.'

'You can choose your friends,' Alison began to quote, 'but . . .'

'. . . not your family,' I concluded. 'Thornie didn't believe that, though,' I told her. 'He always said that the best of friends were those who chose you, and as you saw by the turnout today, a lot of people chose him, and very wisely too. The old aunts,' I continued, 'they didn't approve of me either so we never saw any of her family when

Myra was alive, apart from the odd cousin who fancied a day at the seaside.'

'What did they have against you, for God's sake?' she laughed.

'My mother was an alcoholic. When Myra and I got engaged, there was a family party and my mum got pished at it. The aunts, as you've seen, are real prissy old tight-arses, so we were off their Christmas card list before we were even on it. They'd have been afraid of my father anyway; they regarded lawyers as a class apart. Not Thornie, though; he and my old man were always perfectly civil to each other and they even played a bit of golf together, a big deal, although my father was far too aloof for them ever to become close.'

'You're bitter about your family, Bob,' she ventured.

'No, I'm not. I'm sad about them. Mostly I'm sad for Alex, because I think it's a shame that she can't sit at a big table every Christmas with a dozen so people that are her own kith and kin.'

She reached out and stroked my forearm. 'You may find that Jean and Sergeant Payne start filling that table quite soon. He seems . . . smitten, an old-fashioned word but it works, and she seems suited.'

'Yeah, he's a good guy. I like him. I hope they do settle down. They make a nice couple and Jean'll be a good mother.' I winked at her. 'You do realise they're probably saying much the same about us right now,' I added.

'As long as they don't build their hopes up. They want family, we want careers, and I'm about as broody as a stone.'

'But are you happy?' I asked.

'With my life? Yes, I told you so. It's exactly as I'd like it. Two weeks ago I thought you'd lost interest in me, and I wasn't too chuffed about that. You've shown me I was wrong, and I'm happy about that. I'm looking forward to spending time with you and Alex, but I want to keep her at a certain distance so she doesn't ever start to think of me as a mother figure.'

'And me? What do you want from me?'

She frowned. 'Of you I ask one thing alone. When you are lonely in the dark of night, and when I stop being the one you call first, don't call me at all. Give that promise to me, and I will give the same to you.'

I reached across, took her hand, and squeezed it. 'You've got it.'

Eden Higgins and his son Rory were on board and waiting for us when we arrived at Inverkip Marina. The boat was impressive. It was called *Palacio de Ginebra*, a name that amused me, looked to be about forty feet long and had a couple of masts, with booms and other stuff, like lots of rope that was going to need pulling, and sails rolled up and ready for unfurling, or whatever it was you did with them.

The furniture tycoon looked as if he spent more time at sea than he did in his showrooms. He was lean and weather-beaten and the muscle on his arms was well defined. His hair was frizzy, dark streaked with grey. He wore faded jeans and a T-shirt that proclaimed his love of New York.

'Good to meet you, Bob, and you, Alex.' His greeting was relaxed, and it spoke volumes. I wasn't the first male crew member that his sister had brought along for the voyage, although probably the first one with a teenage daughter in tow.

There was a table on what Alison told me was the afterdeck, with a jug of Sangria, a large bottle of Coca-Cola and four glasses. 'The Coke was intended for the kids,' he said as he started to pour, 'but looking at Alex, she might prefer the other.'

'That would depend on what's in it, Eden.' Sangria comes in many forms, some of them highly alcoholic, and we were on a boat called the *Gin Palace*.

'It's safe, I promise,' he replied. 'Red wine only and that's pretty diluted.'

'In that case, it'll be Alex's choice. But can we change first?'

'Of course. Alison will show you where you're bunked.'

I'd been expecting something akin to a railway sleeping compartment, but I had underestimated Eden's taste and his wealth. The vessel was beautifully fitted out below decks, with a dayroom, a galley, and three cabins. The largest of those was ours and I didn't need to be told that, normally, it was the captain's.

We went casual, and rejoined our host. Alex opted for Sangria. It didn't surprise me since I'd been allowing her that occasional taste since the previous summer. I let her get on with it, even though the base was red, since it was well watered. Rory was a nice kid, he looked a little bit like his aunt, but with some features that owed nothing to the Higgins side of the family. It was evident from the start that he was in awe of my daughter.

When the jug was empty, Alison announced that she was going below to cook, and told the cabin boy that he would be helping. Alex would have stayed with us, but I tipped her a very discreet wink; she read the message and followed.

The evening was calm and warm. I'd checked the weekend weather forecast and, to my relief, it had promised fair. Once we were alone, Eden pulled a couple of beers from a small built-in fridge, popped the tops and handed one to me. Suddenly I realised how Lowell Payne must have felt at the funeral.

'Cut to the chase, Eden,' I said.

His dark eyebrows rose and he smiled. 'Whatever do you mean, sir?'

'You know well enough. Let's skip the opening pleasantries and get straight to what you're bound to ask me sooner or later.'

He had a booming laugh. 'You didn't major in subtlety at Glasgow, did you, Bob?'

'I can do it when I have to, but I prefer the cards dealt face up. It makes the game a whole lot easier.'

'True. I wish there were people like you in business. That's my environment, you see, you keep your hand well hidden. Okay, to it; can I expect to be calling you brother one day?'

'No,' I replied, looking him in the eye. 'Now that we've sized each other up for a while, Alison and I are in the early stages of what's looking like being a very comfortable relationship, one that suits us both. We have a shared outlook on life, we have shared ambitions, and we are very fond of each other. But you should know your sister well enough to realise that if she's offered a choice between marriage and a chief constable's silver braid, then you may phone the tailor and commission the uniform. I'm the same.'

'You're a man, though,' he countered, 'in a masculine world. You don't have to make that choice. I'll bet there isn't one chief in Scotland who's a single man.'

'You'd lose. Two of them are divorced, due largely to the pressures that the job placed on their marriages while they were on the way up, as I am now, as Alison is now. There would be twice the stress if we were man and wife, or even a full-time couple. There is a level of commitment between us, my daughter is happy with the way things are, and that's enough for all of us.' I looked away for a second, then caught his gaze again. 'And there's this. I've lowered one wife into her grave already, I relive it every day, and I have a great resistance to ever repeating the experience for real.'

'Of course.'

'Have you had this conversation with Alison?' I asked.

'Are you kidding?' he replied. 'Am I carrying my balls in a brown paper bag? But you understand, don't you, why I feel that I have to clear the air with you?'

'Sure, and I don't have a problem with it. She's your sister, for a start, and you care about her. On top of that you're a very wealthy man, and you need to be sure that she's not attracting pot-hunters. For the record, I'm nowhere near your level, but I'm not poor.' I paused. 'But what the hell am I talking about?' I laughed. 'You know all that, for you've had me checked out. I knew that as soon as you told me what university I went to, for I don't believe I've ever mentioned it to Alison, only that I'm a graduate. You probably know how much I inherited from my father, and where it's invested. You probably know the value of various insurance policies and death-in-employment benefits that were paid out when Myra was killed. You might even know how much I have in my bank accounts. Am I right?'

He flinched, and I saw him flush beneath the tan.

'Eden,' I told him, 'it's all right. I don't mind. I've just done much the same thing with my sister-in-law's new boyfriend, and I have access to resources that you don't. But . . . I need to know this . . . did your people find out anything else about me, and my family background?'

He nodded. 'Yes,' he admitted. 'They discovered that you have a brother named Michael, who lives in a charitable institution not that far from here, supported by a small trust fund administered on his behalf by a firm of solicitors in Glasgow.'

'Then your investigators have been too good for their own good. Alison knows nothing of Michael's existence. Even my daughter isn't aware that she has an uncle. We might have been born to the same parents, but that man has been dead to me for the last twenty years, as he was to them. Until right now, I had no clear idea of where he was, and I still don't want you to tell me his exact location. I hate him, more than it's safe for me to hate another human being.'

'Christ, Bob,' he muttered, 'I had no idea.'

'Why should you? But now that you do, I need you to promise me two things, that you'll shred every copy of the report your people gave you, and that you'll make sure they do the same. While you're at it, tell them from me that they should forget they ever heard of Michael, for if anyone else ever mentions him to me in the future, my first thought is going to be that it came from them. It'll take me about two minutes to find out who they are, and not much longer for me to put them out of business.'

'Consider all that done,' Eden promised. 'By the way, the report was for my eyes only; it's in my private safe in my office.' He glanced at me, with a tiny smile. 'Bob, if that's what you'd do to people who annoyed you by accident, how would you deal with someone who went out of his way to piss you off?'

I laughed. 'That hasn't happened for a long time.'

He finished his beer and fetched two more. 'Are you sure you don't want to marry my sister?' he murmured, just as Rory appeared to tell us that the food was ready. 'I'd love to have you in our gang.'

Eden and I got on like a house on fire after that. We ate below decks, then took a late evening walk around the marina before we turned in. There were some very impressive boats there, but nothing beat the *Palacio de Ginebra* for sheer class. 'Where are we going tomorrow?' I asked, before we turned in.

'Nowhere too ambitious,' Eden replied. 'Alison and I reckon that since it's your first trip, we might just sail down to Campbeltown, moor there for the night and come back up on Sunday.'

'Great. Like Ali says, I'm only the deckhand.'

I hadn't been sure about sleeping on something that was moving about all night, even if gently. I was still wondering whether I'd manage when I woke next morning, aware of the light that had found its way into the cabin in spite of the heavy curtain over the porthole. Alison was smiling at me, her eyes still fuzzy. 'We're turning into a couple,' she murmured. 'You fell asleep on me.'

'Well, baby,' I whispered, 'I'm awake now.'

Even at that we were still up and ready to go by seven fifteen, although we were the last into the dayroom. I was excited. I couldn't remember how long it was since I'd done something absolutely new, that wasn't related to work. I couldn't remember how long it was since I'd been as separated from the job, mentally as well as physically.

Sailing turned out to be far easier than I'd expected, or feared. Life jackets were mandatory equipment on board, so falling over the side wasn't a big deal, and all I had to do was . . . whatever I was told. Once the sails were set they had to be adjusted every now and then, but mostly the real work was left to whoever was keeping us on course. As Rory proved, that was child's play . . . provided, as his aunt pointed out when I remarked upon it, that the child knew what he was doing.

Eden set a course out of Inverkip that took us west of the Isles of Cumbrae, Great and Little, views I'd never seen before, since my few trips there had been from Largs, on the east, and then out into the open Firth of Clyde. I'm not a hugely travelled man, but I'm a patriotic Scot and every so often I'm struck with a burst of pride in my country's beauty. Too many of us, me included, spend too little time in its contemplation.

The wind wasn't strong but we still made decent time, until Eden decided that we'd moor off Lamlash for lunch. Once we'd eaten, he took Alex, Rory and me across to the Holy Island in the motorised inflatable that the *Gin Palace* towed behind it, leaving Alison on wash-up duty. We walked around the lovely wee island for an hour; my daughter and I each shot a full roll of film. The place is a centre for world peace these days, and I can understand why, although I wonder how its students feel when they see a missile-carrying nuclear submarine go by, out of the base at Faslane.

Back on board, we spent the afternoon cruising round the south of Arran and on towards the Mull of Kintyre and Campbeltown, our destination. We sailed into its loch, which is really a big bay, then found our pre-booked mooring on the pier and tied up for the night. Dinner hadn't been planned, so I went ashore and found a restaurant that had one table left for five, my contribution to the trip. 'You're lucky to get in at such short notice on a Saturday night,' the owner advised me, 'but Paul's not here just now, and so that makes a difference.' At the time I didn't have the faintest idea of what she meant, but Alex explained later.

The food, local shellfish and beef from Northern Ireland . . . we were closer to the Irish mainland than to our point of departure . . . was outstanding, but the greatest memory I have of that night is one of enlightenment.

As I looked at my surroundings, at my companions, and considered how we'd got there, I felt an epiphany, a realisation that I'd been shown a world outside that in which I'd been immersed for the previous fifteen years, and by which I'd become completely consumed. The evening is locked away in the treasure chest of my mind like a movie shot in soft focus, and every so often I close my eyes, take it out, and replay it.

Later, when everyone else had turned in, leaving Alison and me alone on the afterdeck, I told her what I was feeling. My excitement of the morning had grown into an understanding that all things were possible, and that my life need not necessarily be set on a course that was unalterable. 'I could do this,' I said to her. 'I could sell my place in Spain, buy a boat like this, and operate it commercially. It is possible. This is just, so different, so . . . so damn nice.'

She smiled. 'And what about Alex? Do you think she'll settle for a life as a boat girl?'

'In four years' time,' I pointed out, 'Alex will be gone, off to university, to study law, she says, at Glasgow, same as me. A friend of mine at the golf club once said to me that a son will never leave home, truly, until he marries, but with daughters, once they're gone, they're gone. They need their own space.'

'I'll grant you that,' she conceded.

'There you are then. When that happens, I will barely have cleared forty. I will be a relatively young man. I could do this.'

We were still talking about it after we'd turned in for the night; I gave free rein to my liberated imagination, while Alison stayed practical. 'Bob, this is the Firth of Clyde,' she pointed out. 'It's been lovely today, but wet and windy is the norm. I've been out in those conditions, you haven't, and believe me, when the weather is rough, the last thing you want is the worry of bloody passengers.'

That didn't put me off. 'Okay, then we won't charter it out. We'll just live on it.'

She laughed. 'You couldn't, not all the time. You'd go mad.'

'No I wouldn't. If we didn't take passengers, I would write. There are a couple of true crime books I could do right now, and who's better prepared than the likes of me to do crime fiction? Or we could sail the bloody world, and do travel books. I could make television programmes.'

She laid a hand on my chest and kissed me. 'Calm down, big boy,' she whispered. 'If wishes were horses we'd all get a ride.'

'But we can. Maybe we have to, Ali. You talk about going mad; there's a far greater chance of that happening if I stay in the job than if I leave it. I began this week looking at dead people, some left where they had been killed. I saw a man who'd been disembowelled,

in his own home, his own fucking castle. On Thursday I interviewed a kid who'd been systematically crippled with a baseball
bat, for reasons that still aren't entirely clear to me. Later on that
same day I had a confrontation with a guy who tried to pull a gun
on me. I dealt with all that, love. I switched off from all the blood
and the suffering, and I met the violence with greater violence.
Then I went home to my daughter, and we had fish for tea. That is
my life, and it's yours; it's how I live, it's how you live. This weekend
I've been shown a way of changing it, and you're trying to talk me
out of it?'

She stroked my cheek, my forehead, my hair. 'No, lover, I'm not. If
that's how you feel and if that's what you want, then I want it for you.
But will you still want it on Monday morning? And what's this "we" all
of a sudden?'

'Surely you can't believe that I'd save my own life and leave you
lost in the deep, dark jungle.' I kissed her. 'Besides, I'll need someone
to teach me how to sail the thing. Come away with me.'

'Ask me again, when you're really ready to do it.'

'What will you say when I do?'

'Surely you can't believe that I'd let you head off into the sunset
without a bloody clue how to set the sails?'

But I never did buy that damn boat. I never did ask her. If I had, I'd
have saved her life. Ultimately she was someone else I betrayed.

My last great romantic vision endured through that night and into
the morning. It stayed with me well into the afternoon, all through the
cruise up the windward coast of Arran, and until we were within sight
of Inverkip. For all that time, my mind was still set on sailing boats and
sunsets.

And then my mobile sounded. I was in the cabin at the time,
packing my bag. I retrieved it from the jacket I'd worn at the funeral,

where it had spent the last two days. It was at the limit of its battery life, but there was just enough juice left for me to answer.

'Bob, is that you?'

The voice threw me for a second or two, until I realised that it was Sergeant Payne. 'Yes, Lowell, what's up?'

'I've done that checking up for you, on the McGrew family. It's pretty much as reported in the *Tizer*. They lived in a house up Wellhall Road, past the Philips factory, a nice big place; a detached villa. The mother's name was Violet, but there was never any dad around from when they moved in, and that was, oh, about fifteen years ago, when Alafair was at primary school. I had a chat with the neighbours, a Mr and Mrs Shearer; they say that she was a widow, left comfortably off by her late husband. She told them he had been "in business", that was all. Violet died four years ago, when Alafair was about twenty, from cancer. The house was sold a couple of years later. The son kept it on for a while, then he left.'

'She's got a brother?'

'Yes. He's seven years older than she is. The Shearers had a lot of time for him.'

'Did they give you his name?'

'Yes, Peter.'

'Anything else about him?' I asked. 'Do they know what he did for a living?'

'Mr Shearer said that he joined the army after he left school. He came back home when his mother fell ill, but they hadn't a real clue what he did when he lived there after that. Mrs Shearer did ask him once. He told her he was a company director, but no more than that. Their impression was that whatever it was, he worked from home, because he didn't keep regular hours.'

Just as he finished, my battery gave out, so I couldn't thank him for his help. But had he helped me? My gut told me that he had, but I couldn't work out how. Alafair McGrew, the battered Alafair McGrew, had an ex-soldier brother. So was it possible that I'd been wrong about big Lennie? Had she turned to brother Peter, not Manson? Could Tony's mumble about sending a message have been bullshit, to make me think that he was in charge of the situation? Men like him hate to lose face.

In my mind's eye, a couple of bricks had moved, and begun to arrange themselves into a pattern. They were a long way from building anything solid, but it was a start, a move in the only direction I cared about, forward.

I didn't admit it to myself then, but that's when I knew that I wouldn't buy that schooner, that I was what I was for a reason, and that I couldn't run, walk, or sail away from myself.

I turned and saw Alison in the doorway. 'Who was that?' she asked.

'Alex's future uncle, with the result of a check I asked him to do for me. At the moment, it's raised no more than a question, but it could turn into an answer to one of my puzzles.'

'Mine too?' she asked.

'Sorry, no.'

She smiled. 'That's a pity. I'm not looking forward to that helicopter trip on Tuesday any more than you are.'

We went back into the marina under engine power and tied up. We all helped to make the schooner secure; once it was, I thanked Eden for the experience. 'We'll go further next time,' he promised, 'and maybe in more normal weather conditions. You're not a real sailor until you've done a whole cruise in waterproofs.'

I made it back to Gullane just inside two hours from Inverkip. I asked Alison if she wanted to stay, but she'd run out of clothes, and also, she didn't fancy another early start, so she headed back to Edinburgh. Before she left, I asked her to call Shell the next morning, and postpone the oil platform visit by a couple of days. Telfer would keep, and I had some digging to do. I started that evening. At the same course at the police college that John Govan had addressed, I'd met a little man who'd been introduced as Lieutenant Adam Arrow. He was there to talk to us about counter-terrorism; he'd been frank and some of the stories that he'd told had given us all a different slant on Northern Ireland, as well as opening our eyes to coming threats. He and I had bonded, after a fashion, and he'd given me a couple of numbers, office and mobile. As soon as Alex, as bushed after her weekend as I was, had gone to bed, I called him on the latter.

He took a few seconds to answer, time I guessed he was spending identifying my landline number. 'Bob,' he exclaimed when he did pick up. 'How the fook are you?' His Derbyshire accent tended to come and go, but it was genuine. 'Who have you killed and what do you want us to clean up?'

'It's nice to know my phone isn't tapped,' I said.

'Not by us, it isn't. I can't speak for other services, mind you.'

'I don't mind them hearing this. I'm looking for some background on a former army man. His name's Peter McGrew, he's Scottish, home town Hamilton, and I'm told his service began in the first half of the eighties and ended early nineties. That's all I know about him.'

'That should be enough, unless there are two of them. What's he done?' he asked.

'Nothing, I hope. But his sister suffered a bit of domestic violence on my patch and now someone's reshaped her husband's legs. You might have read about it, since the guy's a Scotland international footballer.'

'That hit and run? Lad wi' funny name?'

'That's the one,' I confirmed. 'No vehicle involved.'

'A punishment beating? I wonder if the guy's ever served in Ireland,' he mused. 'It wouldn't look good if it came out that one of ours was copying the Provos.'

'Don't get too excited. There's another strong suspect. Anyway, it won't come out. The victim's not going to change his story. I want to know the truth, that's all, out of old-fashioned curiosity. It's an itch that needs scratching.'

'Then I will assuage it.'

Adam Arrow was always as good as his word. That was one of the things that kept us close to the very end. I made it into the office by a quarter to nine the next morning, to find a message on my desk, 'Call Adam', and a London number.

'Got him,' he said, as soon as he took my call. 'Peter Hastings McGrew, date of birth fifteenth of March nineteen sixty-five . . . the fookin' Ides of March, mate; beware . . . entered Sandhurst in eighty-three, commissioned one year later, served with the Tenth Gurkha Rifles until nineteen ninety-one, when he left the service shortly after being promoted captain.'

'Excellent. Do you know where he is now?'

'Not a fookin' clue,' he replied. 'He could be anywhere in the world.'

'But don't your guys remain on reserve after they leave the service?'

'Not this one. He had an accident while he was on exercise in Brunei. He severed a tendon in his left arm. As a result he can barely grip a cup of tea wi' that hand, let alone a baseball bat. I've seen the medical report, Bob. If this bloke worked his brother-in-law over, then he did it one-handed.'

I sighed. My alternative theory had just gone up in smoke. 'Thanks, mate,' I said. 'I owe you one.'

'Be sure I'll call it in one day,' Arrow promised, and hung up.

I was still itching. I called Martin and McGuire into my office. 'A job for you both,' I told them. 'I want information on a man called Peter McGrew, middle name Hastings, age thirty-one. He's ex-army, ex-Gurkha Rifles, lived formerly in Hamilton, and he is Alafair Drysalter's brother. I want to be fair to the family. Having spoken to her, I want to talk to him now. Andy, get on to the DVLA in Swansea. Let's assume he has a driving licence; it'll have an address on it. While you're at it, find out if he owns a car; if he does, get its registration details. Mario, he told his former neighbours he was a company director. Phone Companies House. Give them his name, find out if that's true, and if it is, what's the company? On your bikes, lads.'

Computer systems weren't nearly as advanced in those days as they are now, but they existed, and they worked. Martin was back to me first inside fifteen minutes. 'He's got a licence, boss, and there's a car registered in his name. The address on both is in Wellhall Road, Hamilton.'

'Fuck it!' I snapped. 'He hasn't changed it.'

'That's an offence; we can do him for that.' Martin smiled.

I didn't. 'What about the car?'

'VW Golf GTI, black . . . what else? . . . registration L712FTG. He's had it from new.'

'That's progress, Andy,' I said.

'Do you want me to put it on a watch list and have it pulled over on sight?'

'We've got no reason to do that. Sit on it for now.' I looked through the glass. McGuire was still on the phone, in deep discussion from the looks of things, but as we watched, he nodded a couple of times and hung up, then swung his chair round and headed for us, beaming.

'Peter Hastings McGrew, boss,' he began, almost before he was through the door, 'is a director of several companies, all tying into a single holding company called Rodatrop plc. Together the group owns pubs all over Scotland, a casino in Glasgow, a video hire chain and three private hire and taxi businesses. McGrew is one of two directors of all the companies; the other's his sister, Alafair Drysalter.'

I whistled.

'It gets better,' he laughed. 'The companies were all set up two years ago, to acquire the assets of an earlier company, called Conan plc. Its sole director was one Perry Holmes. Even I know who he is.'

I leapt out of my chair. 'Come on, you two boys, with me. Fred,' I called to Leggat as we headed for the door, 'we're off out.'

We were in Frederick Street before McGuire ventured the question. 'Where are we going, boss?'

'You're a detective, Mario,' I chuckled. 'You tell me.'

'Back to see Alafair?'

'Good try, but not yet. Andy?'

'Register House.'

'Nearly. In fact, it's New Register House, but you're on the right track.'

I parked in Register Place; on that occasion I did leave a 'Police business' card, with the force crest and the chief constable's facsimile signature, showing on the dashboard. It wasn't there to be abused, but it was easier than having tickets written off. I led the way round past the Cafe Royal and the Guildford Arms, where Charles Redpath had encountered Don Telfer, and through the front entrance of New Register House. It's a fine edifice in its own right, although it was created by the Victorians as a mere overflow from, and is hidden behind, Robert Adam's Register House, built in the previous century, a public building in which Scotland's national archives are housed.

As a cop you make some professional friends, and if you're wise you'll keep them throughout your career. Jim Glossop was one of mine; I'd known him for ten years and during that time he'd cut a few corners for me. I asked for him at the front desk. As we waited, I explained to the boys the reason for our rush from Fettes. 'When Violet McGrew and her kids lived in Hamilton, she led the neighbours to believe that she was a widow. Maybe that was true, but then again . . .'

'Mob-handed, are we, Bob?' Jim Glossop exclaimed, as he appeared through a door on my right.

'New playmates. I thought they should meet you; Mario McGuire and Andy Martin, detective constables both. I need a parentage check, Jim. Two people, brother and sister: Peter Hastings McGrew, date of birth March fifteen, sixty-five, birthplace uncertain, and Alafair McGrew, no d.o.b. but she's seven years younger than him. Mother's name Violet, now deceased; I'd like to know who Daddy was . . . or rather, is.'

'Or daddies,' he pointed out. 'You're making an assumption.'

'There's a good reason for it,' I assured him

He made a few notes on a small pad he was carrying. 'Give me fifteen minutes.'

Rather than wait idly, we went for a stroll down into Princes Street. The two DCs spotted a sandwich stall and headed off in search of coffee; I went in the other direction, to a nearby book store. I was short on reading matter, so I picked up a couple of paperbacks; one of them was called *Let It Bleed*, a yarn featuring the latest adventure of a fictional Edinburgh cop who was beginning to gather attention. I didn't know if he was based on a real-life character, but if he was, I'd worked with a few candidates.

I was a minute or two late returning; Jim and the boys were all waiting for me when I stepped into the foyer. 'Results,' my friend announced. He handed me two photocopied extracts. 'Both children were born in Rottenrow, that's the main maternity hospital in Glasgow. You were right, same father, but he and Miss McGrew never went through a marriage ceremony. Indeed, as you'll see, they don't appear to have lived at the same address.'

I turned my back on the trio and walked across to a corner. I closed my eyes for a second or two as I laid a private bet with myself, then opened them and stared at the top sheet, ignoring everything else and focusing only on the section headed 'Father's name and address.' And there it was: I'd won my bet. Peter Hastings McGrew and Alafair McGrew were the children of one Peregrine Holmes, better known as Perry.

I was smiling as I faced my officers once more. I handed one of the extracts to each of them. 'There you go, lads,' I exclaimed. 'The whole bloody world, me included, thought that Holmes disposed of all his dodgy businesses after he was shot, all the stuff that was linked to the drugs trade, the prostitution, the protection, the money laundering. But he didn't; he simply transferred them to his kids, and nobody noticed. We thought he'd gone away, but he hasn't.'

'So where's Peter?' Martin asked.

'That's one question, but we're cooking by gas here, lads, so let's see if we can answer another first.' I glanced at Jim, and took out my mobile. 'Mind if I make a call?'

'Not at all.'

I found McFaul's number and called it, then jumped on him when he picked up. 'Ciaran, Bob Skinner. I need to know something. The Seagull Hotel: I know there's no CCTV coverage inside, but what about the car park?'

'That's the second thing we checked,' he replied. 'Yes, there's a camera outside, but it's no great help. People come and go all night, it's poorly lit and the coverage isn't complete.'

'Be that as it may, can you access the tapes?'

'There aren't any. It records on to a computer hard disk, stores automatically for two weeks then deletes, a day at a time.'

'In that case we're within the window. Don't get your hopes up, but I'd like you to look at the night we're interested in for the following vehicle: a black VW Golf GTI, registration number L712FTG. See what you get.'

'I'll put people on it. Is this just a kite you're flying, Bob?'

'Some might call it that; I'd call it a fucking jumbo jet. Make sure they're your best people.'

When I finished, Jim Glossop was beaming. 'This sounds like proper police work,' he said.

'And we're not done yet.'

'In that case, I did this as well.' He handed me a third photocopy. 'It's an extract of the father's birth certificate. His parents were Peter Holmes, and Alafair Hastings. That shows you where the children's names came from. Will that be useful too?'

'It might be,' I told him, 'where we're going with this. It could give me an edge. Thanks, mate; till the next time.' I walked back out into the sunlight, my faithful followers close behind.

'Where is next, boss?' McGuire asked.

'For you, lad, back to the office. I need you to try to pin down Peter Hastings McGrew, in case I can't find him by other means. He's ex-army, but they don't know where he is. You've got his date of birth, so start with the DSS; they'll have his national insurance number and a contributions record. It might take you straight to him, but if not, go to British Telecom, and look for subscribers with that name. His car's taxed, so it should be insured. By which company? Find out. Then there's the electoral registers . . .' I stopped; he nodded. 'I'll drop you at the office,' I told him, 'then Andy and I will go to the Murrayfield.

I need to pay another visit to young Mr Drysalter. There's something I have to ask him, and he might even know where Peter is, save us some time. He should be back in the land of the half awake by now.'

He was, but not much more than that; his eyes were still heavy from sedation. The doctor on duty had been hesitant about letting us see him, indeed he'd refused at first, then relented when I'd threatened to call Mr Jacobs. 'Don't be too long,' he said. 'The man's having a hard time. We have to move his knees every so often, and you can imagine, with the fractures, that's a painful process.'

'I hope the physios aren't Hearts supporters,' I muttered.

'Oh no,' Derek Drysalter sighed when we walked into his room. 'Not again. Look, whatever you say, I'm not changing my statement.' The nursing staff had him out of bed, but on a chair with his legs in huge hinged splints, propped on stools and supported by pillows. It was the best they could do, but it didn't look close to comfortable.

I sat on the edge of his bed and looked down at him. 'I don't care about your fucking statement, Derek,' I told him. 'Anyway, you'd be wasting your time if you did change it, and ours, for we'd never get a conviction against the guy who worked you over. All I want is the answer to one simple question. When you found out that Alafair was planning an away trip while you were off on international duty, did you go crying to anyone? Specifically, did you go crying to your father-in-law?' I leaned forward. 'Don't lie to me on this, Derek. Don't even let that idea cross your befuddled mind. You're not important. This is. What future you have left could ride on you telling me the truth right now.'

He turned his head away, looked out of the window and muttered something.

'I didn't hear that.'

'Yes!' he cried out. 'Yes I did. I phoned Perry.'

I moved round to face him 'What did you say to him?'

'I told him Alafair was doin' my head in, and I asked him, please, if he'd fucking talk to her.'

'How did he react?'

'He told me to leave it with him, that was all.'

'How long have you and Alafair been married?' I asked.

'Just over a year.'

'How long had you known her before that?'

'Seven or eight months.'

'Did she tell you right away who her father was?'

'No. I didn't even know she had a father. She told me she'd been brought up by her mother, and that she was dead. She never told me about him till after the wedding. He'd just moved into his new house.' He snorted. 'House? Private nursing home, more like. She took me up there one day, in the close season, and introduced me to him. Poor bastard; spoon-fed by the one guy, lifted and turned and all his tubes changed by the other. He's game, though, Perry. He's still got a smile about him.'

'Do you see him often?'

He nodded. 'I go there about once a month, just to say hello. I feel sorry for him. I take him videos of the Hibs games; the club films them all, for training. At first both of us went, but lately it's just been me. I think he and Alafair fell out about something.'

'Has he ever told you how he wound up in his wheelchair?'

'No, but Alafair did. She said that a business rival tried to kill him.'

'Mmm,' I murmured. 'And did she tell you what happened to that so-called rival?'

'Yes, your lot shot him, didn't they?'

'Well now, that's not exactly true, but never mind. Tell me, Derek,'

I continued, 'when did things start to go wrong between you and her?'

'Oh,' he drawled, lazily, 'it must have taken all of a couple of months. She started to complain about being left on her own when I had to train, then when I was away on Scotland trips. After that it was my gambling, although she never minded when I took her to the casino. I know why that was now. Her and Tony bloody Manson.' He frowned. 'When I get back on my feet . . .'

'You'll what? Derek, these people are in a different world from you. What you should do when you get back on your feet is go and take a coaching qualification, or get a nice job as a TV pundit. You got off with your life. Leave it at that.'

He made a derisive noise. 'Hmmph! That's easy for you to say.'

'You're right,' I agreed. 'It's easy because I don't want to be there when they fish you out of the sea. I don't want to be walking past those new offices at the west end wondering which one you're underneath.' I felt a burst of real sympathy for the poor naive lad. 'You're in an alien world, mate. You're mixed up with some very bad people. You've already seen what Manson can do to people who upset him. Well, let me explain this to you in football terms. Tony's a first division player, sure, but Perry, your wife's old man, he is premier league.'

He stared at me, wide-eyed, and then laughed in my face. 'Perry? You're kidding. He's a property developer.'

'Yes, and Mussolini was an MI5 agent: so what? Derek, you must have friends in newspapers.'

'Of course.'

'Well, you get one of them . . . the *Saltire* would probably be the best source . . . to let you see its file on Perry, the stuff they've printed and the stuff they can't.' I stopped. 'Do it if you can be bothered, but Perry isn't the reason I'm here. You've answer one of my questions.

**346**

This is the other. Where can I find your brother-in-law?'

He blinked and shook his head, as if he was trying to clear it. 'He's in fucking Swindon, and so's my sister, and so are their kids. But what's Jamie got to do with any of this?'

'I wasn't talking about him, Derek. I meant your wife's brother.'

'What the hell are you talking about, man? Alafair doesn't have a brother.'

'Oh, but she does.'

'Then I have never met him, and she's never mentioned him. Neither has Perry. And that's the God's honest truth.' It was, too. He was beginning to realise how far out of his depth he was, and he was scared. 'Look, go away, please,' he begged.

'We will,' I said. 'But you don't want to be on your own. Do you have parents?'

He nodded. 'My mum and dad. They live in Falkirk; that's where I started out. They're just ordinary people, though.'

'So are you, Derek.' He really was a sad figure. 'Shame, but that's how it is now. You want my advice? Stick close to your folks, and to your football club; they're the only ones who'll look after you. Forget you ever knew the crew you've been mixing with.'

Martin and I left him to it. The DC said nothing until we were out in the car park. There he ventured, 'Sorry, sir, but where are we on this?'

'Wait till we make our next call,' I told him. 'If I'm right, it'll become clear then. Fettes first, though.'

We headed back to the office. When we got there, McGuire was looking more downhearted than I'd seen him. 'I'm getting nowhere, boss.' I hadn't expected that we would need his research, but now that we did, I wasn't too surprised by what he told me. 'Peter McGrew's not on the phone, his NI contributions are in arrears, and he's not registered to vote anywhere that I've found. He's vanished.'

There was no good news from Newcastle either, but there was a note on my desk from Fred Leggat passing on a message from, of all people, Tony Manson, letting me know that Marlon Watson's funeral had been set for the following afternoon, a burial in Seafield Cemetery.

It was almost lunchtime, but I wasn't hungry. I sent the boys off to eat, then called Alison. 'Fate is on my side,' I told her. 'It doesn't want me to get on that helicopter.' When I told her what had come in the way, she understood; she knew it was my practice to attend the funerals of murder victims in cases I was working.

As it happened, it didn't matter. 'Fate's working for you on two fronts,' she said. 'The Met Office have given the North Sea operators a bad weather warning for Wednesday, and possibly Thursday as well. All routine flights to platforms have been cancelled.'

'I can smell another weekend on the water looming up for us.'

She laughed. 'I thought that was on the cards anyway. I've been expecting you to take me looking at boats.'

'We've got four years to wait, remember, but I suppose we could start with something small.' What a difference a day made. Less than twenty-four hours before I hadn't been joking.

She went all Robert Burns on me. '*Nae man can tether time or tide*,' she quoted. 'When I see you try, I'll stop believing that, but not before.'

I couldn't come up with a poetic counter. 'Until then you could take up golf,' I suggested.

'You'll roast me on a spit first,' she replied, cheerfully. 'How did Lowell's tip play out?' she asked.

'Pure gold, my love, pure gold.'

'Stop calling me that, it's unsettling. I'm glad you're still moving forward, for I'm bloody stuck. If you were being objective, you'd have removed me from the investigation by now.'

'Alastair Grant would love me to do that,' I chuckled. 'He can wait, though. You just need a bit of good fortune. Tell you what, you can swap Hugh Grant's kid brother for McGuire if you like. He's my lucky charm just now. *Cherchez la femme* indeed.'

As I hung up, I felt the first pangs of hunger. There was still time to go up to the big boys' dining room. That seemed like a good idea, but just as I rose from my chair, my mobile sounded.

No preliminaries. 'I've got your car, sir,' Ciaran McFaul announced. 'It's a shit camera, but there's a clear shot of it arriving at eleven twenty-three, and leaving eleven minutes later. The driver's a lean guy, and judging by his height against the vehicle, he's around six feet. There is no chance of an identification, though. He's wearing a black garment with a hood, SAS-style.'

'That figures. Thanks, Ciaran.'

'I should be thanking you,' he said. 'This is our investigation you're working on. I want to be involved from now on, sir.' He sounded serious. I sensed that I might be on the way to being sandwiched between two warring chief constables, but there was still the major problem of the earlier leak.

I stalled him. 'Let me think about it.'

'What's to think about? You know who the man is, don't you?'

'I know who owns the car,' I admitted, 'but . . . Look, the same man is most probably responsible for ordering a murder here. I'm still staking a prior claim to him.'

'I should be there, nonetheless,' he insisted.

When I thought about it he was right, but not on procedural grounds. He had information and if he took it into his own inquiry, might word not get back to the other side, as quickly as it had before? But what if McFaul was the leak himself? Shit!

I made a decision; I had to trust somebody. 'Okay,' I agreed, 'but this is how it's going to work. Who's viewed this recording with you?'

'Nobody,' he replied. 'I'm at the hotel now, on my own.'

'Then get in your car and drive straight up here. Come to my office in police headquarters. Come on your own, and don't tell anyone. When you get here you can phone your boss and tell him that you've had a tip about something, anything, I don't give a fuck what but not this investigation, and that you need to go undercover.'

'Are you kidding?' He laughed, incredulously. 'He'll skin me. Why the hell should I do that?'

'Because I haven't located this guy yet, and I don't want him to be tipped off before I do, as he has been once before.'

'Hey,' he snapped, 'are you saying—'

'Shut up. I'm telling you what happened, but I'm not blaming anyone, not yet. That's the deal. That's what I want you to do. I'm trying to reach out here and grab the untouchable, and nobody is going to get in the way, or I'll be grabbing them. If you're coming, drive; if you're not, keep your fucking mouth closed in your office. Which is it to be?'

I listened to the silence as he made up his mind. 'Have you got a job for me in your CID,' he asked, 'if I get busted back to uniform?'

I chuckled softly. He was what I liked, detective first, cop second. 'Ciaran, I'll find a slot here for you regardless, if you want it.'

'In that case, I'll see you in three hours, maybe less if the tunnel's flowing smoothly.'

It was the best solution I could devise. Cross-border wrangles are always a pain, but I knew that I'd have to involve my English colleagues sooner or later, leak or no leak. Inviting McFaul to join me was a step towards that, and the way I'd done it took him out of play for up to three hours, time enough, possibly, to run Peter McGrew to ground.

Holmes's son might have proved elusive, but he existed and I had something to pin on him. There was no way he could know it either at that stage, and that worked to my advantage. But to arrest him, I had to find him. How to do that? Yes, I could have driven up to Perry Holmes's place and demanded that he hand over his secret son. Sure, and that would have got me precisely nowhere. But maybe I wouldn't need to.

My next stop was Blackford Hill, back to see Alafair. I suspected that it might be more confrontation than conversation, so I decided to take a female officer along. But which one? The closest was DC Shannon, Alf Stein's gopher. I called him and asked if he could spare her.

'Christ,' he grumbled. 'What is it with Serious Crimes just now? I've had your secondee Higgins on looking for her, not just once but twice, mind you . . . and Grant's giving me grief about his DI being away from his team. Now you're wanting Dottie as well?'

He was in 'awkward old bastard' mode, but I levered him out of it by telling him what had happened in my investigation and why I wanted her.

'Holmes has kids?' he exclaimed. 'He's a fucking dy-nasty?' (He'd been a fan of the TV series and mangled the word as it had.) 'Sure, you can have her. It sounds like a good cause.'

I had planned to go up to Blackford in the Discovery as usual, but I changed my mind, and commandeered a marked police vehicle instead, complete with blue light. That's never been my favourite mode of transport but I felt that it suited the circumstances. I didn't want to turn up quietly at Alafair Drysalter's door, not for a second time. I let Martin drive, with DC Shannon in the back. I knew her well enough since I was a regular in her boss's office, but she and Martin had never met before. Each seemed fairly impressed by the other.

Alafair had remembered to lock the gates. I had to press the entryphone button. 'Yes?' She sounded annoyed, impatient.

'Police,' I announced. 'Detective Superintendent Skinner and colleagues.'

'Oh, go away, will you!' she shouted.

'We're coming in, one way or another,' I told her evenly. 'So choose the easy option.'

After a few seconds, she did. There was a buzz, Martin pushed the gate and it opened. The Afghans were in the garden. They came bounding up to us, barking, their long, high-maintenance coats flying. They'd lost whatever hunter instincts the breed was supposed to have. They were friendly, designer pooches that would have been as much use as guard dogs as the hamster I'd bought Alex when she was six. Shannon made a fuss of them and they fell in with us as we walked up to the door.

Alafair was waiting for us, on the threshold. Any traces of her bruising was covered by make-up, her hair was salon set, and she wore a gold lounge suit that made me think of *Hello!* magazine. 'What the hell's this?' she snapped. 'Three this time? Look, I don't give autographs, okay. Where's the other young guy? He was nice.'

'This is his day for helping old ladies across the street,' I replied. 'Or for taking young ones off it. Invite us in. You need to talk to us.'

'Like hell I do,' she retorted, 'but if you insist, come on. Sasha, Pasha, you stay.' The dogs fell back, obediently.

The house was the type that estate agents were once fond of describing as 'architect designed', all flashy features, but not, at first sight, comfortable. The room into which she led us was enormous: one wall was all glass, a picture window, with doors set in it, that looked up towards the Royal Observatory, and there was an upper level that the sales brochure might have called the 'Minstrel Gallery'. The furniture was there to be admired rather than for comfort.

'What do you want?' she asked. 'Why are you hassling me? Have you found the driver yet?'

'There was no driver, Alafair, as you know very well. Now it's my turn to ask you a question. Has Tony told you about Marlon?'

'Who the hell is Marlon?'

'His driver. A lad about your own age. Solidly built kid, not too smooth, very Edinburgh. I'm guessing he might have picked you up sometimes when you were going to meet Manson. I don't imagine the Ibiza trip was your only encounter.'

He tossed her head back. 'Ah,' she said, airily, hamming it up like the failed actress she was. 'That boy. Was that his name? What about him?'

'He's rather dead, I'm afraid.'

That wasn't in the script. 'What do you mean?' she exclaimed.

'I mean he's not breathing any more,' I snapped. 'I mean he's starting to go off. I mean he's in a box, paid for by Tony for sure, waiting to be put in a hole in the ground. Is there anything about being dead that you don't understand?' Out of the corner of my eye I could see Dorothy Shannon flinch, but I was off and running. 'Your question should have been "How did he die?" Answer, somebody killed him. Next question, "But why, the poor boy?" Answer, because of you!'

'Me?' she squealed; ex tempore she was lousy.

'Yes, Alafair, you.' I took my voice back down to normal. 'This is how it happened. You'd been playing about with Manson for a while, and maybe others but I'm only concerned with him. He asked you to go with him for a week to Ibiza, while your husband was away with his international mates. You agreed, but then you did something fairly stupid . . . the norm for you, I imagine . . . and Derek found out. He didn't have the nuts to face you about it, so he called your dad, the father-in-law that he thinks is a nice guy, Perry, Mr Holmes.' The make-up changed shade as the skin beneath it paled.

'He asked him for help, and your dad in turn asked you what you were playing at. You told him it was none of his business. He asked you who you were playing with, you told him, and you probably said there was nothing he could do about it, the poor old quadriplegic cripple.' I paused.

'Good, you're not contradicting me. I've got it right. Now,' another pause, 'here's what happened next. Your dad can't move much, but he's still got a long arm. He reached out, to an old associate in Newcastle, and he hired two men, thugs, brutes, musclemen. They came up to Edinburgh, they got hold of Marlon, and they killed him. I spent some time thinking they were trying to get information from him, but I don't believe that any more. I reckon they just killed him, pure and simple, to order. You see, Manson himself is too difficult a target, and he might also be too financially important to your dad to be killed. But the word was sent. "Play around with my nearest and dearest and this is what happens to yours." So act your way out of that one, kid. You indulged yourself, and a boy died. How does it feel, Alafair?'

She sat down, abruptly, on one of her designer chairs, then reached out for a box on a table, and found a cigarette and a lighter. I took them from her. 'Not while I'm in the room, please. I detest the habit.' I did and I always will, but that was a . . . a smokescreen, if you like; at that moment I didn't want her finding any crumb of comfort.

'What do you want me to say?' she murmured. 'Because I won't. I know whose daughter I am, Mr Skinner.'

'Yes, I thought you might. But know what? There's another twist. I don't believe that Derek slapping you around had anything to do with him being attacked. Way I see it, Perry sent Tony a message, and Tony sent him one back. Christ, he told me as much, before I really knew why. Now they're quits and Manson won't be lifting your skirts again, lady.'

'Tough,' she whispered. 'I won't be missing much.'

'The story's not done yet, though,' I told her. 'The Newcastle guys were sloppy. They used a traceable van and we got on to them. Your father found out about that. It was a problem for him; if we caught these men, and they talked . . . you can see, can't you? So he took action, and now they're dead too. You might not have had a memorable shag with old Tony, but it sure had consequences.'

She snatched the fag and the Zippo from my hand and lit up. I opened the glass doors.

'Thanks,' she said, tight-lipped, and it wasn't for the fresh air. 'I didn't know any of that, apart from the first bit, about Derek crying to my dad, instead of setting his football team on Tony. But even if it's true, I won't help you.'

'Have you always been so fucking self-centred?' I asked her. 'You'd be no use to us as a witness. I'm not interested in you, Alafair. It's your brother I want. Your dad couldn't have done all that stuff on his own. He can't even make a phone call unaided any more. In the old days your Uncle Alasdair was his executive arm, so to speak. Now he's dead. And so's Johann Kraus, the guy who did the really messy stuff for your father and uncle. So your brother's had to take everything on himself. I can place him at the murder scene on Tyneside: I know he killed those three guys. I need you to tell me where I can find him now.'

She shook her head. 'No chance. Anyway, Hastie's not like that. He wouldn't do that. He couldn't.'

'He couldn't do what? He's an ex-soldier; Christ, he's trained to do that sort of work. Your big brother killed two men in cold blood, close up, and then he found the third and ripped . . .' And then it hit me. 'What did you call him?'

She saw my confusion and knew that she'd made a huge mistake. She realised how, too, and tried to back off from it. 'Nothing. I said Peter, his name's Peter.'

But it was out there. It was in the room. 'Peter Hastings McGrew, Hastings after your granny. You called him Hastie, because that's his family name. I've met him, I've even bloody met him!' I shouted to the room. 'He's hiding in plain sight. He's your dad's nurse.'

She took a huge drag on her cigarette. 'Okay!' she screamed. 'Now go! Fuck off!'

'We're going, don't worry, but you're coming with us. I'm detaining you for formal questioning about a conspiracy to murder. DC Shannon, take Mrs Drysalter out to the car. Cuff her if you have to.'

She kicked up hell about her dogs. She kicked up hell all the way to Fettes. I arranged for Sasha and Pasha to be taken to the boarding kennels where they'd been housed while she'd been in Ibiza with lover boy, and I gave her a kennel all to herself when we got back to headquarters. I'd had a legitimate excuse for taking her in, but I had no illusions about being able to hold her. I didn't need to do that anyway; I wanted only to keep her quiet until I could arrange a visit to her father.

I gathered the team and briefed them. Alf Stein came down to join us after I'd told him what had happened. 'Who's normally in the house, other than Holmes and the man you believe is his son?' the DCS asked.

'Housekeeper, chef and a personal assistant,' I replied, 'but they're background. Then there's the masseur, Vanburn.'

'Is he really a masseur?'

'He's big enough to be muscle,' I conceded, 'but I'd say he's for real. Holmes genuinely does need specialised care.' I pointed to Adam. 'Jeff, your wife's a nurse, isn't she? What's her governing body?'

'The Royal College of Nursing.'

'Then get in touch with them and run the name Vanburn past them. It could be surname or forename, I don't know which. See if he's registered with them.'

Alf frowned. 'How do you want to play this, Bob?'

'I don't have time to be subtle, gaffer. I want to put men at the back of the property to block any exit that way and then I plan to drive straight up there, four of us, me, Jeff, Andy and Mario, at speed. But, I've been in there, and I can tell you the place has a shit-hot security system. The guys at the back can't be too close or they'll trigger movement sensors. So when we're ready to go in, I want the power cut off.'

'Are you going armed?' the boss asked.

'We're after an ex-soldier who's killed three people,' I reminded him. 'I'll be carrying, and so will Jeff. I've seen him on the range.'

Alf frowned. 'Do you really want two young unarmed officers with you in that situation?'

It was a good point; I recognised the hazard. 'No, sir, you're right. I don't want to be looking anywhere but straight ahead.'

'Sensible. In that case, they stay back and I'm coming.'

I stared at him. 'With respect, sir,' I began. 'I know you're trained to handle a gun, but can I suggest that you take a look at yourself in a full-length mirror, then turn sideways.'

DCS Stein peered back at me. 'Are you saying I'm a fat bastard?' he murmured.

'Let's just say you used to be faster on your feet than you are now.'

He sighed. 'Aye, you might be right there. I don't like leading from the back, Bob, that's all.' He grinned. 'I could always go in front and you and DS Adam could hide behind me, then step out and shout "Surprise!" That would make Holmes jump right out of his fucking wheelchair.'

The laughter broke the tension, and an option occurred. 'I can pull in Brian Mackie,' I determined. 'He's our top marksman. Any more than three and we'd be in danger of shooting each other.' I paused. 'But back to this security camera problem.'

'There's a problem with cutting off the power,' Fred Leggat said. 'It would be tricky to do it selectively. You might wind up cutting off the whole of Lothianburn and Straiton. Even then you couldn't be sure it would work. A good security system will have back-up power that takes over within a couple of seconds.'

He was right; even my home alarm had a back-up battery. 'In that case we've got a real difficulty. It's quite a long way up to Holmes's house. On my previous visit, judging by the time it must have taken the guy Vanburn to get from what they call the receiving area to the door, and how long it took me to get there, the cameras must have picked me up almost as soon as I'd turned in off the road.'

'So?' a voice from the doorway broke in. 'Why don't you simply drop in on him? Don't you have a traffic helicopter in this part of the world? Land it right on the guy's lawn.'

Six pairs of eyes swung round to look at the intruder. I laughed; Martin smiled. 'Our friend from the south. Guys, this is DI McFaul, from Newcastle, who thinks he has first claim on our target. Yes, Ciaran, we have a chopper. Are you qualified with a pistol?' He nodded. 'In that case your reward for being a clever bugger is that you'll be on it.' I looked at Alf. 'Boss, that rules you out, I'm afraid. We don't have time to fit extra fuel tanks.'

For all his bulk, the head of CID could make things happen quickly when all that was needed was a phone. The operation was set up and ready to go in an hour. We'd even sourced a drawing from the local authority planning department showing the layout of the place. There was no rear driveway. That made things simpler: no getaway option. There were woods behind the house, accessible from the adjoining estate, and uniformed officers were on the way there, to cut off any escape route. I still had one logistical problem to solve, though; a personal one. Daisy Mears had an exhibition opening that evening in a gallery in Dunbar, and dinner afterwards with the owner and his wife. I called my fallback, privately.

'Of course,' Alison said, when I asked her. I didn't go into detail, or mention firearms; I told her that something had come up and I was committed, that was all. 'It's not a problem. I take it that Alex has keys.'

'Yes, she has. And she knows the alarm combination.' Something came into my head, and I released it. 'You should have a set too. In fact, when you go out, why don't you take a suitcase and leave some clothes in the wardrobe. It'll make it easier.'

She laughed, softly. 'And a toothbrush in your jar?'

'That too. You can even use my toothpaste.'

'As long as it has stripes. When can I expect you?'

'Dunno. I'll let you know when I'm on the way home.'

'Do that. Good luck with whatever it is, and take some good news with you. Things have moved on in my, your other, investigation. You won't have to go in that helicopter after all.'

*That's what you think*, I whispered, just as I hung up.

# Seventeen

'Go on then,' Alison demanded. 'You've eaten, and you've nearly finished your second bottle of red. Are you going to tell us what happened, while you still can?'

'Yes, Pops,' Alex chipped in, 'we've been patient for long enough.'

'Out of deference to our guest,' I reminded her.

DI McFaul was staying over. I'd offered him the use of our spare room, and he'd accepted. A night alone in a hotel room would have been unthinkable. We were both high. It had nothing to do with the Tempranillo either; we were flying on natural fuel, high-octane adrenalin. We'd made it home just after nine and killed the first bottle before we'd even sat down to eat.

'Let me tell the story,' Ciaran said. 'I saw the whole thing; Bob missed the first part.'

I held up a hand to pause him, and checked my watch at the same time: ten past ten. Before I'd opened my mouth, my daughter was on me. 'Pops,' she warned, 'if you say, "Time for bed, young lady," there will be war.'

I gave in. 'One's enough for today; go on, Ciaran.'

'Good.' He looked around the table. 'Are we sitting comfortably? Then I'll begin. So there we are in this chopper . . .'

'What?' Alison exclaimed.

'This helicopter.'

'They got him in a helicopter?' she gasped.

'It was only a wee one,' I pointed out, 'and it wasn't going very far. Ciaran, don't be put off by heckling.'

'I love it when you're merry,' Alex laughed.

'So there we are,' the Geordie resumed, beaming at her, 'in this chopper, coming down in the man's driveway like Robert Duvall in *Apocalypse Now* . . . hinnie, all we needed was to be playing "Ride of the Valkyries" through speakers. We land and the three of us, me, Bob and Jeff Adam, jump out. Your dad goes round the side of the house and the two of us head for the front door. Jeff's got this ram, battering ram, enormously heavy; he can hardly lift it. He hits the door with it. Normally one tap and we're in but this just goes "Boing!" and bounces off, because the door's made out of steel. Remember this, pet, and it'll see you through life: people with steel front doors invariably have something to hide.' He was pushing it with the "pet", but Alex was too engaged to protest.

'So he gives it another thump, and still it doesn't budge. Finally on the third swing it does give, but the ram rebounds again and Jeff lets it slip. Thud! It lands on his foot. And did he scream? Did he ever! Like a Sunderland striker when he gets tackled. They think he's broken a couple of bones. So there we are, this amateur FART team . . .'

'What?' Alex's eyes bulged.

'It's a Tyneside nickname, pet, Fast Action Response Team, except they're not really called that. Anyway, there we are, one of us hopping about on one leg and the other a stranger in town. Not an auspicious start.'

'What happened after that?'

'Ach, by the time I got to where I was supposed to be your dad had arrested the guy; show over.'

I reached across and touched my daughter's hand. 'And with that, love . . .'

She smiled. 'I know, it's over for me too. All right. Night, Pops. Good night, Ciaran. Good night, Alison, and please don't let them keep me awake.'

'I won't,' my occasional bidey-in promised. 'See you in the morning.' She waited until the door had closed and for a few seconds after that, before continuing. 'Now tell me what really happened.' Earlier while I was changing, I had given her a quick rundown on Hastie McGrew, and about the raid on his father's house. I had left out most of the detail but as soon as Ciaran had mentioned helicopters and battering rams, her police officer's brain had drawn conclusions.

McFaul's expression changed; his head slumped a little and the humour left his face, as the last of the action juice wore off.

'What happened,' he repeated, '. . . was that after that bloody sergeant's performance, when I got in there, where I was supposed to be, our man was waiting for me, and he was armed. He had the drop on me. Holmes was in his pool, being floated by his masseur or nurse, whatever he is. That caught my eye first and when I looked at his son he had a gun on me. I was looking right down the barrel, Alison, and I couldn't move. He told me to drop mine, and I did. I saw his eyes narrow and I said the fastest *Hail Mary!* I've ever managed in my life, for I really did think he was going to fire. And that's when Bob shot the gun clean right out of his hand from the patio door. Personally, I'd rather he'd hit him in the head.'

'I could have,' I told him, 'but the hand was the safer target, for you, not for him. He could have pulled the trigger by reflex.'

'You might have missed.' He shuddered.

'I don't, from that far away.'

He chuckled, grimly. 'I didn't know that. All I could think was that I didn't have any spare underpants.'

Alison was anxious. 'He didn't give you any more trouble, did he?'

'No,' I assured her. 'He couldn't. His left hand's pretty much useless, as a result of a service injury. After a year of feeding his father, for a while he's going to find out for himself how that feels.'

'Where's McGrew now?' she asked.

'I had him taken to the Royal A&E, under armed guard, to have his hand fixed. The bullet went through the base of his thumb and out the other side. As soon as they're ready to discharge him, he'll be moved to Fettes. He can have his sister's old room; I released her as soon as we'd secured Hastie.'

'And what about their father?'

'Perry? He's still at home. We'd no grounds to arrest him. Suppose we had, where would we have taken him? No, we left him with his nurse, and there are officers front and back of the house. It's not that he'll be going anywhere but I don't want the press to get near him.'

'How did he take it?'

'Have you ever met Perry?'

'No.'

'Good. He was raging after it had all happened. It was almost frightening to see, all that anger contained in a body that's quite unable to move. He was naked in the pool, and that made him even more furious. Vanburn took him out of the water on a trolley thing that he uses, but he had to sedate him before he even started to dry and dress him. As soon as he was back in his chair and able, I tried to question him, but by then he was back to the old Perry. Same old line that he's been using for years: "I'm a legitimate businessman, and I'm not responsible for the actions of those around me. Now go and prove otherwise, but while you're doing that I'll be calling my lawyers." Nailing Perry Holmes was never an option, love. We've done the best we could. We've got Hastie, plus we found his car round the back. I left a search team going through everything. They won't turn up anything incriminating in the house, but they did find a knife in a scabbard, taped under the passenger seat of the car. It's a Gurkha kukri; an army souvenir, I guess, since that's who he served with. He's bound to have burned the clothes that he wore the night he took care of the guys on Tyneside, but there's a stain on the face of the squab of the driver's seat. The SOCOs were afraid to put luminol on it in case they compromised it, but they're sure it's blood, and the hope has to be that it can be matched to Winston Church.'

Alison picked up the bottle, topped up our glasses and set it back down, empty. McFaul was well and truly down from his cloud. His eyes were starting to glaze over. I didn't mind that; we were probably heading for an argument next morning over the custody of McGrew and it would do me no harm if he had a bad head.

'Interesting stuff, blood,' she murmured. 'Would you like to hear my news now, while you still can?'

I hadn't given it a thought since we'd spoken in the afternoon; I'd been focused on Holmes and son, the family firm. 'Of course, sorry.'

'Well,' she began, pouring herself some white, then leaning back, 'I took your advice. I did some *cherchez*ing. The last time I was in uniform I picked up a little inside knowledge. Do you know that we have a specialist rape unit in the force?'

I nodded. 'Of course; staffed by women officers only, naturally.'

'Almost, but there are specialists they can call in on cases of male rape. However, I went to the women, or rather to one in particular, the team leader, Inspector Martina Chivers, and I asked her about reports on a specific date. Everything they do is very confidential, so much so that if there is doubt, or if the potential victim declines to make a complaint, no report is made, to anyone.'

'Not even to Alf?'

'Not even him; even when there is a complaint, the name's withheld from circulation and only goes to Crown Office. However, Martina was prepared to tell me, girl to girl, that on the day after Weir, McCann and Telfer met up for their boys' night out, a woman was brought into the office in Wester Hailes, in the early afternoon. She was seen by a patrol car, in the street, in a dazed and distressed state, with her clothing dirty and dishevelled. The rape unit was called in, she was medically examined and the doctor determined that there had been multiple rape, and that she'd been sodomised. Semen samples were taken, and in due course these determined that at least three men were involved, each with a different blood type; one was A positive, as are half the population, a second was type O positive, that's one in every three people, roughly. Neither of those is much good as an identifier,' she smiled, 'but guess what? Albie McCann was AB positive . . . as are only three in every one hundred people.'

'The message penetrated my befuddled mind. 'Well done you. And the victim was . . . ?'

'The victim, once she got a hold of herself, refused to make a complaint.'

'She what!' I exclaimed, startling McFaul.

'She said that she had been at a party that got out of hand.'

'Yet she allowed herself to be brought in?'

'Yes, but she was pretty much hysterical when she was found.'

'And she submitted to examination?'

'Yes again, but she said later that she'd been under the influence or she wouldn't have. Then she demanded that they called her a taxi. She wouldn't take a lift home in a police car, even though it was offered.'

'Did the unit take blood samples?' I asked.

'With the rest, yes, of course. Tests showed neither drugs nor alcohol in her bloodstream.'

'Did she give a name?'

'Uh-huh.' Alison rolled her eyes. 'Martina shouldn't have told me, but she did, in confidence. She called herself Mary Whitehouse.'

'Tell me you're ki . . .' I broke off. 'No, you're not, are you?' My mind was working again, and heading in a direction that I did not like at all. 'In a case like this, complaint declined, wouldn't all the evidence be disposed of?'

'Normally yes, but Martina didn't believe her party story, not for a second. She hoped she would change her mind and come back, so she carried on with the lab work, and got those results. The blood types were enough for me; three gentlemen songsters out on a spree on the evening before she was found, and thirty-three to one odds on that one of the sperm donors was McCann. I got an arrest warrant for Telfer; a couple of Grampian officers flew out to the platform this afternoon to lift him and bring him back onshore. He'll be driven down to us tomorrow morning.'

Her initiative made me smile. 'Do we actually have grounds for arrest?'

'Suspicion of rape? How's that?'

'But there's no complaint,' I pointed out.

'There is now, I made one, on Mrs Whitehouse's behalf. Correct me if I'm wrong, but if we believe that a crime's been committed, don't we have a duty to investigate?'

'You could argue that,' I conceded.

She beamed. 'Good, for I told the sheriff you'd asked me to apply for the warrant.'

I drew her a long look. But what could I say? 'You know what this does, don't you?' I murmured. McFaul was watching us, with the flickering eyelids of someone pretending to be sober and alert.

'I think so,' Alison replied. 'But I want you to be the one to say it.'

'Mary Whitehouse equals Mia Watson: same initials. That magazine article. Mia was the victim.'

'A fair assumption, but that's still all it is, a guess.'

'Maybe, but . . .' I stood. 'Just a minute.' I left the room and went upstairs. Alex was still awake, reading Thomas Wolfe . . . the original, not the *Bonfire of the Vanities* man. 'Think back three weeks,' I said. 'Was Mia on air every day?'

She frowned at me. 'No,' she answered instantly. 'She was off air on Thursday and Friday. Period problems.'

'What?' I gasped.

'That was what she said, more or less, when she came back next Monday; she said that she'd had an awkward visit from a persistent friend. Girl talk, Pops. Why are you asking?'

'Never mind.'

Everything fitted, and there was one additional piece of evidence; only I knew about it, and I'd be keeping it to myself. With my new knowledge, Mia's frightened and fierce reaction when I wakened from my nightmare made perfect sense to me if she'd been a rape victim a couple of weeks before. And yet, if she had . . .

I went back downstairs, and repeated the story to Alison, and the bewildered McFaul, who was a few glasses beyond understanding what we were talking about. 'Not such a big jump now,' I said.

'How do you want me to play it?' she asked, suddenly tentative.

I shrugged. 'In whatever way you think best.'

'What would you do?' she persisted.

'If it was me, I'd show Martina Chivers her photo, for confirmation, then I'd pull her in.'

'For what reason, though?'

'Jesus, how many do you need? Subject to Chivers's confirmation we know she was a victim of a sexual attack by three men. We believe that one of them was Albie McCann, and we're sure we know who his associates were. Further testing and comparison of the samples will prove it for sure. Two of them are dead, Ali, and the other one's been out of reach since the attack. On the basis of that alone, you could bring her in for questioning. But if you go back to Wyllie and Redpath, ask them whether the person they saw could have been a woman, and if either one says that it's possible, you could arrest her on suspicion of murder.'

'Seriously?' she exclaimed.

'I said that you could do that. I wouldn't go as far as that, not at first, but I'd certainly be inviting her in for a polite chat. If she refuses, then I'd go looking for a warrant.'

'Shouldn't you get involved if it comes to that?' she asked.

The ground under my feet grew very shaky all of a sudden. 'What?' I laughed; a little theatrically, but she didn't seem to notice. 'Lift my daughter's heroine and alienate her affections forever?' I said. 'You're not on.'

No way could I have been involved in arresting Mia, but not because of Alex; in fact, my blood ran cold at the thought of being cross-examined by her QC in a criminal trial. *Tell the court, Detective Superintendent Skinner, didn't you have an intimate relationship with the defendant? Didn't it end badly? Isn't this whole thing your attempt at revenge?*

'And if I do it,' Alison challenged, 'how's Alex going to feel about me?'

And what would defence counsel feel if he knew about us? *Detective Inspector Higgins, isn't your attitude towards my client coloured by her affair with your partner, Detective Superintendent Skinner?*

'That, my dear, we will deal with if it happens.'

# Eighteen

Beyond all the potential for career damage, I was worried about what Mia would say to Alison about me, if they did come face to face. For all that I was pretty sure I could talk my way out of it, even if she spilled the whole damn tin of beans, still I was unsettled, not by the potential embarrassment itself, but because I realised what a selfish bloody fool I'd been, and most of all because I cared about Ali more than I had realised, and about the comfort that I was finding in our relationship.

That concern was set firmly on one side by a call on my mobile as I waited in a queue of traffic near the office, with a recuperating Ciaran McFaul in the passenger seat of the tank. (And there was I, led to believe that Geordies could hold their drink. That was a joke, by the way; a near-death experience can do that to you.) It was from David Pettigrew, in the Edinburgh procurator fiscal's office. They're the prosecutors in Scotland, and technically we investigate crime on their behalf.

'Bob,' he said, 'I need you to come and see me, in my office now. It's about the Hastie McGrew arrest.'

'Has his dad's lawyer been leaning on you?' I asked.

'What do you expect? He's been shouting about wrongful arrest, attempted murder even.'

'Fuck him. If I'd wanted to kill the guy, he'd be dead.'

'I know that and I've told him as much.'

'Who is his lawyer anyway?'

'Ken Green.'

'Wanker.'

'Agreed, but he's not the problem.'

'So what is?' I snapped, losing my patience.

'I'll explain when you get here.'

'Fuck it, Davie, I haven't begun to question the guy yet.' I was giving him a hard time, principally because invitations to the fiscal's office were never to discuss the time of day; they always signalled a crisis of some sort or another.

'Bob,' he sighed, 'would I ask if I didn't have to?'

'No,' I conceded, 'I suppose not. But I tell you now, if that fucker Green's in the room when I get there, I'm walking straight out.'

'He won't be, I promise; but it's not just you I need. I'd like your English colleague to join us. Can you pick him up and bring him?'

'I don't have to. He's with me. I'll see you in however long it takes.'

By the time I'd extricated myself from my traffic queue and found a parking space, it had taken twenty-five minutes. And I was annoyed. I strode into Pettigrew's office, full of hell, with McFaul tagging along an my heels. 'Okay, Davie,' I began, when I was no more than halfway into the room, 'what the fu—' I stopped short. He wasn't alone. He was sitting at his meeting table with a woman, around forty, slim, dark hair, dark suit, frowning and all business.

He rose, she didn't. 'Bob, Detective Inspector,' he greeted us, 'thanks for coming. This is . . .'

'I know who she is,' McFaul said. 'Morning, Paula. Bob, this is Mrs Paula Cherry, from the Crown Prosecution Service, Newcastle office.'

She nodded, but still didn't crack a smile.

'Is this your back-up, Ciaran?' I asked, not best pleased. 'I thought we'd agreed that I'd question McGrew about the Watson murder then let you take him south.'

'I didn't send for her,' he replied. 'I've got no idea . . .'

'Take a seat, gentlemen,' the fiscal said, 'and let me tell you why we're here. We have a situation. Ken Green is demanding that we release Mr McGrew immediately. Apart from the usual bluster, he is also threatening a civil suit against the police. Bob, it would be helpful if you ran through the circumstances that led you to raid Perry Holmes's house yesterday and to arrest his son.'

I did, in detail, step by step from the finding of Marlon Watson's body in the disused public baths, through McGrew's sister's fling with Tony Manson, to our discovery of his existence and of his true identity, finally tying him to the murders in Newcastle.

'Okay?' I concluded, annoyed more than ever by the woman's silent frowning presence. 'Where's the problem with any of that? Now, can Ciaran and I go and hit the guy with rolled-up Yellow Pages or whatever it is you imagine we do to suspects?'

'The problem, Mr Skinner,' she replied, 'from a CPS standpoint, is that you haven't given us enough evidence to proceed.'

'What the hell are you talking about?' I bellowed, slipping into Taggart mode in spite of myself. She'd set me off. 'We've put him at the hotel for you, we're going to give you Winston Church's blood in his car and we've recovered what I'm certain will prove to be the murder weapon, in his possession. Are your English juries so demanding that they want more than that?'

'The CPS is,' she shot back. 'You've put his car at the Seagull Hotel, but you haven't put him in it, not on that night. You've given us a person of similar build, in a hooded black tunic wearing black gloves, but you haven't proved that it was Peter Hastings McGrew.'

I stared at her. 'Fuck me,' I gasped. 'Where is the reasonable doubt?'

'To my mind it exists. I require an overwhelming chance of conviction before I will commit the Crown to the expense of a trial. I don't have it here.'

'Then you go back to Newcastle, lady,' I told her, 'and send us someone higher up the tree.'

'The decision is mine, and I'm telling you what it is. Until my scientific people can put McGrew in that hotel room, and in Church's house, I won't proceed against him. They say there's no prospect of them doing that.'

I smiled. 'If that's how you feel, you're welcome to take the flak. Because I'm damn certain that Ciaran's force won't let you shift the blame for three unsolved murders on to them, just because you're protecting your conviction ratio against all comers. And don't look to me to keep quiet about it to the Scottish media either.' I started to rise. 'Davie, if that's all, I've got a telephone directory to roll up.'

He waved me back down. 'I wish it was, Bob, but it's not.'

I sighed. 'Oh shit. Not you and all, Brutus. What's your effing problem?'

'It's tied in with Mrs Cherry's.'

'How?'

'Well,' he ventured, cautiously, 'legally, what happened in Tyneside has nothing to do with us, and she isn't giving me grounds to hold McGrew on her behalf. But as far as the Watson murder's concerned, with those guys out of the road, there's nothing linking him to that either, and I doubt if there ever will be. So as things stand, you're not going to get a conviction in Scotland either.'

'In that case, Davie,' I growled, 'I will do him for the attempted murder of a police officer.'

He sucked his teeth. 'He'll have a defence for that too.'

I laughed, in lieu of a roar of rage. 'What do you mean?'

'Ken Green's already floated it. He'll argue that his father, in an interesting and varied business life, has made a few enemies, proof of which being his paralysis and the bullet that's still lodged in his head. He'll say that when he heard someone battering at the front door, his first thought was that his dad's life was in danger, and that when DI McFaul burst through the door, armed, he had no proof, nor even any idea, that he was a police officer. He was defending his father from attack, with a registered and legally held handgun.' He looked at me. 'That will be his story, and to tell you the truth, Bob, I can see a jury going for that.'

I felt my eyes narrow. 'But you've got the balls to give them the chance, Davie, yes?'

'If you dig your heels in, I'll prosecute. But if we lose, then the civil suit will follow. Drop all charges and Green will go away, quietly.'

I stared at the wall, trying to burn a hole in it as I thought. Paula Cherry might be chicken, but Davie was a good guy, and I had learned to trust his instincts almost as well as my own. Holmes and son had me by the balls; I knew it, and I did not like the feeling.

'I'm going back to the office,' I announced. 'I'm going to keep him for as long as I can, and then I'm going to charge him with attempt to murder. Once I've done that, I'll have a night to think about it, and to decide whether we walk away from it.'

Pettigrew nodded. 'Fair enough.'

'Of course I reserve the right—' Mrs Cherry began.

'This is Scotland,' I snapped. 'You don't have any rights here. I'll call you later, Davie.'

'Is she always like that?' I asked McFaul, when I could trust myself to speak. By that time we were within sight of the office.

'That was her being cooperative. She works on a ninety per cent chance of conviction; that's her benchmark. I've never met anyone with a more extreme view of what's a reasonable doubt. We're screwed, Bob.'

'Not necessarily. I'm going to ask our specialists if they can place anyone else in his car. If they can't, that might add a couple of points to her calculation.' I smiled, for what seemed like the first time in a while. 'Mind you . . .' I paused, to consider possibilities more rationally than I had in Pettigrew's office. 'Are you as angry as me?'

'Too bloody right.'

'Then charge him.'

'Eh?' he murmured. 'How can I do that?'

'On the basis of the evidence. McGrew's in Scotland, you're in Scotland in pursuit, with a right to be here. As I told her, she has none. She's invisible to me. You charge him, and I'll use all my media friends to make sure that the story goes national. Then if she wants to stick to her line, she'll have to explain it publicly, instead of hanging failure round our necks.'

He glanced at me. 'I'd love to do it, but there's one major obstacle in the way: Paula Cherry's husband. His name's Norman, and he's one of our assistant chief constables. She may be invisible to you, but he's very real to me. If I charged McGrew, after the meeting we've just had, it would be a disciplinary offence. I've got a wife and three kids, a nice house in Hexham and a pension to protect. I've even got promotion prospects. I can't, Bob.'

'He'd hang you out to dry,' I said, 'even though the man pointed a gun at you?'

'ACC Cherry,' he sighed, 'would hang Mother Teresa out to dry if Paula told him to.'

'You realise that I'm probably going to have to release the bastard?'

He nodded. 'Yes.'

'The fucking Holmeses!' I spat. 'Like father, like son.'

'Having seen him, I wouldn't say that the father's got away scot-free.'

'He's still breathing.'

'We're not judges, Bob,' he said. 'If you judge people, you have no time to love them. Mother Teresa said that.'

'And she'd probably have told us that Perry's Jesus in disguise,' I countered. In spite of myself, I smiled at the image, and at the memory of the scene when we had raided the house, the naked form in the water. 'Would that make Vanburn John the Baptist?'

Back at headquarters, McFaul came upstairs to say goodbye to the team; that done, I walked him back down to his car. We shook hands. 'If ever you get to the point where you can't take any more of ACC Cherry and his wife,' I told him, 'let me know. I'm not a decision-maker here, but I've got some influence with the people who are.'

'Thanks, Bob,' he replied, 'but I'll outlast him. The word is that he's going in a couple of years, and when he does, a lot of people will be after her.' He opened the driver's door, then stopped. 'Hell, I almost forgot.' He leaned in and across, to the back seat, produced a plastic bag, and handed it to me. 'My people went over Glenn Milburn's house. They got no meaningful evidence to help you, but they did find half a dozen pay-and-go mobile phones. They're spares as far as we can make out, unconnected to the investigation and of no use to us, but I seem to recall you saying that you were looking for one. Long shot, but you never know. Sometimes all we can do is keep scratching away; we are all pencils in the hand of God, as Mother Teresa also said.'

I laughed as I took the bag. 'And as Bob Skinner says, right now, fuck off back to Tyneside, and mind how you go.'

I wandered back upstairs, full of the huge frustration that came from the knowledge that in all probability I was going to have to let a triple murderer go free. The more I stared into it, the muddier the water became. Pettigrew had been right: attempted murder would never stick, and even a reduced charge, assault by presenting a loaded firearm, would probably fail against Ken Green's defence.

With Jeff Adam on the ground, McFaul had gone in alone, without anyone to witness that he had identified himself properly, other than Vanburn, the nurse, who had been too busy protecting his patient to remember any of the detail. Yet again, I was stuffed by lack of corroboration. I decided to keep McGrew locked up for the rest of the day without charging him. At least that way I could keep his lawyer out of my hair, for until a charge was made, I didn't have to give him access to a brief.

I gave the bag to Andy Martin, and told him what it contained. 'Go through the call logs on each one, incoming and outgoing numbers, and see if any of them mean anything at all. It's a balls-aching job, I know, but it has to be done.'

I retreated into my small office, nursing a mug of coffee. My team had the good sense to leave me alone. As I brooded, I had the wild thought of calling my friend Xavi at the *Saltire* newspaper, and telling him . . . don't quote me personally, mate, but . . . that I had a man in custody who couldn't be charged with murder because an English lawyer thought there was a one in five chance of an acquittal. I was tempted, but I'd have been taking a chance with McFaul's career, so I stayed my hand. Instead I called Alison.

'How goes your morning?' I asked her.

'Better than yours, from the sound of you. Good and bad, really. As we expected, Martina Chivers identified Mia Watson as the victim. But,' she paused, 'before you start doing a lap of honour, I've spoken to both of our witnesses and they're adamant that the attacker was a man. So any notion of Mia Sparkles turning into Catwoman by night is right out the window.'

I growled at her, but she ignored me.

'That lets me focus on Don Telfer. I'm expecting him inside half an hour; the Grampian car's just handed him over to us this side of the Forth Bridge.'

'Can I sit in?' I muttered. 'I feel the need to eat somebody.'

She laughed. 'That bad, is it? You're the boss. I can have him taken to Fettes if you like.'

'No, I'll come to you. The accommodation here's full of a guy I don't want to see for now.'

I drove to Torphichen and arrived there one minute before Donald Telfer and his escorting officers. Alison had him taken straight to an interview room, while we sat at her desk, with Alastair Grant watching from his kennel in the corner of the CID suite. 'I'm guessing McGrew hasn't confessed,' she began.

'It's worse than that, but let's not go there; let's stay focused on the job in hand. You take the lead in questioning, I'll just sit there and stare him down. The first thing you need to find out is how much he knows about what's happened to his pals, given where he's been for the last couple of weeks. If he doesn't . . . it'll be interesting.'

It's a popular misconception that in the circumstances in which Telfer found himself that morning, the innocent are apprehensive and the guilty are angry. In my experience, the opposite is true, and our prisoner bore that out. He was as nervous as a man in the condemned cell, listening to the trap being tested just along the corridor. He looked up when we walked into the room; his face was white, his forehead was covered in sweat and his hands were clenched together so tightly that the bones seemed to show. I gazed at him, sizing him up. He was a strong-looking guy with clear blue eyes, and a complexion that might have been described as 'fresh' were it not for the day-old stubble on his chin and for two lines on his left cheek, criss-crossing to form a rough letter 'X', standing out pale blue against the paleness of his skin. 'Scar on his face,' Redpath had told us.

'Good morning, Mr Telfer,' Alison began, after she'd switched on the twin deck recorder and identified everyone. 'Do you know why you're here?'

'I've got no idea,' he replied. His voice had a crack in it.

'Then I'll enlighten you. We believe that you were involved just under three weeks ago in the multiple rape of a woman. You were with two other men, Andrew Weir and Albert McCann. The victim hasn't made a formal complaint, but that doesn't actually matter, because we have medical testimony that says she was, and from her clothing and body we recovered forensic samples from the men involved. I'll require you to give us samples of blood and saliva, and I have no doubt that analysis will confirm your guilt, as we're in the process of doing with your old school pals . . . academic as that might be, since it's only you who'll be standing trial.'

He frowned, and I knew that he was about to be given the biggest fright of his life. 'Why?' he protested. 'Have those idiots turned Crown witnesses?'

'My,' Alison said, evenly. 'You have been out of touch. Mind you,' she continued, 'I suppose that you'll only get the *Press and Journal* on your platform. Edinburgh stories might not get the same prominence as in our papers. Your friends will not be tried because they're both currently in the morgue. They were both murdered, one week apart, by the same man. We don't know who he is yet, but we're fairly certain that he's waiting for your offshore spell to finish, so that he can complete the job.'

His eyes stood out, his mouth hung open. She took two photographs from a folder she'd brought with her and laid them on the table. They'd been taken in the mortuary, just before the post-mortems had begun. Until then I'd never actually seen a grown man piss his pants before, but he did. We let him sit there in the wet, and the rising steam, and the shame, his face in his hands.

'Hey,' I called out, 'look at me, Don.' After a while he did. I tapped my left cheek, where his scar was. 'Where did you get this?' I asked. He stared back, mute. 'It goes back to your school days, doesn't it?'

For the first time he showed something other than fear: anger. He nodded, forcefully. 'That wee cunt Ryan Watson,' he hissed. 'He did it with that fucking razor he carried up his sleeve, at the school, in the middle of the playground at a break. The fucking jannie, Ramsay, his name was, he took me to the Royal, and he told me that if I opened my mouth it would probably be my throat got cut next time, so when the hospital called the police I told them I didn't know who did it, not that they gave a shit anyway!'

'Why did he do it, Don?'

His eyes flared. 'Because I tried it on with his sister. The fucking Ice Queen, Mia, who said she never shagged boys, only proper men. The wee bastard came up to me and cut me, and said she'd told him to.'

That threw me. 'Did you believe that?' I asked.

'How the fuck would I know whether it was true or not? Ryan didn't need telling. He was always heading for an early grave, that wee . . . Two weeks later his drugs racket was exposed in the papers and he and his uncle wound up dead because of it.'

'What about Mia?' I continued.

'She left school the day the story about the drugs was in the paper. I never saw her again, until I opened a radio magazine that I read and there she was, Miss Fucking Perfect, back in Edinburgh and a big star. And me, marked for life. Women recoil from me, you know. They do, like I'm some sort of freak. Even the nice ones, I can see it in their eyes. The only way I can get a woman is to pay for it. And it's all her fucking fault.'

Alison picked up the interview. 'So you and your pals decided to teach her a lesson.'

He nodded. 'It was my idea. Andy and Albie came along for the ride, so to speak. They hated that wee bastard too; when we were all at the school he actually made them buy drugs off him.' He paused for breath. 'So, we waited for her to finish her programme and then we picked her up outside her studio.'

'Where did you take her?'

'My place. We kept her there all night. No food, nothing to drink, just us. I wanted to kill her, and hide her somewhere she'd never be found, but the boys wouldn't go for that. So we told her that if she said a word, we'd tell the *Sunday Mail* all about her and her evil fucking family, and then we dumped her in the street. Brutal, eh? Sure,' he spat, 'and you know what? I don't give a toss.'

'I doubt if your friends did either,' Alison murmured. 'Pity we can't ask them.'

# Nineteen

'Where do we take this?' Alison asked, once Telfer's forensic samples had been taken and we'd charged him.

There was only one answer to that, and I knew it; I couldn't avoid it. Well, I could have. I could have gone to Alf Stein, told him the whole story and asked him to put two other senior officers on the case. No, scratch that; I should have done that. But I didn't; instead I ploughed on, taking what was in hindsight a reckless risk, not only with my own career but with Alison's. 'We have to bring her in,' I told her.

She surprised me. 'I'm not sure about that. She's a rape victim, and she's well known. If we arrest her, on the back of the charge against Telfer, and bring her in here, she'll be recognised, and her right to anonymity could be compromised.' She held up a hand before I could say anything. 'I know, I'm sounding like Martina Chivers, but it's a fact. I think we should go to her. Or I should, since you don't want to be involved.'

I made another decision. 'No, I can't dump this one all on you. We interview her together.'

'Okay. Where?'

'I don't know, but not the fucking Sheraton, that's for sure.' I flicked through the options. The radio station? Hardly. That left only one. I took out my phone and called her, mobile to mobile. She must have

381

recognised my number but she answered nonetheless. 'Hello, Bob,' she murmured; she was using her radio voice on me, damn her. 'Do you want to start with a fresh page?'

'I need to see you,' I replied.

'Now?'

'It can't wait.'

'Then I'm at home.' I ended the call and told Alison that she'd given me her home address.

Cross-town at midday, a journey that might have taken as little as ten minutes, took twenty-five. Duplicitous to the last, I parked well away from the house and made a show of checking the numbers. I was nervous as I rang the bell, in case Mia answered in nothing but her T-shirt, but she must have been looking out for me, for she was fully dressed and showed no surprise when she opened the door and found two of us there.

'Mob-handed,' she murmured, with a quick glance at my companion as she ushered us in. 'I'm honoured. It's a pity you didn't bring that dishy detective constable though, Bob. I took a shine to him.'

'A female officer was necessary, Mia. This is DI Higgins.'

She frowned. 'Why would that be?'

'Think back three weeks,' I said, 'and the reason may begin to dawn on you. We've arrested Donald Telfer, and charged him with rape.'

Her eyelashes flickered, but only slightly. 'Who's Donald Telfer?' she asked.

I sighed. 'Please. Have some respect for me as a police officer, if nothing else. You know who he is. He's one of three guys who kept you prisoner overnight, while they raped and sodomised you, repeatedly. The four of you were at school together, and Telfer was getting even for the scars that your brother Ryan left him with, twelve years ago.'

'Wait a minute,' a woman hissed, a woman I'd seen revealed once before. 'I didn't make a complaint. I told that inspector that it was a party that got out of hand, and that it was probably my fault.'

'Your blood was clean, Mia. No drink or drugs. What you say doesn't matter anyway, unless you're prepared to repeat it under oath, and that won't be necessary. Telfer's made a full statement, admitting the whole thing. He's even told us that McCann and Weir stopped him from finishing his revenge by killing you. He'll go to the High Court for sentence and he'll do time, but you don't have to worry, because the law will give you complete anonymity.' She sat down, we stayed on our feet.

'That brings me to the real reason we're here. You're by no means an idiot; you've got a degree in journalism and you must have known that rape victims' identities are protected, so why not make a complaint?'

'I don't know. I suppose I felt sorry for them.'

'Don't make us laugh. After what they'd put you through? If Telfer told us the truth about what happened to him at Maxwell Academy, you didn't feel sorry when he tried it on with you then. He reckons you sent your brother to cut him after he tried his hand with you.'

'Then he's wrong. I told Ryan, but I was laughing about it. Telfer was a spotty wee tyke. I'd no idea that Ryan would decide to defend my honour. Mind you, I suppose I should have. I knew what he was like. My little brother was a psycho, Bob.'

'And your Uncle Gavin,' I added.

'No, Gavin wasn't; he'd never have done anything as stupidly gratuitous as that. Gavin had aspirations, he wanted to be Mr Big, but he was never in the same league.' She said that with feeling. 'In the end he turned out to be Mr Remains Never Recovered.'

'Ryan did defend you, though, psycho or not. Which leads us to ask, who have you turned loose now?'

'What the hell are you talking about, Bob?' she challenged, coolly; too damn coolly, too damn confidently.

'I'm talking about the man who's been taking out the rapists. Andy Weir, attacked a few days afterwards, died ten days later, just after Albie McCann was stabbed to death. Two down and one to go. Telfer was offshore and out of reach or I'm sure he'd have been the first to go. So who was it, Mia? You've run out of brothers, so who's your avenging angel this time?'

'I have no idea what you mean, and I have no knowledge of these things. There must have been a queue of people waiting to kill those three.'

'But not with your immediate motive. Who've you got in your life that we don't know about?' And yet, as I put the question I remembered her saying that it had been a while since she'd had a man in there properly, a man in her bed. I'd believed her then, and I still did. 'Or did you pay someone? Is it as simple as that?'

She shook her head. 'Stop these allegations, please. I'm a victim, pure and simple. You're barking up the wrong tree. I've paid nobody, and I've asked nobody, to do anything to those poor sad clowns.'

'If only I could take your word for that,' I told her, honestly. 'But I can't. I tell you now that we're going to be looking at your bank accounts for cash withdrawals, we're going to be looking at your phone records for contacts and we're going to be following up every possibility.'

'Then do that,' she snapped, 'but you'll find nothing, I promise you. Now please leave. I have to get ready to broadcast this afternoon.' For the second time running she was throwing me out of her house.

If Alison had sensed any frisson between Mia and me, she said nothing about it. 'Do you think we'll come up with anything?' was the only question she asked.

'Honestly? No. But we've got to do it.'

'Is it possible,' she wondered, 'that she doesn't have anything to do with the murders?'

'They say that time travel's possible,' I replied, 'but don't go booking your trip to the twenty-first century and expect it to take any less than three and a half years to get there.'

# Twenty

I had to leave Alison and her small team to begin the trawl through Mia's private life, because I had other things to do. There was the matter of Hastie McGrew to be resolved, but more immediately, there was Marlon Watson's funeral at Seafield Cemetery, only an hour away by the time we left Davidson's Mains. I dropped Alison off at her office then headed for mine, to pick up a companion.

Andy Martin was head down at his desk over a pile of mobile phones, and of course the clumsy Jeff Adam, who'd never have been handling a ram in the first place if there had been room for another large body in the chopper, was at home with his foot in plaster, so I pointed at Mario McGuire. 'You. With me.'

The lad was irrepressible. He jumped to his feet. 'Yes, boss. Where are we going?'

'A funeral.' He smiled, and followed. If I'd told him I was taking him to the zoo to be fed to the lions, he'd have done the same, although that might have been bad news for the king of the jungle.

We made it to the depressing boneyard with ten minutes to spare. The prepared grave was easy to spot. To my surprise there were a few mourners there already: a middle-aged man, fifty-something, probably, four guys, all around the age that Marlon would never exceed, and three women, one of them in black, and ready for a good cry by the looks of her. On closer inspection, the other two seemed to be supporting her. That interested me; Bella had never mentioned a girlfriend, but Bella never mentioned anything to the police, so no real surprise. The younger set knew what we were, if not who. The guys edged away from us as we approached, but the girls stayed where they were. 'Big shock, I expect,' I said to the tearful one. She nodded and dabbed at her eyes. 'Did you see a lot of Marlon?'

One of the ladies-in-waiting actually sniggered . . . at a graveside. I looked more closely at her pal and noted that she was either pot-bellied or pregnant. *The dy-nasty's assured*, I thought. 'He was my fiancé,' she mumbled.

'What's your name, love?' I asked her.

'Lulu. Lulu Ford.'

'Were you with him on the day he died?'

'In the afternoon, later on; he came to see me. He could, because his boss was away.'

'When did he leave?'

'About five; a wee bit after.'

'Do you know where he was going?'

The sniggering girl decided to intervene. 'Hey, leave her alone, you. Can ye no' see she's upset.' McGuire leaned forward and whispered in her ear. She turned, stared at him and backed away. I repeated my question to Lulu.

'To the pub,' she whispered. 'The Vaults.'

'That I know, but afterwards.'

She gnawed at her bottom lip. 'He said he'd a meeting. I asked him what it was about, but he wouldnae say. He said he'd tell me if it worked out all right He was lookin' forward to it, though. I could see that.'

McGuire tapped me on the shoulder. I glanced round, and saw the cortège approaching: a hearse and a single limo. As it grew closer, I could see that Manson had done well by his late employee. The coffin was solid wood, not chipboard, and there were a couple of wreaths on it that must have set him back a few quid.

The small procession drew up a few yards away and the living passengers emerged. Six of them: Bella, stone-faced, in a black suit and hat, Manson, Dougie Terry, Tomas Zaliukas, a surprise to me, and Lennie Plenderleith, newly returned from his wee holiday. They were followed by a minister in a long white robe.

The bereaved mother looked around. She nodded in my direction, more reaction than I'd expected, and beckoned Lulu towards her. And then her eyes fell on the other mourner, the fifty-something bloke. I'd never seen Bella look anything close to tender. In any encounters I'd had with her she'd always been stern-faced, occasionally combative, but when she saw that man her face showed all sorts of stuff I'd never seen on it before. I'm good at reading expressions, but even I was challenged to take it all in. There was shock, instantly; it was replaced by fear, and by curiosity, until they merged together into a grimace of pure hatred. Then she seemed to tear her eyes away from him.

Manson walked round the grave and approached me; his right cheek was bruised, just below the eye. 'For once,' he whispered, 'I'm glad you guys are here. I'm a couple short with the cords. Will you take one each?'

There's a thing we do at funerals, in Scotland at any rate, maybe elsewhere too, I don't know. The deceased is lowered into the grave by up to eight family members and friends, traditionally male, although at Myra's funeral Jean had insisted on being one of the number. There were McGuire and I, on duty at what was, for want of an alternative description, a gangland funeral, and we were being asked to bury the victim. I could have shaken my head and stepped back. Those four would have been enough, and in any event the coffin is always supported by straps held by the undertakers, just in case. But the request wasn't made on practical grounds, or as some bizarre peace offering on Tony's part. It was made out of respect, so that Marlon could be buried by a more or less full complement rather than a scratch team, and so that his mother would have something to remember. 'Okay,' I said. He handed each of us a card with a diagram and a number on it.

And that's how two of the CID's finest came to stand round a grave with four guys most generously described, at that time at least, as pillars of Edinburgh's darker community, an experience which both McGuire and I have kept to ourselves until now. Well, I have, anyway; I suspect there's nothing that Mario hasn't told Paula by now, and that some of it I wouldn't want to know.

The God-botherer was competent, if nowhere near as familiar with his subject as Thornie's minister had been. The service was short and the committal of the coffin to the grave went smoothly. I had cord number two, at Marlon's feet. Manson held number one. As the burden neared the ground, I glanced up and along its length. For an instant, his eyes met mine. I don't know what sort of message we exchanged, but I never thought of him quite so badly after that.

There were no pleasantries afterwards. The hearse was driven away to pick up its next load, and the passengers returned to the limo. Plus one: Bella squeezed in Lulu to join them at whatever post-funeral wake Manson had laid on. I wondered whether she'd known before that afternoon that she was going to be a granny.

That left just McGuire and me, and one other, the man whose appearance had unsettled Bella so much. He was heading for the exit when I called after him. 'Excuse me!'

He stopped and turned, patiently and a shade wearily, as if he'd been hoping to get away unchallenged but recognised that was never going to happen.

'We're police officers,' I told him as we caught up, 'investigating Marlon's murder. Would you mind giving us your name?'

'Not at all. It's Watson, Clark Watson. That was my son you just helped bury.'

Once upon a time, I was in Spain, in L'Escala. Alex was in a cafe with her grandpa, and I was standing on the headland. The Tramuntana, the north wind, was blowing strong and the sea was wild all around me. I'd been looking back towards the beach; in the very instant that I turned, I was hit full on by a giant wave as it broke over the rocks. When Marlon's father revealed himself, I had much the same feeling. I'll swear that I swayed on my feet.

And then . . . this is my day for analogies, so I'll follow one metaphor with another. Remember those imaginary bricks I mentioned earlier? Well, a whole pile of them materialised and formed themselves into a wall. It wasn't quite solid, it was still a bit ephemeral, but it was there.

'Forgive my surprise,' I said. 'Here was me thinking you were dead.'

He smiled. 'Is that what the cow told you? I shouldn't be surprised by that, I suppose. I might as well have been as far as my family was concerned. No, as you see, I'm still alive.' He held out an arm. 'Go on, have a feel; it's solid.'

'Where have you been?' I asked, my mind still swirling in the aftermath of that wave.

'These past twenty years? I've been sailing. I moved on from trawlers and joined the Royal Fleet Auxiliary. I'm chief officer on a support tanker, Leaf class. I live in Portsmouth now, have done for fifteen years.'

'How did you hear about Marlon's death?'

'When I'm on shore,' he replied, 'my newsagent gets the *Scotsman* for me. I read about it in there. I found out about the funeral through the local authority, and came up for it. I thought I might have seen my other two children there.'

Jesus, he didn't know. 'I'm sorry to have to tell you this, Mr Watson, but your other son's dead too. Your daughter's estranged from her mother, and has been for twelve years. She's . . .' I was on the point of telling him where he could find Mia, but I stopped. I had unfinished business there, and I didn't want him getting in the way. Also, I didn't think she'd be too pleased to see him, since he was supposed to be helping Davey Jones sift through his locker.

'I see,' he murmured. 'Lucky Mia.'

'Why did you leave?' I continued.

'Where are my brothers-in-law?' he asked. 'Those fucking Spreckleys?'

I pointed, downwards.

'Both of them? Now that is good news. Billy maybe not so much, but Gavin, yes. If I'd had the guts I'd have put him there myself. He was the reason I left.' He looked at us. 'I was a bit wild in my youth. Check your records and you'll find my name there, although for nothing serious. But I had no idea when I married Bella what her family was like. She was pregnant with Mia and we did the old-fashioned thing, then we had the other two. I was away at sea a lot, so it took me a while to find out what Gavin was up to, with the drugs and everything. When I did, I went mental. I told Bella we were moving away. But she'd have none of it. She did her nut. We had a big argument. A couple of days later, I had a visit from her brothers. Gavin put a gun to my head and said that if I was still around in twenty-four hours he'd pull the trigger. He told me to disappear and not to even think about going to the police as he'd friends who would find me and put me through an industrial mincer, feet first. He scared me all right, enough for me to leave my wife and family behind, and never even think about coming back.'

So: Mia had made up the story she'd told me about her father's departure, but she hadn't been that far off the mark. 'If you'd known he died twelve years ago, would you have?' I asked.

'No,' he admitted. 'I had another family by then, a wife and a daughter. Not bigamous, mind; I divorced Bella as soon as I could when the law let me.'

I wasn't too bothered about that. I had other matters on my mind, for example that mirage-like wall. 'Give my colleague your contact details, please, Mr Watson,' I said. I left them to it. I walked away, across two double ranks of graves, and sat on a long, flat, mossy tombstone, giving myself time and space to think.

Mia had lied to me. She'd told me that after Ryan's murder she'd run off to live with her father, her tragic, lost-at-sea trawlerman father, who'd given her the stability she'd needed, and let her build a proper life for herself away from the remnants of her doomed family. That was all fiction, a farrago of Mills and Boon candyfloss, but she had gone somewhere, that was for sure. It was probably likely that the degree she'd told me of was real, and her CV. She wouldn't have expected me to check any of it, but her bio would have to stand up to the scrutiny of others as her career developed.

So where had she gone when she was barely sixteen? I ran through everything she had ever said to me, looking for a hint. Her contempt for her family had been evident, for her brother Ryan, for Gavin, her uncle. Not a psycho, she'd insisted, but what was it that she'd said about him, only a couple of hours before? I searched for her words and they came back to me. 'Gavin had aspirations, he wanted to be Mr Big, but he was never in the same league.' And the vehemence with which she had spoken them, as if she was speaking from . . .

No, come on, Skinner, stay focused. But couldn't it be? What had she said, according to Telfer? She didn't shag boys, only proper men. Not Gavin, surely? Not her uncle? No, even Bella would have drawn the line there, but did he take her about with him? Did she meet any of the crew he worked for? Could she ever have met . . . Fuck!

'So where did she go?' I whispered. And answered myself, intuitively.

I snatched my phone from my pocket, and searched through incoming calls until I found a number with a prefix I recognised. I knew it was a long shot, one that I hoped wouldn't pay off, but didn't Foinavon win the Grand National, didn't Ali dismantle the monster Liston, then topple the invincible Foreman?

Lowell Payne was on duty when I called. He was surprised to hear from me, but sharp and efficient as usual. I asked him for a telephone number, and he found it in seconds. The lady who answered my call was posh Lanarkshire; her voice was the sort that I'd heard as a child, mostly on my occasional visits to my dad's office, when clients arrived for appointments.

'Mrs Shearer?' I asked.

'Yes.'

'I'm a police officer,' I told her. 'My name is Skinner, and I'm a colleague of the sergeant who spoke to you the other day.'

'About poor Violet and her children?'

'That's right. I need to ask you something else. Can you remember, was there a third child living with them at any point? It would be about ten to twelve years ago.'

'Oh yes, dear. I remember her well. Not really a child, though. She'd be about sixteen when she joined them, about halfway between Peter and Alafair in age. I have to confess I didn't care for her at first.

She was a little . . . well, a little coarse, I have to say. But she improved; Peter, when he was there, and Alafair, were a good influence on her, and Violet, of course. She was a clever girl as I recall . . . I was a teacher myself, you know. She went to Hamilton Grammar with Alafair. Violet told me that she had problems at first, but that she caught up very quickly. She did a very good group of Highers, and went off to university. I don't recall seeing her after that.'

'And her name?' I knew, but still, tension gripped me tightly.

'She had a funny name.' Mrs Shearer laughed softly, genteelly, the way posh Lanarkshire people do. 'But no funnier than Alafair, I suppose. She was called Mia.'

I sat in silence for a while, until I realised that I had to start breathing again. 'One last question,' I continued. 'I know that Violet is . . . was,' I corrected myself, 'a widow. But when the family lived there, do you recall if they were ever visited by a man?'

'Oh yes,' she exclaimed with the enthusiasm of a gossip too long out of practice, 'there was. Violet's cousin, she said,' she paused, 'although, to be honest, from time to time I did wonder. A very nice man. She introduced me once; he was quite charming, in a formidable sort of way. His name was Perry. That was his first name, dear,' she added, 'she never did tell me his surname, and one doesn't like to be nosy.'

I killed the call. I didn't even thank the dear lady, shame on me. The only excuse I can offer is that I was completely stunned. Mia had been under Perry Holmes's wing for twelve years, since she was a precocious girl, disdaining boys, with an eye for proper men. She'd spent two of her formative years with his children and their mother. With Violet, and Alafair and, when he was home, with Peter or rather Hastie, who was sitting in the cells at Fettes, smirking, because he knew he'd got off with . . .

I jumped to my feet. Clark Watson had gone, and McGuire was keeping his distance. 'Come on,' I shouted to him, heading for the gateway and the road beyond where I'd parked. When we reached the car I tossed him the keys. 'You drive. I need to make a phone call. But we're going to the lab, not the office. Do you know where that is?'

'Yes, boss. And the quickest way there.' He wasn't fazed. He eased his bulk behind the wheel and set off as if he'd been driving elderly off-roaders all his life, while I called directory enquiries for the Edinburgh University number. A few were offered, but I called the main switchboard. Inside a minute, I was put through to Joe Hutchinson's secretary. 'This is Detective Superintendent Skinner. Is the prof in?'

'He's lecturing,' she told me. 'He should be finished in ten minutes, though, if you want to call back.'

'No time for that. Ask him if he'd be good enough to meet me at the city mortuary, as soon as he can. I should be there in half an hour.'

I hung up and called Alison. 'Find Wyllie and Redpath,' I said, as soon as she answered. 'I want them both at Fettes, but kept apart. If Redpath's on an away trip, have him brought back.'

'Will do.' She didn't bother to ask why; she knew that I'd tell her in time, and where her priorities lay.

McGuire headed for the bypass, then turned off at Sheriffhall. 'Wait here,' I ordered as he pulled up outside the lab.

I'd been there before but it was new and I didn't really know my way around too well. I asked the first person I saw where I'd find Arthur Dorward. She sent me straight to him and two minutes later we were back on the road again. 'Mortuary?' McGuire asked. I nodded.

We arrived there at the same time as the professor. Indeed our cars almost collided as we swung into the car park. 'What the hell's up?'

the tiny pathologist exclaimed as we met at the entrance. 'Has one of your victims risen from the dead? It had better be something of like importance.'

I held up the object I'd collected from the lab. It was a Gurkha kukri, scimitar-shaped, in its scabbard, an object of veneration among its bearers, covered in fingerprint dust and contained inside a clear plastic evidence bag. 'It is,' I replied. 'I need you to prove that this killed Weir and McCann.'

He blinked, then smiled. Joe loves a challenge. 'Why didn't you say so?' He took it from me, carefully. 'Give me a little while and I'll tell you one way or another.' He looked up at me. 'But Bob, please calm down. I wouldn't want you on my table before your time.'

I took his advice. As we followed him inside I took some deep breaths, to bring my heart rate back to normal and to calm my mind.

Joe's a genius, with few professional peers, if any at all. He was gone for fifteen minutes. When he returned, grinning all over his face, he didn't have to announce his findings. 'Do you have a Gurkha in custody?' he asked. 'If so, he did it.'

'Stack of bibles?'

'One will be sufficient.'

I let McGuire drive us back to Fettes. Alison was waiting for me there, and so was Robert Wyllie; she told me that Redpath was on his way in from Haddington, but I decided not to wait for him. I sent Mario on a trawl of the building looking for five men, in the twenty-five to thirty-five age bracket, slim, clean-shaven and dark-haired. There were plenty of them about, so it didn't take long to set up the identification parade. By that time, Alison had twigged what was happening, but she said nothing, leaving me to get on with it. I had Hastie McGrew brought from his cell. He was puzzled when he saw the waiting line-up, but shrugged his shoulders and gave his escorts a patient, indulgent smile, as he chose his place among the other five, on the extreme left, the first man. I saw his lips move and read the words 'Anything to oblige', although I couldn't hear him, since I was behind a one-way mirror.

When they were ready, I called Wyllie in from the room where he'd been waiting, with Alison. 'Before you do this,' I told him, 'you should know that you will be in no danger from this man, or from anyone else. You've got my word on that. Now, I want you to take your time, and when you're—'

'Number one,' he murmured. 'The man on the left.'

'Are you certain?'

'A hundred and ten per cent.'

'Thanks, Robert. We'll need you to sign a formal statement confirming that you've identified him, then you can go. And I repeat, no worries.'

I left Alison to take care of the paperwork, and to run the second parade when Redpath arrived. I was in my office when she rejoined me forty minutes later. She looked as if her patience was wearing thin. She had no idea who the prisoner was.

I told her.

'The same man?' She was stunned, as I'd been.

'The same,' I repeated.

'But how?'

'Sit down and I'll tell you.' And I did, about Clark Watson turning up at his son's funeral and the chain of circumstances that his appearance had revealed. I didn't tell her everything, though.

'So Perry Holmes . . .' she began.

'You can come with me to find that out, after.'

'After what?'

'After you've charged Hastie McGrew with two counts of murder and taken the press briefing that I've told Inspector Hesitant to set up.'

'But this is yours,' she exclaimed. 'You—'

'I made you a promise at the start of this, and I'm keeping it. It's your arrest, your credit.'

'While he walks on Marlon, and you've got an unsolved against you? No thanks.'

I smiled. 'But yes. It's the rub of the green, Ali.'

'You realise what everybody in here's going to think? That you're screwing me, and that you've thrown me another bone.'

'Listen,' I told her, 'anyone who matters knows that you are a top cop, a class act. As for the rest, do you give a toss what they think? Because I don't. On you go now, do what I tell you and then we'll top and tail it.'

'You know what I'd like to do with you, don't you . . . sir,' she murmured.

'Yes, Detective Inspector, but not here, not now; later on, after the champagne.'

She left, to take her plaudits.

And no, before you ask, I hadn't told her everything. In particular I hadn't told her that I'd got three men killed. No, I hadn't confided in her that I could see as plain as the . . .

. . . that Mia had played me.

She'd swallowed me whole with those bedroom eyes and with those warm, enveloping honey walls of hers.

I'd given her the crucial info that Perry and Hastie needed when she'd heard me speak to Fred Leggat: the fact that we'd made the link to Newcastle, the fact that we'd found the van.

I put the timescale together. Yes, it had been torched after I'd told her, inadvertently, that we knew about it, and Milburn and Shackleton had gone off the radar at the same time.

Then, only after I'd told her that we knew who they were, Hastie had gone down to Tyneside, and removed any threat to him and to his father . . . just to be on the safe side.

And me? The wild reckless bastard that I was, I'd tossed the blame for the leaks to Ciaran McFaul and his colleagues, when all along it had rested with me, and with me alone.

No, I hadn't told Alison that, nor would I; nor would I tell anyone else.

# Twenty-One

It was six fifteen when I parked at Perry Holmes's front door. I noticed that it creaked, and looked decidedly insecure when Vanburn let us in. 'He doesn't want to see you,' he said to my companion and me.

'He doesn't have a say in it,' I replied. 'Take some advice, mate. Get on to your agency and have them find you a new placement. Every time you go into that pool, you're swimming with a shark.'

'A shark with no teeth, Mr Skinner.' The guy had a gentle, sympathetic smile.

'There are a lot of dead people who thought that.'

Perry was in his chair when we walked in. 'You have no right here,' he croaked. 'What do you want?'

'We're here to tell you that your son Hastie's been charged with murder.'

He made a strange sound in his throat that might have been a chuckle. 'Then you'll be embarrassed. My lawyer says you've got no chance, that you'll lose and then we'll sue.'

I treated him to a real laugh. 'Wrong murders, Perry. We're doing him for Weir and McCann, two of the three guys who raped Mia. Don't fret too much about the third one. Hastie might have missed out on him, but he'll do time for the attack.'

I'd been waiting years to see all of the confidence, all of the arrogance, all of the brutality, drain from Perry Holmes's face. It was a wonderful sight, and I found myself regretting that a few of my colleagues, guys who'd spent their working lives trying to skewer him, weren't there to see it happen.

'I've got all the bricks,' I told him. 'I've built my case and it'll stand against any defence. The only question is whether I charge you too, and with what. Are you a paedo, Perry? Are you a beast? Were you fucking Mia when she was only fifteen, when she used to follow Gavin Spreckley around? When you parked her with your own kids, were you grooming her for later when she grew up properly?'

His face filled with rage. It could have been scary if he'd been able to move. 'No!' he shouted. 'Not me! It was Alasdair, my amoral brother, he abused Mia. Her disgusting uncle gave her to him; fifteen years old and he gave her to him, literally, to curry favour with us. As if that would! Gavin told me about it, when I found out that he'd been dealing to schoolchildren. He threatened to expose Al, the stupid bastard, to tell the police; stupid bastards both of them.'

I've never seen anything more ferocious than the look in Holmes's eyes then. 'He was going to die anyway,' he snarled, 'but because of that I told Al to make him watch as Johann strangled his nephew, then cut his hand off with a chainsaw, before he used it to cut off Gavin's fucking head.'

He glared at me. 'I rescued Mia, Skinner, from that awful family, from that den of vermin, from that hard whore of a mother. I'd have fucking killed her too, but for Manson. I wouldn't risk my son against him.'

'No,' I murmured. 'Not Manson. But you must have almost got up and walked when you found out that your daughter was fucking him. Derek came to you, didn't he? He cried on your shoulder, told you she had another man, you confronted Alafair, and she told you who it was. I'll bet you were apoplectic. But no, you couldn't go for Tony, so you did the next best thing. You hired out-of-town talent to kill his driver, and added bonus, he turned out to be a Watson, half a Spreckley.'

'I've sired the wrong daughter,' Holmes growled, a little more calmly. 'Alafair's always been a problem, always trouble. But Mia, once she was away from her awful upbringing, she's treated me like she was my own blood . . . '

His eyes fixed on me. 'You have a daughter, Skinner: I know you have, for Mia told me she'd met her. The way it is between you and her, that's how it is with me and Mia. How would you feel if your kid was picked up off the street by three animals, and . . .' if he had the words he couldn't say them, '. . . for a whole night? What would you do?'

'As much as I could,' I admitted, 'without hurting her worse. In other words, whatever I could get away with. But if I used other people, I'd make sure they were better than your Geordies, or than Hastie, for that matter. He's going to do life, Perry, just as you are in that pathetic chariot. You'd better be nice to Alafair, Daddy, for she's all you've got left.'

He shook his head; it was the tiniest of movements, but he managed. 'I've still got Mia. In spite of you, Skinner, I've still got her.'

'Don't bet on it,' I warned him. 'Mia's on the verge of the big time, and she doesn't need a helpless old geezer in a wheelchair holding her back. You, set against her career? I don't think you stand a chance. So long, Perry, but don't think you're secure. The first chance I get to put you away, I'm still going to take it.'

We left him to his thoughts, to his new life of still, impotent, solitary uncertainty.

Outside, as we stood beside the old car that I was definitely going to ditch, I turned to Alison. 'Love,' I began, 'there's—'

She put a finger to my lips to stop me. 'When you're lonely in the dark of night, who do you call first?'

'You.'

She frowned, then kissed me. 'That's all right then,' she whispered. 'Take me home and let's crack that champagne, and the rest.'

# Twenty-Two

Much of the rest was silence. We shared the champagne and it did me in. After the stress and strain of the day, after its shocks, its triumph and its exultation, I folded; Alison woke me in my chair just after ten and half carried me to bed. So much for my earlier scorn for McFaul.

I think I dreamed of Mia in the night, crouched over Holmes in his chair. If it was her, she had her back to me, so I couldn't see what she was doing, but he had boasted to me that even in his paralysis, he could still sustain an erection, so . . .

It had been easy for him to cast blame on to Alasdair; he wouldn't be offering any denial.

Next morning I took Alison to Torphichen Place. Apart from the final paperwork on what had begun as the Gay Blade investigation, she was back on Grant's team. And I was back with mine, reading their frustration that we'd been thwarted over Marlon's murder, and ignoring the smugness of the returned Mackie and Steele over their 'success'. Hastie's arrest, and Alison's press briefing, were major news in the Edinburgh papers and even made the front pages of the *Glasgow Herald* and two tabloids.

I felt as flat as Richard Branson's latest balloon. I did my duty and went to see Alf, to report the conclusion of both investigations. He was a bit pissed off that he'd read about one of them in the press before he'd heard it from me, but I told him, fairly irritably, as I recall, that he couldn't expect me to be his fire-fighter and his fucking exec at the same time.

'Aye, fair enough, lad,' he conceded, and poured me a mug of coffee that was so strong it should have been seized as a Class A drug.

'One way or another, the job's done, whatever those pen-pushing, bean-counting English tits think about it. McGrew's on his way to Peterhead for the next twenty years, and his old man's fucking helpless. Well done. Now on to the next. Mr Manson; let's see if we can put him in the next room to Holmes's son.'

I drained his rocket fuel and went back to my office. He was right; I should have been moving on, but I couldn't. She was out there, she'd played me, and she'd left me with a couple of guilty secrets. I was hurt, I was humiliated and I was angry.

About a year ago, one of my young CID lads got himself into a similar situation with a woman. Afterwards, a few people were surprised that I didn't crucify him, but I knew, from experience, that letting him live with it was the most effective sanction I could apply.

The guys spent the rest of the morning avoiding me, but a week wouldn't have been enough. When Andy Martin stuck his head round my door at quarter to three, I still bit it off. 'Yes!' I barked although I'd been doing nothing more taxing than contemplating shopping around the boatyards with Ali at the weekend.

'Sorry, boss,' he said, 'but I've come up with something I need to ask you about.'

I sighed, 'Okay, sit down then, and get asking.'

'It's those mobiles,' he began. 'I've been checking through them all, as you said, and the thing is, I think I've found Marlon Watson's. It had to be the one I looked at last, of course; that's life. It's loaded with Edinburgh numbers. I've checked them all, incoming calls and outgoing, and they nearly all fit. There's Bella's mobile, Manson's as well, and his ex-directory line, Dougie Terry's and the Milton Vaults number. But there's a couple that are odd. One's a landline, with a couple of calls to it and from it. I've checked the number. It isn't registered to a person, but to a company, Pentecostal Properties Limited. However, the phone's in a private house. This is it.'

He handed me his notebook, I read his scrawl, and felt as if I'd had another shot of Alf Stein's coffee. I knew the address all right: it was Mia's.

'The other number,' he continued. 'It's a mobile, I haven't been able to find out whose it is, but . . . you know you can send text messages between these things now?'

'So my daughter tells me.'

'Well, there's a message on Marlon's phone, from that number. It says, "My place 9 tonite, chat. M." And it's timed at ten past noon, on the day that Marlon died.'

I felt the blood leave my face. 'Thanks, Andy,' I said. 'Leave it with me.' I didn't bother to ask for a note of that mobile number; I knew that it was logged into my own phone.

I walked out of the office, and left the building, and climbed into my car . . . the BMW, for I'd decided that the Discovery really had served its purpose. I drove out to Sighthill, and was waiting, still behind the wheel, outside the Airburst FM studio when Mia arrived for her show. I waved to her, signalling that she should join me.

We had a brief discussion; no, that's not true, I talked and she listened. When I was done, she got back into her Mini and drove away. I tuned into the station at four; there was confusion, but they coped like professionals. Mia hasn't been seen in Edinburgh from that day on.

I had one more informal meeting that day, at five, at Tony Manson's place. Bella was there as I'd requested, for there was something I wanted to know. 'When Mia left home,' I asked, 'did you know where she'd gone?'

'No,' she replied, 'and I didn't care. I didn't expect to see her again, but when I did, after Marlon saw her in the street and followed her to where she worked, then talked to her and told me about it, I thought she owed me. That's the truth, Mr Skinner.'

I nodded. 'I know it is.' Then I told her where her daughter had been for twelve years, under the protection and in the tender care of Perry Holmes. 'Just as you reckoned she owed you,' I said, 'so she believed that she owed Perry.' I paused, to let that sink in, then continued.

'And guess how she repaid him. Do you know what happened to Marlon, how those brutes from Newcastle got hold of him so easily? He'd given Mia his mobile number. She sent him a message and asked him to come to her place that night, for a wee chat. He went, all excited I'm sure, and they were waiting for him. I don't have pictures, but I know that's what happened. Because Perry Holmes asked her to, your daughter set her own brother up to be killed, and she never batted an eyelid. And why? All because you, Tony, were screwing his daughter.'

'Where is she?' Bella murmured. The way she said those three simple words told me that if she could find her, then she'd be childless.

'I don't know, but wherever that is, she'll be out of your reach. Don't go looking for her. I wouldn't like that.'

I left them to chew it over.

Vanburn is another who hasn't been seen in Edinburgh since that time; he left town a couple of days later, without giving his agency a forwarding address. He may have taken my advice, and found himself a new job in a safer environment. On the other hand, Manson may have paid him a lot of money to be absent while Dougie Terry, or someone similar . . . but not Lennie, not for something like that . . . drowned his patient in his therapeutic pool. Or he may have paid him even more money to do the job himself.

Perry's funeral was private, even smaller than Marlon's, and without anyone like Lulu, anyone who'd loved him. Alafair was there, and a priest. Hastie wasn't allowed to go, and Derek Drysalter was still in hospital. No, Mia didn't show up. I did, though, with Alf Stein. Our main interest lay not in paying our respects, but in ensuring that they filled the grave in properly, after the undertakers had lowered him into it, since there were no men to take the cords.

Life returned to its usual pattern after that. Alex missed Mia for about a week, then realised that the best influences were those around her, not voices from her radio. Alison and I settled into a routine too, living separately, and together, as we chose; it lasted for a couple of years and then it just . . . stopped. Not my doing; Ali never said, but I reckon she'd wanted me to buy that boat after all. We stayed friends beyond the split, but she insisted, and I agreed, that our professional relationship should be entirely formal from that point on.

Me? Well, you know about me. A failed second marriage with the consolation of two lovely kids and one adopted boy, until I was way luckier than I deserved, and another soulmate came along. Now I'm never lonely in the dark of night.

And Mia? What about her? I would say, 'Who knows?' only . . .

A couple of years ago I was playing about online, after everyone else had gone to bed, when I happened upon an English-language radio station that was based in the south of Spain. There was a female presenter on air at the time, with a mature, smoky voice, and an accent that was vaguely Scottish.

I'd clicked on the link because of her name: she called herself Mary Whitehouse. I'm sure that meant nothing to her younger listeners, and I imagine that the older part of her audience thought only that she was having a laugh at the old decency campaigner's expense.

She talked for a bit, about the weather on the Costa del Sol, about which of yesterday's entertainers were appearing at which exclusive night spots, and then she cued up a song. 'This for old friends, old lovers, and even some old enemies,' she breathed. 'You out there, you know this is for you. It's Gram Parsons: "Return of the Grievous Angel".'

'God,' I whispered. 'I hope not.'